RED GRANITE

The Grains of Truth
Beneath the Sands of Egypt

ALEXANDER RETROV

II

LUXOR - KARNAK

RED GRANITE

The Grains of Truth Beneath the Sands of Egypt
II
Luxor - Karnak

Alexander Retrov

Editor: Alexander Retrov
Graphic Design: Goran Djcinovic
Publisher: Renaissance Entertainment Pty Ltd
Printer: Amazon books

This work is 90% fact and 10% fiction.
It's up to you to determine which is which.

To see the truth for yourself and join Krystal or Alex
on one of the Red Granite or Goddess Reawakening Tours
go to the website for more details on the next tour.

www.alexanderretrov.com

© 2018 Renaissance Entertainment Ltd Pty
Second edition
First edition printed in Australia by Eureka Printing
ISBN: 978-0-9943146-4-2

www.alexanderretrov.com

RED GRANITE
The Grains of Truth
Beneath the Sands of Egypt

II

Luxor - Karnak

ACKNOWLEDGEMENTS

My deep gratitude goes to Krystal,
without whose support and patience
this book would never have been written.

I also want to acknowledge Source
for choosing me as the conduit for this work

To my brother in Egypt, Abdou Ashour

This book is dedicated to the truth.

CHAPTER 12 - THE SUN WHO'S RAYS

The great Apis bulls of Ancient Egypt formed a long guard of honour, calling out their sonorous welcome to me as I glided between them, acknowledging each and everyone in turn. The pungent and redolent aroma of fresh incense wafted through the air, infiltrating my nostrils. Levitating, hovering, I slowly and reverently made my way up the gently ascending ceremonial walkway and towards the royal throne. This was a rare ceremony indeed, a great recognition for my deeds and actions.

Seated before me was Hathor; 'Eye of the sun', the daughter of Ra, universal cow-goddess and symbolic mother of Horus and the Pharaoh. Manifest in the form of a thin-nosed naked pale-blue skinned woman with cow's ears, a sun-disc surrounded by cow's horns crowned her head; she was the patron of beauty, love, sexuality, joy, dance and music. There was no greater accolade than to be honoured by Hathor herself.

Having reached the ceremonial podium, I knelt before her, awaiting her revered words of praise and wisdom. She graciously stood and took several elegant steps towards me. This was my crowning moment.

'Moooooo!'

I paused, bemused. But yes, YES, it must mean something incredibly loving and profound, I just wasn't quite getting it.

'Moooooo!'

It took a minute or two before I realized where I was; the vivid images of my dreams were still swirling through my state of semi-consciousness. Firstly I remembered I was the river cascading onwards, then I was flying above it. The river was lush, date palms and green vegetation surrounded the water. This was the Nile and it was Ancient Egypt. It was just as I had dreamed it was the night before, but was different somehow; ancient, yes, but somehow even more ancient, because everything was even newer, if that makes sense?

The barque that majestically made its way down the Nile was the royal barque no less, and sent especially for me. It carried me to the sacred temple where all the Apis bulls gathered in my honour. And Hathor …

'Moooooo!'

The sound of a single cow called me back into full consciousness and suddenly I realized and remembered I was lying on my side, back on the banks of the river Nile in the 21st Century. As I took my first real conscious deep breath of the day, the sleep-induced association with incense quickly dropped into its true context when I slowly opened one eye, not so much to see the cow, rather to eye-ball what the cow had deposited; a healthy, and still steaming, morning ablution less than two-feet away and upwind.

Several metres along the bank, the cow turned its head as if to both acknowledge my awakening and seek an expression of thanks for its 'gift'. I declined, considering myself fortunate that, but for a pace or two, the cow had spared me a truly shit-faced awakening.

As I rolled over in the other direction, preparing to rise and face the dawn, I noticed someone had thrown a blanket over me and slipped a cushion under my head. I was damn sure they weren't there last night when I drifted off, so my first thoughts were that it must have either been Crystal, or that she abandoned me and Saeed had done a midnight reconnoitre.

Further exploration of the bedding revealed a second pillow and blanket closely alongside, so I raked my mind for the most minuscule thread of recollection of what might have happened after I drifted away. But no matter how much I fished, the riverbed was dry.

Climbing to my feet, I had a quick stretch, looking around at the lay of the land. Saeed and Gomar were busily resurrecting last night's campfire and preparing for breakfast, while meanwhile, back on the White Rose, Dwight and Randy were still catatonically comatose on the deck. In a small clearing adjacent to the campsite, Bill was taking Pernille through the basics of Tai Chi, while Pieter, Yuko and Crystal sat several metres away, silently awaiting the impending dawn.

As I made my way towards the clearing, I couldn't help but reflect on the previous evening, especially after I 'tuned out'? Was it Crystal that slept beside me, and if it was, did anything 'happen'? Or was it Saeed, and if it was, did anything 'happen'?

I laughed at the bizarre way my sense of humour connected the dots and speculated on possibilities. In the end, for reasons that should be plainly obvious, I decided in was definitely *not* Saeed that kept me company, and most likely to have been Crystal; by far a more agreeable situation. So, as the sun sparked into view on the horizon, I silently sat beside her, not wishing to disturb her morning ritual. Closing my eyes, I now instinctively shifted my focus first to the touch of the rays upon my face, and then to the sounds of the birds in the air.

If anyone had suggested to me that my first four days in Egypt would have resulted in me 'meditating', and that I would have the encounters and discussions I had experienced, I would have said they were candidates for a straight-jacket and a padded cell; none of what had happened so far actually made any 'real' sense what-so-ever, not to a 'normal' person.

But, contrary to what most people chose to experience, 'normal', or 'the norm', isn't necessarily 'natural'. In fact more than often it is the opposite, and it *had* all happened, so I had no choice *but* to believe it, and that meant I had to accept it, even if some of the concepts being tossed to and fro were way out there. Fortunately that part I *could* choose to take with the proverbial grain of salt. And yet, it all seemed to cohesively meld together.
'Welcome back.'

I opened my eyes to talk to her, but she hadn't moved, not a muscle, so I closed my eyes again and turned back to the east.
'Thanks, and thanks for bringing me a blanket and pillow.'
'Someone had to watch out for you, besides, I was afraid you might have caused a landslide and fallen into the river.'
'My snoring? Was it that bad?'
'Bad? It depends on your perspective. If you compare it to the growling of a nesting Nile crocodile, or the grunting of a herd of hippopotamus in mating season, then it was quite remarkable, but if you compare it to the earthquake that flattened Cairo, though it lasted considerably longer, it was nowhere near as destructive; your

snoring I mean, not the earthquake.'

I opened my eyes and turned to her.
'There was an earthquake in Cairo?'

She remained motionless.
'Several. The most recent one was in 1992 which caused extensive damage to buildings and temples, not just in Cairo, but also in the Nile Delta and further south in the Nile Valley.'

'When were the others?'

'There were ones in 224 BC, and in the 1st Century AD, but the most notable ones were in August and December 1303. The first catastrophic quake was about a magnitude 8 and centred south-east of Cairo. All the buildings in Cairo were damaged, many houses and at least five mosques completely collapsed, any many people were buried under the ruins.

The quake was felt hundreds of miles away; many of the castles on the Island of Crete collapsed, and most of the Peloponnesus Peninsula in Greece suffered serious damage. The town of Rhodes was almost completely destroyed, as were parts of Palestine, Damascus, Syria, and what is now Israel. It was even felt as far away as Istanbul, or Constantinople as it was then known, and possibly even Venice.'

'Were there reports of any tsunamis?'

'Yes, following the quake a massive tsunamis rolled through the Mediterranean hitting, amongst others, Syria, Palestine and the Island of Crete. It is reported that the sea at Akka withdrew ten miles, exposing its sandy bottom, before the tsunami hit and totally wiped out the town.'

'And Egypt?'

'On the Nile itself, boats were thrown up hundreds of metres onto the surrounding land and the advancing sea submerged half the city of Alexandria.'

That was it, I had found the cause of the obliteration of the more modern temples; how they had been buried in metres of silt and sediment. And if it had happened once, or rather twice, then it is highly likely there had been previous quakes of a similar or greater magnitude that marked the end of the 17th Dynasty and the Exodus of Moses. And who knows how many quakes and tsunamis there had been before that? I thought I had better double check.

'Were there any others?'

'Further aftershocks continued for months, including a second major quake that hit in December, its epicentre in the Lybian sea half-way between Crete and Egypt. It affected the whole eastern Mediterranean basin and anything that had survived the first quake was hit and probably destroyed by the a second quake and its subsequent tsunamis.'

'That's amazing, but sorry, I meant any others *before* 1303? For instance, are there any reports of earthquakes or tsunamis from Ancient Egypt?'

Crystal turned to face me.

'All this was at a time when there was no mass media to fully record the impact or damage. So we can only assume it was much bigger than the isolated reports recorded by those fortunate Arabic and Syrian scribes who survived.'

Slowly getting to her feet beside me, I noticed she was wrapped in the same simple translucent sari she had worn yesterday before and after her morning swim. Seemingly adjusting it, she moved before me and towards the river.

'As for ancient Egypt, I am sure there are references to such events in the hieroglyphs and papyri.'

She stopped about six-feet ahead and stood facing me.

'And of course there is the memory within in the stones of the temples, *and* those who were there as witnesses.'

Then Crystal undid her sari and let it fall to the ground, standing absolutely butt-naked in front of me.

'I believe it is important that you can always recall things you have seen, don't you?'

My God, she was stunning; I looked at her from head to toe; down past her full perfect breasts and flat stomach, her gorgeous curved but slender hips, her close-neatly trimmed pubic hair, and down her long slender thighs and calves to her dainty feet.

Then I took my time looking back up again. I knew this is what she wanted to me to do, to look, admire, appreciate, and I made sure I did all that, and then some. When I got back to her sparkling blue eyes I was fixated by them; she had a look of unabashed desire.

'Some images stick in your mind for your whole life.'

'And some, for every life thereafter. Swim?'

Double dipping

I didn't need a second invitation, I didn't even pause to think, before I knew it I was naked and we were paddling around in the water. Moments later we were joined by Bill and Pernille and shortly after that by Pieter and Yuko, all naked and all frolicking around like teenagers.

There was a similar atmosphere in the air to yesterday, all of us enjoying the revitalizing effects of the crispness of the water. The only difference was, that like teenagers, the topic of sex was lurking beneath the surface of every interaction. Actually 'lurking' was not really the right word; bubbling, bobbling, and 'boobling' were more to the point.

Every time any of the girls paddled on her back, or stood in the shallower waters, their nipples, erect and inviting from the cool water and playful antics, aroused similar responses in the guys.

Then, as it had yesterday, it began with Yuko and Pernille having a water fight. However this time there was no prolonged 'wrestling'; within seconds Yuko and Pernille had picked up where they left off the morning before, embracing and passionately kissing. Bill and Pieter were chatting and watching from the deeper water as the two girls moved more into the shallows.

Once there, Yuko stood as Pernille wrapped her legs wrapped around Yuko's waist, their breasts and nipples pressed and rubbing against each other. Yuko grasped Pernille's butt cheeks and squeezed them firmly, pulling her even closer as they kissed.

Again Pieter seemed unperturbed, as did Bill. And who could blame them, front row seats on probably every guy's fantasy. I didn't think it could get much better myself, but I was soon proved wrong when Crystal glided in from her swim and took up a position beside Pernille and Yuko, throwing one leg around Yuko's waist and wrapping her arms around them both. It took me totally by surprise, though I wasn't sure if it was a pleasant surprise or not. For the first time, the idea flashed through my mind that Crystal was a lesbian.

Was I totally wasting my time thinking there could be something between us? Had all our conversations been purely platonic, or had she just been taunting me? Somehow it didn't matter, as the ideas were quickly superseded by my reaction to what was before me.

Seeing these three goddesses caress and kiss each other was extraordinary, they were totally at ease. It wasn't that they were oblivious to our presence, on the contrary they were totally aware of us watching, it's just that they didn't care; they were totally liberated and uninhibited, expressing exactly every desire as the moment presented. Each was kissing the other, grabbing handfuls of hair and heads, kissing necks, sucking ear lobes, sucking nipples, caressing and kneading breasts and butt cheeks, and just below the surface of the water, exploring each others most private of pleasure zones. I wasn't close to Pieter and Bill, who were upriver on the other side of the girls, and given the raging hard on I was sporting had no intention of getting anywhere within eye-shot of anyone.

After a period of time it was clear that Crystal and Yuko were focusing on Pernille, working in tandem to bring her to orgasm. And they probably would have been successful if it hadn't been for Randy, and then Dwight, jumping in beside them. In their defence, their post-alcohol and drug-induced state had dulled their perceptions so much that they were more concerned with recovering their senses, than hoping to 'join in the fun'. But it was like pouring ice-cold water from the Antarctic on a post-party prom date.

As quickly as it had started, it was over, with Pernille left somewhat hanging on the edge. In seeing the way she slowly came back into 'this' world, I had the feeling it was the closest she had been to being 'fulfilled' in a long time, if at all. I knew how she felt; if I didn't have a little release of my own soon I was sure I'd go nuts, and there was not really anywhere private on a felucca trip, on 'the Minnow', to hoist the mainsail. As I swam around waiting for the cold water to have its effect, for some bizarre reason I started thinking about who would have seen the most action on Gilligan's Island?

I eliminated the Professor straight away; he was such a geeky nerd, he was more than likely too busy examining his microscope, and his test tube probably never frothed over. Then I thought it must have been the movie star, Ginger; she would've been able to have anyone she wanted. But she was also pretty aloof and would also have been fussy, so probably only gone for a rich sugar daddy like the millionaire, Thurston Howell the third. As for Mr. Howell, he was supposedly only interested in money. Sure, as the only married man on the island, he always had it on tap from his wife, but why rattle a bag of old coins when you can rifle a fresh stack of cash or two. But then I thought, why would Ginger shag an old dude for cash when there was nowhere on the island to spend it?

Mrs. Howell, or 'Lovey', was next; she was married, old, rich, and would take any action she could get. But who would anchor in her port when there were two younger and prettier wenches of which to partake. But then I thought, she may not be getting as much, if any, from Mr. Howell as he was in love with money, so she may have taken on a toy-boy like Gilligan, or entertained the troops and been splicing the main-brace with the Skipper. Now the Skipper, he could throw his weight around on the island amongst the gals, and the ladies always get excited when the fleet is in port, so it's highly likely he had a safe berth in several harbours. And then of course there are the stories of the antics of sailors lost at sea, and of captains and their first mates, I mean how else do you get the title 'first mate'?

And what about Gilligan, I mean he *was* young and virile? But he was also so dumb-ass stupid he had about as much chance of getting some pussy as a celibate gay monk in a Tibetan monastery. That left Mary-Anne, the farm girl from the mid west, a girl much like our Candy. Yep, Mary Anne would have got it off with everyone, she may well have been the farmer's daughter, but she certainly couldn't keep her calves together.

'My friends, breakfast is ready.'

Saeed stood on the bank grinning like a fox; he'd been observing from the campfire and wasn't shocked in the least, in fact, somehow I think he'd seen all this and then some.

Within seconds we all made our way to shore, though some of us slower than others. Pieter, Yuko, Pernille, Crystal and Bill had no problems exiting the waters, drying off and donning their clothes, whereas Randy, Dwight and myself were not so eager to follow. For the boys it was a simple case of regaining a modicum of *compas mentas,* whereas for me it was more a matter of waiting for the 'tidal swell' to subside. Mind you, the view of three pretty fine asses rising from the water and glistening in the morning light, like triplet embodiments of the divine goddess Venus emerging from the river of life, was delaying the necessary diminution I required to regain my 'composure'.

Whilst the others had headed off to the campsite for breakfast, Crystal remained, a wry smile on her face. She picked up a towel and held it out, open, waiting for me to emerge to dry myself. For a moment I thought of a golden orb spider; she had spun her web and was patiently awaiting her victim. It was a clear and blatant challenge, a response to how she had stood before me earlier, before she entered the water. The question was, was I up to the challenge, or would I shrink away and hide? For me it was rather a case of, could I remain *unaffected* by it?

It wasn't a problem for Dwight and Randy for, despite their stupors, they had entered the water with shorts on. But for me it was crunch time, now or never. I sucked it in, pumped out the chest, gave the crown jewels a quick shuffle beneath the surface to present them in their best arrangement, and, with false bravado and mock nonchalance, strode out of the Nile and into her web.

'Thanks.'

'You are welcome.'

Taking the towel I dried off, pretending to be as unaffected as possible.

'Well, speaking as we were of memorable images, those were a few I won't so easily forget.'

As I pulled on my Calvins, her face lit up.

'Nor I.'

Was she taking the piss out of me, playing me for a fool? I decided it was time to call her bluff, time to stand toe to toe and put her on the spot.

'I must admit, I was a bit surprised, I wouldn't have picked you for a lesbian.'

She laughed.

'The danger with labelling people is you limit your perception and run the risk of looking like a fool.'

I continued to dress.

'You're not a lesbian then?'

'All labels that define difference, or create separation from oneness, from All That Is, are fear-based masculine processes. I am not an *anything*, I am simply all that I express in any given moment of all that I am.'

'OK, so what was all that with you, Pernille and Yuko all about?'

'Pernille is simply in the process of reclaiming her inner Goddess, Yuko and I are merely assisting her through this part of her journey of re-membering.'

'That's some process! And me, are you assisting me to re-member as well?'

'Of course.'

'I best re-*member* that, when next we go for a swim.'

'You can *wait* as long as you *want*, if that is what you desire. As for me, I live the now, and right now I am hungry, *very* hungry, so I am off for breakfast.'

She walked off towards the campfire as Dwight and Randy scrambled onto the bank.

'I think she's hot for you, dude.'

'That's just her hunger, Randy.'

'Hunger, for a serve of the wiener? Man, she wants your balls on toast!'

Eggs over easy

It wasn't the smell of freshly toasted bread that lured the three of us to the clearing; it was the aroma of frying bacon and eggs wafting past the date palms and banana trees that did the trick. As we tucked in for our share, I noticed Bill had picked up on the discussion the previous evening with Pieter about the energy of the Universe.

'I was curious about what you said; that the Universe consisted of the *thoughts of God*, and that's why scientists can't explain the Big Bang, or what was before it, because they *are* it.

'Sure they can explain the by-product, what happened *after* the Big Bang, but only once it exists, not at the point of creation, or the void that was there before it.'

'I like that, I like it a lot, but if it's all thoughts and everything is connected, and all energy is interacting, how does that affect the differentiation into different dimensions?'

I looked at Pieter, not only to see if he had an answer, but to see if he could even understand the question. He did.

'As vibrational energy slows it becomes denser, that's because all energy is ultimately rotational and centrifugal, which means as it slows it compresses, ultimately forming the building blocks of matter at the three dimensional level.'

'So if the third dimensional density is the lowest form of existence, does that mean the religions are all ass-about, that higher dimensions existed first, and that the third dimension is the newest? That would mean the arrow of spiritual development is down, not up? And what about the first and second dimensions, what are they, are they still to come? Are they the 'destination' of the journey? And which came first?'

Pieter laughed.

'That's a lot of questions to answer over one breakfast.'

'I'll eat slowly.'

'OK, firstly, for one to come *before* the other, would imply both the existence of time and time being linear, neither of which is the case or of relevance to dimensional existence, That's because all dimensions from the third upwards *appeared* simultaneously, and *exist* simultaneously.'

'And that's because All That Is means All Is One, right?'

'Yes, but the Source of all these dimensions was initially not aware of them.'

Bill screwed up his face.

'How could God not be aware of what God created?'

'When a child is created and newborn does it, or you, know what it will achieve in its life?'

His face relaxed.

'Fair point.'

'The key is that though it had created them, it had not experienced them; awareness comes from experience, not knowing. It *knew* it had created them, but it didn't know *what* they were until it had experienced them fully, and that is an infinite process.'

'Why is that?'

'Each experience, from the smallest nano-microbe in the third dimension to the largest entity in the highest dimension, whatever that may be, contributes to the experience.'

Bill scratched his chin, putting the pieces together.

'So what you're saying is: the Universe, or the thoughts of God, oscillate like a yo-yo from third dimensions up to the god-knows-what dimensional existence, and then down again?'

'Yes, but I think of it not just as a yo-yo going up and down, but more like a carousel horse going not just up and down, but also round and round. Add to that, the notion that the whole carousel itself is going up and down and round and round as a horse on yet another bigger carousel, and so on and so on.'

'You mean like fractal geometry?'

'You know about fractals?'

'Sure.'

I certainly didn't, and I'm sure Randy and Dwight were in the dark as well.

'What are fractals?'

'They're complex patterns that repeat over and over *ad nauseum* no matter how much you zoom out or zoom in.'

Bill had it sorted.

'So the Universe is just one big fractal geometric concept?'

'That's it.'

Thank God the breakfast was light; if it has been as heavy as the discussion I would probably still have been digesting it for weeks afterwards. But somehow everyone seemed to grasp what Pieter was saying, even Randy. And Dwight came back for a second helping; he wanted even more information.

'Why do things only go down to the third dimension?'

'The first dimension is the singularity, the Source of All That Is; it is nothing but being, it is the Void. It is not empty, just not measurable, for there is no time and no space.'

'How can nothing be something?'

'Imagine the void, the Source of All That Is, is not a *thing* but a sphere of consciousness, of knowing. It has no width, length or breadth, and it exists independent of time. That's why scientists can't explain the big bang, or what was before it, in terms of physics. They're looking for the source of the Big Bang, the centre of the Universe, but how do you find something that does not exist in space-time? You can't.'

I was following it, but there seemed to be a big jump from a non-existent point of pure consciousness to a fully expanding universe.

'OK, I understand the singularity, but how do you get from one dimension to three, or even four dimensional time and space?'

'Knowing is not experiencing. So the singularity, the sphere of consciousness, only *thinks* it knows what it knows. To become aware of what it knows it must shift its perspective, and that is where the second dimension comes in; it is the shift in perspective to see yourself from a new point of view.'

'How does a singularity do that?'

Pieter took a stick, poked a spot in the sand, then drew a circle around it.

'Let's say this is the Void's sphere, or circle, of consciousness. Now imagine the centre of that sphere travels to the edge of its awareness, to the perimeter of the circle, where it creates a new centre for a new circle. Thus it reproduces itself, copies its consciousness, but now from a new perspective on the perimeter of the first circle.'

'Huh?'

He drew a second sphere of the same size, centred on the perimeter of the original circle.

'See how the perimeter of the new circle cuts the edge of the first circle, passes through the original centre, then continues on to again cut the original perimeter. This creates two things; firstly a ufo shape *vesica pesicus*, this is *the light,* the concave mirror that shapes and reflects all back to the point of perspective, and secondly, when the circle is completed, forms a second intersecting circle centred on the perimeter of the first.'

Seeing it drawn was a hell of a lot simpler than the way Pieter explained it. It simply looked like two interlocking circles sharing a common radius. Stick in hand, and undeterred, Pieter wielded it like a cross between Harry Potter and an old Oxford Headmaster.

'The Source, in travelling from it's centre to the edge of its knowing, now has a here and a there; itself and *not* itself; the absence of itself, a mirrored image. This is the duality, the yin and yang, the *positive* and *negative,* the *feminine* and *masculine.*'

That was right up Randy's alley.

'Which is which, which circle is feminine and which is masculine?'

Pieter scratched his head.

'I don't know, I've never thought of that.'

Crystal had; in point of fact she had done more than think of it, she was fully aware of it.

'The original circle is feminine; it is pure creation, it is the Goddess, the womb, it is the state of BEING, of unconditional Love. The second circle is the birthed child, the product of thought, it is the offspring of BEING, it is the *absence* of love, the separation *from* Love that generates all fears, it is the masculine that questions its very BEING, as it knows it is a thought, an illusion, it is God.'

'God is an illusion?'

'The thoughts of God are illusions, only Goddess exists.'

Bill couldn't resist.

'Boy, would you have been a hit in the 60's, you would have made Germaine Greer look like a misogynistic sympathizer.'

Crystal looked at him with a wry smile.

'What makes you think I wasn't?'

Dwight brought us swiftly back to the topic.

'So the second dimension is the duality?'

Pieter quickly got back on track, pointing back to the scrawled circles in the sand.

'Travelling from here to there creates two things, firstly separation, then the *time* it takes to go from here to there. This is what creates the second dimension, the Source and the mirror, the duality, here and there, everything I am and everything I am not. So the second dimension is separation, separation between the void and the reflection of the void. This it what produces the concept of *time*, for it requires a shift of perspective, and that can initially only occur from a shift of perspective from *this* moment, to another perspective, which occurs by definition, at *another* moment or place. And that shift of perspective is the first step in the expansion of consciousness of the Source, and thus the perceived expansion of the Universe.'

'What do you mean *perceived*, surely the universe is expanding?'

'That is the illusion; it is simply the expanding consciousness and awareness of Source; it increases with each experience, whether it is at the micro or macro level. But all parts are not *expanding* from one point as scientists would suggest, but rather *pushing away* from all points simultaneously.'

I wasn't so convinced, but it did spark a thought.

'If that's the case, then it would explain why the scientists can't explain gravity, because it's not a law of attraction at all, but rather one of compression into lower densities, and that's why it's denser in the centre of large masses like planets and stars, because the vibrational dimension is slower and lower, even though the particles may appear faster and energized.'

There was brief pause, as those of us who were previously in the dark as the day dawned, finished our breakfast and absorbed the information. That done, Dwight wanted to know the next step.

'So what happens from second dimension to third?'

'The perspective then rotates along the surface of the first sphere to a new point of interest, that is how it maintains separation. It rotates to a point where both circles intersect. This creates three points of reference and thus three-dimensional *space*. It also creates the basic building structure of *matter* and the principal that all *matter,* or rather energy, is rotational in it's purest essence.'

He kept drawing new circles.

'And so the process repeats, rotating until another new sphere is created from a new intersecting point on the circle. This continues around the perimeter until we come full circle back to the second circle. This takes seven steps in all; seven *days*, the first of which creates *light*, the rest of which describe the formulation of the materialistic world.'

Bill almost leaped to his feet.

'Whoa, whoa, wait a minute; I've seen that before. That's an ancient image which supposedly describes the structure of all life, all being, including the creation of the torus, all the crystalline structures of mass, the shape of all the geometric solids, the angles and molecular bonds of atoms and molecules, the very structures of this and all other universes. I read all about it in a book called ...ah? '

Crystal chimed in.

'*The Ancient Secret of the Flower of Life*, by Drunvalo Melchizidek.'

'That's it, The Flower of Life.'

I'd never heard of it. Neither had most of the others.

'What's the Flower of Life?'

Bill took the stick and proceeded to draw another ring of circles, budding them off from the ones drawn already, then he added another layer outside that.

'It's exactly what Pieter was talking about. Ultimately you finish up with an image that looks exactly like the arrangement of cells in an early embryo, and within it, the structure of every element and atomic structure in the universe.'

He drew a final circle closely surrounding the whole scrawl.

'Wow!'

Dwight, Randy and I looked down at the confusion of scrawls; while I could follow the logic behind the first few circles I'd be buggered if I could see what all the fuss was about now. Maybe it would make more sense later on down the track.

'Well, my friends, I am hating to interrupt your most interesting discussion, but as breakfast it is now over we need to be get sailing.'

'How long, Captain Jack?'

He glanced at his watch.

'Ten minute; it is now 7.35, let us try to be on board, ready to sail, by 7.45.'

'Egyptian time?'

He grinned in my direction.

'Mister Indy, unless you wish it to be left behind for a second time, and risk missing out on meeting up with Mister Jacques and Miss Candy, I suggest you best be keeping to western time.'

As if on cue everyone laughed, briefly contemplated the return of Napoleon and Mary Anne, then stirred into action, packing their gear and taking the mandatory 'pit stop'. At 7.45 precisely we pulled out from the bank and set sail for Esna.

Not tonight Josephine

It's strange how humans gravitate so easily towards being creatures of habit. As per the previous trips on the boat, Pieter and Yuko positioned themselves at the bow, where Pernille had taken out her tarot cards and was preparing to give them a reading. I was hoping to do a little 're-membering' with Crystal but, the enigma she was, she chose to sit beside Saeed and chat to him.

That left Bill, Dwight, Randy and I gathered amidships in our now traditional huddle. At first Bill oscillated between Pernille and us, but was eventually reassured by her it was fine for him to spend time with 'the boys'. Off to a steady start, I wondered what would be the topic of the day, and, thanks to Randy, it didn't take long to resurface.

'So, where's the treasure?'

'It must still have been there at the end of the 18th Century.'

I turned to Dwight.

'What makes you say that?'

'Well firstly there was a famine in Egypt in 1784 where about a sixth of the population perished, and then in January 1791 a terrible plague raged through Cairo and elsewhere in Egypt, killing many of the ruling family; not really the sort of place you would want to be. So why would Napoleon Bonaparte invade Egypt in 1798?'

'Napoleon invaded Egypt? Why?'

'Supposedly, it was to reinstate the authority of the Sublime Porte, and suppress the Mamluks. Napoleon argued that all men were equal except as distinguished by their intellectual and moral excellences, and declared that he revered God, Muhammad, and the Koran far more than the Mamluks reverenced either.'

Randy had his own view.

'That's bullshit; I bet he discovered there were treasures buried in Egypt.'

Bill was on a similar thread.

'Or maybe some ancient knowledge for the benefit of all mankind?'

'Yeah, but how did he know?'

'Pretty simple really, think about it, when the French Revolution happened Napoleon would have gained access to all the documents and secrets of both the French aristocracy *and* probably even the French church; he's bound to have found out about the persecution of the Templars and their secrets about the scrolls. God, who knows, he may even have been part of an underground Templar movement that developed after the Knights Templar were officially abolished, who actually instigated the French Revolution.'

'How long was Napoleon in Egypt?'

'Not long; less than three years later, in March 1801 the English, effected a landing at Aboukir, and proceeded to invade Alexandria. Consequently, with the destruction of the French fleet at the Battle of the Nile, and the failure of the French forces sent to Upper Egypt, where they reached the first cataract, the French were eventually repulsed six months later.'

'What were the British doing getting involved?'

'Ah, now that's a good question. My guess is that over time, those Templars that escaped to Scotland transformed into the beginnings of the Illuminati and the Freemasons. They had been the major bankers in Europe from around 1130, and realized that whoever controlled the flow of money in countries, controlled the politicians, to a certain extent the church, and thus controlled countries and the people who lived in them.

So they infiltrated the English aristocracy, so much so that years later, in 1875, the Prince of Wales, later to become Edward the Seventh, was elected as the Masonic Grand Master. I think the British thus knew about the ancient Egyptian treasures and seized the opportunity to invade Egypt on the false premise of coming to the aid of the Mamluks and ousting the French.'

'Fuck, that's exactly the sort of bullshit that Bush and Blair pulled on Iraq.'

'Nothing changes in history, just the players.'

'So it's the British who controlled Egypt, they have all the loot?'

Dwight pondered Randy's thoughts.

'Possibly, but not initially. The expulsion of the French was followed by four years of anarchy where the Ottomans, Mamluks, and Albanians wrestled for power. Out of this chaos, the commander of the Albanian regiment, Muhammad Ali, seized power and established a dynasty. And no, Randy, it wasn't *that* Mohammed Ali, this one lived a hundred years earlier.

Having witnessed the technology and advances of the British, Ali was keen to learn more about their military and industrial techniques, so he sent students to the West and invited training missions to Egypt. Subsequently he built industries, and a system of canals for irrigation and transport, specifically introducing long-staple cotton in 1820 that, by the end of the century, had transformed Egyptian agriculture into a cash-crop mono-culture. It led to the concentration of agriculture in the hands of large landowners, particularly a large influx of foreigners who exploited Egypt's resources.'

'Let me guess, they had connections back to the British and the Illuminati.'

'Probably, Randy.'

'And it's still happening; it's exactly what all the major corporations are doing with third world countries now, exploiting their natural resources, and exploiting the common people. Exxon, BP, Coca-cola, the list goes on and on. I'm surprised the Catholic Church didn't have talons in the carcass.'

Bill interjected.

'They probably did; did you know the Vatican sent an archaeological expedition to Egypt in 1841?'

That got my interest.

'Really? Now, you've got to ask yourself, "What on earth was the Vatican doing in Egypt?" Unless of course you knew what we all know, that they were looking for hidden treasures.'

'The question is, were the Illuminati, the European bankers, in partnership with the Vatican, or competition?'

'That's a good question; I'm guessing a bit of both.'

Ideas started flowing thick and fast, and it was Randy who was leading the way.

'So do you think they used the cotton industry as a cover-up for looking for the treasure?'

'Wow, that's a brilliant question...'

Like Bill, Dwight and I were similarly impressed. Bill mulled it over.

'...I guess it's possible. I know that's part of the reason why they built the Suez Canal, so that all the corporations could ship their stuff around the world easier. In fact part of the *rules* of the Suez Canal are that it can be used in times of war, as in times of peace, by every vessel of commerce, or of war, without distinction of flag. So, even during conflicts, the battleships and destroyers of all countries could go back and forth, so long as they didn't interfere with the rich bankers trade and commerce.'

'Fuck, what sort of bullshit is that?'

'It tells you who really runs the world, that's for sure.'

'When was it built?'

'It was started in 1859, and completed and opened ten years later in 1869. But the irony is, it was built in partnership with the French. But, no points for guessing that the massive cost of constructing the Suez Canal left Egypt in enormous debt to the European banks, *visa vi* the Illuminati, and, lo and behold, in 1875, the Egyptian leader, Ismail, was forced to sell Egypt's share in the canal not to the French, but to the British Government.'

Randy was confused.

'I don't get it.'

Bill painted it as plain as day.

'By then, the French and English governments, and the US for that matter, were all owned and controlled by the money mongers, the Illuminati bankers. Countries were literally just different shop fronts, different outlets or brand names. Within three years of seizing control of the Suez, British and French *controllers* were sitting in the Egyptian cabinet, and, with the financial power of the Illuminati bankers behind them, were the real power in Egypt.'

Dwight followed on.

'But the people's dissatisfaction with Ismail's rule, and with the European intrusion, led to the formation of the first nationalist parties in 1879. Three years later, a nationalist-dominated ministry committed to democratic reforms, including parliamentary control of the budget and thus the country, forced the hand of the British and French. Fearing a reduction of their control, the British and French governments called in their military and bombarded Alexandria, crushing the Egyptian army at the battle of Tel el-Kebir. That done, they reinstalled Ismail's son as the puppet leader of a *de facto* British protectorate.'

With broad strokes Bill painted another insightful overview.

'It seems the manipulation and power-mongering that was happening in Egypt in the 19th Century had been happening for thousands of years, and was rivalled only by that of the total corruption of the Catholic Church through the middle ages. And somehow it's all connected to some sacred knowledge the ancient Egyptians knew, and that everyone else seems to want to know, but keep secret. And by the time we get to the Victorian era, it's the Brits turn at bat.'

As usual Randy was frothing at the mouth.

'So what did the British do?'

The Dam Truth

Bill and Dwight exchanged glances, then included me, seeing who would answer. I bailed straight away; on this topic I was about as much use as a perky set of tits on a rodeo bull. Though Bill clearly had more to say, he left it to our resident Middle Eastern expert, Dwight, to get the ball rolling, though he did fill in a few blanks along the way.

'Several years after the invasion, in 1898, the British proposed building a dam across the Nile, downstream of the island of Philae, at the site of the first cataract at Aswan.'

'It was designed by Sir William Willcocks, and involved the eminent engineers Sir Benjamin Baker and Sir John Aird; all of whom were Freemasons.'

Randy reacted straight away.

'It figures, I knew the Freemasons would have their grubby mits all over it.'

After we'd all had a good chuckle, Dwight continued.

'The annual floods from Ethiopia and the East African drainage basin, which at their peak could increase the flood's volume as much as sixteen-fold, also brought high water levels and tons of natural nutrients and minerals. They enriched and rejuvenated the soil, keeping it fertile along the full length of the river and making the Nile Valley and the Nile Delta ideal for farming...'

I wondered if that could really explain what I had seen on elephantine? I kept it in the back of my mind as Dwight forged ahead.

'...But suddenly the British wanted to control the flood, supposedly because Egypt's population was increasing, and it wanted to protect and support the farmland so as to prevent droughts and famine.

But the reality was, it had nothing to do with the welfare of the locals, it was all to do with protecting the economical importance and business interests of the cotton fields; high-water years could wipe out the whole crop, while in low-water years a drought could do the same.'

'The bastards did a similar thing in the US.'

'What do you mean, Randy?'

'They protected the cotton industry in the United States by passing legislation prohibiting the cultivation of hemp; not only did they ban marijuana to protect the pharmaceutical industry, marijuana, which by the way has huge medicinal benefits, but they banned *all* hemps, because hemp was a major threat to both the cotton and paper industries.

And the fuckers are doing the same thing now with fossil fuels and free fuels; the Illuminati, the Freemasons, the Templar bankers, they control all financial markets so they control all the major governments, and that means they control the legislation. One day we'll all wake up to the fact we're all being screwed up the ass and hang the fucking pricks by their testicles from razor wire fences.'

Bill stirred the pot.

'Come on Randy, don't beat around the bush, say what you really think?'

'Well, if the Freemasons were involved in the building of the dam, then you can bet your bottom dollar there was probably even another ulterior motive for the dam other than just to help the impoverished local farmers.'

'You might be right, Randy, the construction of the dam meant a serious threat to the temples at Philae. The island had become quite a tourist escape for the aristocracy of Victorian England, and the proposed height of the dam was at first restricted because of the protests made by people interested in preserving Philae, and the other temples and monuments upstream, from being submerged.

Despite their protests though, work on the dam commenced in 1898, though the protests delayed construction somewhat. That was until 1901 when Winston Churchill stepped in and spoke out against resistance to the dam. He supposedly couldn't give a shit about ancient Egyptian cultural heritage, and, having spoken, effectively gave the dam the rubber stamp.'

Bill chipped in again.

'That's really interesting, because not only was Churchill's father a Freemason, but Winston himself was initiated into the Studholme Lodge around that very time, in fact on May 24th 1901.'

'The Freemasons *did* have their grubby little paws all over it.'

Randy was like a starving ferret on a rabbit's leg, and he hung on Dwight's every word.

'Well, even though Churchill's speech gave the dam the go ahead, it also brought about more talk of relocating the temples, piece by piece, stone by stone, to a nearby island such as Biggeh or even Elephantine. But instead of moving the temples, Captain Henry Lyon, who was the chief engineer, strengthened the foundations and consolidated the supporting superstructures so that they could withstand the *seasonal* effects of water flow from the dam.'

Bill was chuckling away and shaking his head.

'You know, Captain Henry Lyon was a Freemason as well.'

'Really, well it looks like Randy was right, the whole thing was a Freemason plot.'

I mused over it.

'Yes, so what were they really after?'

'Interestingly enough, in the course of his excavations Lyon discovered the remains of several Christian churches built behind the Temple of Isis.'

'One can only wonder what else he found.'

I thought about my time on Philae, about my thoughts of what may still be under the water, under the original temples on P'aaleq. It made me ponder, that given their connection to the ancient scrolls of the Essenes, and through them back to the sacred knowledge of the Tat Brotherhood and the secrets of Seqenenre, did the Freemasons have a totally different agenda all together? Was the building of the dam just an excuse to dig up, and then cover up, what was really on the island of P'aaleq? And while I pondered, Dwight pontificated.

'Once the dam was completed and opened, though thanks to Lyon's work the temples endured for another seventy years, it sounded the death knell for the stunning wall reliefs.'

'And guess who officially opened the dam; none other than His Royal Highness Prince Arthur, the Duke of Connaught and Strathearn, a grand master of the United Grand Lodge of England, which just happens to be the oldest Masonic Order and Grand Lodge in the world.'

I had to say something.

'Geez, Bill, you know a hell of a lot about Freemasonry.'

'That's because I *was* one, for over twenty years.'

Randy almost fell overboard.

'Jesus H, we've been sleeping with the enemy.'

Bill laughed.

'WAS one, Randy, the more I delved into its history, the more I became disillusioned, just as I had been with the Catholic Church when I was younger.'

Dwight was putting the pieces together.

'Oh, wait a minute, it gets even better. Somehow, the initial design of the dam, by the most reputable firm in England, was soon found to be inadequate, and so between 1907 and 1912 it was raised again by the same Freemason affiliated engineers John Aird & Co. However after the First World War, sick of their colonial rulers, the Egyptian people rebelled in Egypt's first modern revolution. That resulted in Great Britain issuing a unilateral declaration of Egypt's independence on 22 February 1922. Consequently, in 1923, the new Egyptian Government drafted and implemented a new constitution, one based on the British parliamentary system with Saad Zaghlul popularly elected as the first Prime Minister of Egypt in 1924.

But the British must have done some sort of clandestine deal with Zaghlul, because, rather than ousting the British, he approved the raising of the dam a second time, by John Aird & Co, from 1929 to 1934. Despite that, in 1946 the dam almost overflowed yet again, but rather than raise its height a third time, the decision was made to build a second, bigger dam, six kilometres further upriver.'

I had it!

'I think the real reason they built the dam was to cover up the excavation work they wanted to do on P'aaleq.'

They all looked at me dumbfounded.

'Where's P'aaleq?'

'It was the original island the Temple of Isis was on before they moved it to Philae, or Aglika as it was called in ancient times. The whole cotton industry thing was just a convenient bullshit justification that they also managed to benefit from financially. It must have taken them nearly thirty years to find everything, excavate it all and secretly remove it.'

'The treasure, you mean the treasure don't you?'

Randy looked crest-fallen.

'I'm afraid so, Randy, at least at Philae.'

'Do you think that included Elephantine Island? I mean maybe they were looking for the Ark of the Covenant as well?'

He'd done it again.

'Of course! They were probably looking for everything they could get their hands on, but the Ark of the Covenant, hell now, that *would* have been a prize. I don't know about that though, somehow I feel it was moved from Elephantine Island well before the 20th Century.'

'Where to?'

'I have no idea. But my guess is they must have removed all they needed from P'aaleq, from the original Temple of Isis.'

Dwight was one step ahead.

'So why did they build the High Dam in the 1950's then?'

'That's a good question, maybe there was more left behind at other temples further upstream?'

Randy still had gold in his eyes.

'Surely the British built it so they could get the rest of the treasure?'

'It's a good thought, but the continued instability in the Egyptian Government, which was due to the remaining British control, led to a military coup d'état in 1952, which was led by Gamal Abdel Nasser. Nassar was part of a group known as the Free Officers Movement, which was strongly controlled by the Nazis and the Muslim Brotherhood. It ousted the monarchy and resulted in a dissolution of the parliament.

The next year the Egyptian Republic was declared, and the year after that, in 1954, Nasser put the elected president, General Muhammad Naguib, under house arrest, forced him to resign, and took control.'

'How the fuck did the Nazis get involved?'

I wasn't sure, nor was Dwight, but thankfully Bill had the answer.

'Hitler was preoccupied with ancient artefacts, such as the Spear of Destiny, which he acquired from a museum by annexing Austria, and no doubt he knew of the stories of the Ark being back in Egypt, that whoever had the Ark before their army was invincible. My thinking is that's why Germany invaded Egypt during World War II, for the same reasons as everybody else throughout the centuries.'

Dwight was slightly confused.

'Yeah, but weren't most of the Nazis locked away after World War II?'

Now we were totally in Randy's territory.

'No, exactly the opposite, the Nazi scientists were all whisked out of Germany to the US, where they firstly formed the core of the nuclear and rocket programs, and then became the backbone of NASA. The Nazis wanted a one world government, and so do the Illuminati, that's a little more than a coincidence, don't you think?'

The pieces were slowly coming together in my mind

'I see where you're coming from Randy, but why would the Nazis team up with the Muslims?'

'They had a common objective, to eliminate the Jews.'

I made the connection.

'And that would be because they're the cursed race, the ones responsible for assassinating Seqenenre and stealing the Ark of the Covenant and lots of other sacred objects from Egypt.'

'You got it, dude.'

'So it was the Nazis and the Muslim Brotherhood who built the new dam.'

Dwight jumped in.

'No, it was the Russians.'

'What?!'

While I may have been keeping up and able to follow the discussion until now, Dwight's introducing of the Russians into the mix threw me completely.

'I guess if Hitler wanted the ancient technologies, it makes sense that Stalin would have as well, but how did the Russians get involved with Egypt?'

'It wasn't until Nassar took power in 1954 that proper planning for a new dam started. Now we would assume that Nassar was aligned with the either the Nazis or the Muslim Brotherhood, or maybe both, and yet in September 1955 Nasser announced an arms deal with Czechoslovakia, who were just acting as the middleman for the Russians. Interestingly, a few months later, despite Nassar's deal with the Russians, the US and UK pledged fifty-six million and fourteen million dollars respectively towards construction of the dam.'

'Clearly they were trying to protect their *investment*.'

'Nassar must have been pretty shrewd though, he didn't accept the US and UK offer and upped the ante six months later in May 1956 when he recognized communist China, an act which was in direct conflict with the US. Then, a month later, the Soviets offered Nasser over a billion dollars US at 2% interest for the construction of the dam.'

Bill shook his head.

'The Soviets were in a cold war against the US, why on earth would they spend over a billion dollars in Egypt on a dam? What could they hope to gain?'

'Nassar was clearly playing one side against the other. Then in July 1956, when The United States' State Department announced that financial assistance for the High Dam was not feasible, Nassar responded within a week by nationalizing the Suez Canal, in effect *stealing* the canal back from the creditors and thus negating the debt.'

'I don't think the Illuminati bankers would have been too pleased about that.'

'They weren't; in fact it prompted the 1956 Suez Crisis and the Suez War. The UK, France, and Israel all tried to invade Egypt, but they failed and were forced to withdraw from the Suez.'

'I can't imagine they gave up that easily.'

'Maybe they didn't.'

We all looked at Bill, wondering what he meant.

'Well, think about it, who was it that provided the weapons to Egypt merely a year before hand?'

'The Russians.'

'And where did the Russians get the weapons?'

We all shrugged our shoulders so Bill answered his own question.

'From the weapons merchants.'

'And who were they?'

'It all goes back to the Templar bankers who were the original weapons merchants and traders, and have been ever since. So long as there are wars, it's a very lucrative market. So if you're the Illuminati, how do you sell more weapons?'

'You create more wars and conflicts.'

'Right. And who goes into wars?'

'Countries.'

'Yes, but more than that, the governments that *you* control.'

I needed to get it clearly in my head.

'So the Illuminati control the governments, then set them in conflict with one another, all the time, supplying weapons to both or all sides. They don't care who wins because they own all the combatants, so the more they fight, the more money they make.'

'It certainly ain't rocket science.'

'Bill, I think you've just explained the real cause of every war since about 1300.'

'My friends, we will be arriving at it Esna in just a few minute.'

It was 8:50 am and the time had flown; Saeed maintained his position at the rudder, a relaxed Crystal beside him, as Gomar and Mohammed moved towards the bow readying to tend to the sail. On the fore-deck Pernille had finished her reading and was happily chatting with Pieter and Yuko.

Further ahead on the west bank, numerous cruise liners were lined up four and five deep at the dock. Though partially obscured by the flotilla of tourist hotels, the city of Esna slowly drifted into view and we all started to break from our groups, stretching and preparing to disembark.

'Wait an minute, wait a minute....'

Randy had a bemused sort of mentally constipated look on his face.

'... if I've got it right, then the Illuminati owns every government, every religion, every financial system and major corporation on the planet, and uses them purely to control the masses and make even more money for themselves.'

Bill winced.

'They make the money, then they lend the money to you at interest, you spend it with them to buy weapons, houses, drugs, food, oil and all manner of other goods, all of which they own, and all of which have an elevated profit margins attached, and then to top it off they create wars to escalate prices through accelerated demand and restricted supply. Welcome to the western economic hamster wheel, aptly referred to as *the rat race*.'

We pulled into a grassed section of the bank just upstream of the main docks and eagerly clambered ashore, all laughing and in great spirits. Mohammed and Gomar stayed with the boat as Saeed led the way along the riverside road towards the ticket office, Crystal still by his side. I quickened my pace to join them, leaving Pernille, Bill, Pieter and Yuko chatting next in line, and the two boys a few more paces back, bringing up the rear.

Esna

At first sight the village of Esna appeared like most other small Egyptian villages along the Nile, a shit-hole! Now maybe that was unfair, but the more we walked, the more my first impression held firm.

In ancient times the city was called Iunyt or Ta-senet, and was probably a beautiful city, but now, as Esna, it was dusty, dirty, with garbage in the streets, in the canals, in the river; the standard of living hovered between a third-world slum and second-world hovel. Maybe it was partly because most of the side roads were dirt and those roads that were sealed look more like the pock-marked cratered surface of the dark side of the moon.

There were no gutters, probably because there was no rain to speak of, and no drainage. The buildings had the same slap-dash approach to construction standards and I think only two, or maybe three rules applied; use what you can find, close enough is good enough, and, if it remains standing for more than a year then that's a bonus.

And yet the place was full of joy, you could see it on the faces of the villagers, especially the children who ran up and walked along side us. In particular, they were fascinated by Crystal; captivated by her.

'You very pretty lady.'

'You princess.'

Resting her hand on their shoulder, or cupping their cheeks and heads in her hand, Crystal was like the Pied Piper, except she never said a word, everything was conveyed in looks, smiles and touches. Within minutes there must have been fifteen to twenty of them ranging from five to ten years old scampering along at her feet. The overflow gravitated to my side.

'Hello. What is your name?'

I smiled back.

'Alex, what is *your* name?'

They couldn't have been more than seven or eight, and hadn't learned to fully respond yet, so they scurried alongside like bewitched little rodents repeating the game parrot-fashion.

'What is your name?'

'You have quite a way with children, Mister Indy, maybe it is your hat?'

I laughed at Saeed.

'I don't suppose they see many people like me here?'

Suddenly, but calmly, Crystal interjected.

'These beautiful children have all seen a crocodile, in fact they have seen many of them, but they have never seen an antelope.'

'And yet we protect the crocodiles, the cold blooded reptiles that lurk beneath the surface, while we claim the forests and grasslands for our own greedy purposes and push the antelopes to the brink of existence.'

She turned to me and smiled, then, as if I hadn't fully heard the melody, played another tune on her flute.

'So what behaviour will they copy, can they copy, only that which they can see.'

It resonated strongly in my heart; as a high school drama teacher for fifteen years I had tried and tried to instil a sense of self-belief, confidence and purpose in the kids, only to see it undermined by the overwhelming pressure and tide of the education system. Only the strongest few survived; the rest were swamped, left stranded, washed down river, smashed against the rapids, or even drowned.

'I guess the children here are no different to the children all round the world; how can we teach them what is right when we haven't even learned that ourselves?'

'There is no right or wrong, nothing to teach, nothing to learn, just *all* to remember.'

As we reached the ticket office it was fairly quiet; no queues to speak of, just the tourist police milling around in the street, leaning back on the riverside railings in their now familiar relaxed manner, their ever present high-tar cigarettes in one hand and nursing their Russian built kalashnikovs in the other.

I half expected Jacques and Candy to be standing there waiting, Jacques expressing his indignation at the manner in which he had been treated, but the two of them were nowhere to be seen. No doubt he was giving Mary Anne a damn good rogering in Luxor.

I purchased my ticket, a bargain at only twenty pounds, then waited with Saeed as the others bought theirs.

'Indy, I have been listen to you with it great interest to your discussion with Miss Crystal and the others. I think it you should talk with my uncle.'

'The one back in Australia?'

'No, the one here in Luxor.'

'OK, and why's that?'

'My uncle he is retire now, but for many year he was chief supervisor at Medinet Habu.'

'Medinet Habu? The Temple on the West Bank at Luxor?'

'Yes, but as a young man in the 1960's he work in Aswan relocating the temple from P'aaleq to Aglika.'

'I bet he has a few stories to tell.'

'Oh, yes, many of them I think you may find *most* interesting. He was also the long time childhood friend of Mister Zahi Hawass until several year ago.'

'Now that *is* interesting.'

'If you wish it I will make the arrangement for you to meet with him once you get to Luxor.'

'I would like that very much, thanks, Saeed.'

That sorted, everyone had their ticket and we were ready to see the temple at Esna. Saeed pointed tenuously towards a darkened alley.

'Very good. This way it is the temple. It is now 9:20, I will be meet you back here at 10:30 am western time.'

I felt we were about to enter the abyss, in truth we were about to negotiate the rapids otherwise known as the Esna Market.

The Esna Market

Crystal boldly led the way down a short narrow street, or rather dingy alley that led away from the falsely perceived safety of the river. Within metres of entering we were all sucked forward, nay thrust, into the swirling cacophony that was the market.

Entering the abyss I looked for parallels between this, the Aswan Bazaar, and the Edfu arcade, and there were many: the similar goods on sale; statues and statuettes, scarves, linen, clothing, papyri, oils, and the meticulously attired local merchants, each donning samples of the local goods, crawling over the emerging tourists like harvester arts at a family day picnic.

'So, Dwight, who did finish up paying for the dam?'

We dodged the first bank of stallholders.

'The Soviet Union; in 1958 they stepped in and funded the whole project. Though Egyptian engineers had some input, it was primarily designed by the Soviet Hydroproject Institute. That raised concern with archaeologists because the design meant that numerous major historical sites, including Philae, were about to become submerged. Clearly drastic action had to be taken as soon as possible or they would be lost.

So construction began on the enormous rock and clay dam in 1960, with twenty-five-thousand Egyptian workers forming the backbone of the workforce, and with the Soviets providing not only all the technicians and heavy machinery, but twenty-thousand soldiers as well. At the same time, UNESCO began a rescue operation; sites were surveyed, excavated and twenty-four major monuments were moved to safer locations or gifted to countries that helped with the works.'

Pushing by a scarf seller who had lassoed a boatload of Chinese tourists, Randy rallied.

'UNESCO? That was the fore-runner of the United Nations, they were not only totally Illuminati, but they were controlled by the Dracos as well.'

I'd never heard of them before the trip, and now, within two days they had surfaced twice. Originally, when Crystal talked about them, I thought it must have been just another myth, or one of Randy's secret conspiracy organizations. But now I was more than curious, I was putting pieces of a gigantic galactic puzzle together.

'Who are the Dracos again?'

Like a marauding pack of desert jackals, the hawkers quickly singled out the weakest of the herd, Pernille and Yuko, allowing the strongest to pass through. Pieter had teamed up with Bill and they left the two girls to their bartering fate, preferring to keep up with the discussion that had started on the White Rose and continued to unfold. The last I saw the two girls they had been encircled, and each of the hawkers was taking his turn nipping at their heels, trying to lure them into their lairs.

Crystal turned back. I thought, as the clear spiritual matriarch of the Minnow, she had glanced back because her 'girls' were being tempted with bright coloured scarves, baubles, bangles, and beads. I was wrong.

'The Dracos are a race of reptilians who originated from Alpha Draconis in the constellation Draco. They are the oldest reptilian race in the universe, having been around for seven-billion years. They believe they own everything, including the planet Earth.'

She clearly didn't like these Dracos guys one iota. Having vented her thoughts, Crystal paused momentarily, seemingly contemplating whether to return and protect her flock. I had visions of returning later to find nothing but their bones, picked clean of every last coin of baksheesh. But then I knew Pernille didn't have any cash, and Yuko had been back-packing for months, so I guessed they were pretty safe after all; they would just be a little delayed in getting through the mayhem of the crowd and to the temple. I guess Crystal must have been of the same mind and turned, continuing forward.

With Pernille and Yuko now totally abandoned to shopping nirvana, Crystal weaved her way through the obstacle course of shop owners and tourists like a champion slalom skier vying for Olympic gold. Closely in her wake, Randy pranced around like a lapdog about to go on a walk.

'See, I told you.'

Dwight chuckled away to himself.

'Come on, Randy, aliens? We've talked about this before. Don't get me wrong, I've got an open mind on pretty much everything, but The United Nations run by an alien race of reptiles seven-billion years old, it's a bit far fetched?'

Bill was less attached to his 'educational' conditioning.

'Wait a minute, Dwight, don't be so hasty, I mean look at all the stuff we've discovered over the last couple of days, if anyone had even suggested half of that before the trip we would all have said they were dreaming.'

'True, but reptiles running the United Nations? If it wasn't just after 9:00 in the morning and I hadn't seen what you and Crystal had for breakfast, I'd have bet my last dollar you were both either drunk as skunks, or you'd been in the sun too long; it all sounds like science fiction. Now if they'd actually dug up some real evidence, that would be a different matter.'

'Randy may be right, there are reptiles all though our mythology. There was Quetzalcoatl, the feathered serpent creator god of the Aztecs, the Chinese had a dragon king, Hindu mythology had the Nāga, a reptilian race that lived underground and interacted with human beings, and the Sumerians had statuettes of reptilian gods who came from the stars.'

I threw in my two cents.

'If it looks like a duck, walks like a duck, quacks like a duck.'

'Then it's probably a pterodactyl.'

Bill and I shared the joke, as Randy and Dwight continued their sparring. Then my mind clicked into another gear as I remembered an old TV show.

'Hang on guys, maybe there's more to it.'

They all looked at me right at that moment when, barely two-hundred metres from the river, we emerged from the market and stood before the entrance to the site of the Temple of Esna.

The Esna Temple Site

Though the site had only been partially excavated, the large hall stood in a big squarish pit in the middle of the modern town about nine to ten metres below the surrounding houses and street level. From the distance of the street and entrance gate above, it appeared well preserved.

The temple was not so much a complete temple but rather just the Hypostyle Hall which would have stood outside the main temple, as it had at Philae and Edfu, plus a few minor ruins of some later and earlier buildings.

It had been excavated by Auguste Mariette and was dedicated to Khnum, the ram god worshiped throughout this area, who fashioned mankind on his potter's wheel using mud from the Nile. I figured out it was not oriented exactly East/West, but about ten to fifteen degrees anticlockwise, east/northeast. It was not hard to deduce that the remains of the main temple and the rest of the ancient city complex were still buried beneath the surrounding buildings of the modern town.

Handing over our tickets, we went through the usual token security screening, and down the steep steps into the forecourt, the discussion flowing as we made our way into the site.

'I don't think Hitler was the only one interested in finding and recovering ancient and possibly alien technology, I think Stalin was as well.'

'What makes you say that?'

'I remember a documentary type show from the seventies called something like '*The Secret UFO files of the KGB*' or something like that; it was hosted by one-time James Bond, Roger Moore. Clearly, because of the information they would have gleaned from Nazi files found when they took Berlin, and their extensive spy network, the Soviets would have known about Hitler's agenda, and about the potential findings of ancient technologies in Egypt.

So, sometime after the end of World War II, probably in the late 1950's, and coinciding with their entry into Egypt, the Russians instigated a project called Project Isis, which was specifically set up to discover advanced knowledge left by an ancient Egyptian civilization.'

We stopped in the centre of the forecourt, near the ruins of what looked like an early Christian church, waiting for Pernille and Yuko to join us, however they were still trapped somewhere in the abyss.

'Did they find anything?'

'They sure did. In July 1960 a Bedouin trader supposedly stumbled across the tomb of an ancient God that wasn't supposed to exist, and the Soviets went straight into action, ordering the military to the site. In order to avoid drawing attention to the activity, they dressed their archaeologists as soldiers and set about excavating and opening "The Tomb of the Ancient Visitor", as it was found to be titled.'

'The building of the Aswan Dam would have been a perfect cover.'

'It was, and in 1961, unknown to the rest of the world, the Soviets finally entered the tomb; as far as I know, the first intact tomb opened since the discovery of Tutankhamun's tomb.

Inside, they discovered an unopened sarcophagus and reported that one of the walls exhibited magnetic repulsive forces. Written on the walls were references to "The Followers"; those who were charged with keeping the knowledge taught to them by Osiris, and to keep that knowledge sacred and secret until Osiris returned.'

'Do you think these "followers" were the same as the Tat Brotherhood or the Brotherhood of Thoth?'

'It would certainly make sense. The hieroglyphs referred to the prophecy of the return of ancient winged gods; the second coming of Osiris, that it would herald a new age.'

'That sounds just like the second coming of Jesus.'

Randy was right, it did, and Bill could explain exactly how it came about.

'It doesn't take much vision to see how the knowledge of the ancient Egyptians concerning the second coming of Osiris could be misinterpreted by those who hijacked the teachings of the Essenes and created Christianity.'

Finally the two girls appeared at street level, having temporarily escaped the clutches of the market, and made their way down the steps to join us.

'What happened to the treasure?'

'According to the Russian KGB records, they removed fifteen crates of "relics", eight samples of hieroglyphs, and one stone sarcophagus containing one partial mummy; taking the samples back to Moscow.

On examination, several of the radioactive metallic samples were found to be composed of metals and synthetic compounds of unknown origin, but dating to before 10,000 BC.'

'Was the mummy a reptilian?'

'No, but it wasn't human either. When they examined the mummy they found it was humanoid, with a large cranium, large eyes, small chin and mouth and a long neck. The "being" was supposedly from the constellation of Orion.'

Dwight asked the obvious question.

'You think it was Osiris they found?'

'I doubt it; all reports and ancient Egyptian myths suggest he was dismembered into fourteen pieces and scattered around Egypt. But who knows, you could be on the right track.'

'What happened to the tomb, to the mummy?'

'Following their initial discoveries, the Russians refocused on finding further technology, and, using ground imaging radar on the passage and tomb, discovered a vertical passage under the tomb that led down to a large ovoid chamber deep beneath the surface.'

'What was in it?'

'That's just it, no one knows. The presence of the underground cavity divided the scientists; some wanted it opened, others feared it may unleash some dreaded curse, others formed a group calling themselves "The Followers". In the end the chamber was left unopened.'

'So what happened to the scientists?'

'Especially, "The Followers"?'

'That's where it gets *really* interesting, you see Project Isis officially ended in 1981, but in April 1985 a group of Russian tourists vanished somewhere in the Egyptian desert just outside Cairo. When an investigation was carried out as to who they were, it turned out the tourists were mostly made up of the Russian scientists who had been part of the original opening of the tomb.

They arrived at an unknown restricted site somewhere out in the desert, got off their bus, and waited looking up into the evening sky. Then, a bright light approached at speed from the heavens, hovered for a moment, and they all disappeared. Then the light retreated back into the sky at speed. It was if they had arranged to go there at a predetermined time specifically to be picked up.'

Pernille and Yuko finally rejoined the group and we all stood looking at each other and at our location, much as the Russian scientists had done twenty-five years earlier, wondering what to do next. Were we all 'followers' waiting to reawaken, waiting to be picked up by some alien creator race and whisked off to who-knows-where?

'Well, we've got about an hour, so let's explore.'

Pieter and Yuko walked off to the left, Bill and Pernille to the right, whereas Randy and Dwight headed straight inside. Crystal waited until the others had gone then turned to address me.

'There may not appear to be that much here at Esna, but if you have your eyes and heart open, and look below the surface, you may be surprised at what you discover...'

She then sauntered majestically away several steps, before pausing and briefly turning back.

'... or re-member.'

Then she continued in through the entrance, leaving me to contemplate where to start. Since I was outside, and near to the ruins of a Christian Church, I decided not to stalk Crystal, but to go solo and have a look around the forecourt. The modern nine-metre brick retaining walls to the east of the compound probably masked what would have been the buried ruins of the first pylons. Inside them, sections of a Coptic Church had been erected in the forecourt.

There were other bits and pieces of walls and columns from differing times, some from the Roman period, some from the Greek era, others from the 18th Dynasty, and some even earlier; all strategically placed as if to suggest this is where the Christian Church would have been.

It was a mish-mash, and clearly just tourist-driven Egyptian opportunism, not the informed, professional archaeological restoration one would have expected. This modern 'remedy' was reinforced by the material used in covering the forecourt and total temple surrounds; grit and river stones, much as they had done at Kom Ombo, just a lot worse.

Despite my disgust, I checked my notes, remembering from my research that the temple at Esna, or rather the Hypostyle Hall at Esna, was one of the last temples built by the ancient Egyptians.

'The Temple of Esna has the last known hieroglyphic inscriptions ever recorded; completed by the Roman Emperor Dios in 250 A.D. and includes one with an inscription from Emperor Decius on the back decreeing that Christians will suffer death if they don't make sacrifices to the pagan gods.'

I started looking around the blocks, searching specifically for it, but to no avail. What I did find was a beautiful black granite statue of whom I thought was Sekhmet, but who turned out to be the little known lion-headed goddess, Menheyet, the consort of Khnum. I just thought – a rose by any other name. In any case, it clearly didn't belong where it had been placed, neither chronologically nor aesthetically, but it was a major clue to me; granite meant old, very old, and black granite had some special importance, though I had no idea what it was.

Further around to the south were two more groupings of blocks placed randomly along the retaining walls. Amongst the second; two pharaonic busts of heavily worn red granite, one resembling the statue of Queen Tiye in the Cairo Museum, as well as sections of red granite and black granite columns, bases, and pieces that looked like preparatory tables or altars. And there was one totally incongruent, shaped column section made of alabaster. Where did they all come from? The answer was right in front of me.

I knew that the current temple was begun by Ptolemaic rulers and finished by the Romans, for their names were apparently recorded all over the temple walls. The Hypostyle Hall itself, or the Temple of Khnum as it was now called, was the latest addition.

'Built by the Roman emperor Claudius in the 1st Century AD. The Temple of Esna sits atop the ruins of a preceding sanctuary built by Thutmoses III in the 18th Dynasty, which itself was built over the ruins of even earlier temples.'

So how did the red granite get to be where it was now? Quite simply.

Between the arrangement of stones and the temple was a round drain-covering; a little over four-feet in diameter. It was clearly a 20th Century addition to the site, and apparent that when they were digging out the channels for the drainage of the 'submerged' temple they unearthed various 'bits of rubble' which were invariably cast to one side.

The drains and pipes in place, they simply filled in the ground with grit and river-stones, levelled it off, and, not having a clue what to do with the older stones, placed the flotsam and jetsam 'strategically' to the side.

It totally reinforced my idea about the tsunami. And, if I had any doubts before, the nine metres of sedimentary deposits that stared me in the face, that marked the difference between the lower level of the old temple and the level of the modern city above, quelled every single one of them.

The southern exterior wall of the Hall had a reasonable well-preserved huge relief of one of the later pharaohs, probably Ptolemy III as he was the major restorer of the temples, followed by a tame lion. The pharaoh was smiting the assembled chiefs of his enemies before the blessing of Khnum, holding what looked like a feather of truth or a curved knife, and a lion headed god, either Sehkmet, or Khnum's consort, Menheyet.

Moving around to the rear of the Hall it was easier to see the layers of sediment from which the temple had been excavated, as there was no brick retaining wall. Somewhere under all this mud was probably the actual inner sanctum temple from the Ptolemaic era. I stood there taking it all in, feeling the rock, shifting my perspective under tons of debris; here was the living proof so to speak, more so than at Kom Ombo or possibly at Edfu.

This was no minor flood, this was nine metres of sediment from a *major* tsunami, and it swamped EVERYTHING. And that was just since the building of *this* structure, who knows what was buried below that, or when *it* was buried?

This temple had to have been buried *after* the Roman era that's for sure, and that made me lean strongly towards the earthquakes Crystal had talked about in 1303. That sorted in my mind, I concluded there was not really anything else to discover here at Esna and moved on.

The rear wall was all that remained of the Ptolemaic era, the exterior façade containing reliefs of Horus and Khnum dragging a net full of fish from the Nile. Everything else *forward* of that belonged to the Romans.

Instead of entering the hall through the rear entrance, I continued around the perimeter, passed the northern façade, which was basically a mirror of the southern side, passed another drain cover, and back to the front entrance, where I stood back, taking in the view.

The 'Temple' was built from red sandstone, measured about forty metres wide, was over fifteen metres high and had the same decorated inter-columnar screen wall frontage as the Hypostyle Hall at Edfu. There were two smaller outer doorways at the edges, probably used by the priest for access, a third door in the right wall that appeared to lead to a small inner room, and then the main large opening gateway in the centre. For some reason I checked my notes before entering.

'There is an inscription carved on the wall of the temple that those who enter the temple are expected to cut their fingernails and toenails, remove other body hair, wash their hands with natron salt, dress in linen, as opposed to wool which was forbidden, and not to have had sexual intercourse for several days.'

Having calculated that I passed three out of the five, I felt comfortable to enter the Hall.

Inside the Temple of Esna

The building echoed to the chirps of birds and coos of pigeons. On the left side of the gateway was a relief of the sky goddess, Nut, and several constellations; one being Orion's belt, though I wasn't sure exactly what the others were.

'That's Orion.'

'Hmmm?'

Pieter stood beside me pointing to the reliefs.

'And that's Sirius, the Dog Star; most of the ancient Egyptian mythology is linked to it, or Sothis as they called it. And over here is Alpha Draconis; the Dragon Star.'

'Alpha Draconis? What does that mean to the ancient Egyptians?'

Pieter shrugged his shoulders.

'I don't know.'

'Pieter, do you think the United Nations really could be run by reptiles?'

'Cold-blooded, self-serving, power-hungry reptiles secretly manipulating the world through a puppet organization that pretends to have the best interests of the human race as its priority? It wouldn't surprise me.'

My mind started ticking over as I moved further inside, the floor, like the courtyard, composed, not of sandstone blocks like at Edfu, but the same grit and river-stones as the forecourt. It also had the same appalling lighting system installed throughout to illuminate the columns.

As I wandered left, passing a small room inside the entrance like those in the Hypostyle Hall at Edfu, which probably served as a storeroom or change room for the priests, I wondered what *really* lay below the ground. Flanking the door was a relief of the Roman Emperor, Trajan, carried in a litter by six priests wearing masks of Anubis and Horus. Suddenly I started getting images in my mind of an old TV series about reptiles coming to Earth.

Further on, there was a strange hieroglyphic text to Khnum, written almost entirely from rams, just inside the front corner of the hall and next to the door used by the priests for access to the temple. But still the TV show lingered in my mind.

Hitting the southern wall, I ran into Bill and Pernille in one corner, Randy and Dwight in the other.

'Hey Bill, do you remember back in the early eighties they made a series about a race of reptiles that came to conquer Earth?'

'Sure do.'

'What was it called again?'

'"V"'

'That's it!'

From the other corner, Dwight corrected him.

'No, that's a recent series.'

Then Randy corrected us all.

'Actually it's a remake of the 1983 miniseries, and in the remake the reptilians have been on earth all along.'

That was a little too much of a coincidence for my liking, and, as I examined the southern wall, which was covered with four rows of relief's, showing Ptolemaic and Roman Emperors dressed as pharaohs making sacrifices to Khnum, I considered the similarities.

'You have to wonder where they got the idea from?'

Unseen by the rest of us, Crystal spoke from behind a column.

'It's called seeding; the information, truth, is sub-consciously seeded by higher entities into the consciousness of "humans" during the dream state, just like the whole Star Trek idea was seeded through Gene Roddenberry.'

As we circled round to join her, Randy was the first to react.

'What about *Stargate, Star Wars, Predator, Alien I, II and III* and heaps of other movies?'

Quickly followed by me.

'*Close Encounters, ET, Species, Contact, Red Dwarf, The Hitchhikers' Guide to the Galaxy, Mars Attacks*?'

Then Bill.

'*Lost in Space, Battlestar Galactica, War of the Worlds, The Day the Earth Stood Still, Day of the Triffids, The Blob, The Thing*?'

'*Armageddon*?'

Crystal just smiled.

'Ultimately every idea comes from the Source, but they have to come *through* someone.'

Whilst Bill and I might have been slightly flippant, Dwight was thinking a little deeper.

'You mean there really is a Galactic Federation?'

Crystal walked slowly though the Hall, and, like the disciples of Aristotle, Plato or Jesus, we dutifully followed.

'Of course; they were the ones who negotiated a truce with the Dracos, deigning this planet to be a planet of healing; a place where races could come to work out their karmic issues. Hence the scenario that is being played out throughout the world; that of choosing between fear, or love.

The reptilians believe that fear is the best way to rule, and that love is weak, the Galactic Federation believes the opposite. Ultimately though, it is all one, just the duality of All That Is.'

We stopped in the very centre of the Hall, looking up at the central image on the back wall, once part of the older Ptolemaic pylon. It still had much of its colour, though now somewhat muted, and appeared to be an image of Khnum in a large central disc.

Below and above were images of the winged disc and double uraeus. Was this a connection, did it refer to an alien creator-race coming from the second sun, Nibiru? Randy was on the same tack.

'So what you are saying, is that the "V" series was seeded by the Galactic Federation to help us remember the truth about the Dracos, that they've always been here?'

'Possibly, or maybe it was deliberately put there by the Dracos themselves; to keep us held in fear, and to trigger the activation of the alien reptilian DNA in all of us.'

'What happens when it's activated?'

'How you choose to react is determined by the level of your own vibrational energy; if it is low, it will respond and react to fear with fear. If it is high, it will, in effect, short circuit the activation of the reptilian DNA, and keep you in your heart.'

She moved on, towards the northern wall, and like sheep, or perhaps lambs to the slaughter, we followed. To the right, on the inside of the front wall, was another interesting text to Khnum, or more likely to Sobek, written almost entirely with hieroglyphs of crocodiles. Hidden meanings were everywhere, in the reliefs, in the words Crystal said, in the places we had visited, the events that were happening, all supposedly by complete coincidence. But that was it exactly: co–incidence: incidents occurring in concert. Everything had meaning, everything was exactly as it was intended. I was here, right here, right now, for a specific reason, a specific purpose. All I had to do was grasp the meaning, and to do that, all I had to do was shift my perspective, broaden my awareness.

As we reached the northern wall, the reliefs depicting the pharaoh netting wild fowl made me wonder if I was just a sitting duck, or a pigeon, or was Crystal really a hawk, or even a vulture, luring me into an ambush, casting her net for me to blindly fly into.

'How do you get your energy high enough?'

Bill had asked a simple question, and the answer was just as elementary.
'Simply let go of fear.'
'And how do you do that?'

I knew the answer to that and laughed as I shared it with the others.
'You shift your perspective.'
'And how do you shift your perspective?'

At first I didn't know what to say, I mean I had Nemo, but I could hardly tell them to imagine a cartoon fish. I looked to Crystal for support and she looked back as if to say, 'Well, what are you going to tell them?' Eventually I looked around and up at the columns that supported the roof; twenty-four twelve-metre high columns in six rows of four, beautifully decorated with lotus and palm capitals. I felt like I was gazing up into a primordial antediluvian forest, and I had an idea.

'Look at the columns. At first they all look the same, regularly placed merely to support the roof. But look closer, each one is different in its own way.'

I pulled out my iphone and led the way as we walked back towards the southern wall, but this time weaving around the columns in a snakelike fashion. Thankfully the temple was virtually empty, apart from us.

'Choose one; notice each column has a different capital, some form of lotus or papyrus. Make your choice, then imagine that's who you are; that individual column.'

They spread around the hall, each making their selection, Crystal standing centre stage like an examiner, assessing my performance.

'Now, look at your column closely, what do you see about yourself?'

They each turned and scanned the reliefs.
'Mine has a image of Horus and Khnum.'
'My one has rearing cobras alongside strange images that look like electrical transducers.

'Mine's got this strange ugly looking creature near the top.'

I'd seen that image at Kalabsha and Philae.
'That's Bes, the god of singing.'
'There's this strange creature like a horned bird with a hawk's beak on mine, but it's also got additional clawed hands, and beside it is the image of a star.'

I thought the transducer image was strange enough, but the bird creature really had me guessing. I put it aside, and continued talking as I walked among the columns.

'Each column is just like each of you; some may seem a little more timeworn, while others have retained more colour than the others. Some are adorned with texts

34

describing the religious festivals of the town, while others depict various Roman emperors before the gods. One even shows the Emperor Trajan dancing before the goddess Menheyet.'

'Other columns record that there are, or rather were, four smaller temples in the nearby region; one of which was dedicated to Isis and built on the east bank near el-Hilla, another at Kom Mer, south of Esna, but which can't be excavated because, like here, a modern village has been built over the top.'

'Each of the columns tells a different tale, and if you were that column, and *only* that column, then you would only have that tale to tell. But now move to a different column.'

They dutifully obliged my request.

'By repeating the process of examination, by shifting you perspective, ultimately your awareness increases as now your knowledge includes alternate stories, alternate perspectives. Once you've incorporated all twenty-four you are in a position to realize that your purpose is more than your original single view, for now you see the purpose of each column is not just to retell its own individual tale, but also to act in concert with all the other columns, to support the roof, and ultimately the stories that *it* tells.'

'Cool.'
'I get it.'
'Wicked, Dude.'
'Brilliant, Alex.'

I strolled over to Crystal and whispered an aside.

'So, how did I do?'

'Very well, but perhaps you might have considered suggesting that they also *feel* the stone. Oh, and you missed the roof, or rather what *its* story is.'

I'd realized there was more-than-often something additional to be learned from Crystal's words. As I gazed to the heavens wondering what she might have meant, Bill checked his watch.

'Oops, it's nearly 10:15, maybe we should start heading back; I'd like to check out the market before we leave.'

He had a strange look in his eye, and I think I knew what he had in mind. Knowing Pernille had no money on her, I was sure he wanted to buy her something in the market.

'And I could murder a soft drink.'

Randy and Dwight were quick to join them; they were still suffering the after effects of the previous evening, and had seen enough for one day. I looked back at Crystal, who glanced at the ceiling. What was it up there she was referring to?

'I think I'll skip the market and spend a little longer here; there's a few things I haven't seen yet.'

I didn't know exactly what they were, but I had a feeling it had something to do with the reliefs on the ceiling.

'Pieter? Yuko?'

'I think we'll stay a little longer as well.'

'OK, we'll see you all back by the river.'

Thus four departed, and four were left behind.

35

I turned my attention to the ceiling, to the scenes running between the columns. What was I missing here? What was Crystal directing me too? Then, as I shifted between the ceiling, the columns and the walls, I got something; I knew the images on the ceiling were most often representations of the heavens of the ancient Egyptians, everything that was on the ceiling related to events in the sky, otherwise it would have been put on the walls. So what were the images?

I looked along the panels for something familiar, a place to begin. Then I noticed symbols that reminded me of the zodiac. Firstly I spotted a scorpion, Scorpio, in front of that was a woman with a set of weighing scales that I easily associated with Libra, then there was a horned figure I couldn't discern, but further along another woman carrying a feather which I assumed was Virgo; all surrounded by five-pointed stars.

Ahead of that was what was probably a Lion, Leo, with a snake underneath it. I wouldn't have thought about that had it not been for Pernille and Pieter mentioning Ophiuchus. At the very front was a barque with four human figures on it, the later of whom was seated on a throne.

Behind the scorpion were a few smaller figures, one possibly a crocodile, then a set of twins, Gemini, and another pair of snakes. I must admit that had me scratching my head a little. Next was the half-horse half-man archer of Sagittarius, though interestingly upside down compared to the others and again surrounded in five-pointed stars, then a number of other human figures including a throned one, all a little too faint to make out from ten metres away on the ground. But here were at least six of the modern signs of the Zodiac, and, as I called the others to my profound discovery, I stood proudly pointing to them.

'Hey, guys, check this out, it's the signs of the Zodiac.'

They gathered around as I indicated each one in turn.

'There's Scorpio, the scales of Libra, Gemini the Twins, Sagittarius ...'

Yuko wasn't so convinced.

'What are all the other figures in between?'

'I don't know.'

Pieter had the answer, and it changed the perspective completely.

'Actually I don't think it's a representation of the zodiac at all, I think it's a depiction of star constellations.'

'I thought the zodiac were star constellations?'

'They are, but there are more than just the twelve used in the zodiac. Around the time this Hall would have been built, say 100-200 AD, there was a guy called Ptolemy who catalogued up to eighty-eight constellations that formed the basis of modern astronomy and astrology.'

'Ptolemy? One of the Egyptian Ptolemy pharaohs?'

'No, this was Claudius Ptolemy, he was a civilian who lived in Egypt some time under the Roman rule around 140-160 AD. So this is exactly the sort of *modern* decoration you would expect in a new Roman temple building.'

Again Yuko needed further explanation.

'So what do the figures on the barque at the front represent?'

Pieter and I both pondered the answer until suddenly it hit me.

'Wait a minute, they're not *just* star constellations, they're more than that; this is the story of the procession of the figures on the barque at the front, *through* a number of star constellations. It's the story of a journey through the stars. After all, the Gods were always associated with the stars, because that's where they came from, and that's where they went. Of course that begs the questions: who were they, where did they come from, why did they come here, and where are they now?'

Crystal smiled.

'Now, that would be quite a story, don't you agree? Maybe you'd better incorporate a few more columns into your perspectives.'

And she walked off, back to the northern part of the temple from whence we had started our conga of shifting perspectives. As she did, my mind was filled with a scene from *The Rocky Horror Picture Show* where Frank 'n' Furter says, 'I see you shiver with antici.....' and as we hung on her every word, we trailed after her awaiting the inevitable '...pation'. Instead she silently stood, once again, looking to the heavens.

Given the symmetrical aspects of the building, I expected the southern half of the ceiling to be similarly decorated, however I was surprised to see that the images were very different indeed. Rows of Egyptian gods, each standing upon what looked like a small barque, covered the ceiling. These were definitely not star constellations of any sort.

'What do you make of these Pieter?'

He screwed up his face.

'I'm not sure; it's very different to the other side. This is more focused on the ancient Egyptian gods.'

'Yeah, it sure is.'

'Well, if it we assume the boats represent some sort of vehicle of travel, and that the ceiling is to do with the sky, or the heavens, then that would mean the boats must be spacecraft and that the gods are travelling through space.

'What about this one?'

It was an image of Osiris lying on a funeral bier that in turn sat on a barque.

'I guess that's Osiris and either his body or his spirit returning to the stars.'

'And the big one here?'

The main relief present was that of Khnum, the creator god, standing within a large circle with the eye of Horus above him, overseeing things. The circle sat in the centre of a long barque that also contained eight other gods, four at the front, one of whom appeared to be Isis, another Hathor, and four more astern. A row of fourteen gods, including Anubis, Amun, and Thoth reading a scroll, were each standing on a series of small discs before the barque.

Pieter mused it over.

'Well, maybe the circles the gods are standing on represent individual planets, after all, each of the gods has a very different appearance.'

I wondered if this meant that each of the gods came here from a different world? Were the fourteen gods somehow related to the concept of the twelve tribes of Israel; were the twelve tribes really twelve different alien races that came to Earth?

'Maybe it's a representation of the Galactic Federation?'

'And the main boat?'

'Well, if that's Khnum in the large circle, the creator god, then that must be the home planet of the creator.'

'Or maybe the home planet of the Federation? Or maybe it's Nibiru?'

'Possibly, and that would make all of the ancient gods Annunaki.'

I pointed to the large relief on the back wall.

'And the winged disc that's over on the wall there, then it's definitely connected, right?'

'Yes, yes it would all be connected to Nibiru.'

Pieter returned to the image overhead.

'That also looks like Isis on the large boat. You know, I think that this is some sort of royal barge, or federation starship, that was either travelling from planet to planet, or coming to earth to visit all of the races.'

'Maybe this is the first depiction of the starship Enterprise, Isis is Lieutenant Ahura and Khnum is Captain Kirk.'

As we were laughing, Crystal interjected.

'So, shall we boldly go where no man has gone before?…'

We stopped and looked at her.

'…Well it's nearly 10:30, and we still have to weave our way through the minefield that is the market.'

Running the gauntlet

So, just who were the gods? It seemed they were beings from the stars. Where did they come from; which stars? Apparently from Orion, Sirius, Alpha Draconis, and a dozen or so other constellations. Why did they come here? Not just to create a slave race to mine gold, but, on a larger scale, to play out some massive galactic karmic issues. And where are they now? Hmmm, that was a good question. According to Randy, some of them, the Dracos were running the United Nations. The others, who knows?

As we exited the temple and crossed the forecourt to ascend from the pit, I felt confident that I had done the same; I had passed the test. I'd been able to shift my perspective sufficiently enough to broaden my awareness, and now could comfortably move forward. Then I thought to myself, move forward to where? That was yet another question and Crystal must have sensed my thinking.

'How is Nemo doing?'

'I'm not sure if I've found him yet, but at least now I think I'm on the right path, or at least swimming in the right river.'

'Then you'd better keep swimming, and don't forget to come up for air once in a while.'

Hitting the top of the stairs, we came back into view of the merchants in the market. Most of the cruise-ship tourists had filtered through and were now back on their floating hotels waiting to head upstream to Edfu. That meant the market was virtually tourist free. It also meant the odds were massively stacked against us; we were outnumbered at least twenty to one.

Tourists only passed this way but once, and the locals only had two chances to lighten them of some baksheesh; on the way in, and on the way out. And whilst the local merchants may have allowed us to get *in* reasonably easily, getting out unscathed looked like it was going to be another matter altogether.

I had two visions. In the first, it was clear that making our way back through the market was going to be like a salmon swimming back upstream to spawn; hungry Grizzlys were poised at every vantage point, at every turn in the river, waiting to pounce. Each had their own territory and knew that the salmon had only one way through, and had to pass eventually. In the second, the wildebeest in Kenya were massing and waiting to cross the crocodile infested Nile. Neither image filled me with the confidence that we would all make it through unscathed.

So, did we split and try to confuse them by going in four different directions at once, and were we prepared to lose one or two in the charge? Or did we run as a group, using an impetus of mass and the safety-in-numbers strategy? It was too late for discussion, for having seen us emerge from the pit, the merchants instantly clicked into overdrive.

Crystal didn't wait to consider the options and confidently strode into the abyss, the rest of us quickly following behind; first Pieter, then Yuko, and I brought up the rear. I guess that answered that question.

Yuko had a previous history and experience with them, so she seemed to be their prime target, and most in need of protection, so Pieter and I ran interference patterns. It felt like we were at the Running of the Bulls in Pamploma, only this time *we* were the bulls; polite bulls I have to say, but bulls never the less.

Ahead, confident and gracious, Crystal scythed her way through the cascade of silks and necklaces like a hot knife through butter, cutting a path through the shop-owners like a fervid missionary macheteing her way through the darkest jungles of Africa.

'You buy, very good price.'
'Shukran, la.'

At one time she resembled Bill doing his Tai Chi, passively fending off the advances and offers of dresses, scarves and ornate bottles of scented oils.

'Pretty scarf for pretty lady.'
'Assalaam Alaikum, La, shukran, la.'

But we were losing momentum; the crocodiles had clamped their mighty jaws on us and were about to drag us beneath the surface. I felt like the weight of numbers of the attacking pride of lions would bring even the mightiest of buffalo to the ground, and feared that we would fall and be swallowed up like lizards caught in the path of a swarm of harvester arts.

But then, at the final knell, when all seemed lost, we suddenly and safely emerged from the abyss without a scratch. We all breathed a deep sigh of relief, well, I know I did, and together we headed across the road towards Saeed, Bill and Pernille, who was fussing over and sporting a new lilac headscarf that was clearly a gift from a very chuffed Bill.

'10:35, thanks for waiting, I'm sure if Jacques had been here, I bet we would've been finding our own way to Luxor.'

As usual, Saeed chuckled away.

'Indy, we are back on Egyptian time now. Besides, I have had a call from Mister Jacques; he and Miss Candy are not meeting us here after all; they have decided to meet the bus when it arrive in Luxor.'

Over by the ticket office, Mohammed and Gomar stood beside a mini bus. Inside, Randy and Dwight were stowed away finding relief from the escalating heat, quenching their respective thirsts with bottles of lemon soda.

'So, Indy, is it to be the bus, or do we need to be put you onto the train.'

Everyone's bags had apparently already been transferred from the boat while we were away at the temple, and, even if Candy and Jacques weren't absent, there still looked as if there was plenty of room for the eight of us, that is if it *was* only the eight of us.

'Just us, or are we picking up all your sisters and cousins and aunts along the way?'

'No, it will just be the eight of you and the driver.'

'What about you?'

'No, I will sail down through the lock with Mohammed.'

'Why don't I come with you, we could talk more on the boat?'

'I am sorry, Indy, tourist they are not allowed to go downstream through the lock, not beyond Esna, only upstream on the cruise ship. I will meet you tonight in Luxor.'

'Any particular spot?'

'On the esplanade, opposite the Luxor Temple, where the road from the railway station it curve to the left around the square and meet it the river. I shall be see you there at 7:00 pm tonight, western time.'

'OK, you'd better give me your cell number just in case.'

'Of course.'

We exchanged numbers as everyone climbed aboard and we prepared to depart.

'So is it to be the bus, or the train?'

'How long is the trip?'

'Only about forty-five minutes.'

I'd survived the last bus trip, and that was with twenty-odd people crammed into a sardine can for over four-and-a-half hours; this would be easy. Besides, it was probably my last chance to spend any time with Crystal, so I wanted to make the most of it and find out what her movements were once we hit Luxor.

'I'll be fine on the bus with everyone else.'

'Very good , then you had best be join the other.'

On the buses

There were several seat options available, however I was disappointed to see that Crystal had been monopolized by Yuko and Pernille in the back row, so I took a spot in the second row behind Randy and opposite Dwight. Behind me, Saeed stood in the doorway, beaming as always.

'Well, my friends, thank you for sailing with Captain Jack and Mohammed. I have left you a cooler with it some orange, banana and some water for the trip, please, to help yourself.

Unfortunate that our time together on the Nile it has now come to an end, and now it is time for you to please dig deep into your heart and also into your pocket to thank your Captain Jack and his crew for the last few day.

We have safely taken you passed the tomb of the noble at Aswan, then to Kom Ombo and the seldom-visited quarry and Temple of Horemheb at Silsila. You have visited the mighty Temple at Edfu and also the pyramid at Kihl Gharb.. After that we stopped special at El Kab, which most tourist not only do not know about it, but they never get taken to see it, or the tomb and temple at Wadi Hillal. And finally here to Esna, and all the time the most wonderful sailing on the Nile, with cooked breakfast, lunch, the most delicious dinner.

You have all met them new friend and had it the great adventure, and of course you have had it the best and most wonderful of Egyptian hospitality. So please I would ask for you to consider all these things when you most kindly when you are settle it your most wonderful of journey.'

Bill laughed.

'I have to give it to you, Captain Jack, you certainly know how to seal the deal.'

Everyone sprouted compliments and thanks as they recalled specific moments and started diving into their wallets. The normal price for the trip was four-hundred, and though Saeed had quoted me three-fifty, I weighed up all the bonuses I had received along the way and pulled out five-hundred; that was about a hundred Aussie dollars and an absolute bargain for four extraordinary days on the Nile. Then I realized how tough they were doing it at the moment with the lack of tourists, and pulled out another hundred. Even that seemed a bargain.

At the back of the bus, Pernille started softly sobbing; clearly she was not only upset but also embarrassed.

'Captain Jack, would you mind if I could take care of it when we get to Luxor?'

Bill came to the rescue.

'It's OK, I'll cover for Pernille.'

She tried to talk him out of it, but Bill was not to be dissuaded, and ultimately he convinced her.

'If you want to pay me back when we get to Luxor, that's fine, but it's not fair on Captain Jack and Mohammed to keep them waiting. *I* can wait.'

'What about Candy and Jacques?'

Saeed tried to settle things.

'Their luggage it is on the bus, when they come to pick it up they can pay it then.'

'No, that's not good enough....'

The change in Pernille was almost instantaneous.

'... I don't know about Candy, but Jacques can go to hell. I think you should keep his bags on the boat and make him come to you in Luxor and pay you personally.'

Suddenly everyone was throwing their two cents in, and it looked like it was going to become a real bun fight, until Bill spoke up and saved the day yet again.

'How about I cover for Candy and she can pay me when we get to Luxor, and Saeed, you take Jacques bags back on the boat as Pernille suggested; after all, as he's not here and she is the only appropriate one to speak on his behalf, we should respect her wishes?'

That settled it. Pernille happily jettisoned Jacques' bag, and his energy, from the 'magic bus', and we all prepared to depart. Out of the corner of my eye I caught Bill slipping Saeed several thousand pound notes; either Bill was just a really nice generous guy, but somewhat of a fool when it came to money, or he was strapped to the eyeballs and hid it damn well. In any case Saeed's grin touched the horizon east-to-west.

'Have a safe trip, my friends. This he is your driver, Saleem. When you are arrive in Luxor, just to please tell him what hotel you are stay and he will take you direct to there.'

There were lots of hugs, kisses and handshakes as we all bid first him, then Mohammed and Gomar, farewell. I saw Bill slip each of Mohammed and Gomar an additional healthy tip as well, and I followed suit with an additional fifty each of my own. And that's how the castaways kissed the Minnow adieu; sure we'd lost Mary Anne overboard so to speak, taken by a shark, or a crocodile after all, but we still had one more road trip together.

As the bus pulled away, I called out back to Saeed.

'I'll see you later tonight, Inshallah.'

'Yes, Mister Indy, of course, by it the river at 7:00 pm.'

'Egyptian time, or western time?'

'Dinner time.'

Everyone laughed. What a great trip.

The Magical Mystery Tour

Within minutes we'd all settled down and were bouncing our way along the potholed road to Luxor. Since I couldn't get to Crystal right away, I decided to catch up on my memoirs of the trip and pulled out my laptop.

'Anyone mind if we have a little music along the way?'

Randy looked back over the seat.

'What you got?'

'You name it, opera, classical, rock, pop, 70's, jazz, Michael Jackson?'

'Puff Daddy?'

'Ah, No.'

Crystal suggested Wagner; she thought 'the ride of the Valkyries' would be appropriate, either that or *Aida*. Bill went for Men at Work's, 'I come from a land down under'. Pieter opted for Kraftwork. With so many diverse tastes on board it was a miracle we settled on anything, however a consensus was agreed upon with The Beatles – a mixture of the *Magical Mystery Tour* and the *Sgt Peppers* albums.

It had only been a little under two days since I had made any notes so initially I didn't think there would be much to note down. I mean, it was just two evenings ago that we were talking about Isis and the genetic manipulation of primates by the Annunaki to create man, and about the Dracos and dinosaurs. Then over night there was the Jacques and Candy incident, and the next morning Pernille was sleeping with the Crystal and the others. That led to a dawn talk about mediation and the energy of the universe, and about being the eye of the hurricane, about shifting perspective to broaden awareness, about becoming the river, about Nemo. I certainly was on a Magical Mystery Tour, that was for sure.

Then everyone went skinny-dipping and Crystal taunted and teased me with her amazing body, alluring eyes and double entendres. How ironic that the next song was 'Fool on the Hill'; I simply *had* to connect with her again, and couldn't bare the thought of leaving Egypt without seeing where it could go.

I thought back over the chat during yesterday's breakfast that covered Hinduism, Buddhism, and led to a discussion on reincarnation and how it works. Somehow that led to contemplation on the missing books of Thoth. Was Thoth in fact Imhotep, and, if he was/is, where are the books hidden? Are they part of the legendary Hall of Records supposedly under the feet of the Sphinx? That in turn led to a talk about the Essenes and Jesus, about the Dead Sea scrolls and the Copper scroll.

Then there were Candy's tits; how could anyone, having seen them in their glory, ever forget them, or Jacques' preoccupation with them? Jacques behaviour was nothing less than appalling as was his lack of respect and consideration for Pernille.

But despite those distractions, the topic soon returned to where the treasure was buried, and to the 'prophet' Mohammed and the origins of Islam.

The time I spent at Edfu reinforced my thoughts on the real origins of the red-granite blocks and raised my suspicions on the buried city alongside. Information about the eruptions of Santorini, and the tsunami that would have gone up the Nile, fuelled my thirst to discover the truth, but my strange reaction to the Chinese tourists, seeing them as reptiles, was quite disconcerting.

The readily recognizable introduction to 'I am the Walrus' cranked in. I never really understood what the hell it was all about. Did anyone? Lennon and McCartney must have been on much heavier shit than Saeed and the lads had smoked last night.

My discussion with Crystal in the sanctuary, about facing truth, the absolute truth of the moment, about feeling the stone and the different levels of consciousness and memory in the stone, left me in the same state, and it challenged me to totally see the world a different way. That led to the mind-blowing concept of me seeing my Higher Self as a scriptwriter that was creating the most interesting scripts it could for my lower-self ego to play out.

'I am here as you are here as you are me and we are all together.'

Suddenly the first line seemed to make total sense. It led me to try and remember who I really was in those other lives, and who Crystal was. But so far I wasn't having much success, I didn't know if I was the eggman, or the walrus.

Deciding to visit the Edfu pyramid turned out to be, on the surface, just as much of a fizzer as my attempts to remember, or rather re-member, who I was. But digging deeper showed there *was* something to be discovered, and when Crystal implied that Imhotep was in a reincarnated form, but waiting somewhere for the appropriate moment to reappear, I even contemplated if she may have been metaphorically referring to me? She certainly wasn't referring to Jacques, who we left behind shagging Candy in a field. Although that did finally bring Pernille to her senses, and, having heard her life story, I for one was glad she had made the split. Just at that time 'Hello Goodbye' started playing on the laptop and I stopped typing and chucked away to myself, amazed at the synchronicity.

When 'Strawberry Fields' followed on, I tried to make a connection between it and El Kab; it was tenuous at best, the never-ending infestations of camel thorns hardly qualified as a field of strawberries, black-berry bushes maybe. But my time at El Kab was totally unexpected and it proved to be a real bonus. It sparked the search for the Ark of the Covenant, a discussion on Ahmose and his abdication to become the admiral of the navy, and, after visiting the Temple of Amenhotep, a contemplation on who Akhenaten could really have been.

The rest of the afternoon delved into the actions and motives of the Roman Catholic Church during the middle ages, the crusades, as well as the role of the Knights of Templar and their discovery of the Essene scrolls. Then how Philip IV of France subsequently persecuted the Templars and forced the survivors to escape to Scotland and the US. But some must have remained in Europe, running their banks, and somewhere along the line they formed not only the core of the Illuminati, but got 'labelled' as pirates, making the flag of the skull and crossbones famous. Meanwhile, the church was continuing to screw the truth, and twisted the death shroud of Jacques de Molay into the Shroud of Turin. A day is a long time in history!

As if totally on cue, 'All You Need Is Love' clicked in. I looked back at Pernille, seated in the back corner, and Bill sitting sideways in the seat in front of her. They were chatting like two teenagers on a school bus trip. Their budding relationship was a breath of fresh air and I subtly turned up the volume.

Bill started waving his hands like he was at a concert, singing at the top of his voice; the more I saw of the man the more I liked him, his sense of humour, his laid back approach to life, and his honesty and generosity. As everyone in the bus joined in the chorus, I hoped something really happened between them.

'She loves you, yeah, yeah, yeah. She loves you, yeah, yeah, yeah.'

It was subtle, but I did notice I wasn't the only one directing it towards the back corner of the bus. As for Jacques; boy did he deserve Candy; it might be fun for a while, but sooner or later the mid-west porn star from LA, twenty-years his junior, was going to bleed the tight-arsed Frenchman's wallet and testicles drier than a dehydrated dingo fart. And that was fine with me. We all let out a great cheer and laugh at the end of the song and, as we did, Sgt Peppers followed straight on.

We may well have all considered ourselves to be Sgt Peppers Lonely Hearts Club Band and the sing-along continued with Bill transforming into our resident rock star, standing in the aisle as best he could and miming the songs. I thought, 'I bet he does a mean Elvis as well'. As it segued into 'A Little Help From My Friends' he directed more and more of it to Pernille, the rest of us singing the chorus lines.

'Do you need any body?'
'I need somebody to love.'
'Could it be anybody?'
'I want somebody to love.'
'Would you believe in a love at first sight?'
'Yes, I'm sure that it happens all the time.'

Pernille was loving it, and so was Bill. In fact we all were.

Next track up was 'Lucy in the Sky with Diamonds', a song written when The Beatles were experimenting with dropping tabs of LSD. Who knows what was going on in their minds? As if in cosmic sympathy I turned my thoughts to last night's discussion of third dimensional existence. It was pretty heavy I must admit, but I really got the point about being exactly where our Higher Self chooses to be, and that Love was a force, and judging by what I had seen brewing between Bill and Pernille, and, dare I contemplate it, between Crystal and myself, it was indeed a force to be reckoned with.

Was Crystal my Lucy in the sky? To find out, maybe I just needed to filter some of that information and action down into my 'lower' self so I wouldn't go completely round the bend. And to do that I just had to find Nemo. And yes, though I didn't quite know why or how, 'I had to admit it's getting better, getting better all the time'.

This morning's dream was like no other I had ever experienced, and I was still trying to figure out what it meant, though I suppose it did have some familiarity with the previous night's dream about Ramses II. Things sure were shifting, getting shaken up, and Crystal's information about the Cairo earthquake nearly rocked me as much as seeing her naked and then cavorting in the water with Pernille and Yuko.

Initially I was disappointed when the frolicking aquatic proceedings were interrupted, but the discussion over breakfast that followed on from the previous night, about the Universe being the thoughts of God, about being one huge-fractal-geometry of pure feminine creation, totally intrigued me. Pieter's circle drawing initially helped me to understand about the second dimension being light, and how the expansion of the universe was the expanding awareness of consciousness of God, but once he added the second and third layers of circles I was a befuddled as the diagram in the sand.

Getting back on the boat, Randy got us back to where the treasure might have been; the French invasion of Egypt by Napoleon, then the British ousting Napoleon and bringing in the Freemasons to build the first dam at Aswan, which was not only to protect their interests in the cotton industry, but more than likely built to cover the robbing of the temples on P'aaleq. As 'For the Benefit of Mr. Kite' began, I wondered just who was really benefiting from proceedings in Egypt.

'For the Benefit of Mr. Kite there will be a show tonight on Trampoline.'

First it was the various religions having a go; the Theban Priests, then Moses and his Hyksos Jews, followed the Christian Roman Catholic Church, and then the Muslims; all vying for power like four clones of Jaba The Hut bouncing around on a trampoline in a tag-team world championship wrestling match.

'Over men and horses, hoops and garters, lastly through a hog's head of real fire. In this way, Mister K will challenge the world.'

After that, it was the turn of the Illuminati-controlled puppet governments of Napoleon, the British, and then the Soviets. And that was probably the real reason for the building of the second dam by the Russians, after Nassar, the Nazis, and the Muslim Brotherhood had seized power, to access the buried treasures in the temples.

But when I got to Esna I remembered Project Isis and the Soviet search for ancient technologies; so maybe there were other reasons why the Russians wanted to get into Egypt. And when Saeed implied that his uncle had some first hand stories from the building of the High Dam, and about Zahi Hawass, the face of the Supreme Council of Antiquities, I made a point to follow through on his invitation to meet up with his uncle in Luxor.

Then, seeing how much below the street level the Hall at Esna was situated, and the nine metres of layers of sediment behind it, that surely contained the rest of the temple complex, it confirmed my tsunami theories completely. Further, the red and black granite fragments of columns and statues excavated from the drain below the temple level convinced me there were even earlier temples below, waiting to be discovered.

Inside the Hypostyle Hall, though many images were similar to those at Philae and Edfu, there were several images that were very different, especially on the ceiling. They triggered a discussion about the 'V' TV series about a reptilian race on earth, and of a galactic federation that travelled the stars. And all of that in about thirty hours of being a simple tourist on the Nile.

To the strains of the reprise of 'Sgt Peppers', the bus pulled up outside the Luxor Train Station, and I found it hard to believe not only how remarkable the felucca trip had been, but that it was over. As I shut down my laptop and packed it away I thought to myself, 'So, where to from here?' and 'Would I get to see Crystal again?'

CHAPTER 13 – CROCODILE TEARS

It was 12:10 and Jacques and Candy were waiting outside the station, though if the body language was anything to go by they were definitely not waiting together. I gave Bill a quick look back over the seat.

'Well, this should be interesting.'

Without hesitating, Bill got to his feet.

'You all stay on board, I'll take care of things.'

It was said to us all, but he was really directing it to Pernille, who now had a look of concern, even fear on her face.

Bill picked up Candy's luggage and, before Candy and especially Jacques could even think of taking a step on board, he bounced out onto the street.

'Hi ya, Candy, Jacques, how was your adventure?'

'Have you got all my bags?'

She was a single-minded girl, and even that may have been giving her more credit than she deserved. But Bill quickly reassured her.

'Of course, girl.'

Needing to be certain, Candy did a quick count; though I'm not convinced she had much mathematical capacity, as she counted them at least three times. Any more than three bags and I'm sure she would have been severely challenged. She clasped her makeup bag to her chest; how she had survived without it for a night was a mystery beyond comprehension. However, having satisfied herself that she had accounted for all her belongings, Candy searched through the bus windows.

'Where's Captain Jack?'

'He's back on the White Rose, but he'll be here in Luxor later tonight.'

'Oh, no, I won't be here, and I still owe him for the trip.'

She may have been a thick, inconsiderate, self-centred, selfish, exhibitionistic, bimbo of a nymphomaniac porn-actress farm-girl, but at least she was honest; that was our Mary Anne.

'It's OK, I covered for you.'

'Oh, thank you again, Bill, how much do I owe you?'

'Well, what ever you agreed with Captain Jack, plus each of us gave Mohammed, Gomar and him a tip, but that's up to you.'

She pulled out four-hundred-and-fifty pounds and handed it to him.

'Do you think that's enough? Does it cover what you gave them for me?'

'That's fine.'

She started handing the bags to a taxi driver waiting off to the side. Bill gave her a hand.

'Where are you staying?'

'I'm not, I'm heading out to the airport, I fly out later this afternoon to New York.'

'What about seeing Luxor?'

'I saw it before I came up to Aswan for the boat trip. Thankfully my hotel let me leave some bags with them.'

Christ, she had more? I could see Bill was chuckling as well.

'OK, well have a great trip back to the US.'

She jiggled aboard the bus, in turn giving each of us a brief saccharine hug and LA kiss to each cheek, her pendulous breasts similarly waving farewell as she did.

'Thanks for everything, Alex, you were sweet, *really* sweet.'

She raised both eyebrows, giggled, and licked her lips. I know for the last few days I'd been tuned in to double entendre mode, but I didn't credit Candy with that level of subtlety. But then again, for her, it probably wasn't a double entendre at all. At least she had some sense of respect and conscience and just waved at Pernille, or maybe it was because Pernille was in the back corner and out of reach. In any case, with that done, she exited the bus, gave Bill a similar adieu, then, totally ignored Jacques, climbed into the taxi and disappeared into the streets of Luxor.

My last image of her was of her ass, still in a tight-fitting pair of cut down denim shorts, disappearing into the back seat of the taxi. To think I was so close to having that ass ride me like a rodeo bull. I was fairly confident that, if ever I *was* to see her again, it would be adorning the cover of some girly magazine in a plastic cover on a newsstand, or frolicking around as part of *In the Laps of the Gods – The Second Coming.*

Meanwhile, throughout the whole melodrama, Jacques just anally stood back, waiting for Pernille to disembark. When she was nor forthcoming, he stuck his head briefly inside the door, then turned his haughty disposition loose on Bill.

'And where are *my* bags?'

'I'm not a porter, mate, they're not here; Captain Jack still has them has them on the White Rose.'

'That is illegal; you know he left me abandoned somewhere out in the middle of nowhere.'

'I wouldn't know about that, mate, I'll be blowed if I can understand if there are any laws in Egypt, let alone doing what you're instructed, or holding on to someone's bags who owes you money. And as for leaving you stranded, well, as you said many times, my dear friend, *we can't wait.* Captain Jack and the rest of us were only following your lead; I was sure you would have not only understood, but been supportive. Anyway, I'm certain you've had an interesting time and plenty to keep you busy.'

'I suppose you paid for us as well?'

'No, I only paid for Pernille; *she* didn't have any money. You're a big boy, I'm sure you can take care of yourself.'

Realizing Bill was probably a formidable opponent, and rather than confront him, or pay him what was due, at least for Pernille, Jacques tuned his attention to the bus.

'Pernille!'

Bill looked to see if she would shift; so did all of us. After a quick lap of the eyes in the bus, Pernille calmly sat back and looked out the opposite window.

'PERNILLE!'

When she didn't react the second time, Jacques made a move to step on to the bus, but Bill headed him off at the pass.

'I don't think that's a good idea, mate, the lady doesn't want anything more to do with you.'

'Stay out of this; it is none of your business. PERNILLE, COME!'

'Jacques, you need to understand something. *I* decide what's my business or not, not you, and I'm *making* this my business. Now the lady has made her choice, so be a good chap and run along.'

'I will call the police.'

'Yes, let's do that; let's call them right now, and then each of us here will testify that you are harassing the lady. Do you really want the local police to know what you've been up to the last few days? It may be a Muslim country, but I don't think even they would condone your behaviour. So best make the best of a bad lot and get on your bike.'

Jacques tried to fob it off, at the same time stirring fears within Pernille.

'Where will she go, what will she do? She has no money.'

'That's not your concern any more.'

'How will she support herself? Where will she live?'

'Again, that's not your concern. I'm sure she'll be in contact with you at some time in the future, through her lawyer.'

Jacques was smug.

'She *has* no lawyer.'

Bill leaned in slightly, smiled, and spoke softly but directly.

'Then she'll get one; and a *good* one too.'

'And how will she pay for it.'

'Jacques, you're not listening, *that's ... not ... your ... concern.*'

'We shall see. She will come back, you will see.'

'Maybe she will, maybe she won't; but for the moment, it's she won't.'

Jacques was seething, but smart enough not to risk making a scene in public, or to get physical with Bill and what would have been the rest of us. I knew Bill did Tai chi and could probably take care of himself, but if there had been any confrontation I would have been right there should Bill need assistance, and I am pretty sure the others would have as well.

Realizing he was outnumbered, and that discretion was probably the better form of valour, with smug indifference Jacques screwed up his face, like someone had super-glued a fresh dog turd under his nose as a moustache.

'So, where will I get my bags?'

'Captain Jack will be on the esplanade at 7:00 tonight, I'm sure he's looking forward to returning your bags and getting his payment.'

'I'm not paying for Pernille; you paid for her, so you can keep her. And good luck to you.'

As he stormed off you could imagine him taking out his frustrations by kicking a puppy or stray cat. I don't think he took rejection well, most control freaks don't. Candy had rejected him, probably when she realized he wasn't a wealthy millionaire, but a tight-fisted miser. Though she probably enjoyed a little rough sex, she wanted a Sugar Daddy, not an anally-retentive sadist.

And now Pernille had rejected him. His poor over-inflated little ego must have taken quite a pounding; our little Napoleon thought he could have his cake and eat it as well; instead, Josephine had left the boudoir and he got left holding an empty plate.

Pernille was upset, of course she would be, that was understandable, but as Crystal comforted her I got the feeling it was more tears of relief, that it finally was over, mixed with a certain trepidation about the future. Having made sure Jacques was not going to backtrack for a second assault, Bill climbed back into the bus.

'Right then, I think that's sorted, where's everyone staying?'

'Randy and I are at the Nubian Oasis.'

'Alex?'

'I haven't booked anywhere yet, I was going to play it by ear.'

The truth is, I was hoping to lay my hat wherever Crystal was bedding down. But Randy was keen to keep 'the boys' together.

'Why not come with us?'

'Maybe. Depends where else is available. Saleem, do you know the Nubian Oasis?'

'Yes, yes, Nubian Oasis, very good.'

I wasn't penny pinching, but I also didn't want to blow my money staying in a five-star hotel. I turned back to Randy.

'Do you know how much is it?'

'Yeah, we stayed there before we went to Aswan; it's about five bucks a night.'

'Sounds perfect.'

Dwight gave a little more background information.

'The rooms are pretty basic, but they have a wicked rooftop hangout with a bar and hammocks, and the guy who runs the place, Seleh, is pretty cool, he'll look after you.'

'It sounds like paradise.'

Meanwhile Bill checked on the others.

'Pieter, Yuko?'

'We're the same as Alex, we've been taking things one day at a time and were going to find a place once we arrived, so the Nubian Oasis sounds perfect for us as well.'

'Well, that's easy fixed. Crystal?'

'The Nefertiti Hotel.'

As soon as she said it, shivers went up my spine. Nefertiti, she *was* Nefertiti; it made total sense to stay in a hotel named after yourself.

'How much is it a night there?'

'A little more than the Nubian oasis; about twenty Euro I think.'

'That might be a little more my speed guys, no offence, but I think I might check that out first.'

They knew exactly what my real motives were, I think everyone did, but thankfully they didn't voice them.

'That's cool dude. What about you Pernille?'

She was uncomfortable with the circumstances.

'Well, Jacques and I were supposed to be staying at the Princess Hotel, but I don't really think that's an option now.'

'It's all taken care of, I've organized a room for her at my hotel for the next few nights while she adjusts and thinks things through.'

She was grateful, excited and embarrassed all in one.

'Bill, are you sure?'

'I won't hear another word on it.'

'Right then, let's go Saleem. I shall leave it to you; Nubian Oasis, Nefertiti Hotel, or the Winter Palace?'

Saleem fired up the engine.

'First, Nefertiti Hotel, then Nubian Oasis, last, Winter Palace.'

And that was it; we were off through the streets of Luxor.

Where ever I lay my hat

The city was bigger than Edfu and Esna, much more like the hustle and bustle of Aswan. Streams of shiny black kalashes lined the streets beside the station, waiting for any westerners brave or adventurous enough to walk the streets. I'm sure it wasn't true, but if the shops down the main street were anything to go by, then Luxor only had one industry - tourism.

A minute or so down the road we passed the main square and caught a glimpse of the Luxor Temple. Even from the window of the bus it looked beautiful.

'I'm going to the Luxor Temple this afternoon if anyone would like to join me.'

I didn't want to seem too eager to jump at Crystal's invitation; I was hoping instead that one of the others would accept first. Randy and Dwight quickly declined as they'd seen it before they went to Aswan, but thankfully Yuko accepted on behalf of herself and Pieter, which opened the door for me.

'Yeah, you can count me in as well.'

Crystal turned to Pernille.

'Pernille?'

'I'd like to, but I'm not sure I should.'

'There is nothing to be afraid of, in fact, it would be the perfect time.'

'Go on, Pernille, I'll come with you if you want.'

Bill's encouragement, and probably his presence, convinced her to go.

'What time?'

'It's now 12:35. Let's all meet outside the main entrance at 2:30 pm. That gives us all plenty of time to check in, have a proper shower to freshen up, and a bite to eat.'

That decided, we arrived at the Nefertiti Hotel, quickly said our goodbyes, and headed inside. Bill, however, wanted some insurance.

'We'll just wait here and make sure you have a room.'

And just as well they did, because there were no rooms at the inn; a spiritual tour group had booked out most of the hotel. Crystal had a double room, but I didn't think it appropriate to invite myself into her bed, at least not before I had explored other options at the Nubian Oasis. I grabbed my backpack and threw it over my shoulder.

'No problems, I'll try my luck with the others. In any case, I'll see you at the temple at 2:30.'

As I jumped back on the bus, Bill let me have it.

'Boy, they must be getting really fussy.'

'All booked out by a spiritual tour group.'

'They must've known you were coming.'

'Well, hopefully there're a few vacancies at the Nubian Oasis.'

'If not, we might have to find a camel stable for you, I just hope the camels are not as fussy as the hotel managers.'

A few laughs and some light banter later we turned into a side street and pulled up outside the Nubian Oasis. Randy and Dwight grabbed their stuff, said their farewells to Bill and Pernille, and traipsed in. Pieter, Yuko and I followed right behind, fingers crossed they had vacancies.

It was nowhere as glitzy as the Nefertiti, but the lobby was clean, and it looked comfortable, most of all it was highly affordable. The guy behind the counter was obviously Seleh, and he welcomed the two Yankee lads back like they were long lost brothers. Dwight asked him if there were any other rooms free, and it seemed the gods were indeed smiling on us because they did have vacancies.

As they checked in, I stuck my head out the door and gave Bill the thumbs up, that we all had a roof over our head, and that Pieter, Yuko and I would see them outside the temple at 2:30 as arranged. That done, Bill and Pernille took off in the Magical Mystery Bus, and I headed back inside.

'Is the bar open, Seleh?'

'Not presently, Mister Randy, sir, but if you allow it for me five minute I can open it for you.'

Having seen how Randy was putting them away on the boat, he was clearly a good customer. So, having checked in, the lads headed straight up the stairs.

'We'll see you on the roof, Alex, after you've checked in.'

'Sure guys.'

Pieter and Yuko took a room with an ensuite for the grand price of three Euro each, that was around five bucks.

'I think we're going to pass on the roof; we'd like to meditate before going to the temple. We will meet you here in the lobby about 2:20.'

'No worries.'

I opted for an ensuite room as well for the same price, who knows, I might strike it lucky with Crystal, and climbed the stairs to my room. It took all of two minutes to dump my bag, take out my laptop and plug it in so it could recharge, check out the bathroom, and the comfort level of the bed. It was basic living, but it was clean, comfortable and all I needed; a bed, a power point, a toilet and a shower.

I could never understand why people spent massive amounts on expensive hotel rooms just to spend eight hours horizontal. The point of travelling and exploring a new country and culture wasn't to sit in a westernised room watching television, ordering room service, and tucking into the mini-bar; you could've been in a hotel anywhere in the world and not known what was going on outside your door.

My way was to spend as much time out and about with the people, absorbing their culture and to use the room purely to keep my bag secure, sleep, and shower; which was what I decided I needed right at that moment to refresh myself.

The warm humid air was like walking through a car-wash, and that made a cool shower the most refreshing experience I'd had since arriving; almost as good as a morning dip in the river, however I did make a note that I didn't have three naked women with me. A few minutes and a change of clothes later, I was making my way up the stairs to the roof.

The flat roof was loosely divided by cloth partitions and decorated with all sort of flags and, of all things, pirate decor; Captain Jack would have been totally at home here. Shade cloths protected most parts of the roof from the direct sun, while underneath a myriad of cushions and sofas filled the spaces. It was a very chilled-out lounge environment.

In one corner, Seleh was behind a makeshift counter which clearly functioned as the bar. In another corner were two hammocks, stretched across a section of the roof covered with beach sand. Lazily swinging away in them were Dwight and Randy, beers in hand. They looked like they'd settled in for a lengthy session, and I had to admit, if it wasn't for the prospect of spending more time with Crystal, I think I would have joined them for the afternoon.

'Hey, Alex, grab a beer and pull up a cushion.'

'I'll take a rain check on the beer, but I could go a soda.'

'Pepsi?'

Seleh was off the mark faster than a ferret up a Scotsman's kilt.

'That would be great, thanks Seleh.'

Within seconds it was in my hand, I had settled down on a sofa, and Dwight was picking my brain.

'Randy and I have been talking about the Dracos and the Aswan High Dam. I was thinking; if the whole thing was built just to get access to not only Philae but all the temples upstream of Aswan, all the way to Nubia, then that's a major operation.'

'Major? It's Massive.'

'If means that if the whole temple rescue program was set up and run by UNESCO, then they had to have done it in conjunction with, and with the approval of, both the Russian and Egyptian governments, which, if Nassar was Prime Minister, means the Nazis and the Muslim Brotherhood were involved as well. And we also know that UNESCO was the fore-runner of the United Nations, and that both UNESCO and the United Nations are really run behind closed doors by the Dracos.'

'There must have been a lot of treasure.'

Randy was right, it *was* a lot of treasure.

'Twenty-four temples worth, and a lot of history too.'

That set Randy right off.

'It's been happening since before the Battle of Independence. Just look at history. If the first white Americans were really those Templar guys, who escaped from France to *la Merica* and Scotland, but now called themselves Freemasons, then they'd make sure they could never be persecuted by the church or government again. They knew that money ruled, so they set up and ran all the banks, and because they owned almost everything in sight, especially the weapons manufacturing, all they had to do was infiltrate the monarchies, or replace them with their own financially backed governments, whether that be a democracy where they *owned* both parties, or a dictatorship.

And that's what they did; they set up the major world banks and infiltrated the British government and European monarchies. The US people *think* they won the War of Independence, but in reality the bankers used the *British* to create a conflict and seize power forever.'

'What do you mean?'

'The US Congress had no money to pay its debts; they couldn't pay the twelve-million owed to European nations and bankers, mostly the French, or pay the forty-million owed to the individual states, nor the twenty-five million owed to the American soldiers, merchants and farmers who had been given promissory notes for providing food, horses, and supplies to the revolutionary forces during the war. Then, in 1787, out of the blue, a group of nationalists calling themselves the "Federalists", convinced Congress to call the "Philadelphia Convention" and adopt a new Constitution that provided for a much stronger federal government; one with an executive management committee, financial accountability, legislation and judiciary policing.

And after some fierce debate over the nature of the proposed new government, the new Constitution was ratified and, in 1789, the new government under George Washington took charge.'

'Who were they, these Federalists?'

'Who else, the Freemasons.'

'George Washington was a Freemason?'

'Yep.'

'So the British won anyway?'

'When Paul Revere rode through the streets yelling that the British were coming, little did he know it was the same Freemason-ruled British that would later invade Egypt.

'So if George Washington was a Freemason, then the *true* Americans were being duped into thinking there was actually a war, when it was just an excuse for a *corporate take-over,* and for the Illuminati to sell weapons to both sides?'

'They took over because they made the United States into a corporation, and though it may *appear* to have it's own system of government, the US, as a corporation, is ruled by British common and maritime law. It's a huge scam.'

I had to do a double take, Randy wasn't a moron after all, he actually was quite switched on, and it seemed that conspiracy theories, as they related to the US, were his area of expertise. As Seleh brought the boys another beer, I decided to delve deeper.

'So what was the American Civil War about then?'

'Slavery. No, no it wasn't ...'

His face had that look of sudden enlightenment.

'...Oh, wow, the Civil War was about cotton too, about bringing the southern states under the rule of corporate law.'

'So it had nothing to do with freeing slaves?'

'No, that was just another fucking cover up. The rich plantation owners in the south were bucking the system and producing cotton using slave labour, thus under-cutting the northern and European competition. That was driving the price of cotton down, not up, and the major corporations, the Illuminati traders and bankers, didn't like that at all. They weren't going to stand for that, so they went to war, supposedly to *free* the slaves.'

'But why, so the blacks could work for a wage and pay taxes?'

'Sure, that was part of their plan, but the reality was, the corporations wanted total control of the cotton industry, and the land. What better way than to declare a war.'

Dwight added his thoughts.

'It seems to have worked for Philip IV when he kicked out the Jews, so why not use a similar tactic.'

On a roll, Randy rabbited on.

'They owned all the money anyway, and supplied the weapons to both sides, so they couldn't lose. The corporations wanted a monopoly on the industry and they wanted the land, and that meant putting the landowners out of business. It was just another corporate form of slavery that the rest of us have been imprisoned under ever since. Whenever they have an agenda, they just tweak the system to create the problems that they already have the solutions worked out for.'

'Such as?'

'The great depression, Pearl Harbor, JFK ...'

'Whoa, one at a time; how did they create the depression?'

'They caused a crash in the stock market deliberately by pushing prices up, getting everyone over extended, then pulling out all their stock. That caused a panic, prices plummeted, everyone rushed to sell, the banks called in their margins on everyone etcetera because they couldn't meet *their* margins. That was October 1929. After the stock market hit rock bottom, the rich Illuminati vultures stepped in and bought everything up at bargain basement prices. But that was just bonus fodder; their real agenda was to shackle the United States by setting up the Federal Reserve, a private corporation, which lent money to the government.

What's also interesting is that the Vatican State was established earlier that year. It may be unrelated, but in any case, I think they knew exactly what they were doing.

The Illuminati created banking, and interest loans, they created the real estate market; you borrow money from the bank at interest, money that doesn't really exist, just a figure on paper, and use it to buy property. Then over the next twenty years you work, getting paid money they are already making interest on, and in a company they probably own.

You get maybe three-quarters of your *loan* paid off, then they push up interest rates and about thirty percent of people have to foreclose on their mortgage, loosing everything back to the bank. You see, you don't own your house until the last cent is paid off. That's why banks will lend the full one-hundred percent of the cost of the house; they know they own the property and are going to hook you like a baited fish and play you along for the next quarter of your life. They've done it before, and they'll do it again.

The Financial Crisis of 2008 was another example; while they abandoned most average workers and home-owners to be crippled by the banks, the government bailed out major companies, including the banks, to the tune of eight-hundred trillion dollars. And that money was borrowed from the Federal Reserve, the Illuminati bank, at interest; interest the US Government can *never* repay. But that was just the set up, because they passed legislation preventing the government from any further bail-outs of companies, and that includes the big banks. So when the next crunch happens, and it is *when,* not *if,* then the major banks will collapse bringing the US and most parts of the western world to it's knees.'

It was pretty convincing, but perhaps just coincidental. I needed more.

'And Pearl Harbor? How were they involved in that, I thought the Japanese attacked.'

'They did, but the whole thing was orchestrated by the Illuminati, the bankers, to bring the US into the war. They needed to get the US in so they could sell lots of weapons. But the American people didn't want a part of it, so they set up the attack on Pearl Harbor to *force* the American people into the war. They also needed an excuse to test out their new atomic technology on a mass of innocent people.'

That caught me off guard.

'You mean Hiroshima and Nagasaki were just massive lab tests?'

He finished his beer.

'Sickening isn't it, just goes to show you how they'll murder hundreds-of-thousands of innocent people just to achieve their goals.'

'I have to admit, Randy, you do sound like a bit of a conspiracy theorist at times.'

'It ain't no theory, and if it's a conspiracy, then it's being propagated by the Illuminati. After all, weren't the Nazis the master of propaganda?...'

He had a point, and he continued to expand on it.

'... And look what they control: the Pharmaceutical industry; drugs and vaccines that are really infections designed to weaken the system and keep you hooked for life. Do you know how they dispose of all the toxic by-products created when they manufacture drugs?'

'I've never really thought about it.'

'It's too expensive to dispose of them, they did it once, into the rivers and streams, and garbage dumps, but now they can't, so they put them back into other drugs. They get legislation passed allowing them to put so-many parts-per-million in as *safe* "filler" and they have no disposal costs. That's why all these drugs have so many dangerous side effects.'

'Why don't people speak up against it?'

'How are they going to find out? The media is totally controlled by the Illuminati, and they're certainly not going to tell you the truth.'

'And look at today's presidential elections, the way the campaigns are run, the use of the media, the fact it's nearly impossible to break the two-party systems that are in place in the US, the UK, all over the world.'

'We've got the same basic two-party system in Australia.'

'Anything that came from the corporate English system of control is poisoned. Just look at the world today; how can almost every government on the planet be in massive debt? Debt to who? Not to other countries, but to the money-lenders. If each of the governments decided to create their own money and run their own economies, they could get out of debt instantly, and everyone could live in prosperity. But the Illuminati don't want that, because that would mean people are happy and not fearful, and they rule by fear because they are controlled by the Dracos.'

'Why don't they do something?'

As Seleh delivered yet another round, Dwight, who had been silently chilling while Randy went on his rant, murmured from his hammock.

'Most people are just mindless puppets. I proved it once; a group of guys and I did an experiment; four of us stood on a city corner pointing up at nothing in the sky, pretending we could see something weird, like a UFO. Within five minutes we had about twenty people around us, all gazing up looking and pointing, asking what it was we were looking at. People stopped their cars and looked out the window, some even got out to look. Traffic got held up and the more it did, the more people gathered.

Ten minutes later we all stepped out of the group and watched from a distance as maybe forty or fifty people gathered and looked mindlessly into the sky. None of the original four guys was there, but that didn't matter, the crowd continued anyway, and lasted for over half-an-hour.'

'Yeah, but surely someone knows the truth and has spoken up against it all.'

'Oh, there have been, many, people like JFK, Robert Kennedy, Ghandi, Anwar Sadat, Martin Luther King Junior, and look at what happened to them.'

'Come on, Dwight, there are hundreds of theories on who killed JFK, surely it had to have been Lee Harvey Oswald?'

Randy was on a roll.

'He was just the fall guy.'

'So the Illuminati killed JFK? How do you figure that, why would they kill him?'

'They control the CIA, the secret service, NASA, all the major organizations in the world. JFK made a speech in 1962 that put the target on his back. He exposed the secret societies in the US and was going to tell the world three things; firstly he was going to expose the Illuminati, secondly he was going to introduce the American dollar...'

'I thought that was already in place?'

'...No, that dollar was lent to the United States by the Federal Reserve put in place by the Illuminati in 1929, it resulted in the US being in perpetual debt.'

'And that got him killed?'

'We are talking about trillions and trillions of dollars, people have been killed for a lot less.'

'But why Kennedy, wasn't he part of the Illuminati?'

'Joseph Patrick Kennedy Sr., JFK's dad, was part of the Illuminati. He wanted his eldest son, Joseph Patrick Kennedy Jr., "Joe" as President, and was grooming him that way. But when Joe was killed in World War II, JFK, as next in line, was thrust into the fold. But JFK was not like his father, and when JFK got to office he actually wanted to do the right thing, so did his brother Robert. When they discovered the truth, they decided to expose things, so the Illuminati took them out.'

'So was it actually Oswald who shot JFK?'

He shook his head.

'The first bullet perhaps, the one from the back that also hit the governor of Texas, or maybe it was someone else in the book depository. In any case, Oswald was the fall guy. Just look at the evidence; the car went into a tight curve, meaning the car had to slow considerably, and the secret service were not on the rear bumper, they would have blocked the first shot. But it didn't kill him, it missed its target, so they had a secondary, a back-up, closer, to make sure the job was executed. So the real shot that killed him, the one from the front, came from the driver of the car, William Greer.'

'What? I've never seen that.'

'That's because it was edited out of the footage released to the public. But you can see it in the original film. The movement of Kennedy's head at impact shows the bullet must have come from close range and below, because his head went up and to the right, and it blew out the upper back right part of his head.

At that very time the car had slowed almost to a halt. Now the driver is trained that if anything happens, he should speed up immediately, so, after the first shot, you would expect a trained CIA secret service operative to hit the pedal and floor it. But no, he slows down. Not only that, he turns around to look into the back seat. But, and here is the real proof, when Greer turned to look in the back seat he kept his right hand on the wheel and took his left hand off.'

Being an Australian and driving on the other side of the road I had to mirror it.

'What's so strange about that?'

'Well most people would keep their left hand on the wheel, and take their right hand off to turn and look at the back seat, otherwise you cross your self. What you definitely wouldn't do is push your left arm under your right, as Greer did, pointing something at Kennedy. And at that point, Kennedy is shot in the head, Greer turns back to the front, and speeds off.'

'But what about the investigation, it never said all this?'

'That's because the people doing the investigation, were the ones who set the whole assassination up.'

'Shit! What else was he going to say, you said there were three things?'

'He was going to tell the world that man was already on the moon.'

'Hang on, what year are we talking about?'

'1962.'

'But the Americans didn't land on the moon until July 1969.'

Randy just shook his head.

'The "Americans" might have, but the Illuminati have been there since 1959.'

'OK, now you'll have to explain.'

'The highest levels of "Government", and the Dracos, have been in contact with aliens since the late 1940's and the Roswell incident. The whole NASA Apollo program was a cover up.'

'But isn't NASA a government department?'

'No, NASA is a private company owned by, guess who, you guessed it, the Illuminati bankers. They get allocated billions of dollars of Government money every year to carry out their covert black operations; money that is all borrowed from the Illuminati bankers in the first place. Pretty clever really; the Illuminati lend it to the US at interest, then the US government gives it back to them in payment to run projects through NASA. And the US people still have to pay back the original loan plus interest. No wonder the country is trillions of dollars in debt.'

'But what about the moon landings, the photos, the video broadcast?'

'They knew they couldn't show what was really on the moon.'

'What is there?'

'Alien bases and mining operations; that's what it's all about, mineral rights to the moon.'

'Jesus! How did they do it?'

'They went to Stanley Kubrick, who was shooting 2001 at the time, and used the studio to film a fake moon landing and take all the photos. Then they broadcast the fake footage via satellite to Australia, and then via television to the world. And everyone believed it.'

'Christ, Randy, what else are they responsible for?'

'The Vietnam war, the gulf wars and invasion of Iraq, 9/11, the Civil Rights Movement, …'

'How could they be responsible for the Civil Rights Movement?'

'The African Americans were becoming the largest population in the states and potentially a major problem. By offering them the right to vote as equals, they were able to bring them into the work force as tax paying citizens. It was just a form of corporate slavery, the same as they have done with many people over the centuries.'

'Who else have they killed?'

'Robert Kennedy, Marilyn Monroe, Michael Jackson?'

'Michael Jackson?'

'He was going to speak out against them as well.'

'Why?'

'His early music had satanic references and stuff on it when you played in backwards. But once he became famous in his own right he tried to break free from SONY; check them out, they're one of the most evil organizations on the planet. It started around the time of *'All I wanna say is they don't really care about us'*, and that's why they tried to destroy him with allegations of being a kid molester. But it didn't work, because there was no proof, so they tried to break him financially through continued accusations. But that didn't work either. Then, when he was going to go on his comeback tour, they topped him and made billions out of the resales of his records.'

'What else do they have their grubby little fingers into?'

'Fluoride in the water, Aspartame, Swine flu, the AIDS virus, the feminist movement ...'

'Come on, the feminist movement?'

'Two reasons, firstly to get women into the work force as taxpayers so you can make money out of them. But more importantly, to separate them from their children and indoctrinate the children through the education system, which they also created, so as to control people's thinking; fill their heads with an overload of useless information so that they have no time for any free thoughts of their own.'

I was overwhelmed by all the information, could it all be true, could *any* of it be true?

'Mister Randy, I am just going down to the reception desk, do you wish it another beer before I am going?'

'Thanks Seleh, that'd be great.'

It was hot and humid, but Randy and Dwight were perfectly placed to handle it. Normally I would have pulled up a beer and spent the rest of the afternoon picking Randy's brain, weighing up the possibilities of what he was saying.

'Anything else?'

'How long have we got? Nutrition, chem-trails, the illicit drug trade.'

He'd already said so much, and I was sure there was lots more, I checked my phone; Shit, 2:15, time had flown and I had to get to the temple.

'Hey guys, I have to get going, but will you be around later on? I'd like to talk more about the Illuminati.'

'Sure, dude, we ain't going no place.'

They readjusted their positions in the hammocks as Seleh presented them with another round, then he and I headed off down the stairs. The truth was, at the pace they were downing the amber fluid, at the rate they were knocking them over, by the time I got back they would probably be pissed as farts and barely able to speak their names. No matter, I could probably catch up with them sometime tomorrow.

As Seleh and I arrived in the lobby, Pieter and Yuko were waiting at the counter.

'Ready to go guys?'

'Nearly, we just want to book some bicycles for tomorrow.'

I knew that Crystal and the others would wait, but we had less than ten minutes to get to the temple, and the thought of missing out on reconnecting with Crystal was an option I did not wish to entertain. Fortunately Seleh leaped into action.

'Bicycles, yes, of course, what time?'

'7:30.'

'7:30, gee that's early, are you planning to ride all the way to Cairo?'

'No, we're going to the West Bank and the Valley of the Kings. It's slightly uphill towards the end so we want to get there before it gets too hot.'

'Sounds like fun, how much is it Seleh?'

'Ten pounds....'

That was about two bucks, what a bargain, and damn cheaper than a taxi or the organized tours, which were around three-hundred plus.

'...Shall I book it one for you as well?'

I certainly wanted to see the West Bank; the Valley of the Kings, Hatshephut's Temple, the Colossi, and doing it on a bike really appealed to me, but I wasn't sure what Crystal had planned tomorrow, so I hedged my bets.

'Can I let you know later tonight?'

'Yes, yes, but of course.'

'Cool. OK, let's hustle to the temple.'

As we walked to the temple, every passing kalash or taxi asked us if we needed their services. It didn't matter, we were only going about half-a kilometre, they still wanted to give us a ride. I took the opportunity to throw a few things at Pieter.

'Hey Pieter, these Annunaki guys, do you think they're connected to the Dracos?'

'It's possible, but I don't think so. From what I have learned in the last few days I think the Dracos have been here way before the Annunaki.'

'What about Nibiru, do you think they're a part of that?'

'Not specifically, no.'

I was beating around the bush, the real thing that was playing on my mind was the girls frolicking in the water and Pieter's reaction, or rather lack of reaction, to it.

'How long have you two been together?'

'About six years.'

'You guys seem pretty open in your relationship.'

'What do you mean?'

'Well, that was pretty intense stuff this morning, hardly a splash and tickle.'

'Just a natural expression of love.'

'Not the sort of love I've had in relationships.'

'Love is a state of being, not a set of rules and regulations based on your own insecurities.'

'It didn't bother you, the girls playing and fooling around this morning?'

Pieter just smiled as Yuko took control.

'We believe in living the moment, about being totally in your heart; that spiritually you don't even own your own body, let alone have any right to tell someone else what they can or can't do with theirs. Each of us is just a passing caretaker.'

'But what if it was another guy she was mucking around with?'

'If you love the other person unconditionally, then wouldn't you want to see them happy, pleased, pleasured and fulfilled?'

'Sure.'

'What if you couldn't do that fully yourself? What if you partner had desires beyond your capabilities?'

'What about trust?'

'If you need trust, it is coming from a core belief of *mis*trust and *dis*trust. When you have no conditions or expectations in your relationship, trust is not an issue. Each person lives their life in their highest possible state of awareness at all times.'

'But what if you're not happy with your partner being intimate with other people?'

'Then that's about you, not them. You are being selfish, because you are not allowing them to fully and openly experience what they believe is in their best interests to be happy and fulfilled.'

'So that means anyone can do what ever they want? Drugs, sex, violence?'

'Of course it does, everyone must make their own choices, and they do. No one else has the right to tell you how to live your life, but that does not mean each person is not fully responsible for their actions; they are.'

'So you guys have done this sort of thing before?'

'Many times.'

'Other girls? Guys?'

'Yes, even couples; sometimes groups.'

'No jealousy?'

'If there is, then you probably shouldn't be in a relationship with anyone, let alone an open relationship, because you are insecure, possessive, emotionally dependent, or obsessive.'

'I have to say, that's pretty *out there*.'

'It may not be normal, but that doesn't mean it's not completely natural. We only wish it *was* the norm. Think about it, if the whole world was in bed with each other, then there'd be no wars; why would you try to kill someone who you could fuck instead?'

'I guess the hippies and John Lennon had it right in the sixties, "Make Love, Not War".'

'Yes, but we didn't get the message.'

'The world would be a very different place if we had, that's for sure.'

Luxor Temple

Crossing the main square, we approached the entrance to the temple, where Crystal, Bill and Pernille were waiting by the ticket office. Crystal had changed into the all-white outfit she had worn when I first saw her at Philae, and, as ever, she looked captivating. She stood confidently, holding the space, holding my attention. She, Bill and Pernille had already purchased their tickets, so the three of us each quickly paid our fifty pounds and we set off to explore the temple and its surrounds.

We decided to start outside the temple at the Avenue of Sphinxes, and it seemed my trusty notes were coming in handy once again.

'Built by Nectanebo I in the 30th Dynasty, on top of an older route, it was used at festival times to carry the sacred barque of Amun from the temples at Karnak to Luxor Temple. An inscription of Nectanebo reads *"I have built a beautiful road for my father Amun-Re surrounded by walls and decorated with flowers for the journey to the temple of Luxor"*. The Avenue was around twenty metres wide and lined on both sides by the pharaoh headed sphinxes of Nectanebo; each on a plinth evenly spaced about ten to twelve feet apart and about ten foot high. They had been discovered several years ago during an excavation to create a car park in the forecourt area, and it was soon realized they extended from the entrance of the Luxor Temple an astonishing three kilometres north-northeast to the temple complex at Karnak.'

The Egyptians had done some of the restoration, but they still had a long way to go; my understanding was the Supreme Council were 'acquiring' houses and land that covered the Avenue and were hoping to restore the full length of the Avenue and open it up at some time in the future.

Having explored about a hundred metres up the avenue, we walked back and into the Court of Nectanebo situated before the temple. I couldn't believe it! It was flooded with Chinese tourists again; not just one bus-load, but more like three or four. They were gathering like a pit full of squirlling vipers, you know the ones you see in the Indiana Jones movies. I looked for an escape.

To the right, in the northwest corner, were the remains of the Chapel of Serapis, a Graeco-Egyptian god invented during the 3rd Century BC by Ptolemy I Soter as way of trying to unite the Greek and Egyptian people under his realm. By now I knew exactly what I was looking for, and what time frames they related to, however, whilst I was initially only mildly curious, the chapel served as a welcome repose from the cacophony of high pitched squeals, so I tagged along with the others as they explored it.

It was similar in size to those at Wadi Hillal, though surrounded on three sides by half columns, and made of smaller mud bricks, all common in the later periods. As we explored, Bill and Pernille were almost inseparable, at times arm in arm, other times hand in hand, but never more than a few feet apart. She seemed a changed person, laughing and acting like a teenager, although I got the distinct impression she was not one-hundred percent at ease, always looking around and over her shoulder to ensure Jacques was not about to vent his anger on her. At all times Crystal was not far from her either, reassuring her and encouraging her about facing her fears and freeing herself to charter a new course in her life.

Through it all, we pressed on, and, though there were other minor ruins in the courtyard, the Chapel of Hathor and the Kiosk of Shabaska, neither warranted much examination. So we moved on and prepared to enter the temple itself. Fortunately the writhing oriental mass that once obscured the entrance had invaded through the pylon and, in the distance through the gate, I could see them dispersing in different directions.

Whilst I knew almost nothing about Silsila or El Kab, I had done a lot of reading up and research on the main sites at Luxor, as clearly it was going to be one of the major stops on my journey. I'd seen heaps of photos, but being here was different; it had a feeling about it, maybe that was because of its location by the river. I was only a third of the way down my journey on the Nile, but the Luxor Temple, dedicated to Amun the creator god, had to be, along with Philae, one of the most picturesque temples in Egypt.

At the risk of sounding like Jacques, I shared some of my knowledge with the others.

'The temple, as we know it now, dates back to the 18th Dynasty during the reign of Amenhotep III, in the New Kingdom around the 14th Century BC. But it was built on the site of a smaller 12th Dynasty Middle Kingdom temple to the god Amun.

In the time of the 18th Dynasty, it was known as Ipt-Rsyt, meaning *southern shrine*, to differentiate it from the temple at Karnak, which was the *northern* house of Amun Ra; the creator god Amun often being fused with the sun-god Ra into Amun-Ra.

At the time Amenhotep built the temple it was only a hundred-and-ninety metres long and fifty-five metres wide, however over the years other pharaohs such as Horemheb and Tutankhamun added columns, statues, and reliefs. Akhenaten even installed a shrine to the Aten.'

Right at that very moment Crystal looked deeply into my eyes.

'That would be a great place for us to experience.'

Whoa, something weird happened; when she said 'us', I know she didn't mean 'all of us', she specifically implied 'her and me'. All of a sudden I had images of Crystal as an Egyptian Queen and the whole façade of Luxor ablaze with colour and celebration.

'So who built the entrance?'

Yuko's question brought me back to the present.

'Huh? Oh, ah, the main entrance pylon in front of us, as well as the obelisks in front, and the courtyard beyond, were built by Ramses II in the 19th Dynasty.'

As we stepped up to view the sole remaining obelisk, I continued with my background info, this time referring more to my iphone notes...

'There were once two twenty-five-metre pink granite obelisks, but the western one was given as a gift to King Philip Louis of France by the Egyptian ruler, Mohammad Ali, in the 1830's. It's now at La Place de le Concorde in Paris.'

'You would think after a hundred-and-seventy years, the French might return it to its original owners and to its original place.'

Bill was being flippant, Pernille not so forgiving.

'If they are all like Jacques, forget it.'

We left the obelisk and strolled across the front of the pylon.

'The pylon is over seventy-feet high and decorated with scenes of Ramses' military triumphs against the Hittites, particularly the *famous* Battle of Kadesh. Later pharaohs also recorded their victories here too.

It was originally fronted by six colossal statues of Ramses, two standing in front of each side of the pylon and two seated statues flanking the entrance...'

I pointed to the fragmented pieces on the ground, then to the seated statues, and the sole remaining standing figure.

'...but only these three remain.'

I stood there trying to see if there was any resemblance between the statues before me and Jacques, apart from them both being heartless and having a cold hard exterior that is.

'Well, shall we go in then?'

Crystal's voice brought me back to the moment.

'Ah, sure, that's why we're here, right?'

'Indeed it is.'

There was something in the way she said it that made me think this was not going to be another touristy sightseeing trip.

The pylon gateway led to a rhomboid, but almost rectangular, courtyard, surrounded by a double row of over seventy papyrus-topped columns. It had been built at an oblique angle to the remaining part of the temple, presumably to accommodate three pre-existing barque shrines located in the northwest corner.

'The triple shrine was built during the reign of Queen Hatshepsut and Thutmoses III, and dedicated to the sacred boats of the *Triad of Thebes*. Once a year, the divine image of Amun, along with his consort Mut and their son Khonsu, would journey in their sacred barques from Karnak to the temple at Luxor to celebrate the Opt festival.'

I looked at it closely: more red granite. Not only were all the papyrus-topped columns that fronted the three shrines made of red granite, but so was the façade of the central shrine. Had Hatshepsut resurrected the granite from a pre-existing structure belonging to her grandfather, Amenhotep I? Perhaps even utilizing the columns from that structure? It was possible. It got me back into detective mode and I wondered if there was any further evidence.

There was. The two shrines on each side were not made of red granite, rather, they were made of sandstone. To me that meant something, firstly, that there was something significant about Hatshepsut that connected her to a much older time, and secondly, that the two adjoining shrines were built later, and belonged to someone *not* considered to be well-versed in the 'powers' of the *sang réal*, and that fitted her step-son Thutmoses III. But was there more?

The answer was right before my eyes; a red granite altar stuck out in the middle of the courtyard like a shag on a rock. Where did it come from, where did it belong? Was it part of the Hatshepsut façade? I started looking for even the smallest scraps of evidence.

It may have meant nothing, but I suddenly realized the original temple was almost exactly aligned north-north-east, whereas the new temple was angled further east to align exactly with the Avenue of the Sphinxes and Karnak.

'What's that door up in the middle of nowhere?'

Yuko's question reluctantly jolted me back into my role as self-appointed tour guide.

'On the opposite side of the courtyard is the Islamic mosque of Abou El-Hagag...'

On the eastern side about eight metres above the ground, a doorway led out into thin air.

'...According to the Egyptologists, the mosque was built in the 13th Century atop the columns of the courtyard, after the whole complex had been buried underneath accumulated river silt.'

'Or the mud from a tsunami.'

I gave Bill a smile.

'Just my thinking exactly. Most likely it was built after the Cairo earthquake in 1303.'

We continued deeper into the temple and I took note of the ground, looking for blocks of red granite. There weren't paved stones in the courtyard, as you might expect, but the same grit and river-stones as there had been at Kom Ombo and Esna.

That told me there was probably something else underneath, because this definitely was not part of the original temple.

The southwest part of the courtyard was incomplete, with many of the columns missing their top halves. But the left corner was the opposite, with numerous massive statues of, guess who, Ramses II, positioned between the columns and guarding the entrance to the next part of the temple. Sure, they were made of granite, but there was something else that didn't add up.

'That doesn't really make sense to me; that Ramses II built this courtyard and then put these statues where they are now, between the columns.'

Bill looked around.

'Agreed! Where do you think they should be?'

'I don't know, maybe in front of the columns, I think the modern Egyptologists have just put them there neatly out of the way so they look good for the tourists.'

Bill was examining them more closely.

'They *are* made of granite though.'

'True, but so far, no blocks on the ground, just gravel.'

'Then we'd better keep looking.'

As we exited the courtyard and travelled deeper into the temple, we entered a section referred to as 'The Colonnade' Just as we did, positioned between the first pair of columns and the rear wall of the first courtyard, on either side of the path, were two paired statues made of alabaster. One was in a poor state, however the right hand one was remarkably well preserved.

Checking my notes, I found some discrepancy between who the 'experts' believed the statues were of; some maintaining they were of Tutankhamun, whilst others believed they belonged to the Middle Kingdom, and to one of the 12th Dynasty pharaohs, namely Amenemhat I, II, or III. They certainly were out of place; not so much stylistically but because they were made of alabaster.

My own thoughts were the Middle Kingdom, though I wasn't really sure why, just a hunch. In any case, I made a mental note and set off down the Colonnade.

I could feel the energy increasing: the tension, the level of expectation. And that increase in energy was reflected in the increase of the size of the columns. They were massive, at least twice as tall as those in the preceding courtyard; set out in seven pairs of open-papyrus capital columns that stretched out fifty metres into the temple, creating a processional avenue.

I thought about the Annunaki: was this confirmation that Amenhotep III was either Annunaki himself, or descended from them, and that he built the Colonnade to accommodate their size? It certainly looked that way.

'The Colonnade was built in the 18th Dynasty by Amenhotep III, a hundred years earlier than the previous courtyard...'

'...The reliefs on the accompanying outer walls describe the stages of the Opt Festival, from sacrifices at Karnak at the top left, through Amun's arrival at Luxor at the end of that wall, the twenty-four day feast, and concluding with his return on the opposite side to Karnak.'

Crystal walked slowly ahead, pointing off to the side walls, showing she knew a few details herself.

'The decorations were put in place by Tutankhamun, and his image can be seen in several places along the walls, although his name has been erased and replaced by that of Horemheb.'

The others moved off to examine the walls and columns, however Crystal remained and held her course, slowly and elegantly making her way down the centre of the Colonnade. I added a few extra tit-bits as they dispersed.

'You should also be able to see the cartouches of some of the later pharaohs as well, such as Seti I, Ramses II, and Seti II; they all recorded their names here.'

Having said that, I quickly joined Crystal in her procession.

'This all seems so familiar.'

'Seems? Feels? Or *is*?'

'Well, yes, it feels familiar; like I've been here many times before.'

'What makes you think you haven't?...'

I turned in to face her but she stayed centred and kept walking.

'...Close your eyes, *feel* the stone, tap into its memory.'

No sooner did I close my eyes, and picture Nemo, than I was transported, and the images I had seen minutes earlier returned almost instantaneously; vivid colours, sounds and even smells flooded my mind.

The Colonnade was resplendent in colour as flags and banners waved in the air. Fragrant scents of flowers, incense, and food cooking wafted through my nostrils as, along the Colonnade and between the columns, novice priests chanted praises and threw handfuls of flower petals and offerings before us.

Yes, it was *us*, we were together; she was a queen and I was right beside her. That jolted me back to reality.

'We've walked this path before haven't we?'

'Many times.'

'I meant in other lives; specifically some time during the 18th Dynasty?'

She smiled.

'Good, you are re-membering.'

'And you were a Queen, weren't you?'

'There you go, doing it again?'

'Doing what?'

'Making a statement of truth, and then questioning it.'

'OK, What I meant to say was, "At some time in the past you were an Egyptian queen; you were Nefertiti".'

'I have told you this before.'

I quickly summed up the implications.

'Are you saying I was an Egyptian pharaoh?'

'It is not for me to tell you who you were or were not: it is you who must re-member. And what makes you think you have been just one?'

She walked on, leaving me open mouthed.

'Just one?'

We'd reached the end of the Colonnade, and, as Crystal transitioned into the second courtyard, I stood as motionless as the statues of Ramses II in the previous courtyard. What did she just say? 'Just one?' So, I'd not only been 'a' pharaoh, but possibly several; that was really freaking me out.

'Come on, Alex, you look about as life-like as Tutankhamun's mummy.'

Bill wrapped his arm around my shoulder, and, as the others caught up, we exited the Colonnade and entered the open space of the second courtyard.

Tutankhamun? As a child I'd always been fascinated by Egypt, and particularly the boy king. Is it possible that I was him, that I was the son of Nefertiti and Akhenaten?

'So where are we now, Alex?'

I gathered my thoughts.

'Ah, this is the Sun Court of Amenhotep III.'

The Sun Court was close to square and a little bigger than the first courtyard; about fifty metres wide and a little bit longer. Like the first courtyard, it had a double row of papyrus-topped columns, though only on three sides, and the ones on the northern side where we stood were incomplete.

Crystal had stopped in the centre of the courtyard, waiting for the rest of us to catch up. Walking toward her, I noticed that again the ground was covered in grit and river-stones, and made a mental note that something else may well have originally existed beneath the surface. All around the yard, the bus-loads of Chinese tourists had scattered like a swarm of locusts sweeping across the fields.

They snapped photographs of everything in sight, and their incessant nattering made it almost impossible for me to focus on finding Nemo. I neither wanted to have to endure the Chinese, nor visit the side columns, what I wanted was to spend more time alone with Crystal and question her about our past lives together.

'How about we continue into the inner temple before it gets over run with Chinese tourists?'

Bill was right with me.

'Good thinking, Alex.'

We made our way from the centre of the courtyard towards the inner temple.

'Hey, Bill, check it out!'

'I'm right with you, matey.'

At the far end of the courtyard, on either side of the entrance, sat large rectangular 'chunks' of worn red granite.

'Now where do you supposed *those* came from?'

'Probably dug up with the rest of the courtyard.'

He was right; I seemed to remember reading something about a whole lot of statues discovered under the ground in the courtyard here some time in the 90's. I wondered what else they'd found. Luxor was revealing more secrets with each step, and the set we had just scaled took us into the Hypostyle Hall. Though its ceiling was missing, it was similar to those at Edfu and Esna: there were thirty-two columns arranged in four rows of eight. On the walls were reliefs of Amenhotep III in front of various gods, including one of him hunting and killing a gazelle before Amun Ra.

In each of the rear corners a small doorway led to the remains of two long chapels; the chapel of Khonsu to the right, and the chapel of Mut to the left. However it didn't take long before the hoard of Chinese started flooding in, so we pushed deeper into the temple towards the inner sanctum.

We hit another open section with the ceiling missing. Apparently, during the Christian era, its eight existing columns were removed by the Roman Emperor, Diocletian, (well, not him personally, but you know what I mean) and it was converted into a Roman church. On the walls, Amenhotep III's reliefs had been plastered over in places with Roman stuccoes and painted with Christian themes. While everyone else was checking out the walls and the juxtaposition of religious decorations, I was preoccupied with the floor.

Not only had they plastered over the walls, it seems, just like at Edfu, they, or some one later, had covered or replaced much of the floor with paving stones. But what captivated my attention were the several sections where the paving stones were missing. What was underneath were 'small' but very worn red granite stones.

I stood there contemplating several things; why were they covered, why were they there in the first place, and what was underneath them?

Suddenly Pernille started getting very anxious.
'I'm not sure I want to keep going any further inside.'

Bill grabbed her hand and supported her arm.
'It's OK, I'll take you back to the hotel.'

Yuko offered her some water, and Crystal quickly stood supporting her other side.
'Or, she could have a drink, take a few deep breaths, and keep going. It would be a shame to have come so far, to get this close, and not get to the heart of the temple.'

I paused, we all did; there was something in what Crystal had said, in the way she had said it. It made me think there was a lot *more* to it. "It would be a shame to have come so far, to get this close, and not get to the heart of the temple." She *wanted* Pernille to keep going, almost *insisted* that she continue, continue into the inner sanctuary. Crystal knew something, and Pernille reacted as if she knew it too.

'Sometimes you have to face you fears, right?'
'It's the only way to truly conquer them.'

Pernille stood strong.
'I'll be fine. Thanks. Let's keep going.'

With Crystal and Yuko beside her, and Bill and Pieter following behind, they entered the realm of the inner sanctum. I took a step as if to follow, then paused as I noticed the ground; it had changed to small chipped fragments of red granite, just like those I had seen used as the retaining wall on the Island of Philae.

For me it was confirmation, something was under the ground here. In fact, a cache of 26 statues dating to the New Kingdom had been found under the floor here in the inner sanctum area in 1989. It's not sure when they were buried, or why; perhaps by the Theban priests at some moment of upheaval or invasion, or maybe by the later pious Roman Catholic priests who subjugated the temple. It didn't really matter, the real question was, what else was there under the ground?

The Daughters of Isis

The three girls passed through a small four-columned offering hall and into the central sanctuary that at one time was commandeered and rebuilt by Alexander the Great, who removed the four columns, added a rear doorway, and turned it into a walk through shrine that supposedly once housed a gold-plated statue of Amun-Ra.

Inside the sanctuary was a circle of about seven or eight women, all dressed in white, doing some sort of ritual prayer or meditation. The leader of the group lifted her head to acknowledge the new arrivals.

'Welcome, sisters.'

Crystal turned back to face Bill, Pieter and me.

'Would you boys mind leaving the three of us for about ten to fifteen minutes.'

We looked at each other; we could hardly say no, and exited through the door to the left, leaving the girls to their 'secret women's business'.

The doorway led to two rooms each with three columns. The northern one, the Birth Room contained scenes depicting the birth of Amenhotep III. Unfortunately they were in poor condition, as were the reliefs in the adjoining room. Not wishing to disturb the women in the next chamber, Pieter whispered in my direction.

'Who do you think those women are?'

'I haven't got a clue, but Crystal sure seemed to know them, and they sure seemed to be expecting our gals.'

From the side rooms we circled behind the central sanctuary and into a wide offering hall containing the remnants of twelve columns spaced in two rows of six across the room. We could hear the women singing in the adjacent chamber. Actually they weren't so much singing words, as singing notes. And not all the same note, but harmonies: at first simple ones, but progressively they became more and more complex; ahs, oohs, ees, aws, it was like a symphonies of angels reverberating through the temple.

The three of us had no idea what they were doing, but we all wished we could have been in there with them. But we weren't, so we moved on and into the original sanctuary at the rear of the temple; the private quarters of the gods and the Birth Shrine of Amenhotep III.

Surprisingly it was a small chamber, with only four clustered papyrus columns, but the walls were decorated with scenes depicting Amenhotep III's claim to have been fathered by Amun, and therefore of divine descent, and of him dancing before the God Amun-Ra. For some reason, I felt I had to stand silently in the room and close my eyes. No sooner had I done so, than Nemo swam into view, and within seconds I was the river, the eerie chords of the women's voices washing over me in an almost hypnotic effect.

Around me the walls of the stone chamber started humming in resonance with the chorus of voices and I felt the room come to life. I shifted my perspective to expand and include the stone itself, to be one with the temple space. As I did, I was sure I heard a low-pitched growling and hissing sound underpinning the women's chorus. I opened my eyes and looked around. I was surprised to see Bill and Pieter also standing silently, as if they were meditating.

'Did you hear that?'

Bill opened his eyes.

'You mean the girls singing?'

'No, that growling and hissing.'

Pieter joined in.

'The growling sounded like a crocodile.'

'And the hissing was like a snake.'

'So you did hear it.'

'Hmmm, very interesting.'

I closed my eyes and 'logged back in' as quickly as I could. There was something not very good about this place; the air was laced with fear, it latched on to you like spider-webs and a walk through a dark forest. In the shadows I caught glimpses of strange figures lurking with evil intent, not just in the corners and behind the columns, but under the floor, especially under the floor.

I expanded my awareness even further, downwards, below the floor. Suddenly I was in a dark candlelit chamber that contained an altar, a black granite altar, like the one that sat in the centre of the temple at El Kab or those at Kom Ombo. On it was a young girl, a priestess, an ancient Egyptian priestess. She was nearly naked and in a semi-conscious state, like she had been drugged.

In from the surrounds stalked several beings, not human; they were reptilian, two-legged hominid lizards about eight feet tall. Holding her down, they spread her legs as another, whom I perceived was the alpha male, moved in and proceeded to sexually molest and rape her.

'Shit! We have to get back to the girls.'

Bill and Pieter followed as I led the way back through the people who had gathered in the Offering Hall watching, passed the voyeurs in the doorway, and into the central sanctuary. The women, still chanting, toning, had closed ranks and, in the centre, Pernille and two other women were bent over, crying and being held up, Pernille by Crystal and Yuko.

On the other side of the chamber, the Chinese were pressing in, impatient, wanting to claim the sanctuary as their own. They had no respect for what was happening, all they wanted to do was snap a few pictures, and the thought that someone else was doing something in the room that they were not a part of was totally unacceptable. They could have circled, as we had done, and explored the rest of the temple first, but, no, they had to see the sanctuary, and they had to see it now. In that moment I saw them morphing, shape-shifting they called it, and each and everyone of them suddenly looked reptilian.

Leaving Pieter to guard the rear doorway, instantly Bill and I circled the women to block the opposite side, to guard the door, to protect the women until they completed what they needed to complete. We didn't say anything, just stood there, staring the outsiders down. They weren't happy, trying to look past. Then their guide tried to push passed us and into the space. I raised my hand.

'No! Wait!'

He tried again, this time through Bill, who stepped forward, at first laughing. 'Maybe you didn't hear my friend here... '

Then he changed his tone; firm, authoritative.

'.... NO! WAIT!....'

Before returning to his charming self.

'...Why not come back in five minutes when the ladies have finished what they are doing?'

His shifts of tone had the desired effect and the 'aliens' temporarily retreated to other parts of the temple, but not before snapping a few photographs. As it turned out, the women were just finishing, stopping their chanting and toning and opening up the circle. At the centre, Crystal, Yuko and the lead woman were embracing Pernille, who in turn was crying tears of both exhaustion and exhilaration. Breaking from the group, the leader walked up to Bill and I.

'Thank you for escorting our sister here, and thank you for your protection, we will see you again soon.'

Then, without a word, they filed out between Bill and I and out of the temple, each one nodding their head in turn and thanking us. Our girls brought up the rear, and, as they reached us, Pernille gave Bill a huge hug, bursting into tears again, though this time it was tears of absolute joy. When Yuko also embraced Pieter I glanced at Crystal, who smiled right back at me, affectionately cupping my cheek with her hand.

'You did well.'

After several seconds that felt like an eternity, she dropped her hand.

'Our work is done here.'

Then she simply, but ceremoniously, walked straight out of the sanctuary, following the other women towards the Colonnade on the other side of the courtyard; it seemed our time in the temple was at an end.

The lads regrouped and followed her across the courtyard, through the Colonnade and into the first courtyard.

'What do you think all that was about?'

'I don't know, Bill, but I think it had something to do with the Dracos.'

'You believe all that stuff about reptiles, and them running the United Nations?'

'Bill, to tell you the truth, by now I don't know what to believe. But what I do know, is we haven't even scratched the surface.'

CHAPTER 14 – REPUTATIONS IN RUINS

Leaving the temple, we gathered outside the main pylon in the Court of Nectanebo then headed towards the exit and the main square; it was just after 5:15pm.

'So, where to now?'

Bill was still somewhat concerned.

'I'm going to take Pernille back to the hotel for a sleep, and then get some dinner later.'

'I think Yuko and I will do the same.'

'Maybe we can all meet for dinner?'

I liked Bill's thinking, and I was starving, but then I remembered I had a previous appointment.

'No can do; I've got to meet Saeed by the river at 7:00; unless we could make it 8:00?'

'No; we have all been invited to join a spiritual circle after dinner, tonight at 8:00.'

We all looked at Crystal; we knew who had invited us, that was obvious.

'Where?'

'At the Nefertiti Hotel.'

'I guess we'll all go our separate ways until then.'

At that moment the call to prayers sounded out from the minaret standing tall above the mosque of Abou El-Hagag. It was soon echoed by other mosques in the city. I can imagine how, once, the sound of solo voices calling from the heavens in various corners of town would have been hypnotic, even angelic, but heavily amplified voices blasting out and invading the atmosphere was an invasion of not only my sanity, but my religious beliefs: even though I didn't have any.

There's no way they would allow this in Australia, and to me it just reinforced the intimidating aspect, as well as the indoctrination and conditioning, of all religions, not only Islam: 'Come to pray, or else; or else you'll go to Hell! No excuses!'

Any further conversation was now impossible.

'OK, we'll see you in the lobby of the Nefertiti at five to eight.'

Bill and Pernille climbed aboard a kalash, while Pieter and Yuko elected to walk up the main street back and to the Nubian Oasis. That left Crystal and I strolling across the square.

To the right, inside the perimeter fence of the temple, unidentified 'surplus' stones had been laid out in rows. Many of them probably belonged to the Roman period as, during Rome's domination of Egypt, the temple was converted into a Roman fort and centre for the Roman emperor cult of Emperor Augustus.

'Hungry?'

'It depends what for.'

She was doing it again, teasing me, taunting me. It was all good humoured, all done with a wicked smile on her face, but it was driving me crazy.

'Would you care for dinner?'

'That's a good start.'

'Do you have a preference for food?'

'Food would satisfy *part* of my appetite. How about over there?'

I couldn't believe it; across the road directly overlooking the temple was the all too familiar image of the golden arches.

'McDonalds?'

'No, just kidding, let's go over there.'

She pointed a little further along, to a treed area just before the corner, which turned out to be a 'local' restaurant, or rather a pub, The King's Head Pub to be precise.

The outdoor decor was bohemian; large comfortable chairs dispersed around tables. In the centre of the 'dining area' was a large tree from which large canopies stretched out to protect the dinners from the sun, which was now making its way towards the hills in the west. This was a perfect place to chill out and relax; hopefully the food was just as good.

We placed our orders; for drinks, a pineapple, coconut and mango juice for Crystal, and, though I was tempted to have a beer, a lemonade lime and bitters for me. For dinner, Crystal ordered lentil soup with lime and an omelette, and I opted for spaghetti Bolognese.

I sunk back into the chair; in many ways it felt like it was the first chance I'd had to relax since I arrived. But it was just a twisted and perverted illusion, for though my body was relaxing, my mind was wound tighter than a coil.

'Who were those women in the temple?'

'You didn't recognize them?'

'No, should I have?'

'Then why did you protect us?'

'I.. er … well you were busy doing whatever it was you were doing and looked like you didn't want to be disturbed.'

'That is true; we would have preferred not to be disturbed. But that is not what you were doing, you were protecting us.'

'Well, yes, I suppose I was.'

'What from?'

'The Chinese tourists.'

'And how would a group of Chinese tourists have harmed us?'

I was getting confused. She was going somewhere with all this, I knew it, but I had no idea of either the destination or the route. Hell, I wasn't even sure where we starting from.

'I guess they wouldn't have actually harmed you.'

'Then why did you feel you had to protect us?'

I debated whether or not to tell her about my vision in the back chamber, about the reptiles and the rape, then thought 'What the hell', and blurted it all out as best I could. She listened intently as I went into every detail, not taking her eyes from me.

'So, am I crazy, or do I just have an over-active imagination?'

She let out the most adorable smirk.

'Are they my only choices?'

As our drinks arrived, Crystal took a sip and then a more contemplative attitude.

'Let me see; are you crazy? Not that I am aware of. An over-active imagination? I would hardly see that as a disability. Have you considered the possibility that perhaps you were acutely perceptive and aware?'

'You mean, all that was real? How?'

'The stone has memory, re-member? All you have done is tune in.'

'Tune in to some past event, some sort of bizarre ritual or sacrifice? To some past time, a time when you were Queen Nefertiti.'

'Oh, just because I lived a life here as Nefertiti, doesn't mean there weren't temples here before then, and that I wasn't someone else.'

'But the Luxor temple only dates back to Amenhotep III...'

Then I thought about it, there was a previous temple in the 12th Dynasty.

'...Or do you mean these rapes happened back during the Middle Kingdom, when there was another temple on this spot?'

She shook her head; clearly I wasn't getting the message.

'They have been happening for millennia, even before the Ancient Egyptian culture.'

'I don't get it.'

'What do you think all those women had in common?'

I thought about it.

'PMS?'

She wasn't amused, so I quickly move to redress the situation.

'I suppose they were all victims of the reptilians.'

She shook her head again.

'There are no victims; their Higher Selves agreed to undergo the bodily invasions, the tortures, mutilations and experimentation.'

'They volunteered?'

'Their *Higher Selves* agreed.'

'And why would they do that?'

'To experience the experience; to test their resolve in the face of fear.'

'But why them?'

'Why do you think?'

I scratched my head, but couldn't think of an answer.

'I don't know.'

'They were all priestesses; Queens and High Priestesses of Ancient Egypt.'

'So which queen was the leading woman?'

'Hatshepsut.'

It figured.

'And what do you think we were doing in the shrine room?'

'I don't know, singing, chanting, praying, secret women's business, a Tupperware party.'

I wasn't sure if she was appreciating my sense of humour, or just tolerating me. Maybe they didn't have Tupperware in Germany. She leaned in to me.

'They were reclaiming their Goddess awareness *back* from the Dracos.'

'And why do they need to do that?'

Our dinner arrived, briefly interrupting our discussion, however, once served, Crystal swiftly returned to the topic.

'There was a time, once, a long time ago, when women ruled this planet; actually it was not so much *ruled* as governed under benevolent caretakership. There were no wars, no hunger, Mother Earth truly was mother earth. Then the Dracos used fear and intimidation, bribing the priests, by giving them power over the women, if in turn they surrendered and turned a blind eye to the Dracos experimentations on the priestesses.

The priests then created powerful rituals, which can be seen echoed in many ancient cultures including the Aztec and Incan civilizations; rituals where virgins were sacrificed to the great *winged serpent*. These virgins were the bloodline goddesses that the Dracos had experimented on.'

'Why would the Dracos want to experiment on them?'

'The Dracos are masters of genetic engineering. They knew, that when the human race was created, the carrier genes for the higher spiritual vibrations of humanoid existence were unknowingly implanted within the DNA, and subsequently carried by the female of the species.

They were trying to *crack* the spiritual code within the humanoid DNA, so that they could splice and integrate it into their own DNA.'

'How does that happen?'

'Are you aware that the female has two X chromosomes and the male an X and a Y?'

'Yes.'

'Well the Y chromosome is a broken or rather incomplete X chromosome, and it is this missing piece, that is only carried fully in the female of the species, that carries the encoded DNA of Higher Spiritual awareness.'

'But why just the priestesses and queens, why not other women; servants, slaves?'

'The Genes of Isis, the original thread of DNA, is carried through the female, and because of close inbreeding it was kept very strong and active in certain bloodlines.'

'The Holy Grail; *Sang réal!*'

'Pardon?'

'*Sang réal*, it's French for royal blood.'

'Yes, the gene was carried through the royal blood line of the Egyptian queens.'

'So those women in the temple were all Egyptian queens at some time in the past?'

'Yes.'

'And the Dracos carried out genetic engineering experiments on them? On *all* of them?'

'They harvested the eggs, manipulated the DNA, then implanted the fertilized eggs back into the priestesses, thus creating hybrid children, which were usually removed prior to full term.'

'Why?'

'To produce a new hybrid reptilian/humanoid form, that would enable them to gain access to the higher dimensional vibrational levels of consciousness.'

'Why can't they do that now?'

'Two things. Firstly, DNA is a holographic blueprint, not just of what is physically created, but more so of the spiritual vibrational state of consciousness. They

74

cannot crack the code because they cannot *see* the code; it is a case of trying to put the cart before the horse. Secondly, fear. It is the lowest vibrational form of consciousness, the second dimension from which the Source of All That Is created as a mirror to view itself. It is the absence of Love.

Some reptilians have managed to raise their energy as high as the fourth dimension, but their belief that fear rules life is always pulling them back to their lower state; like a length of elastic anchored to the third dimension, the more they pull away, the more the tension pulls them back. They hope that in decoding the higher consciousness humanoid aspect of *Love*, they will be able to cut the elastic and catapult themselves to the highest spiritual levels.'

'Why do they want to access the higher states?'

'Quite simply, so that they can conquer them. The Dracos believe they own this universe and everything in it, including all the higher levels of consciousness that exist, and that with their knowledge and power they can rule the entire universe, not just the lower realms.'

'How many levels are there?'

As I twirled a long strand of spaghetti around my fork, Crystal laughed.

'How long is a piece of string?'

Mirror Mirror on the wall

I chewed it all over. It was meaty, though the flavours were unfamiliar and exotic and it seemed heavily spiced. However, despite that, it was totally palatable; I was just finding it hard to swallow. I wished the Bolognese tasted as rich, but unfortunately it was rather on the bland side.

'So what actually *were* you doing in the temple with all those women, why all the singing. And what happened to Pernille, was it something to do with her being Tausert or Queen Inhapi?'

'That's a lot of questions, perhaps we should look at them one at a time.'

'OK, first, what were you doing in the temple?'

She finished a sip of her drink.

'You don't remember? Why not shift your perspective and go back to the temple, back to the chamber.'

I closed my eyes. Within a few seconds the images reappeared, and, not long after, I started getting a feeling.

'You were connecting with the temple, with the stone; connecting back to the time when each woman was first invaded.'

'Very impressive. And why were we doing that?'

'To face your fears, because to dispel a fear, you must first confront it, and that means going back to the time and place when the fear was first created, or first implanted in your mind.'

'Excellent.'

'And the singing had something to do with reconnecting to the stone. No, it was more than that, you were singing what the ancient priestesses used to sing.'

I tried to focus on what it was they were singing, but nothing clearly stood out; it was more like a wash of sounds.

'I can't make it out; it's as if you're each singing different notes and different sounds, but there are no words.'

'That's because there aren't any; it is called toning.'

I opened my eyes and looked questioningly towards her.

'Toning; isn't that what you do to muscles?'

She glanced at my physique, towards my arms and then down at my stomach.

'It is what *some* may do, and what others may *need* to do, but in this case is has to do with voicing specific pitches and specific sounds.'

I subconsciously pulled in my gut as she continued.

'From ancient times the knowledge of vibration has been sacrosanct. And vowel sounds were the most sacred, as each sound and each pitch had a specific relationship, which is why they were only uttered in the inner sanctums. This is also why all the ancient *written* languages consist of only consonants; the vowel sounds were sacred and reserved for the use of the priestesses in the temples.

'That's what you were doing at the altars in the temples at Philae, Kom Ombo and Edfu; toning.'

'Yes. With these tones, the priestesses knew how to unlock the codes in the DNA and activate the higher realms within each woman. But the reptilians were unable to tone, the best they could manage was to growl and hiss.'

'I've heard it, I heard it when I was in the rear chamber of the temple.'

'That is because you are awakening and re-membering.'

'So what was it about, what were they doing?'

'You tell me.'

I closed my eyes again, returning quickly to the darkened chamber.

'The Dracos growled and hissed, but they were incapable of toning, that's why they needed the priestesses, that's why they needed to keep the priestesses and the priestess cults alive, while at the same time using them to create hybrid reptilians with the appropriate DNA sequences; the Dracos were unable to access the *knowledge* about how to reach the higher realms.'

'I am very impressed.'

'But what about the children that were born, what happened to them?'

'Many of the embryos were grossly deformed and many did not survive. Of those that did, the male offspring were useless in accessing the codes, so as they grew they were placed in positions of power, and thus soon became the governments of the world. They also raised them as novices in the priesthood, who ultimately took control, forming the core of the Amun priests.

Thus the Amun priests, who were now totally controlled by the Dracos, and had a different agenda to the original priesthood, caused a split in the priesthood, into the Priests of Amun on one side, and the Tat Brotherhood, who were the true protectors of the priestesses and the bloodline, on the other.

As for the female hybrid offspring, they *still* couldn't access the codes; it was the very reptilian DNA spliced into the women's genes that was keeping them at lower vibrational states, a sort of short circuit. So they were sacrificed as part of the new blood rituals they had created; it served to keep them silent and also keep the others in obedient fear.

But the Dracos still needed to keep the original bloodline pure, to use it as a resource until they could find the access codes, so they permitted the highest priestesses, who were also the true pharaonic bloodline, to breed according to the sacred knowledge of the priestesses and the Tat Brotherhood.'

'And it was the Amun Priests, and not the Tat Brotherhood, that went on to become the Illuminati.'

'Yes. Over the years, unsuccessful in bridging the dimensional gap, the toning of the priestesses was hijacked by the Amun priests who, not knowing the true power of the sounds, added words in an attempt to reflect the meaning and intention, and raise the spiritual energy. Thus the tones were turned into, or rather distorted into, the sacred hymns, prayers and plainchant of the modern religions. And it did have some effect, allowing the Dracos to reach the lower realms of the fourth dimension, and also to access the knowledge and ability to shape-shift.'

'Shape shifting; I think I've heard of that.'

'Fourth dimensional shape-shifting is the interim stage between the *solid* state of the third dimension and the free ability to manifest anything and anywhere at will in the fifth dimension.'

'But that's as far as the elastic would stretch, right?'

'Exactly.'

I thought I had it.

'So toning is something like Sound Healing, like the ancient Greek *Theory of Effects*, where every musical mode, every note, had an accompanying response. Or is it more?'

'It's more. The Theory of Effects is part of it, as is Colour Therapy and Aromatherapy, but you are on the right track; everything is in a harmonic relationship to everything else.'

'You mean like the Harmony of the Spheres.'

'Again, that is part of it. But you must shift your perspective much further than musical notes and sound, and the rotational frequencies of the planets. You must include *all* vibrational frequencies; molecular and sub-atomic spin resonances, light, radiation, *everything*.'

'I get it, so something is either in harmony or dissonance, right; sort of cosmic Feng Shui?'

'Except there is no such thing as dissonance, that is a judgment based on a given perspective. Everything is in harmonic relationship to everything else, period! That relationship may interact similarly to music, and range from unison, octave, fifths, etcetera, through to the semitone of modern music, but there are also microtones and fractional tones, like beat frequencies that create certain effects.'

'Beat frequencies?'

'Specific frequencies and combinations of frequencies have specific effects on not only the human body, but also the human mind, as well as the human spirit. Just like in music, nothing is truly dissonant; it just has a different *colour*, a different affect on the listener. Some make you happy, some make you sad, others make you angry, while others make you feel at peace.'

I tried to relate it back to what happened in the temple.

'All that toning certainly had an effect on Pernille. Was it something to do with when she was Tausert, or Queen Inhapi?'

'In this case it was as a young girl, as Ashotep, before she became Queen Inhapi. Being here in Egypt, and visiting the temples, triggered both Jacques' behaviour and Pernille's remembering of her sexual abuse in the temple at Luxor. You see Jacques was also a reptilian hybrid, as were all descendants of the Ramses bloodline.

It was important for Pernille to confront her fears, as it was for several of the other women, and their fears were rooted here in Luxor. Once we were in the temple, and started toning, it activated all their cellular memory and they connected with the reptilian energy within the stone, within the temple.

The reptilians tried to gain access to Pernille and the other women, as they had in the past, up through the vagina and into the uterus and ovaries. As the toning continued, the women were compelled to relive the experiences and naturally they broke down. That's probably when you were also triggered to recall the Dracos.

Then, we shifted the toning and raised the spiritual energy above that of the Dracos, we supported the women, physically and spiritually, to stand up to the Dracos and reclaim their goddess energy.'

'What about you? I mean, what about Nefertiti? Was she molested.'

'We were all interfered with in some way. Only the strongest were able to stand up spiritually and physically to the Dracos.'

'How do you do that?'

'Awareness. Spiritually you cannot do anything that is against the will of the Higher Self of another being. What the Dracos don't realize is that Higher Dimensional Entities have agendas for the *Human* consciousness way beyond those of the Dracos.'

'But these Dracos guys are still in the temples, right? I mean, their spiritual energy is still resonating in the stones?'

'That's correct.'

'Then why don't you girls all just gang up on the Dracos, tone up a storm, and kick their scaly butts out of there?'

'Because we, the goddesses, the priestesses, were not the ones who invited them in there; it was the priests, the pharaohs.'

'So how do you get the priests to kick them out if the priests themselves are all hybrids controlled by the Dracos?'

'It takes someone who is not Dracos, but someone the Dracos fear, and whose decisions they have to abide by.'

'You mean a pharaoh that was not infected with the Dracos bloodline; perhaps a pharaoh that came from the Annunaki?'

'Exactly.'

'Like Imhotep, Amenhotep I, Akhenaten?'

She smiled.

'That's interesting; out of the hundreds of pharaohs, what made you choose those three?'

Before I'd arrived in Egypt I don't think I'd really considered who Imhotep and Amenhotep I were, or that they were Annunaki gods, or that they could have been one and the same person. Up until then, Akhenaten wasn't just the *first* pharaoh that came to mind, he was the *only* one that came to mind, and he'd been on my mind since I was a child, since I first saw an image of him.

In fact Akhenaten had been on my mind from the moment I landed in Egypt. And there were even stronger reasons why he came to mind, but I wasn't sure I wanted to go there for reasons of my sanity. I took the safe path.

'Well Imhotep and Amenhotep were both referred to as deities, but Akhenaten was different, he was labelled a heretic. You see, when Akhenaten assumed the throne, he knew the Amun Priests were really the ones in control, but he also knew they were totally corrupt, and by instigating the worship of the Aten, he effectively removed them of all their power.'

'Akhenaten also knew the Amun priests were controlled by the Dracos, as did Imhotep and Amenhotep I.'

'How do you know?'

'You are forgetting, I was Nefertiti.'

'That explains knowing about Akhenaten, but what about Imhotep and Amenhotep I? How many Egyptian queens *have* you been?'

She sat back, and having finished her omelette, sipped on her juice.

'Let me see, going backwards: Cleopatra Selene...'

'Not *the* Cleopatra?'

'No. Cleopatra Selene was the *daughter* of Cleopatra, Cleopatra VII and Marc Antony; and though she wasn't technically a queen, she should have been. Before that I was Nefertiti, daughter of Amenhotep III and wife of Akhenaten...'

'Wait a minute, I know Nefertiti was Akhenaten's wife, but I thought it was Akhenaten, Amenhotep IV, who was the child of Amenhotep III and Queen Tiye? I thought Amenhotep III was Nefetiti's father-in-law.'

'No, he was her father,...'

I was quickly running through in my mind Nefertiti's ancestry; married to Akhenaten, who was thought also to be the son of Amenhotep III, thus making Nefertiti his daughter-in-law. But Crystal seemed so sure she wasn't, and if she really had been Nefertiti, then she would know the truth.

'..., and Queen Tiye was not the mother of Akhenaten.'

That took me back for a second.

'Yes she was.'

'Is that what you believe?'

'Well, all the Egyptologists say she was.'

'All the Egyptologists are wrong; they are just guessing. You should know that.'

She was right, I should have, I *did*. But she was really confident, sure of herself, like she had been when confronted by Jacques.

'The only thing they have correct is that Queen Tiye was married to Amenhotep III and they had a son, Amenhotep IV. What the Egyptologists don't know is that Nefertiti was also the daughter of Queen Tiye.'

'How do you know that?'

'I would hardly not know who my own mother was. Besides, the royal bloodline was through the women, not the men, that is why Akhenaten married her.'

'So Nefertiti married her brother?'

'No, Amenhotep IV was *not* Akhenaten, they were totally different people, totally different beings.'

I got all excited.

'I knew it, I knew they weren't the same person.'

'Of course you did.'

Then I asked for her reasoning.

'OK, I know it, but you might have to explain it for me.'

'Why? Don't you remember?'

She'd thrown down the challenge, so I decided to meet it. I sat back and closed my eyes.

'Amenhotep IV was meant to be the next pharaoh, and meant to be married off to his sister, Nefertiti, but his father, Amenhotep III, abdicated when Akhenaten returned.'

'Very good, and why did he abdicate to Akhenaten, and not to his own son?'

She was leading me, guiding me.

'Because Akhenaten was...., because he was Annunaki; he was a god.'

Then images started to open up even more and I had a major awakening.

'The Annunaki were also not on very good terms with the Dracos; there was no war as such, but the Annunaki totally distrusted them. So Akhenaten arrived not only to bring the truth of the *one god* concept back to the human race, but in particular to put a stop to the corruption of the Amun Priests and the genetic experiments of the Dracos. Before Akhenaten arrived, Amenhotep IV would normally have married his sister, Nefertiti, and, upon the death of his father, assumed the throne, but when Akhenaten arrived and claimed the throne, that all went out the window.

Knowing the bloodline, the *sang réal*, was through the women, Nefertiti was married off to Akhenaten, and several years later Amenhotep IV was reduced to marrying Khiya, a younger sister of he and Nefertiti.

However, because of the genetic problems of interspecies breeding between the Annunaki and human race, only female offspring were produced. So Akhenaten and Nefertiti produced only daughters, six in total, the third eldest of which was Ankhesenamun. Meanwhile Amenhotep IV and Khiya produced a son, Tutankhamun, whom they named in honour of the Annunaki pharaoh, and who was then married off to his first cousin, Ankhesenamun.

What the modern Egyptologists haven't realized is that the heritage, the bloodline, was through the women, not the men; the males indeed became pharaoh, but legitimacy was through the female bloodline. But Akhenaten did, and once on the throne, he then went about instituting worship of the Aten and removing the Amun priests from their corrupt positions within the temples.'

Then I had another flash.

'Also, with the Amun priests ousted, and the worship of the Aten now in place, it allowed for the resurrection of the spiritual work of the priestesses, of the toning. So Nefertiti, who was a High Priestess within the temples, became instrumental in the resurrection of the sacred tones and the spiritual work of the priestesses.'

Crystal was beaming like a proud mother who had just been told her son had topped the Dean's list.

'And where did you read all that? Which of the modern Egyptologists has such profound insight?'

'I didn't read it anywhere, I just know it.'

'And how could you know it?'

'Because I was there?'

'Of course you were. And who were you?...'

I hesitated; she'd not only thrown down the gauntlet, she'd slapped it in my face.

'...Well? You can say it.'

There was only one person I could have been.

'I was Akhenaten.'

It resonated through me like a canon shot through the Grand Canyon. Saying it was a massive release; like admitting I was an alcoholic or drug addict. And in stating it and accepting it, it opened the door to even more insights and more importantly to re-membering.

'So we have been man and wife before.'

Matter-of-factly she finished her drink and called for the bill.

'Does the idea appeal to you?'

'Very much.'

'Good, then now we can move forward.'

Rising to her feet, I checked my phone, 6:52pm.

'Great timing, just over five minutes until I have to meet up with Saeed.'

'Would you mind if I came with you to meet him?'

'No, not at all.'

No sooner had the waiter placed the bill on the table than Crystal picked it up. My chivalrous upbringing instantly sprang to the fore.

'I'll get that.'

'That is very kind of you, but we are not married in *this* life, not yet. And until such time as we are, I shall pay my own way, thank you.'

I wasn't sure if it was a reproach or a green light, if she was a feminist or just fiercely independent.

'No problems.'

The bill settled, we left the restaurant and strolled across the road towards the river. I'd been so engrossed in the conversation I hadn't even noticed that the sun had set. Another romantic opportunity missed, I attempted to make up for lost ground.

'So what's the deal with this group of women we are meeting?'

'We are not meeting them, we are joining them.'

'OK, why are we joining them?'

'That depends on you.'

'Me? Why does it depend on me?'

'Because of who you are.'

'They know who I was?'

'Of course, that is why you were invited.'

Talk about laying the pressure on; it was only moments ago I had openly accepted who I had been in a previous life, and now I was being told that a group of total strangers, of ancient Egyptian priestesses, were waiting on me to join them in a spiritual circle.

As we arrived on the upper part of the esplanade, I had to chuckle away to myself; my ex-wife would be flabbergasted at the changes in me, though I doubt if she could even comprehend what had happened. It made me contemplate a lot of what-ifs.

What if I'd opened up to all of this earlier, would we still be together? But then, if I *had* shifted, we may have stayed together, and that meant I may never have come to Egypt, never have met Crystal, never have taken the boat trip, never had met Bill, Pieter, Randy, Dwight and the rest of the castaways, and never have truly awoken to all the things that had unfolded in the last four days.

It's amazing how hindsight can help you see the wisdom in how and why things have happened to you in your life. If only we could have the benefit of hindsight *while* it was happening. Then I realized, we can, and Nemo was the key: by shifting our consciousness and expanding our awareness we could BE the river and everything in it.

I'd also finally realized that time was *not* linear, that all things happen in the moment because the moment is all there ever is; it's just that the moment we choose to focus on is often all that we see, but not All That Is. And finally, I totally got the concept that *we are exactly where we are meant to be in every second of our life*, and that we should be grateful for all that we have, all that we are, and all that comes, for it is the measuring stick by which we evaluate how near or far we are to BEING a *part of* All That Is, rather than being *apart from* All That Is.

Dock of the bay

We didn't get a chance to discuss things any further, as, just ahead, from the lower esplanade, the sound of Jacques voice cut through the balmy twilight like a chainsaw in the forest.

'I don't care what you say, I'm not paying you a cent.'

We looked over the fence to the lower level of the waterfront where Saeed and Jacques were facing up toe to toe.

'I am afraid, Mister Jacques, that I cannot return to you your bag without it the payment.'

'Then I will call the police.'

I turned, half laughing, to Crystal.

'It seems like Jacques takes a long time to get the message.'

The thing was, Crystal wasn't there, she was already half way down the stairs before I could even take a second breath.

'Captain Jack, how was your trip down?'

'Ah, Miss Crystal, yes, very good, thank you.'

'I see Jacques has found you as well. That's fantastic, now he can pay you what he owes you for the trip.'

'I will do nothing of the sort, he left me stranded in the middle of the desert.'

'Hey, I was left stranded at Edfu, and you don't see me complaining.'

I wanted to help Saeed get his money, but I needn't have bothered, as Crystal effectively nudged me aside, tagged Saeed, and stepped into the ring.

'Oh, I wouldn't call beside the river just north of Edfu *the middle of the desert*. In fact there are some lovely green fields there, especially between the Edfu pyramid and the river.'

I stood beside her like a ringside second, watching her dance around, jabbing like a prize fighter, setting him up for a body punch, a right hook, or a uppercut. Jacques had two predictable strategies; ducking and weaving, and arrogant intimidation, neither of which was effective against his more accomplished adversary. Unperturbed, Crystal kept jabbing away.

'The way I understand it, Jacques, you were the one who insisted the boat *always* leave on time.'

'Captain Jack had a responsibility for our safety.'

'You look safe to me. By the way, where is Candy?'

'How should I know?'

'Did she catch her flight?'

'Who cares about that tramp?'

'Well, I might be wrong, but there seemed to be many times during the trip when you seemed very concerned about whether she was happy or not.'

'I was just being friendly. And that does not alter the fact you were supposed to wait for me.'

He had tried to switch the duel back to Saeed, but Crystal was having none of that.

'Saeed why don't you go and get Jacques' belongings, while I help him

82

understand his position?'

'Of course, Miss Crystal.'

He grinned like the proverbial Cheshire cat, before disappearing down the dock; though I'm sure he would have loved to stay and watch the battle unfold.

Having positioned her artillery, Crystal fired her first salvo.

'Maybe, if you had been watching the time, rather than being so *friendly* to Candy, you might have made it back on time.'

'What are you talking about?'

'Well, I'd already made arrangements with Saeed to stay longer at Edfu Temple, and to catch up with the boat at the pyramid. Alex decided to keep me company and we made our way to the pyramid, but then, when we were walking back along the road to the river admiring the scenery, you will never guess what we saw in the paddock, or rather *who* we saw, and what they were doing.'

Jacques' face changed immediately, betraying his vulnerability, but he ducked and weaved, feigning ignorance.

'I have no idea what you are rambling on about?'

Oh, he knew all right, he was just in denial. And that's somewhere I wanted to throw him right then and there, into 'de Nile'. I hardly needed to bother though, as Crystal was setting him up for the knockout blow.

'I am sorry you don't understand me? Let me simplify things for you. You owe Captain Jack four-hundred pounds; it should be eight hundred, for you *and* for Pernille, but another man has graciously stepped up and offered to cover for *your* responsibility.'

'Where is Pernille?'

'Oh, have you forgotten, *that is none of your concern.*'

'Where is she staying? Is she with that antipodean gorilla, Bill?'

Now he was really getting on my nerves, but I bit my tongue and left Crystal to deal with him.

'You should be happy for her; she's somewhere really nice, somewhere she really deserves, somewhere really safe, with someone who really cares for her. And she is happy; truly happy.'

'I want to talk to her.'

'I'm sure you do, but the thing is, she doesn't want to talk to you.'

'Well, we are flying out tomorrow, so she had better return to the hotel.'

'I wouldn't be so certain about that. As far as I know, she won't be on that flight and you'll be flying back to Zurich alone. But before you go, you personally owe four-hundred pounds, which is, let me see, about fifty Euro. I think you would pay an awful lot more than that back in Zurich for the sort of *friendly* interaction you and Candy were indulging in, so I'm sure you got more than your money's worth on the trip.'

'I was cheated of a day.'

'That would be about a hundred pounds for the day, right? So that means you do admit you owe Captain Jack three-hundred for the first three days then.'

'I admit nothing of the sort. He left me behind and he deserves nothing.'

'I hardly think Air France would hold up one of it's flights, or reimburse your money, if you missed your flight, because you were getting a head job from a working girl on the *Pigalle Place*.'

'What is that supposed to mean?'

I'd had enough of his bullshit.

'Look, Jacques, let's cut to the chase; the reason you missed the boat was because you were too busy pounding Candy's ass while she was bent over in a paddock. Why don't you be a real man and just take responsibility for your actions; if you want your bag and your belongings back, simply pay Saeed the money you owe him.'

At that point Saeed returned with the bag and Crystal looked to Jacques.

'Well?'

He stood there about as animated as the statue of liberty with a cucumber up its ass; there was no way he was going to fork out a cent. But Crystal had one more ace to play.

'Very well....'

She reached inside her sarong and pulled out several notes.

'... I will not see Saeed out of pocket.'

She gave him five-hundred pounds and took Jacques' bag in return.

'Now, if you want your belongings, you shall now have to *buy* them back, from me.'

'You cannot do that, it has my passport and personal effects; I will call the police.'

She had him exactly where she wanted him, by the visa.

'You do that, and I will tell them exactly how you have behaved; everything! And in the end it will be the three of us against the one of you; who do you have to back up your story?'

'Pernille.'

'If I were you, I wouldn't be counting on Pernille for anything any more.'

He must have realized he was not only out numbered, but he'd been out manoeuvred.

'Very well, but on one condition, that you tell me where Pernille is.'

'Certainly.'

I thought there would be no way Crystal would tell him, but I was wrong. He waited for the information, but Crystal was no fool; she calmly held her ground waiting to see the colour of his money. Finally he conceded, reluctantly handing her the cash and receiving the bag in return.

'Pernille is staying at The Winter Palace.'

'And where is that?'

'I am not your tour guide, I suggest you ask a taxi driver.'

He stormed up the stairs and out of sight, no doubt to collar the nearest taxi and hightail it to the Winter Palace.

'Thank you, Miss Crystal.'

'My pleasure.'

I was still slightly mystified.

'Why did you tell him where Pernille was, surely he's going to head straight there and cause a scene?'

'That is between Pernille and Jacques, and not for us to interfere. And not interfering also means not blocking, or preventing from happening, that which has to occur. Just like your meeting now with Saeed.'

'Have you eaten it the dinner? My uncle he has it a very good restaurant here.'

'Is this the uncle who knows about Zahi Hawass and the Aswan Dam?'

'No, this it is his brother.'

'Saeed, you must related to half of Egypt.'

He chuckled away.

'No, no, Indy, this is not it at all. I am related to the other half.'

Crystal was gracious.

'I would love to join you, but we have already eaten and have another appointment in about forty minutes I also have some business to attend to before then, so perhaps we can dine there another time?'

'Yes, yes, but of course.'

She went to leave, I presumed to the Winter Palace.

'Will Pernille be OK?'

Crystal just laughed.

'Pernille will be perfectly fine. I would be more worried for Jacques; his massive ego is about to get the shock of its life.'

Then she gave me one of her knowing looks.

'Enjoy your chat, I will see you at the Nefertiti Hotel at 8:00 pm.'

We both watched as she elegantly glided up the staircase; that woman had the most amazing ass I had ever seen, and legs like a stairway to paradise.

'OK, where shall we go?'

'Please, to come to my boat and have it a beer, or shall I make for you some hibiscus tea?'

'Tea would be great.'

The man from uncle

I followed Saeed along the riverfront, down a gangway, and within minutes we were back on the familiar deck of the White Rose, where he quickly 'put the kettle on'.

'Where's Mohammed and Gomar?'

'Gomar he is out with some friend and Mohammed he visit one of his wife.'

'How many does he have?'

'Three.'

'Three?'

'One here in Luxor, one in Aswan, and another in his home town Fayoum.'

'No wonder he spends so much time on the river, I couldn't cope with one wife.'

'Maybe, Indy, you need it an Egyptian wife, or perhaps a German wife?...'

He had a wicked glint in his eye.

'...Well, you and Miss Crystal do make it quite a couple.'

'She's one in a billion, that's for sure.'

I settled in for a chat.

'Saeed, what do you make of her, of Crystal?'

He took his time, choosing his words carefully.

'I have only met her a few days ago, but I feel that I am knowing her all of my life, or perhaps it is I have known her in some other life. And it is not just that I am knowing her, but that I am serve and honour her.'

'So you believe in reincarnation?'

'Oh, yes.'

'Who do you think you were, and who she was?'

He handed me a tea.

'My father and my grandfather they have always talk of the tradition of it the Tat Brotherhood, that we are descend from the High Priest who were the keeper of the ancient knowledge and truth of Thoth....'

He chuckled away.

'...But unfortunate that it would seem that over the many year the ancient secret they have been long forgotten.'

I was quick to correct him.

'Not forgotten, just not re-membered.'

'This I do not understand.'

'Crystal showed me; it's about shifting your perspective, expanding your awareness and feeling the rock.'

'Ah, I use it the shisha for that.'

'I would think that might be the reason you *can't* remember.'

'Perhaps, you may be right, Indy. I do know that we were also the protector of the High Priestess in the temple, and I am being sure that I was one of these priest, of the Tat Brotherhood, and I serve Miss Crystal when she was being the High Priestess and Queen of Egypt.'

'Do you know which queen?'

'There are two that come to my mind; maybe just be because they are famous, but I believe she was Nefertiti and Cleopatra.'

'I agree with you, I think she *was* Nefertiti, but I'm not so sure about her being Cleopatra, not the famous one anyway. Maybe you did indeed serve Cleopatra, but possibly Crystal was not *the* Cleopatra, but perhaps Cleopatra's daughter?'

He mulled it over a little.

'Very interesting, Indy, what is it that makes you say this?'

'It's what she told me herself.'

'Then I am guessing she would know. And what about you, Indy, where is it do you fit in?'

'What do *you* think?'

This time he took a little longer to choose his words.

'You are like it a brother to me, perhaps you were also the High Priest and member of the Tat Brotherhood? And yet, there is it more to you, more to your relationship to Miss Crystal. Perhaps you have also been it the pharaoh, and such a rebel too.....'

He laughed away.

'... Yes, yes, perhaps you were the husband of Nefertiti, the heretic pharaoh, Akhenaten.'

That was the second confirmation in less than two hours, one more and there was no way I could have any more doubts.

'That's not the first time I've thought that.'

'Then this trip it will be quite the eye-opener for you, especially when you visit it the temple here at Luxor and Karnak.'

'I've already been to the Luxor Temple.'

'Really! And how was it?'

'Pretty weird actually; I had all these images, flashbacks.'

'The Lizard People?'

I was surprised at what Saeed had said.

'You've seen them?'

'No, but my grandfather he sometimes would talk of them. He say they are lived in the ancient vault beneath the temple.'

'He may have been right.'

'If you have been see them at Luxor, who is knowing what it is you will be see when you are visit Karnak.'

'What's at Karnak?'

'You are know about the Priest of Amun?'

'I'm finding out more each day.'

'The Temple of Karnak it was their stronghold; from here they ruled the Nile....'

He pointed his glass of tea at me.

'....That is until Akhenaten he come along.'

'I know, he removed all their power when he introduced the worship of the Aten.'

'He removed nothing; he merely forced them to go underground, and once underground they become more trouble, corrupt and manipulate of everything.'

'What do you think will happen when I visit Karnak?'

'I do not think you will be welcome, that is for sure.'

'And what about the West Bank; the tombs in the Valley of the Kings and Queens?'

'The only interest the Amun Priest have in the dead, is to rob them.'

'What about the Dracos, the Lizard People?'

'They have it even less interest; they have only the interest in those who are living. My grandfather he used to say it was to feed on the blood of the virgin priestess.'

'I think your grandfather was a wise man.'

I held my tea up and we toasted him.

'So, Indy, where else is it you are going after Luxor?'

'I haven't planned anything really. Originally I was going to do Abu Simbel, Aswan, the felucca trip, all around Luxor, Denedera, Abydos and then head down to Cairo and the Giza Plateau.'

'Are you plan to visit Tel el-Amarna?'

'I wasn't going to.'

'If you were Akhenaten, then you must visit it Tel el-Amarna.'

'I think you may be right, Saeed.'

'What about Miss Crystal, she will go with you?'

'I don't know what her plans are.'

'Then maybe this you should find out.'

I nodded and held up my glass.

'I'll drink to that too.'

Saeed was proving to be more than just a simple felucca pirate, and his family history was providing some useful information and corroboration.

'So tell me about your uncle.'

'Which one?'

'The one who worked on the relocation of the Philae temple.'

'Kareem; as a boy he live in Aswan, and when the High Dam it was being built he got work in the relocating of the temple from P'aaleq to Aglika. He say that first they built it a giant reservoir around the island to protect it from the rising water, then they start to remove the temple, stone by stone.

After the ceiling and wall had been removed, they start to work on the floor stone, but soon they discover much older ruin under the floor, that have been covered in it sand and silt. Many of the worker they are one day told they are not needed. My uncle he is one of the few men asked to remain, and as they dig it out they find it the top of a gold statue. They are all told to keep quiet about the statue, that they will be reward with it land, or money, to keep quiet, which they do.'

I got even more excited.

'He might be able to prove my theory about other temples underneath the present ones, when can I meet with him?'

'Let me to give him the call.'

Saeed pulled out his cell phone and within seconds was conversing in Arabic with whom I assumed was his uncle. He turned to me.

'What is it you are doing tomorrow?'

'I was going to visit the West Bank, but I can change that.'

'No, no, this it is perfect, my uncle he is officially retired now, but he still go out to Medinet Habu each day. What about you will meet him at West Bank ticket office tomorrow around 3:00pm?'

'That would be great. How will I know him?'

'He is seventy-year old Egyptian in a galabeya...'

Saeed laughed, then continued.

'...You will not know him, but so long as you wear it your hat, I am sure he will recognize you.'

He finished the call, and it was all arranged. But time was racing and before I knew it the clock had ticked over to 7:50.

'How long will it take for me to get to the Nefertiti Hotel?'

'Only four or five minute; it is just along the river.'

'Ok, well I'd best be going. Thanks for the tea, and thanks for arranging things with your uncle.'

'It is my pleasure.'

'Are you going to stay long in Luxor?'

'A few more day.'

'Great, maybe we can do dinner tomorrow night at your *other* uncle's place?'

'Yes, yes, if that it is what you wish.'

'I'll give you a call.'

I skipped the handshake and gave Saeed a huge hug, how could I not, then hightailed it up the stairs.

The inner circle

No sooner did I hit the esplanade than a kalash driver tagged me for a soft touch.

'Kalash; you need driver?'

It was a great night to walk, but to tell the truth I wasn't exactly sure where the hotel was, so I thought a few pounds was a wise investment in making sure I wasn't late.

'Nefetiti Hotel, how much?'

'Yes, Nefertiti Hotel, please to step in.'

'How much?'

'Yes, Nefertiti Hotel, fifty pounds.'

At first you get angry that they are trying to rip you off so much. I mean, I knew that the going price was only about a tenth of that for such a short trip. Then you remember that not only are they trying to support a family at a time when tourists are becoming as scarce as hen's teeth, but that bargaining is the normal way of doing business.

'La, la, I walk.'

'Nefertiti, yes, forty pound; very good price.'

After walking about fifty metres and bartering back and forward we settled on ten pounds. I jumped aboard and had virtually just settled in when two turns later we were pulling up outside the Nefertiti Hotel. I smiled and laughed; the seat had barely got warm, before disembarking and handing him the ten pounds.

'Shukran.'

'Yes, cowboy, something for the horse?'

They never miss a chance to milk you dry of every pound they can. So, do you give them a note and encourage the behaviour, or brush it off? Given he was already getting about five pound a minute for the trip, I decided to just shake my hand and head, and hustle into the Nefertiti.

The Nefertiti, whilst not five star, was at least a star or two above where I was staying; Crystal had good taste. The others were waiting in the reception area; Pernille showed signs she had clearly just had another encounter with Jacques; though thankfully this time she wasn't flustered, so much as liberated, empowered and energized.

She and Bill were relating the whole experience to Pieter and Yuko, who both looked well rested. Crystal was speaking to two women whom I presumed were from the circle in the temple.

No time for idle chitchat, within minutes we were led to a largish lounge room within the hotel where the rest of the women were waiting.

'Welcome, my name is Diane. We are both delighted and honoured that you have all chosen to join us. Please make yourself comfortable.'

Diane was the leader of the group from the Luxor temple; an attractive brunette around five-foot-seven or eight, in her mid-thirties with a soft American accent. After introducing us to the rest of the ladies, she invited us all to sit in one large circle. Large cushions were scattered around the room as ambient music played in the background, one of those nature relaxation CDs with the sound of water and humpback whales. The air was fragrant, a mixture of frankincense, lavender and sandalwood.

It was only once we had settled, Crystal to my immediate left, that I took a moment to look around. Diane sat directly opposite us, Pieter and Yuko diagonally across the circle to my left, whilst Pernille and Bill sat opposite them to my right. In fact somehow we had managed to divide the group into three equal segments, with three women seated between each of the pairs.

Was it just coincidence or divine orchestration? The women varied in age, most from their early twenties to mid thirties, a few in their forties, plus one women in her late sixties who I instantly felt, whilst not the leader, was the spiritual matriarch of the group. Diane gathered everyone's attention.

'Right then, let's get started.'

She held out a large clear-quartz crystal in both hands.

'Divine Aset, Highest Goddess, we gather here in your name that we may fully re-member our Highest Self and our true purpose here on this planet at this time. We meet in the eternity of this moment to fully embrace and embody the creative Goddess Source that is at the heart of each and every one of us. We once again welcome to our circle, our sisters Yuko, Pernille and Crystal, and extend a warm and loving special welcome to our brothers and protectors, Pieter, William, and Alexander...'

Hell, no one called me that, not even my mother. I know it was a logical assumption, but no one really knew that was my full name. I wondered if Bill and Pieter were as perplexed as I was about what was happening and what may have been going to happen. Time would certainly tell.

'...I think we would all agree that was quite an interesting visit to the Luxor Temple this afternoon, extremely powerful and liberating.'

I wasn't sure whether I was supposed to contribute to the discussion, or just be a witness, so initially I sat silently as Pernille and the two women, who had been at the centre of the circle in the temple, related their experiences.

Each in turn took the clear crystal and held it in their hand, retelling their tales. Their stories were very similar, of feeling oppressed, watched, fearful, used and violated, of having to face an unknown fear in the darkness. Pernille allowed the other two women to speak first, then, having the crystal passed to her by Diane, took a deep breath and slowly began sharing the full details of her time in the temple.

'My experience was initially very similar to the others, but I had more detail. At first I was very anxious, I knew I had to be there, but I didn't know what was going to happen. Then when everyone started singing and the other two girls walked to the centre, I felt I had to join them; what ever it was that had happened to them, I was a part of it as well.

I quickly became aware of someone else, something dark and sinister around me; the lizards. I could hear them growling, hissing, their yellow eyes peering through the shadows. As the singing changed they came out of the cracks in the walls, it was like it lured them out, oozing like black blood from the heart of the stone, from the ceiling, and especially up through the floor. I was terrified, but I knew I had to stand strong, to face them.'

The other two women confirmed her thoughts and visions.

'Yes, yes, I remember now, it was like they were coming at me from every side, grabbing at my hair, arms, my body.

'I felt them creeping up my legs, inside my thighs. But I had to stand strong too, show them I wasn't scared, even when they lunged at me and breathed in my face.'

Pernille continued her retelling of events.

'It was the same for me; they were clinging to me like parasites. The floor was covered in blood, thick and sticky, pooling ankle deep around me. Then, before I could do anything about it they had reached up deep inside me. That's when Crystal and Yuko rushed in to support me, and that's all I needed to fight them off.'

I figured that's when the guys and I rushed in, and I was going to add my thoughts, but Crystal headed me off at the pass.

'The Dracos were trying to get to your ovaries, to get to your eggs. They knew you were all priestesses, that you each carry the Goddess bloodline, and they were trying to manipulate your genes. They did it to you in the past, and they were trying to access you once again. But this time you said no, you faced your fears.'

Diane chimed in as Pernille passed the crystal to her.

'And this is the first step in reclaiming your goddess empowerment. You must not only go back to where your fears were first triggered in *this* life, but to truly dispel them, you need to go back to the life where you first manifested and absorbed them, and for most of us here it was with the Dracos in the temples of ancient Egypt.'

One of the other women piped up.

'But how do we drive out the Dracos, how do we get rid of them forever?'

This was a topic Crystal proved to be very knowledgeable about, and Diane clearly was aware of that, so she passed her the crystal.

'The Dracos can never be defeated; they have been around for too long and are too dispersed through the universe. Nor is it our role to go into battle against them, or even to drive them out, this is not the role of Goddess. They have just as much right to be here as we do; in fact if you asked them, they would say that it is we who have no right to be here.'

'Why is that?'

'They see humans as fodder, as cattle, to be grown and bred for a variety of purposes.'

'Then who can stop them from doing what they are doing?'

'I think that's where we come in....'

I hadn't said anything until that moment, neither had Bill or Pieter.

'....We have to make them respect us, but not respect who we are, but rather what we are.

Crystal smiled and handed me the crystal. I paused momentarily, then realized the spot light was well and truly shining on me and, if I was to win Crystal's respect, it was now time to not only talk the talk, but walk the walk.

'The only way the Dracos can control us is through fear, and it's fear that keeps us trapped in the lower dimensions, which are ruled by the Dracos. But humans are beings that can connect and ascend to the Higher Realms, the realms of unconditional love, realms the Dracos cannot attain. If we raise our energy to those higher levels, by expelling all fear from within us, then the Dracos cannot reach us, and if we are not fearful of them, then they have no power over us.'

I briefly paused, gauging their response, before I was compelled to continue.

'But it is not the women who are the most fearful, they are more connected to the Source of All That Is, it is the men who are the most susceptible to fear, the easiest to manipulate, because of their incomplete DNA, because they lack the double X chromosomes of women.

Look at the world, it is full of fear, and who runs the world? Men. It is men who cause wars, men who allow children to starve to death by the millions, men who let millions die of thirst or disease, men who rape the planet of its riches and pollute the skies, lands and seas in return.

So if the human race is to break free from this dimension it is the men who must stand up and face their fears; the men who must face not only their own demons, but face the Dracos and say *enough is enough*, the men who must tell the Dracos to steer clear, to get out, that they have no right to interfere with our women, and never have.'

One of the women offered an option.

'Shouldn't we show them love?'

'Of course we should. But all the Dracos understand is warrior mode; survival of the fittest and exploitation of the weakest. So treating them just with love will have no effect other than to confirm their beliefs. The Dracos will not respect love, they do not understand love, they see it as a weakness. So the role of men is to protect our women from the Dracos by standing toe to claw with them, with love in our hearts, and let them know in no uncertain terms that life on this planet is not based on *their* rules, but on *our* rules. Besides, it was the men who invited the Dracos into the temples in the first place, because of their own fears and insecurities, so it is the men who must tell them to leave.'

I'd said enough and handed the crystal back around the circle to Diane. I couldn't believe that I'd even said what I'd said, but I did.

As the crystal made its way from person to person, I looked around the room and realized I could see each and every person as they were, who they were, at the time of Akhenaten. This was his family: his mother, his sisters-in-law, his wife of course, and his daughters. Bill and Pieter were High Priests of the Tat Brotherhood. For some reason they had all chosen to incarnate at that time in history, for it was a key time in the re-establishment of Goddess energy, as they had chosen to incarnate in this time, and that is exactly what Diane followed up with.

'Gaia, our Mother Earth, has reached a crucial time in her being; she is on the verge of coming of age. The teenage years have been full of experimentation and self realization, and now, as she nears the end of her turbulent adolescence, she offers us the chance to join with her in ascending to the next phase of our being.'

She changed the music on her ipod to a choir of women's voices, much as they had sung in the temple, starting simply and progressing in complexity.

'I invite you to close your eyes, make yourself completely comfortable, tone along with the sacred recording if you wish. Gentlemen I would request that for now you refrain from toning, as the frequencies and masculine energy, whilst providing incredible grounding, can also have the effect of retarding the energy.'

That suited me fine; I wanted to be free to fully experience the toning first hand.

Some of the women laid down on the floor, as did Bill and Pernille, others including Yuko and Pieter assumed meditative poses. It had been a long day for me so I chose the horizontal option. Once we were all settled, Diane continued.

'Let us fully go within our hearts. Picture your heart opening like a blossoming flower; each petal unfolding to both offer its sweet fragrances, pollen and nectar, and in grateful reception of sunlight and the caressing breezes that bring the many birds and insects that will spread your seeds of truth and wisdom around the globe.

It is time for Goddess energy, the pure creative energy of Love, to reclaim the planet. This it must do through the feminine, through the women, who must first fully awaken and embrace their own Goddess energy before men can see it in themselves, remember not to fear it, before awakening it fully within themselves.

Now, in the centre of your heart, the centre of your flower, visualize the eternal flame of creation that burns within you, from which you have emerged. See its flickering flame rise from the deepest red, through orange, yellow, green, blue and to the highest violet light of knowingness. See it extend out through your feet and out through the top of your head, infinitely reaching into, and connecting you completely with, the Source of All That Is. This Goddess awakening does not require you to acquire anything, nor to *learn* anything, for the answers are not external. Nor are they internal, for there are no answers to seek, only truths of which to become aware.

It is the questions you ask that define who and where you are, and the events you experience that are the mirrors for you to see that perspective of your Self. Your responsibility is to *be*, nothing more, nothing less, nothing else.'

And then Diane's voice started to drift into the background and I sort of tuned out. Actually it was more that instead of being tuned in to just one station, I was now tuning in to hundreds of them. I became aware that I was out of my body, not in the sense of actually being out and looking back at myself like what is talked about as astral travel, but not *of* the body. It was like I was here in the room, yes, but I was also everywhere. And when I mean everywhere, I mean the whole universe. My river had become a vast ocean bigger than the Milky Way galaxy.

In front of me appeared a face, a face I was very familiar with, Akhenaten; it was as if I was looking into a mirror. I felt myself being drawn into it, closer and closer, then specifically into the left eye. As I passed through the iris into the pupil, it was as if a whole new universe opened up. No sooner did that happen than another eye appear before me and I was drawn towards and into it. That opened into yet another universe and the whole process repeated again, over and over.

After several episodes I realized they were not separate universes but different lives. One after another they rolled along accelerating with each new eye. In the distance, a star system appeared; the constellation of the Pleiades.

I remembered as a child of maybe eight or nine staring up into the sky at night, specifically at the Seven Sisters, and feeling incredibly homesick, that was where I most wanted to be. And here I was, suddenly speeding towards it at a million miles a second. I suddenly got the overwhelming feeling this was home; this was where I had originally come from. I expected that as I would draw nearer I would slow down and focus in on one star then one planet, but no, I whooshed straight through the whole constellation and the whole process continued.

Streaking through more and more eyes, I cascaded further 'back' in time, into and through new galaxies, alternate lives, until once again a constellation appeared, approaching in the distance. This was Andromeda. This was not just 'home', now I felt I was going way back to my origins as a being, as a human, or rather humanoid, consciousness. As I headed into the heart of the constellation, again I anticipated a deceleration and zeroing in to one planet. But once again I flew straight through the galaxy and further back into the *past*. Now I was completely lost.

I churned back, faster and faster, further and further, with no idea where or when I was going to stop. I don't know how long or how far I travelled, when all of a sudden I came to a halt, and I found myself face to face with God, Allah, the alpha and omega, the Source of All That Is.

Actually I wasn't so much face-to-face, as face to presence, face to *being*. I couldn't describe what God looked like, as it had no form, but I could describe the feeling; total euphoria. I have never felt such an overwhelming experience of Love and I didn't want it to ever end.

Then it was as if God slowly placed its hands on my shoulders and turned me around to look back from whence I had come. It was like looking back through a tunnel of rings, hundreds, thousands of eyes, tens-of-thousands of lives, each one a life I had lived. At the far end of the tunnel was a small figure, a fractional part of my Self, known to others as Alex. It was merely a caretaker, an extension, a role. And in between, every existence I had ever lived and the reasons why I had chosen that existence.

The more I looked the more I saw; hundreds-of-thousands of lives on tens-of-thousands of planets, in thousands of solar systems in hundreds of galaxies. And right back at my end of the tunnel, where it all began? This was who I truly was, this was my Cosmic Self, this was my Highest of Selves, and it was mind-blowingly beautiful.

Then God whispered in my ear.

'Look around, see as I see.'

As I shifted my gaze, I saw millions, billions, of sparkling shafts shooting off in all directions. At that moment I became one with All That Is, seeing what it saw, hearing what it heard, feeling what it felt, knowing what it knew, being what it was, EVERYTHING.

I don't know how long I had been out of it; all I became aware of was voices calling me.

'Alex? Come back.'

I found that highly amusing. I hadn't gone anywhere, I was right there; the difference was I was also everywhere else at the same time. And yet they sounded concerned. But nothing could have been further from the truth; I was in complete ecstasy, and could have remained there indefinitely. Then my Higher Cosmic Self spoke, not to me, but to the others in the room.

'We are fine. We are binding.'

I knew exactly what it meant; the fractionalised parts of my self, or selves, were reconnecting, re-membering. However, most of the others in the room had no idea what was going on, including Diane. To them, I guess it looked like I was possessed. As several of the women started to gather around, focusing their energy towards me, I could feel their unfounded fears escalating, so, I had a short internal dialogue with my Cosmic Self.

'Can we do this later, at any other time?'

'Of course.'

And with that I opened my eyes.

'Hi folks, nothing to be alarmed about, everything is fantastic.'

I was euphoric, floating about a stratosphere or two above cloud nine. To my surprise I soon discovered the session had concluded about fifteen minutes earlier and it was now nearly 10:30. My how time flies when you are zooming through the universe. I looked for Crystal and found she was beaming, glowing, not just from her face, but from her whole body, huge shafts of golden light were shooting out from her head and her hands. Before I could say anything to her, Diane came up to check on my condition.

'Are you OK?'

I was beaming.

'Never been better.'

She gave me a warm embrace.

'Thank you so much for coming, I hope we will see you again.'

'How long are you in Egypt?'

'Another week or so. We're off to the West Bank tomorrow, Karnak the next day, then, the day after that, a Nile cruise up to Aswan and the Temple of Philae, and finally down to Cairo and the pyramids. We usually have a short gathering in the morning before we head out, and one in the evening around 8:00. You are more than welcome to join us.'

'Thanks, I'm sure we're bound to cross paths then.'

And that was the end of the circle; the women returned to their rooms and Crystal walked the rest of us back to the lobby.

In the Depths of the Temple

Bill threw an arm around my shoulder.

'You had us worried there for a minute. What was going on?'

'You know, Bill, I'm not really one-hundred percent sure yet. Can you believe all this started when we jumped on a felucca for a simple four day sailing trip?'

'I know what you mean.'

Crystal had different thoughts.

'Or maybe it started earlier than that?'

'Perhaps it all started when I first saw you in Philae.'

'I am flattered, but your journey began way before that.'

'You mean when I landed in Egypt?'

'Before that.'

'When I boarded the plane in Australia?'

She gave me her now mandatory 'I am not amused' cold glare, so I wound back the clock all the way.

'Maybe it was when I was born into this life?'

'Did you not absorb anything from your experience in the circle?'

I looked closely at her; did she know what had just happened to me? She must have.

'It goes all the way back to the Source, doesn't it?'

'There you go again, making a statement, and then questioning it.'

'OK, my journey began when the universe began; all my other lives are just stages, as are all the parts of this life, it just depends what perspective you choose to take.'

'While it may be good to know where you have come *from*, and that your lives are just stages, what is more important is where you are *now*, and why you are here...'

She gave me a kiss on the cheek and pushed me out the door.

'...Your journey is not over so you had better move along; you have things to do.'

'Will I see you tomorrow?'

'That depends on whether you have your eyes open or not. Now go.'

Everyone said their farewells and we set off into the streets of Luxor. It was a beautiful night, balmy, exotic, so we decided to give the taxis and kalashes a miss, and walk back along the riverfront to our respective hotels. As we did, we passed the Luxor temple, beautifully lit up in the night. Heading beyond the Roman ruins that surround the temple, we stood facing the western wall, ironically covered in reliefs of Ramses II's Battle of Kadesh.

'It's so pretty, who'd have thought that such terrible atrocities were committed inside?'

Pernille was still slightly apprehensive.

'Do you think the Dracos are still in there?'

'Well, if they are, it's about time we booted them out.'

Bill was right; it was time to give them their marching orders. And so I led the way.

'Right then, let's all close our eyes and connect to our Highest Selves.'

I allowed a minute or so for everyone to focus.

'Now, project yourselves inside the temple, to the inner most sanctuary. We are going to systematically sweep them out of the temple chamber by chamber, courtyard by courtyard.'

Again I waited a few moments until I felt us all gathered in the back chamber.

'Members of the Dracos and Priests of Amun, listen to my command. You are not welcome in this temple and must leave at once. You are hereafter evicted, exiled, and banished from this temple forever.'

The others repeated my words.

'You are not welcome in this temple.'

'You must leave it at once.'

'You're evicted.'

'You are banished from this temple forever.'

I upped the ante.

'Let's move 'em out.'

Within the temple I felt us form a line and advance.

'You are not permitted to re-enter without the permission of the priestesses, the goddesses of the temple.'

'You must leave at once.'

'You're not welcome.'

'Get out.'

'You're banished forever.'

Systematically we cleared out the temple, the inner courtyard, the colonnade, outer courtyard, and finally booted them out of the gateway between the first pylon.

'OK, girls, it's all yours. Feel free to reclaim it, and redecorate to your heart's content.'

And the two girls had lots of ideas.

'Lots of fresh flowers; roses, carnations, lotus blossoms.'

'And scented oils; lavender, sandalwood.'

'Lots of fluffy cushions.'

'Chiffon and feathers.'

'And pillows.'

'All in pink.'

'Automatic vacuuming systems and washing machines.'

'And dishwashers.'

'All manned by a tribe of hunky eunuchs.'

'Toilet seats that never go up.'

That made the two of them laugh.

'Walk in wardrobes in every room.'

'With built in sections just for shoes.'

'And hand bags.'

'Mirrors that always make your figure look perfect.'

'Massage tables with an endless supply of Adonis-like masseurs.'

'With endless supplies of chocolate.'

'That doesn't make you fat.'

'And coffee.'

'No, champagne.'

'Both.'

By now the girls were cackling away like happy hens. Bill chucked in a few suggestions of his own.

'What about non-stop ABBA music piped through the temple; Dancing Queen, Mamma mia.'

'No, Tom Jones.'

'Elvis Presley.'

'Michael Jackson.'

'Jon Bon Jovi.'

'Yummmmm.'

Bill thought they were getting a little *too* carried away.

'Sounds like the girls would need vibrators with batteries that never run down.'

Pernille shook her head.

'What would they need them for, they have the eunuchs.'

Everyone was in hysterics, everyone except me that is; I was still uneasy.

'Something's not right.'

'What do you mean?'

'The Amun priests are gone but the Dracos are still there. They're not just *in* the temple, they're in the chambers and stone *under* the temple.'

'What are you saying?'

'We cleared out the *space* in the temple, but we didn't clear out the *stone*, or the underground vaults.'

Pernille was suddenly stoic and deliberate.

'Then it needs you boys to get back in there and kick them out once and for all; the spirits of the priests *and* the Dracos.'

'Getting rid of the spiritual energy of the priests was one thing, that was easy, getting rid of the Dracos could be another matter all together.'

I closed my eyes and tuned in to the rock.

'We have to head to the oldest, darkest part of the temple, at the rear.'

We walked down to the far end of the temple and stood behind the fence, looking at the rear of the inner sanctum. Bill looked at me, one eyebrow raised and both hands out stretched.

'Now what?'

'We need to lure them out.'

'How?'

I paused, thinking, then looked at the girls.

'We need to tone; we need the girls to tone.'

Bill was a tad concerned to say the least.

'You want to use the girls as bait?'

Pernille was quick to step forward.

'No, it's OK, we have to do what we have to do; we have no other choice.'

With a resigned nod of the head, Bill agreed, then turned his attention to me.
'What have you got in mind?'

'We let the girls start toning on their own to lure them out; but stay outside the fence, don't project into the temple, or let them drag you in. Think of it like you are fishing, you are here with the pole, but the line, the hook and the bait are inside the temple. Let your tones be the bait.

Then when I give the word, Pieter, Bill and I will join in the toning, sweep them up in a net, and blast them the hell out of here. OK, spread out, not too far, about ten metres between each of us, with the girls in the middle of us guys.'

We spaced ourselves evenly around the fence; Pieter, Yuko, me in the centre, Pernille then Bill. I gave a nod and the girls began.

It didn't take long; within ten to fifteen seconds I could hear faint growling noises from below the sanctuary.
'Keep going, it's working.'

The girls raised the pitch slightly, drawing the Dracos from the depths of the temple and into the inner sanctuary. But we had to make sure we got all of them.
'Higher, change the vowel sound to *ee*.'

Having previously been toning to *aw,* they made the shift, with instantaneous effect. The Dracos flew out of the temple and prowled along the inner part of the fence hissing at the two girls like hungry lions behind the bars at the zoo.

I took the opportunity to project within the inner sanctuary. It was empty; the Dracos were all stalking the fence-line. It was now or never. I projected into Akhenaten, I became him, I was him, and gave the signal.
'Now guys, blast them. Ah!'

The guys joined in as the girls shifted to *Ah* and raised the pitch yet again. For several minutes, the Dracos swirled around in a fury, in frenzied anger, trying to both intimidate the women and retreat back into the temple.
'Begone, you are not welcome here. You are trespassing. You no longer have authorization to inhabit this temple, or the stone that comprises it. I, Akhenaten, Prince of the Annunaki, Pharaoh of the ancient Egyptians, command you to leave.'

In one fell swoop we gathered up all the Dracos in a huge net and dragged them from the temple grounds. Within seconds they were scurrying off into the shadows like rats deserting the proverbial sinking ship. And then all was silent.
'Well, that's that done!'

Pernille was transfixed.
'That was amazing.'

Yuko had one last thought.
'I'd like to do one more thing before we leave. I'd like to fill the whole complex with golden light.'

We took a minute to do that, then could feel the night was over, though Bill clearly wanted to connect again the next day.
'What are you all doing tomorrow?'

Pieter answered for himself and Yuko.
'We're off to the West Bank in the morning. What about you?'

Pernille took Bill by the hand.

'I'm was supposed to be flying back to Cairo, but I won't be doing that. I'm going to keep out of the way until Jacques has gone, then I'm going to spend a little time with Crystal in the afternoon.'

'Alex?'

'I think I might join Pieter and Yuko and head to the West Bank, if it's still OK?'

'Sure.'

Bill wrapped it up.

'Why don't you all come to the Winter Palace for afternoon drinks around 5:00?'

'Sounds great.'

We all nodded.

'OK, see you then.'

We split, Bill and Pernille walking off hand in hand along the esplanade, while Pieter, Yuko and I made the short walk back to the Nubian Oasis.

It was nearly midnight, but Seleh was still up behind the reception counter. Pieter doubled checked arrangements for the next day.

'Seleh, are the bicycles booked for the morning?'

'Yes, but of course. They will be here ready for you at 7:30 in the morning.'

'Is it too late to book another one for me?'

'Not at all, what time would you like for it?'

'Same time, 7:30?'

'This it is not a problem.'

'OK, time to hit the sack.'

'See you in the morning.'

'Seleh, what about breakfast?'

'Yes, on the roof, what time would you be like it?'

'How is 7:00?'

'Yes, no problem.'

We climbed the stairs, bid each other good night, then I made my way to my room and laid down on the bed.

'What the hell sort of day was that?'

I was tired, but I knew that if I didn't note it all down I wouldn't get a winks sleep. I probably wouldn't anyway, but it was best I noted it all down while it was fresh in my mind.

Firstly there were all the conspiracies theories of Randy; UNESCO and the relocating of the temples, the whole Cotton industry thing, Pearl Harbor, 9/11, the assassination of JFK, the Apollo moon landing, Michael Jackson's death.

If that wasn't enough to mull over, then there was the event in the Luxor Temple, in fact the whole Dracos thing; the genetic experiments, the toning, the codes, me being Akhenaten, Saeed and the Tat Brotherhood, connecting to my Cosmic Self and being face to face with God, then seeing things through God's eyes, and finally evicting the Dracos.

I shut down my laptop, plugged in my iphone to charge it up, and set my alarm for 6:40. I collapsed on the bed, who knows what tomorrow would bring and what Saeed's uncle would have to say.

CHAPTER 15 – HOW GREEN IS MY VALLEY?

'ALLAH U AKBAR, ALLAH U AKBAR.'

'What the fuck?!'

'ASH-HADU AL-LA ILAHA ILL ALLAH - ASH-HADU AL-LA ILAHA ILL ALLAH.'

I fumbled around in the dark for my phone, then, having located it, peeled back an eyelid and tried to focus on the time; 5:45. Christ, what an ungodly time of day to pray.

'ASH-HADU ANNA MUHAMMADAN RASULULLAAH.'

I mean this wasn't the lilting sound of someone standing atop a minaret and serenading out into the pre-dawn half-light, this was the deafening explosion of an amplified voice blasting out from a speaker set on top of the building across the street, right outside and into my window. And no sooner did he get rolling than three or four other mosques in town fired up in the distance, creating a canonic chorus of chaotic cacophony that sounded more like four or five amazonic mosquitoes on steroids dancing the watoosi.

'ASH-HADU ANNA MUHAMMADAN RASULULLAAH.'

I buried my head underneath the pillow hoping the muffling effect might reduce the adumbrately undulating melismatic phrases that ricocheted around in my head like bomb blasts through the Grand Canyon.

'HAYYA LA-S-SALEAH - HAYYA LA-S-SALEAH.'

It was not so much a 'Call to Prayer' as a demand, an 'or else'. Roughly translated through the half-dazed consciousness of a non-religious quasi-atheist, it sounded like 'Get your lazy heathen asses out of bed and high-tail it down here to the mosque straight away to pray, because if you don't you shall all be cast down into the flames of eternal hell and damnation', or words to that effect.

'HAYYA LA-L-FALEAH - HAYYA LA-L-FALEAH.'

Why do they have to pray five times a day, and at specific times? Does Allah only have certain business hours? 'Sorry, prayers are only received at dawn, midday, three in the afternoon, sunset and just after din-dins'. Why not just once a day before niy-niys, before they go to bed, or is that just reserved for the Catholics?

Funny how kids are told to pray before they go to sleep with the Lord's prayer, and yet, as they grow older, most people reject that option, choosing instead to dispel all their sins and get a top-up of holy righteousness all-in-one hit on a Sunday morning at church; or if you're a Jew, once a week on a Friday night at the synagogue.

'ALLAHU AKBAR, ALLAHU AKBAR.'

Does God, Allah, Yahweh, Yoda, Obiwan Kanobi, whoever, set aside different times to listen to each of the different religions? Muslims at dawn, Catholics at 10:30, Muslims again for lunch, Jews after dark, that sort of thing. And if that's the case, then the different time zones around the planet must really give him a head ache; assuming of course that God, Allah, Yahweh etc is in fact a male, which is what the main religions would have us believe. Or is it all just another man-made set-of-rules by which to control the masses and say 'My way is right, your way is wrong, so therefore not only *must* I kill you, but it's all OK, above board and legit, because God/Allah/Yahweh tells me it's the kosher thing to do'?

'LA ILAHA ILL ALLAH.'

In the end I concluded it was just another technique by which you firstly controlled the masses, and then, having corralled them into a holding pen, systematically brainwashed them with more of the same sort of rhetoric. Like an ostrich in the desert, I buried my head another five miles beneath the sands of my pillow, hoping they would all go away, and attempted to reclaim the remaining three-quarters-of-an-hour before my alarm went off.

However, it seemed that no sooner did I close my eyes again than my alarm summoned me to start my day, only on this occasion it was on western time. I dragged myself from the bed and into the shower, which thankfully had enough hot water for me to exfoliate the grungy layer of nocturnal sweat that was a mandatory by-product of dozing through the hot and humid evenings of Egypt.

Only the five-star hotels had air conditioning; the three-star ones, a ceiling fan. And the Nubian Oasis? Louvered French doors that opened on to a two-foot balcony three stories up and directly opposite the mosque! However, with the obligatory, shit, shower and shave out of the way, I headed up the stairs to the roof and breakfast.

Pieter and Yuko were already sitting at a table, about to start eating; they had obviously done their meditations earlier on, probably under the canopies.

'Good morning.'

'Ah, Mister Alex, for you, some breakfast?'

'Yes thanks, Seleh.'

He quickly went to work behind the bar as I sat down to join Pieter and Yuko.

'Did you sleep well?'

Was she kidding?

'Until the sound of the *Call to Prayers* exploded in my room, I did.'

They laughed, then, each in turn added their thoughts.

'Yes, it was rather loud.'

'Fortunately for us we were already awake, but had not yet started our meditation.'

'Lucky for you, but not really how I was hoping to start the day, that's for sure.'

Pieter shook his head.

'That was quite an amazing day yesterday.'

'That's an understatement; the whole trip has been amazing. What's your plan for today?'

'Firstly we're going to take the ferry across the river, then ride north up through the region of the Tombs of the Nobles, and inland to the Valley of the Kings. From there we will come back down to Hatshepsut's Temple, the Ramesseum, Valley of the Queens and the Colossi of Memnon. You are more than welcome to tag along.'

As Seleh placed my breakfast on the table, I thanked both him, and then Pieter and Yuko for their invitation.

'Shukran. Sounds like a great plan, though I may not be able to ride all the way with you; I'm meeting Captain Jack's uncle at Medinet Habu at 3:00 pm.'

'That's fine, just be in the moment and see what happens.'

I wanted to follow up with Pieter on something he had said during the trip about Amenhotep I, so, as I tucked in to breakfast; an omelette, a slice of goat's cheese, boiled egg, mandarin, a banana, tub of yoghurt, bread bun, jam and a glass of black tea, I posed him a question.

'Pieter, you were saying the other day that these Annunaki guys lived tens-of-thousands of years, right?'

'Perhaps even hundreds-of-thousands, maybe more, but that's our years, not theirs. The Annunaki don't operate in our time frame. The yearly orbit of their planet around our sun is around thirty-six-hundred of our years, so they live to be over hundreds-of-thousands of our years: to the Annunaki, one of our years is the equivalent of only about an hour.'

'Do you think they built Atlantis?'

'Most certainly.'

'When?'

'That's a good question; at least fifty or sixty-thousand years ago, probably more like hundreds-of-thousands.'

'How do you know that?'

'It was written in the Emerald Tablets by Thoth in 34,000 BC.'

'Thoth, not the *son* of Ptah, but actually the *grandson* of Ptah?'

'Yes, and the true builder of the Great Pyramid.'

'Are you saying the pyramids were built at least thirty-five to forty thousand years ago?'

'Probably more.'

'Well that's a total contrast to what the Egyptologists say.'

'It sure is.'

'Where are these Emerald Tablets now?'

'Well, supposedly in 1925 they were returned to a sacred chamber beneath the Great Pyramid by a loyal follower of the Tat Brotherhood. But it is said that one day soon, the books will be unearthed by members of Ptah's ancient priesthood who have reincarnated into modern-day life, and, at around the same time, reincarnated priestesses from the Daughters of Isis will make similar discoveries in the sanctuary of Isis at Philae.'

I knew he meant the original site of the sanctuary of Aset on P'aaleq, rather than present day Philae, because if anything had been discovered at the present temple it would have been well and truly stolen by now. What ever it was awaited beneath the waters, back upstream at Aswan.

'Do the tablets say when Atlantis disappeared?'

'No, they were written in 34,000 BC, way before the demise of Atlantis.'

'How do you figure that?'

'Firstly, Atlantis was not so much an island, as a world civilization of the Annunaki that existed from at least 52,000 BC to as late as, I think, 8800 BC.'

I'd read books by Bauval, Hancock and West, who all indicated dates for the building of the Sphinx and the last pole shift at around 10,000 BC. But could they have been slightly off?

'Why 8,800 BC?'

'Nibiru returns every thirty-six-hundred years, but I think the level of destruction varies with each passing, depending on its position relative to the earth. If it's on the same side of the sun as the earth, it's at a maximum, but if it's on the other side of the sun to the earth, then I think the crustal displacement and pole shift is reduced.

My guess is that every third pass, every ten-thousand-eight-hundred years there's a complete one-hundred-and-eighty-degree flip of the crust, huge destruction, and thus a perception of a pole shift; that would be around 8,800 BC, 19,600 BC, 30,400 BC, 41,200 BC and 52,000 BC.

'Plato said Atlantis sank in 9,600 BC.'

'True, but he was writing around 360 BC, that's three-hundred-and-sixty years *before* Christ, so how does he figure that date when Christ hasn't even come along yet? And even today we don't really know the exact dates when Christ lived. Plato only had to be out by eight-hundred years, that's less than a ten per cent error margin, and 9,600 becomes 8,800.'

'Plato also plagiarized his data from writings by other people, who had in turn derived their information from their time in ancient Egypt over two-hundred years earlier, in the 6th Century BC.'

'There are further sources that say it was 9,565 BC and others that it was prior to 8,570 BC. Both would fit around the date of 8,800 BC, more importantly they correlate to a passing of Nibiru and a pole shift.'

'But is there any evidence to support it; any actual physical evidence?'

'Lots. Scientists, geologists, they all agree the Pleistocene epoch ended around 10,000 BC; that's *around* 10,000 BC. But that's just a guess based on things like the end of the ice-age, the demise of the Woolly Mammoths, Sabre-Tooth Tigers and orogeny.'

'Orogeny?'

'Mountain building; the formation of mountains. Geologists postulate that, contrary to early theories, the Himalayas, French Alps, Rocky Mountains, Andes, and the mountains around Kabul in Afghanistan were all created rapidly, possibly within the space of hours.'

'How is that possible?'

'Crustal displacement and pole shifts; Macchu Pichu was once a seaside village; Lake Titicaca is a salt-water lake fifteen-hundred metres above sea level. And when the crust flips, some things go up, which means some things go down. So I think Atlantis *sank* in stages; parts of the civilization went under around 30,400 BC, more submerged at the next passing, around 19,600 BC, and finally all traces of the civilization of Atlantis disappeared beneath the waves in 8,800 BC.'

I'd been steadily munching away throughout our breakfast chat, but now I sat back and paused; this was quite a bit to digest. Annunaki, Thoth, Emerald Tablets, Nibiru, Pole shifts, Atlantis. If you had thrown it all at me before I arrived in Egypt I would have found pretty much all of it hard to swallow. But now it gave me cravings; I was rapidly becoming a *New Age* junkie. Meanwhile, Pieter finished his tea and got to his feet.

'Well, it's now 7:24, so we'd better get a move on.'

Alas, time was moving on and I had to be patient until my next snack, or feast as the case may prove.

'Pieter, I'm not sure if I can fully comprehend what you've said, but it's sure quite a bit to for me to chew over while we ride along. I'll see you downstairs at reception.'

I grabbed the banana and mandarin for later on, and headed down the stairwell, stopping briefly at my room to slop on a layer of sunscreen and pack the banana and mandarin into my backpack, all the time running through my mind the implications of the lineage of Thoth.

Ticket to ride

When I joined Pieter and Yuko in front of the hotel, the bikes were waiting. They looked like relics from the Second World War, the bikes that is, not Pieter and Yuko: black, basic, with a rear parcel rack. As I sat astride my valiant beast and tested the air pressure in the tires, I had visions of getting a puncture in the middle of the desert and having to wait for a passing taxi to come to my rescue. Never the less, after a few adjustments to the seat and handle bar heights, we were ready to ride off into the sunrise, or rather with the sunrise at our shoulder.

'OK, Pieter, I've been thinking, and it's pretty far fetched, but hear me out. If the Annunaki come from Nibiru every thirty-six hundred years or so, that's 1,600 BC, 5,200 BC, 8,800 BC, 12,400 BC and so on, then there must have been other earlier civilizations, other than Atlantis, before and during ancient Egypt?'

As we peddled away from the hotel it was Yuko who was the one to respond.

'Lots of them; Sumer, the Himalayas, The Minoan Civilization, China, the Maya, just to name a few.'

'That means there's plenty to explore along the way, so I'd better stock up on supplies.'

I figured it was going to be a long hot ride, and didn't want to pay the exorbitant prices for water that they charged at the sites, so stopped a hundred metres down from the hotel at a little local shop. The lady spoke very little English but eventually we agreed on a price of four pound for a one-and-a-half litre bottle of fresh water. Locals could probably get them for two fifty, maybe three, but four was a good price for a tourist. I settled on three bottles of water, added in a packet of potato chips, stuffed them all into my pack along with the fruit, and readjusted my akubra.

'All set. Let's go!'

Riding through the alleys and streets of Luxor on a beaten up old push bike was actually lots of fun; dodging cars, kids walking to school, taxis, kalashes, vendors on bikes piled high with freshly baked buns and bread, horses, carts, donkeys, cats, dogs, potholes, speed bumps, and piles of fresh horse shit. Even the locals stopped to smile at the three westerners 'slumming it'.

Pulling alongside Pieter, I picked the conversation back up.

'Dwight mentioned Sumer the other day, but I'm not that flash on exactly when and where it was?'

'According to experts, the Sumerian Civilization began in the Indus Valley around 5,300 BC. That fits in with what you were saying before, so it's not as far fetched as you would think.'

'But you were saying Atlantis went back fifty-thousand, maybe a hundred-thousand years.'

'I think civilizations go back over four-hundred-thousand years.'

'What! *Four-hundred-thousand years*!?'

'At least.'

'How do you know that?'

'The Sumerian clay tablets indicate that four-hundred-and-forty-thousand years ago, six-hundred Annunaki arrived on Earth from Nibiru, led by Enlil, his half brother Enki, and his sister Ninmah.'

'That sounds to me exactly like the Egyptian Zep Tepi, the first time, the time of the Gods ruling Egypt, where the rulers reigned for thousands of years at a time.'

'That's it exactly; the Sumerian King Lists go back four-hundred-thousand years.'

'OK, so tell me all about this ancient Sumerian civilization.'

'According to the Sumerian tablets, the ruler of the God race was Anu. '

'Who the Egyptians would have called called Ptah, right?'

'Right. Anu had two sons, Enlil, the eldest, whose mother was Ki, and Enki, whose mother was Antu. He also had two daughters, Enki's twin, Ereshkigal, and a younger sister Ninmah, or Ninhusag.'

'That would be Set, Osiris, Isis and Nephthys?'

'Exactly. Anu initially sent Enki, Ninmah and Enlil to earth. Although the Annunaki have male rulers, as did the Ancient Egyptians, they were a matriarchal society, with all inheritance passed on through the female lineage.

'The *sang réal*.'

'Yes, and although Enlil was older than Enki, his mother was younger than Enki's, and therefore the rightful inheritance of the throne should have gone to Enki. However when the Annunaki arrived on Earth, Anu appointed Enlil *Lord of the Earth*.'

'I dare say that would have caused a little friction between the two brothers.'

'To say the least; it's what ultimately caused Enki to leave Sumer and set up his own civilization in Egypt.'

'And I bet that's the basis of the story of the fight between Osiris and Set.'

'I agree.'

'Wait a minute, if they arrived four-hundred-and-forty-thousand years ago, how did they split, and then Enki set up ancient Egypt in 3,000 BC. Are you saying the Egyptian gods were over four-hundred-and-forty-thousand years old?'

'At least. But remember, they are Annunaki, they lived about one-hundred-and-twenty sars, which, as one sar, one of their planets revolutions around our sun, equals three-thousand-six-hundred of our years, means the average life span would have been four-hundred-and-thirty-two-*thousand* of our years.'

'That means Thoth, Imhotep, Enki from Sumer, they could have lived in many places on Earth going back over four-hundred-thousand years.'

'Yep.'

Minutes later we arrived at the river and made our way down the stairs, bikes in hand, to the lower esplanade. Of course the locals offered to help us, but they would have then wanted a little baksheesh in return, however we all declined; it wasn't going to tax any of us, even Yuko, to escort our bikes down twenty or so steps, going up at the end of the day, perhaps, but certainly not down at the beginning.

The ferry was basically a motorized boat that operated continuously during the daylight hours ferrying workers, farmers, traders, housewives, back and forth between the two banks. It cost a massive two pounds each, about forty cents, one pound each for us and one pound for the bike, but it *was* a return trip ticket so that was a bonus. And it was a damn site more appealing than the alternative, which was to ride a fair distance out of town to cross the nearest bridge upstream, or take a mini-bus or taxi which could have cost anywhere upwards of three-hundred pounds for the day. This was perfect.

Within a couple of minutes we were fully loaded, and the skipper, who looked about twelve, steered us out into the river. I turned to Pieter.

'I'm slowly putting all this together, but how does it all relate to the creation of the human race again?'

'According to Zacheriah Sitchin, who translated all the cuneiform tablets from Sumer, there was a lower class of Annunaki called the Igigi and they made up about half of the original landing party of six-hundred. For tens-of-thousands of years they did all the mining and manual work, but then they revolted and refused to do the work any more.'

'They went on strike.'

'Basically, yes. So, as Enlil was leader and in charge of farming and mining, he came up with the solution to genetically create a worker race, the humans, from the early hominids that were on the planet.'

'The Neanderthals and Cro-Magnon?'

'Yes, you see when the Annunaki arrived on earth, they discovered the technology of the Dracos, they may even have been assisted by them.'

'Why would the Dracos help them?...'

Then I had an idea.

'... No, wait, I know. The Dracos had their agenda of producing a humanoid/reptilian hybrid that would enable them to access the higher realms, and in having access to the Annunaki DNA, by adding it to the gene pool, they could get closer to their goal of conquering the universe.'

'It's a wild idea, but it wouldn't be the first one on this trip.'

I thought I'd finally got a handle on the origins of the human race, but that made me wonder where the beings they replaced, finished up.

'So what happened to the Annunaki workers, the Igigi?'

'Once the humans were created, the Igigi were subsequently cast aside and became the *fallen angels* referred to in *The Bible*.'

Another piece of history dropped into place; it was yet another way the religions of the world corrupted the truth to suit their agendas.

'So Enlil was the one responsible for the human race?'

'Not exactly. Enlil came up with the idea, but he passed the actual project over to his half-brother Enki, who was second in command, and who, with his sister, Ninmah, *fashioned man in their image.*'

'So Enki and Ninmah were Osiris and Isis?'

'No, Enki may have been Osiris, but Ninmah was most likely Nephthys.'

'And all this is in those Sumerian tablets?'

'Yep.'

'So who was Isis?'

'Enki's twin sister, Ereshkigal. Enki and Ninmah did the actual engineering but it was Ereshkigal who provided the genetic material and carried the embryos. I guess that's why Enki's emblem was two serpents on a staff; the winged caduceus, the rod of Hermes.'

'The double helix of DNA. Or do you think it referred to the Dracos?'

'It could be a bit of both.'

'So Enki was Thoth.'

'No, I think Enki was more than likely Thoth's father; Thoth probably just borrowed the emblem from him.'

'Like a family coat of arms?'

'Yeh, that's a good way to look at it.'

On board, the locals continued their fascination with why three obviously wealthy foreigners would bother to not only ride bicycles, but take the people's ferry across the river. While they gawked, I continued with my fascination on the lineage of

106

man.

'So who was Thoth's mother then?'

'According to the Sumerian tablets, Ereshkigal, Enki's twin sister.'

'So Thoth was the product of Osiris and Isis?'

'I think so.'

'Which means Thoth was Horus.'

'No, I don't think so, it's possible, but Thoth was around way before Horus.'

'And what happened to the Igigi?'

'They probably went about their own business, farming, waiting for the next return of the home planet.'

'But in the meantime they bred with the human females.'

'Yes, and created the Nephilim, or Elohim; the Giants referred to in the Bible.'

'What happened to the Nephilim?'

'Most were wiped out by great flood, but they have found skeletons of them buried in various places around the world.'

I was pretty blown away.

'Wow, that basically explains the whole history of man.'

'And the more you dig, the more you find.'

'Meaning?'

'The Igigi weren't the only ones impregnating women, Enki and Thoth also found them attractive, and one of the prodigy of Enki was a man called Ziunsudra, whom, when the return of Nibiru was imminent, was told by Enki to create an ark to survive the impending flood.'

'The story of Noah?'

'Exactly.'

'So, if humans had served their purpose well in doing the mining and farming, why didn't the Annunaki save all of mankind when the pole shift came around?'

'When Enki created man, he must have *tweaked* the gene pool somewhat, and created a race with higher consciousness and IQ than Enlil had originally requested. Consequently the humans became more aware, more rebellious, more defiant and more quarrelsome.

By the time Nibiru returned, Enlil had grown weary of the troublesome traits of mankind and decided to leave them, and the planet, to be obliterated by the geological catastrophes and tsunamis that would unfold. Enki, Ereshkigal and Ninmah on the other hand, who had considered the humans like a cross between children and pets, decided to return after the passing of Nibiru and help the humans build their own civilizations.'

'Sumer, ancient Egypt, Central America, etcetera?'

'Yep.'

Having safely docked on the opposite bank, we jumped ashore, negotiated ourselves through the local market, and set off northwards towards the Valley of the Kings. Another adventure awaited, another chapter in the journey of my life.

Into the Valley of Death rode the ... three

So much had happened in the ..., how many days had I been in Egypt? I was losing all track of western time; I didn't even know what day of the week it was. There was a great sense of liberation and joy as we pedaled away from the river and through the streets into the early morning countryside; the farmers and traders all out and about, going about their daily routines.

'Sabah al khair', which meant, *Good morning*.

'Marhabbah', *Hello*.

They would stop what they were doing, smile and wave as we rolled passed, and called out.

'Assalaam Alaikum', meaning *Peace be up on you*.

Through the northern sector of the west bank we wheeled, closest to the Nile, through and passed the village of Qurna, and what is often referred to as the Tombs of the Nobles region, heading ultimately to the supposed burial place of over sixty pharaohs, including the boy king Tutankhamun.

I would suppose most people think the tombs are all in the Valley of the Kings, in particular Tutankhamun's tomb. In fact there are currently sixty-three tombs that have been discovered, mostly for the pharaohs, in the East Valley, as well as an additional five in the West Valley. But the reality is, there are over eight-hundred tombs in total, spread across five different sub-zones of the West Bank. There was no way we could visit them all.

As we cycled northward along the road, it turned to the left, towards the Valley of the Kings. On the right side of the road, to the north, we approached a large row of tombs dug into the hillside and I stepped into tour-guide mode.

'This is el-Tarif. These tombs were dug during both the late 17th Dynasty of the Second Intermediate Period as well as the early Middle Kingdom, the 11th and 13th Dynasties.'

First Pieter and then Yuko pulled over to the side of the road.

'What do you think, should we stop and take a look?'

As I looked at the tombs in the hills, I checked my notes.

'Most of the tombs here are of officials and priests, and it's fair to assume that if the hieroglyphs and tomb reliefs here were more impressive than those in the Valley of the Kings, then we would certainly know about them. But I'm guessing if there was any evidence in these tombs it was now long gone. '

Yuko was the one who quickly put things into greater perspective, and in the process made the decision for us all.

'They're probably very similar to the ones at Wadi Hillal, so I think we should save our time and money and focus on the tombs in the Valley of the Kings and the Valley of the Queens.'

And with that, she pushed off and headed inland into the hills, Pieter quickly following suit. I took a moment to think; if what Pieter and Crystal had said during the trip, about the Annunaki genetically creating the human race, was all true, then we really *were* the children of the gods. That, in turn, took me back to Thoth, or rather Imhotep, then to the end of the 17th Dynasty and the origins of the 18th Dynasty. I quickly pedalled up alongside Pieter.

'Hey, Pieter, yesterday, you suggested that Ahmose might have abdicated, that Amenhotep might have taken over as ruler because Amenhotep was Annunaki, and that they had returned around 1600 BC when Nibiru returned. Do you think it's possible that Amenhotep could have been any number of pharaohs going all the way back to Imhotep?'

'It's possible: Imhotep was around, what, 2600 BC? And Amenhotep 1500 BC; that's a little over a thousand years, or about two months in Annunaki time. Why, what are you thinking?'

'So Imhotep could have been in Egypt from the beginnings of the 1st Dynasty around 3000 BC, through to the end of the 3rd Dynasty and the reign of Huni around 2650 BC?'

'It's possible. What makes you think that?'

'According to the ancient Egyptian texts he advised at least four pharaohs over a period of three-hundred-and-fifty years, so it's most likely he was; helping to build and develop the civilization.'

'I like your reasoning.'

I shrugged my shoulders.

'So where did he go after 2650 BC, and why?'

'I guess the best place to look is other spots around the world where civilization suddenly developed.'

'Any thoughts?'

Yuko volunteered her knowledge; little did I know she had studied the history of many ancient civilizations. What she said was like gold.

'Three civilizations immediately spring to mind. Firstly there was the Minoan Civilization. It started around 2700 BC and was a society of traders; ruled by priestesses, with female deities and female officiaries, with all inheritance passed on through the matriarchal line.'

I couldn't believe it.

'The *sang réal*, there it is again!'

'Pardon?'

'The importance of the bloodline being through the women.'

'Yes, though unfortunately the Minoan Civilization ended with the Thera eruption around 1500 BC.'

'Thera? That's Santorini, right?'

'Yes.'

'So that could have ended around 1600 BC? I mean all the dates are just approximate guesses, right?'

'I suppose so.'

'And the second civilization?'

'Next would have been the development of the Mayan Civilization around 2600 BC. It ran to 900 AD with its high point from 250-900 AD.'

'I guess that's how the Mayans are connected to the ancient Egyptians; the Mayans knew all about Nibiru and the movements of the stars because they learned it all directly from Imhotep; from Thoth himself.'

'To the Maya he was known as Queztalcoatl.'

That had me confused.

'But wasn't Queztalcoatl the feathered serpent, the winged god? That sounds more reptilian, more like the Dracos.'

'The Maya refer to two gods, Thoth and Queztalcoatl, which people have believed were one and the same being.'

'But perhaps they were separate beings, one Dracos, the other Annunaki, initially arriving in the earlier part of the Mayan Civilization, each trying to rule or control the people, the humans, and later over time becoming fused into one persona?'

'That would make sense.'

As we approached a right hand curve in the road, a temple appeared, virtually out of nowhere, nestled between a palm grove, a green field, and the road. Without a discussion we all intuitively stopped and took in the view.

'I didn't think there were any temples out here.'

I checked my iphone notes, which just happened to include a map of the West Bank

'According to the map, it's a memorial temple to Seti I, who also built the Hypostyle Hall at Karnak and the temple at Abydos.'

Yuko was curious.

'Should we go in?'

There wasn't that much to see, more than at el Kab but not as much as at the Luxor Temple, basically an open courtyard, with a few foundations to the side and before the temple, with its façade consisting of ten papyrus-like columns. I wasn't really aware of it, I doubted many visitors were, but I checked my notes none-the-less and was surprised to find I actually had a few lines about it.

'The memorial temple of Seti I on the west bank at Luxor and dedicated to Amun-Re, was severely damaged by torrential rain and floods in 1994, though it has recently been restored. The first and second pylon, constructed from mud-bricks, and the court, remain in complete ruin, though the walls of the colonnade to the west of the temple, and those of the Hypostyle court beyond it, contain some well carved reliefs.

Off from the Hypostyle courtyard are six shrines and to the south is a small chapel dedicated to Seti's father, Ramses I, with scenes showing the barques of Seti I, Ahmose-Nefertari and the Theban Triad, as well as portrayals of Seti and Ramses II making offerings to various deities. The barque pedestal of Amun is still in situ, behind this is the *holy of holies*, with many scenes of the king celebrating the temple rituals and a partly reconstructed false door of the king at the rear on the western wall.

At either side of the door to the Hypostyle hall are stelae of Amenemesse, which were later usurped by Merenptah-Siptah.. Further excavations have revealed the foundations of the Pharaoh's palace, just south of the court. This is the earliest found example of a palace within a memorial temple, and its plan is similar to the better-preserved palace at the memorial temple of Ramses III at Medinat Habu. However, despite its picturesque location, the temple sees few visitors.'

Pieter was cut throat.

'If it's similar to the temple of Ramses III at Medinat Habu, and that is better preserved, then I'm happy to give this one a miss and ride on.'

Yuko and I nodded in agreement and we all put the pedal to the metal. As we set off, I returned to our discussion.

'Yuko, before we stopped, you mentioned there were three civilizations that Imhotep could have gone to; the Minoan, the Mayan, and...what was the third?'

'The Harappon Civilization in the Indus Valley. It arose around 2500 BC and ran until around 1700 BC, around the same time that Nibiru returned. It had advanced architecture, sewerage, drainage, dockyards and warehouses.'

'So what was Thoth/Imhotep called there?'

'I don't know, there's no evidence of palaces or temples, or of any kings or priests.'

'So basically Imhotep set up a civilization in Egypt, then, with that done, he went to Greece where he did the same thing for the Minoans, then he went to India, to the Indus valley, set up another civilization, and with that done headed down to Central America and did it all over again for the Mayans.'

Pieter was nodding away.

'Sounds like a good theory.'

I was trippin'.

'Man, it's revolutionary! So where would he have gone after setting things up in Central America?'

'Who really knows, China, Nepal, Japan? But probably back to Egypt to see how things were going.'

'When would that have been?'

'Maybe around 2300 BC.'

I couldn't believe it.

'There was a pharaoh called Montuhotep who reigned at the beginning of the 11th Dynasty from 2130 BC. Montuhotep; pretty coincidental don't you think? Maybe that was Imhotep returning?'

'It certainly fits your theory.'

Suddenly realizing there was more to it, as I rode along I pulled my iphone from my pocket, and checked my notes.

'In fact, there was a whole string of Montuhoteps in the 11th Dynasty, Montuhotep I from 2130-2117 BC, Montuhotep II (2049-1999 BC), Montuhotep III from 1999-1987 BC, Montuhptep IV from 1987-1983 BC. Then as many as nine Sobekhoteps, three Neferhoteps, a Seth, and another two Monuthoteps, who all reigned during the 13th Dynasty between 1741 BC and sometime after 1638 BC. I mean, am I just clutching at straws, or is this real evidence of the Annunaki presence throughout the dynasties of ancient Egypt?'

'It is to me.'

Yuko was more pragmatic.

'What hard evidence is there: texts, statues etcetera?'

I scanned my notes.

'Unfortunately there are no records of the actual dates of the pharaohs from the middle of the 13th Dynasty, around1638 BC, through the 14th Dynasty and 16th Dynasty, until the beginning of the 17th Dynasty.

I wondered if that was that because a massive tsunami obliterated almost everything, including all the records of the time? It would make sense. It was Yuko's turn to be cutthroat.

'So it's all a massive period of guess work?'

'I suppose so; the Egyptologists are really just trying to fit all the pieces together around then.'

'Where anything goes.'

'Historical *'join the dots'.'*

We chuckled as we calmly rolled along, scanning the tombs set into the hillside.

'This is Dra Abu el-Naga. There are about eighty numbered tombs dug into the hillside here, most of them belonging to priests and officials from the 17th through to the 20th Dynasty, including some rulers of the 17th Dynasty.'

'Do you think there are any tombs worth seeing?'

'I don't think so. The best tombs are supposedly in the Valley of the Kings. We could stop and spend time and money here, but I guess most people don't visit these tombs for a good reason, they're not as impressive as the ones in the Valley.'

We decided to ride on by, but as we left Dra Abu el-Naga in our wake, I started having second thoughts. Sure the best tombs were in the Valley of the Kings, the resting place of the 18th Dynasty rulers, everyone knew that. But, was I overlooking something in the 17th Dynasty? It had never occurred to me there was any real interest there; that was until I pulled over, took out my notes and ran some of the names through my mind.

'At the beginning of the 17th Dynasty, Rahotep reigned from 1616-1613 BC, then there was Djehuti, which translates as Thoth, sometime between 1597 and 1596 BC, although no specific dates were given. They were followed by Montuhotep VII in 1596, then Nibirau I, 1595-1576 BC, and Nibirau II in 1576, which was about thirty years before Seqenenre.'

Ra-hotep, *comes in peace from the sun*, Thoth, and the similarity between Nibirau and Nibiru was unquestionable. Was this a clear sign the Annunaki were present at key points in Thebes around 1600 BC, the exact time when Nibiru was returning? There just had to be a connection. I quickly stuffed my iphone away and pedalled after Pieter and Yuko.

The road started weaving through the wadi, but, though the gradient had increased slightly, it wasn't the French Alps. Mind you I certainly wouldn't have wanted to have been riding it later in the day with the sun pelting down overhead.

As taxis loaded with tourists started passing us, heading into the valley, the three of us swapped ideas.

'So I guess from there, Imhotep would have gone back and forth between Egypt, Greece, the Indus Valley, and Central America for the next five-hundred years or so, until Nibiru approached around 1600 BC; perhaps then returning to Egypt first as Rahotep around 1600 BC, then Djehuti/Thoth, or Montuhotep VII, and perhaps naming his children, Nibirau I & II, after the approaching home planet of Nibiru. But where does he go then, while all the shit is hitting the fan?'

'He would have briefly gone *off-world* and gone back to visit his home planet, thus avoiding the geological upheavals that would have transpired on Earth.'

'And after the earthquakes, volcanic eruptions and tsunami subsided, say around 1500 BC?'

'He would have returned to Earth.'

I was putting the pieces together.

'And he would have returned to Egypt, specifically to rebuild the Egyptian Civilization, and in the process taken over the role of Pharaoh from Ahmose, and, seeing that the Priests of Amun had used the confusion to seize control, called himself

Amenhotep, *one who comes from Amun.*

Then he remained in Egypt for about twenty-five years, overseeing the rebuilding of the temples and marrying Ahmose-Nefertari, who was most likely the daughter of Seqenenre and the sister of Ahmose, with the union resulting in a daughter, Ahmose, who in turn had a daughter to Thutmoses I, that being Hatshepsut.'

Yuko was following my thinking.

'But Amenhotep would have known there were other parts of the planet that needed rebuilding as well, so he wouldn't have stayed in Egypt for very long. He probably left to set up the Mycenaean Civilization in Greece, which originated sometime around 1600 BC, after the Thera eruption.'

'I'm right with you. With the reconstruction of the ancient Egyptian Civilization well underway, Amenhotep handed the sovereignty back to Thutmoses I, who was the son of Ahmose, and the original bloodline of Seqenenre. Then he took off to Greece, instigated the Mycenaean Civilization and changed his name to Hermes.'

Pieter had a different thought.

'No, I think he changed his name to Apollo.'

'Apollo? The sun-god? Of course. But how is that possible, when according to the epics of Homer, *The Odyssey, The Iliad,* Hermes and Apollo were half brothers?'

Yuko had the answer.

'Yes they were. But Homer was writing around 750-700 BC about events almost five-hundred years earlier, he could easily have confused the two stories and separated Amenhotep into two separate characters, one more godly, the other more humanistic.'

'The opposite to what happened with the Maya.'

'Or Hermes and Apollo could have been the half-brothers, Enki and Enlil.'

I was playing a huge mind game of join-the-dots; there were distinct connections in ancient Egypt between Imhotep, Apollo, Asclepius and Hermes, and the possibility they were all one and the same being was so radical it was bound to meet with rejection and ridicule.

'OK, so let's say he rebuilt the Mycenaean Civilization and called himself Apollo, I mean it makes sense, Apollo was the son of Zeus and Leto, and had a twin sister, Artmeis. That part coincides with Osiris and Isis. But as Hermes, he was the son of Zeus and Maia, herself one of the pleiades, the Daughters of Isis. That would totally correlate with Thoth being the son of Ptah and the mother coming from a race of star beings. The question is, how long was Apollo/Hermes in ancient Greece?'

'Oh, only about a hundred-and-fifty years.'

'Really, where did he head after that?'

Pieter looked strangely at me, then laughed.

'Why back to Egypt of course.'

I was baffled.

'A hundred-and-fifty years after Amenhotep? Who was he, Amenhotep III, Amenhotep IV?'

'He came back and reinstated the worship of the sun, of the Aten.'

Then it hit me; like a sledgehammer, like a road train crashing through a greenhouse.

'Apollo, the sun-god was....He was Akhenaten.'

It was one thing to connect Thoth to Imhotep, Montuhotep, Rahotep and Amenhotep, even to Quetzlcoatl in Central America and Enki in Sumer, and then to connect them to Hermes, Apollo and Asclepius. But to add in Akhenaten, well, that was me, and that was freaky! He was ...me. I was .. him. Surely I wasn't ... ALL OF THEM!'

As we curved around the next bend, the check-point and car park for the Valley appeared.

'So Apollo was Akhenaten. Do you think that's why he built the city at Amarna, to worship the Aten?'

Pieter shook his head.

'Possibly, but I think he had a more powerful motive. Akhenaten knew the Dracos had not only corrupted and infiltrated the High Priests of Amun, but that they had also imprinted their energy into the very stones comprising and below the temples at Luxor and Karnak.'

'So by ordering a new city to be constructed at Tel el-Amarna, he could start afresh.'

'Exactly.'

'No wonder the Amun Priests were pissed off.'

'Maybe that's part of the reason why he used sandstone blocks rather than granite. Sure it would have been easier and quicker to build with sandstone, but maybe there is also some sort of major difference between the resonant qualities of sandstone and granite that would make it harder for the Dracos to gain access to the priestesses.'

It suddenly became another reason for me to consider including Amarna in my trip; there may well be answers there.

'Sabah al khair, Assalaam Alaikum.'

As we passed through the checkpoint, calling and waving to the bemused faces of the Antiquities and Tourist Police guarding the road, I thought to myself, 'There may well be answers here as well'.

'Hey Pieter, do you think Akhenaten died in Egypt, like the Egyptologists would suggest, or do you think he left Egypt again?'

'Good question.'

Yuko was confident.

'Akhenaten clearly did as he had done before, and returned to Greece.'

'I agree, though this time he left Egypt in the rule of his wife, Nefertiti, who must have been of the royal bloodline of Seqenenre.'

'And once back in Greece, he continued as Apollo, the god of light and sun, becoming the patron of Delphi.'

'And what do you think happened to Nefertiti?'

Yuko paused momentarily before sharing her thoughts.

'Maybe you had better wait until we get back and ask her yourself?'

I chuckled.

'I might just have to do that.'

We chained our bikes to the fence outside the visitors' centre and prepared to enter the valley. I looked at Pieter and Yuko and had a very strange feeling come over me.

'Pieter, you know how you were talking about how someone returned Thoth's writings to a chamber under the Giza plateau?'

'Yes.'

'Well, do you think it's possible you might be one of those reincarnated members of the Tat Brotherhood?'

He paused reflectively.

'Perhaps, I'm not one-hundred percent sure yet, but there are certainly some very strong reasons why we are here, why we are *all* here.'

'Yuko?'

'Until yesterday I was much like Pieter, not sure, but after my experiences yesterday in the temple, and last night in the circle, I now know I am a Priestess of Aset, a daughter of the gods, and I am here to reclaim my goddess heritage and birth right.'

'So you think you might be descended from the Annunaki?'

'Alex, in some way we are *all* descended from the Annunaki.'

The Valley of the Kings

As soon as you enter the Visitors' Centre, the Antiquities Police are waiting not only to screen you for pistols, submachine guns, knives, bombs, probably even for tweezers, but also for cameras and video recorders. There were several aspects to that which made me laugh. Firstly, the 'logic' behind it.

The Egyptians are concerned that too much flash photography will break down the pigment of the reliefs and they will deteriorate. OK, fair point, so you strictly ban any form of lighting. And yet many of the tombs are apparently illuminated – constantly, day in, day out. Secondly, with modern technology, almost everyone has a mobile phone capable of not only taking snaps, but also video footage – *without* flash or extra lighting.

So maybe their reasoning for banning photos and video is because they are tombs, as a sign of respect for the departed. That's a joke, because you can snap pix in many of the other tombs, such as those at Wadi Hillal, and in the Tombs of the Nobles we had just ridden through. The reality probably is, that the Egyptians totally exploit absolutely anything they can, so, by banning photography, they pressure tourists into *buying* the images from the Visitors Centre, just like they had at Abu Simbel.

So, do they check you for plastic explosives, assault rifles, spray cans, anything that might *really* damage the reliefs? No, they just want to know if you are carrying a camera of any sort. I didn't have a camera as such, but my trusty iphone took a fair snap or ten. But they could hardly confiscate my mobile phone now, could they, so they made me promise not to take any photos or videos.

Sure. Great security that one. I wondered if it would work at the airport.

'I see you are carrying a bomb, Mohammed.'

'Yes, it is the latest in anti-aircraft, mid-air, suicide triggered devices.'

'Well, if you promise not to set it off, we will let you on to the plane.'

'Oh, I promise, cross my heart and hope to die.'

'OK, through you go.'

By now I knew that if I really wanted to snap a few pix, then a little baksheesh would go a long way. In the end, after not even bothering to search my backpack, they let the three of us in.

The Visitors' Centre was great, all around the walls they had photos dating back to the beginning of the 20th Century as well as touch-screen information displays and video presentations. The focal point of the room though, was a large three-dimensional see-through diorama depicting all the tombs and how far they disappeared beneath the surface of the hills and valley. It really gave a great overview of just how many tombs there were, and how deep some of them actually went. Pieter stopped beside me.

'Do you know which tombs you want to see?'

'I'm not sure which ones are open, apparently they rotate them to reduce wear and tear, but I was thinking of trying to see at least six of them.'

'Which ones?'

The ticket office was out the rear door, so we headed out to get our tickets.

'I was thinking of seeing them in chronological order; Amenhotep I, Thutmoses I, Thutmoses III, Hatshepsut, Amenhotep II, Thutmoses IV, Amenhotep III, Ay, Horemheb, Seti I, Ramses II, and Tausert.'

'Not Tutankhamun?'

'No, from what I've read, it's one of the smallest tombs and grossly over-rated and over-priced.'

'What do you mean?'

'Entrance to the Valley is eighty pounds, and for that you get to see any three tombs except Tutankhamun's tomb. If you want to see that, it will cost you an *extra* hundred pounds just to see that one tomb.'

'But I thought that because you'd been Akhenaten, you'd want to see the tomb of your son.'

'Tutankhamun wasn't the son of Akhenaten, he was the son of Amenhotep IV and Kiya.'

While they stood there slightly dumbfounded at what I had said, I purchased two tickets to cover six tombs and then the guy in the ticket box tried to sell me a four-pound ticket to the people train that took tourists the two-hundred metres up the road to the beginning of The Valley proper. I declined: I much preferred to walk. I could see how elderly tourists would take it in the heat of the day, but I was fit, healthy and it was still only just after 8:30 in the morning.

After absorbing my revelation, Yuko stepped up to the ticket window leaving Pieter to continue the discussion.

'We'd like to see as many tombs as you, but Yuko definitely wants to see Tutankhamun's tomb, and we're on a bit of a tight budget.'

'I understand; that's cool.'

Pieter and Yuko also declined to join the road-train, so, as the three of us set off walking up the road, I perused my trusty notes.

'Biban el-Muluk, or Wadi el-Muluk as the locals called it, or, to give it its official name, 'The Great and Majestic Necropolis of the Millions of Years of the Pharaoh, Life, Strength, Health in The West of Thebes', or more usually, 'The Great Field', was used for nearly 500 years from around 1539 BC to 1075 BC. It contains over 60 tombs, built for the pharaohs and nobles of the New Kingdom, starting with Thutmoses I and ending with Ramses X or XI.'

The hills and slopes vary in colour from grey, through pale yellow to ochre, even reddish orange. Depending on what angle the sun is striking them, they transform like a chameleon; it reminded me of Ayers Rock, or Uluru as it's now referred as, back in the heart of the Australian desert. Maybe it was a trait of all sacred sites, except Stonehenge perhaps, it was just drab gray, like most of the weather in England.

As we walked up the road, the hills started to close in more and more on either side.

'You know, this was supposed to be a secret and sacred place; sentries were placed at the entrance to the valley, as well as all along the top of the hills in the hope of discouraging tomb robbers. And yet, despite the pharaohs being buried in secret tombs and protected by the best security of the age, all the royal tombs, except Tutankhamun's, were plundered by grave robbers.'

'How do you think they did it?'

'It's quite simple when you consider the possibility that the ones who robbed the tombs were the very ones who were responsible for guarding it.'

'The priests?'

'Of course; they knew exactly what the layout of each tomb was, all the traps designed to block and capture thieves, and the contents of the tombs. They would be able to carry on unnoticed, because they could prevent any normal person from entering the valley, and be able to remove all the artefacts without suspicion.'

'But why?'

'Greed, power.'

'But wouldn't they be desecrating the tombs?'

'I think by the time the ancient Egyptian civilization got to the 18th Dynasty, the priests had no respect for the pharaohs; they purely saw them as puppet figureheads by which they could manipulate and control the masses.'

'But why go to all the trouble of digging out massive tombs and mummifying the bodies?'

'I'm not sure, but I'm hoping to find a few answers here amongst the tombs.'

'If you want to see all those tombs, I know you'll finish up spending longer here than us, but do you mind if we tag along for the first few tombs at least?'

'Not at all, which tombs are you planning to see?'

'We were thinking of Thutmoses I, Thutmoses III, Ramses VI and then finishing off with Tutankhamun.'

'OK, why don't we just go with the flow and see where our paths lead us?'

'Sounds like a good plan.'

We'd passed three paths that led off the main track. The first two headed off to the right to the tombs of Ramses IV and VII respectively. The third tracked left to supposedly one of the best-preserved tombs in the valley, the tomb of Yuya and Tjuyu, who were possibly the parents of Queen Tiye. Further down that track was the tomb of Ramses XI, which I had absolutely no interest in seeing.

Continuing on, we approached the main *square* in the valley. I stopped outside KV5 (Kings Valley Tomb No. 5). I had read up quite a bit about this tomb, and here it was a few metres before me.

'Why are we stopping, Alex, this tomb is closed?'

'It may appear closed, to us that is, and the entrance may seem unimposing, but this is the biggest tomb ever discovered in the Valley of the Kings. It was built for the sons of Ramses II and had originally be *lost*; covered in the rubble removed from the excavation of other tombs. But in 1995 they re-discovered it and started re-excavating. By 2006 they had cleared over a hundred-and-fifty corridors and rooms, including at least sixty-seven burial chambers, and they're still going. They think there may up to two-hundred rooms and corridors to it.'

'Why is it so big?'

'Each time a new pharaoh is crowned, they would start a new tomb specifically for him. But Ramses II ruled for sixty-six years so I guess at first they started digging a tomb for his successor, but as he had over a hundred children, I guess they converted it into a tomb for all his sons.'

'Have they found anything?'

'Not yet. It supposedly housed the remains of fifty-two of his sons, but no sarcophagi, mummies or mummy cases were ever, or have currently been, found in it. But they're still digging, so who knows what may lay within?'

'Do you think they will ever open it to the public?'

I laughed.

'Sure, once they've stripped it bare of anything and everything of value.'

A little further along was the entrance to KV6, the tomb of Ramses IX, and across the path, located at the foot of the northern side of the main valley, was the entrance to KV7, the tomb of Ramses II. This was one tomb I really wanted to visit, especially since my encounters with Jacques. But, alas, it was also closed.

However that wasn't going to deter me as I really wanted to gain access and check it out, but I surmised it would only be possible on my own, without anyone else around, so that I could safely bribe the guard. I earmarked it to return later, and we moved on.

A few paces further into the valley and we were at the tourist resthouse; a large open-roofed area clearly designed for folk to shelter from the Egyptian sun and partake of refreshments. I scanned the large map of the valley erected outside the shelter, surveyed the surrounds, and quickly figured that it was totally impractical to visit the tombs in chronological order, as that would require criss-crossing back and forth and up and down the paths like a nomadic zombie in a pinball machine.

The solution was basically to visit the furthermost tomb and work your way back. That meant heading south to our first destination: the tomb of Thutmoses I. So, off we set up the path, Yuko keeping pace with me.

'Alex, do you know much about Ancient Greece?'

'A little; Zeus was the father of the Gods, Poseidon was his brother, then there was Aphrodite, Apollo, Artemis, Athena, Pluto, Hermes....'

I paused and pondered; for the first time I directly compared them to Egypt and then also to Sumer and the Annunaki.

'... Hang on, Zeus would have been Enlil/Osiris and Poseidon, Enki/Set.'

'Or vica versa depending who you believe was the leader of where.'

'True. Enki ruled Egypt, so *he* would have been Osiris and Enlil would have been Set. Akhenaten and Nefertiti were Apollo and Aphrodite, and that means they were also Thoth and Ma'at?'

'Possibly.'

'And Artemis, Athena and Pluto must have been....'

It was all getting a little confusing.

'It's a bit like trying to put one of those 3D wooden puzzles together, you know the pieces all fit, and you know what it's supposed to look like, but all the pieces seem to be similar.'

'I know what you mean, but actually by ancient Greece I meant Classical Greece, from around 600 BC onwards.'

'You mean the time of the first Olympics, Socrates, Plato, Aristotle, those guys?'

'Yes.'

'OK; Well, let me see. I know all about Homer's Epics, *The Iliad* and *The Odyssey*, and all about Achilles, Heracles, about Jason and the Argonauts. And then there's Aesop and his Fables, the dramatist, Aeschylus, the plays of Euripides and Sophocles, and the characters in the plays, Agamemnon, Clytemnestra, Orestes, Electra, Oedipus. Of course there's Herodotus, the creator of History, and Hippocrates, the father of modern medicine, not forgetting good old Pythagoras, the father of mathematics; $A^2 + B^2 = C^2$. That's about it, I think'

Pieter added his own Greek hero.

'There's also Democritus, who invented atomic theory some time around 400 BC.'

'Seriously, 400 BC, the atomic theory?'

'Yes.'

'Whoa! Wait a minute, did he discover it, or rediscover it?

'Good point.'

I was sudden busy linking the concept of atomic structure to the genetic engineering and knowledge of the Annunaki, when Yuko fired a salvo at me.

'I was thinking; if Amenhotep left Egypt and went to Greece as Apollo, then came back as Akhenaten, then when he returned to Greece the second time, say around 800 or 700 BC, this time as Hermes, then it's possible that over time he could have directly tutored all of them, particularly Democritus, Hippocrates, Socrates and Plato from around 450-350 BC.'

'Wow, it wouldn't surprise me.'

Pieter added to the possibilities.

'It would also mean that Socrates and Plato could possibly have been members of the Tat Brotherhood.'

'I guess it would. It certainly makes sense where they acquired all their knowledge, wisdom and philosophy. Now you're really freaking me out.'

Yuko dropped another bombshell.

'And it was Plato who tutored Aristotle, who in turn tutored Alexander the Great.'

I stopped dead in my tracks.

'Whoaaaa! That would mean that when Alexander invaded Egypt, it wasn't so much an invasion, as an invitation to return? That's why the Tat Brotherhood was still strong, through Alexander the Great, through Plato. The Brotherhood didn't die out, they just went *underground* so to speak, they went to Greece.'

Pieter had his curiosity sparked.
'But why didn't they stay in Greece?'

Yuko had a possibility.

'There was an ancient Athenian lawgiver called Draco who lived around the 7th Century BC. He believed every offence should be punishable by death. It's where Draconian views come from; from ancient Greece.'

'They're pretty heartless, cold, ruthless perspectives. Do you think it's possible that not only was Akhenaten, or Thoth, around then, but so were the Dracos.'

'It's possible; if not directly, then certainly the hybrid offspring they'd placed into positions of office.'

Detouring right, into a desolate part of the valley, we passed the tomb of Siptah, KV47, who succeeded Seti II, then KV14, the tomb of Tausert and Setnakht, and arrived at the entrance to KV38, the supposed Tomb of Thutmoses I, which was situated at the base of a shear cliff.

'According to some Egyptologists, this is the earliest known tomb of the New Kingdom, originally thought to be the initial burial place of Thutmoses I, from which he was later moved to another tomb, KV20, the tomb supposedly excavated for Hatshepsut. However others have suggested KV38 was built *after* KV20.'

Whatever the case, it clicked us into another gear, and, to be honest, it was a welcome relief from the intellectual onslaught my sanity was being subjected to. Handing our tickets to the guardian, he punched a hole in the corner and granted us permission to enter the tomb.

Thutmoses I

According to the Egyptologists, and it depends which source you choose to believe, Thutmoses I was either the son of Amenhotep and Ahmose-Meritamen, or the son of Ahmose and Ahmose-Nefertari. Of course it's highly probable that Meritamen and Nefertari were not only sisters, but sisters of Ahmose, or even one and the same person. But to me, it was more likely Thutmoses I was the son of Ahmose and Ahmose-Meritamun, and that Amenhotep married Ahmose-Nefertari.

It's hard to know exactly who was begetting whom: brothers married sisters, nieces married uncles, aunts married nephews. There was so much incest going on it made 'Kissin Cousins' look like a training film on marital techniques of foreplay. It was the ultimate family pastime. I mean when these guys kept things in the family, they *really* kept things *in the family*.

All we really know is that Thutmoses succeeded Amenhotep and ruled from 1484-1472 BC. But I was convinced Thutmoses was appointed to the throne by Amenhotep when Amenhotep left Egypt, because Thutmoses was married to the *sang réal*, to the daughter of Ahmose and granddaughter of Ashotep and Seqenenre.

As we silently and carefully descended the steep crudely cut steps, we passed through a small doorway into a descending corridor that curved gently to the left. Why? I have no idea. Maybe the slaves who dug it out were drunk, or blind in one eye. There may have been some significance, but I certainly couldn't see it. In fact there wasn't much to see at all, parts of the ceiling and walls had collapsed, probably due to water damage from one of the rare floods over the millennia, and so I was somewhat disappointed. Never the less, I was sure I would find some answers further in.

The curving corridor led to an irregularly cut room, wider on the right, again a collapsed ceiling and no decorations on the walls. In the centre, the steps continued to descend, this time very steeply via rough-cut steps and a ramp, leading into a large burial chamber in the shape of a cartouche and about eleven metres in length. To the left was a small opening in the wall, leading to a crudely cut storage annex, of course now empty.

In the centre of the chamber I could just see traces of where the ceiling had once been supported by a single, square pillar, though now it was missing. I must admit I had momentary thoughts and concerns about what was stopping the roof from caving in as it had for most of the other parts of the tomb, but it had lasted thirty-five hundred years without collapsing, so I was fairly confident, excluding sudden earthquakes, it would last another ten minutes or so.

Parts of the walls of the burial chamber showed the traces of a watermark indicating the level of flooding, about seven feet deep. Once they would have been covered with plaster, as high up, near the ceiling, I could see traces of some sort of mud plaster and decorative friezes still visible. It was also clear some of them had been removed, probably by early 'Egyptologists' and museum 'providers' of the 19th Century.

At the rear of the chamber, on the floor and adjacent to the annex, was a smallish niche, probably for the canopic jars. In the centre of the floor was a larger niche where the sarcophagus would have resided. I checked my notes.

'Carved from yellow quartzite and inscribed for Thutmoses, the sarcophagus found in tomb KV38 had been removed to the Cairo Museum along with the canopic chest.'

I guess that's logically why the tomb had been ascribed to him. Overall it was only about thirty-five to forty metres long, had virtual no reliefs apart from a few crude inscriptions, and was hardly the grandiose site I had expected to encounter, in fact it was more like one level up from a cave. But though the tomb was basic, it was definitely a tomb, not much of a step on from the 'rooms' I had seen at El Kab, but, to me, it was a signpost. I didn't know one-hundred percent where it pointed, but I was going to find out. I took out my notes to check why I'd held such grand reasons for visiting it.

'Graffiti within KV38 suggests that it was opened around the beginning of the 21st Dynasty when the two wooden coffins of Thutmoses were removed and appropriated for the use of Pinedjem I, a High Priest of Amun who ascended to the throne around 1070 BC. The coffins were *appropriated* because there was a belief they held divine power. The coffins were later discovered, redecorated and inscribed for Pinedjem I as pharaoh, in the cache of mummies found at Deir el-Bahri in the Valley of the Queens.'

From that, the logical assumption was that the mummy found inside the coffin was not Thutmoses; it seems more than likely that it belonged to Pinedjem and that Thutmoses' body is missing, or is one of the as yet unidentified mummies from the Deir el-Bahri cache.

'It's also believed, because of the large size of the two wooden coffins, that there was originally a third, inner coffin made of precious metal that was subsequently melted down for bullion.'

That was it! To me, it was proof that the Amun Priests were responsible for the tomb robbing; they even left their calling cards bragging about it. But what was the time-line? My time here done, I retraced my steps back up the stairs; Pieter and Yuko close behind me. With each step my mind ticked over like a precision Swiss watch.

If the tomb robbing started in the 21st Dynasty by the Amun Priests, then that would explain why Tutankhamun's tomb was untouched. As head of the Amun Priests, Ay had briefly seized power after the death of Tutankhamun, and it was probably Ay who instigated the erasure of Akhenaten and Tutankhamun from history, as a reaction and revenge for what they had done to disempower the Amun Priests. But when Ay died around 1300 BC, Horemheb claimed the throne and that led to a long line of military, non-'sang réal'-related, pharaohs running through the 19th and 20th Dynasties.

That meant the *sang réal* was lost, or perhaps had just gone underground. But then I thought of what Yuko had said about the other civilizations: 'No, it must have gone to Greece with Nefertiti and some of her daughters'.

Meanwhile, back in Egypt, the 'military' took over running the country. But they only knew some of the aspects of pharaoh-hood, and, much as it is today, I doubt the Amun Priests would have shared their secrets with the military. Then, at the beginning of the 21st Dynasty around 1070 BC, after two-hundred years and two dynasties of military rule, some event or theological disagreement caused a split between the Priesthood and the military, the church and the state, and the country was divided into the Military rulers of the north, and the Theban Priests, the Amun Priests, of the south.

Having regained power and control of the throne, Amun priests then broke into the old military king tombs, appropriating all the treasure, the golden caskets, and dumping all the previous mummies in a single tomb, not in the valley of Kings where they belonged, but a short distance away over the hill in the Valley of the Queens. But over four-hundred years had passed, and tombs such as Tutankhamun's were forgotten, or missed, while other tombs of non-military pharaohs fell under the umbrella and were just robbed as a matter of course.

It sounded just like the people's revolts in modern Iraq, the gulf war, and any number of uprisings of the people against military dictatorships that had happened through the millennia, including Egypt. I guess history truly does repeat itself.

As I emerged back into the morning air and natural sunlight, it felt like a new dawn. I knew what I was looking for now. From behind me, Pieter's voice briefly shifted my focus.

'Where to next?'

I looked around, gathering my bearings. The tomb of Seti II, KV15, was further up at the end of the path, but not on my agenda, whilst KV14, the tomb of Tausert was right beside us.

'Well, the tomb of Thutmoses III is back down this path and then further up the other fork. But I also want to see the tomb of Tausert, which is right here, so maybe you should go on ahead without me?'

'No, you go in, we'll wait for you.'

'Are you sure?'

'Yes.'

'OK, I'll be as quick as I can.'

'We're in no hurry.'

Tausert

Checking my notes, I quickly presented my ticket and entered the tomb, this time via a modern entrance and wooden ramp, not down crude steps as in the previous tomb.

'Tomb, KV14, is one of the largest tombs in the Valley, encompassing two complete burial chambers, one for Tausert and a second for Setnakht, the father of Ramses III. Tausert was a female pharaoh, the wife of Seti II, and granddaughter of Ramses II. She ruled at the end of the 19th Dynasty, three-hundred years after Thutmoses.'

I expected to see quite a difference in the two tombs, and, as I walked down the descending wooden walkway, I wasn't disappointed. The finished walls of the first corridor were covered in reliefs of Tausert before numerous deities such as Horus, Osiris and Anubis. There wasn't much colour in them, just the occasional traces of blues and brown. It was obvious that some of the images had been doctored to show a king rather than Tausert herself; that was probably a reflection of the interment of Setnakht in the tomb at a later date. But, still, the reliefs were very impressive. One could only imagine what the now-faded colours would have looked like in their heyday.

'Construction on the tomb began when Tausert was still simply the queen. After the death of Seti II in 1195 BC, Siptah, who was ten or eleven, briefly assumed the throne. The identity of Siptah's father is currently unknown; though some Egyptologists speculate it may not have been Seti II, but have been Amunmes, who was possibly a brother of Merneptah, son of Ramses II and uncle to Seti II, and that his mother was a canaanite called Sutailja.'

That would mean that Siptah would not have been of the true royal bloodline, the *sang réal*, because his mother was a foreigner. And that explained the next passage in my notes.

'Unlike Merneptah and Seti II, both Amunmes and Siptah were specifically excluded from Ramses III's Medinet Habu procession of statues of ancestral kings. This suggests that Amunmes and Siptah were inter-related in such a way that they were regarded as illegitimate rulers and thus probably father and son.'

That meant that Seti II must have died childless, and that Siptah, the young first-cousin of Seti II, had been placed on the throne. Clearly it would not have been a popular decision and it also may have explained why he didn't rule for long, and didn't rule on his own.

'Around 1190 BC, perhaps because of Siptah's dubious lineage or failing health, Tausert became co-regent alongside him. Then, several years later, around 1187 BC, Siptah died, and his stepmother, Tausert, was left to ascend to the thrown of Egypt as Pharaoh in her own right.'

A doorway led into a second corridor, decorated with images from the 'Book of the Dead', or more correctly the 'Book of Emerging Forth into the Light', or as I preferred to call it, the 'Book of the Path to Resurrection'. It was an ancient funerary text that dated specifically to the New Kingdom, although it had developed from the Coffin Texts of the Middle Kingdom. They in turn had developed from, and were basically an update in a newer language of, the Pyramid Texts that were discovered in the 6th Dynasty tombs of Pepi I, Pepi II, three of his queens, and Teti. They dated back at least to around 2400 BC and the Old Kingdom tomb of the 5th Dynasty pharaoh, Unas, at Saqqara. To me that meant they must have been formulated, or in practice, for some time before that, and that very possibly put them around the time of Imhotep three-hundred years earlier.

The purpose of the pyramid texts varied considerably, but basically it was all ultimately concerned with an afterlife in the sky. There are around two-hundred-and-twenty-eight known pyramid text spells, including; protecting the pharaohs remains, reanimating his body after death, helping the dead king ascend to heaven so that he can take his place amongst the gods, and reuniting him with his divine father, Ra.

As far as I know, the texts weren't illustrated, but written in old hieroglyphic text on papyrus scrolls and placed in the coffin with the deceased king or, as for Pepi I and Teti, on the walls of the burial chamber. To view those, I had to wait until I got to Saqqara. For now I had to focus on the 'Book of the Dead'.

The second corridor led to a third corridor that descended and contained more images from the 'Book of the Dead'; of which there are just under two-hundred spells known to appear at present, although no single manuscript or inscription contains them all. Perhaps that's because they have such a range of purposes: mystical knowledge in afterlife, protection, guidance, weighing of the heart.

The further I went down the corridors the more colour was evident; browns, yellows, reds, in addition to more shades of the blues. Most of the decorative plan here was the same as the first corridor, except for the places where the queen's image or name appeared. They had been plastered over and painted with king Setnakht's image and name.

The third corridor led to what was referred to as a ritual pit, with a huge winged-sun disk on the lintel across the doorway. This was supposed to be a booby trap for would be tomb robbers, with a deep pit dug into the ground that would have preceded a false wall in the corridor. I could see how the builders of the tomb would have dug this out last, after the sarcophagus and all the loot had been stashed inside. Once the pit was dug, it would have been covered with a thin false floor and left for the unsuspecting criminal to fall through, probably resulting in broken legs, arms or even death.

The walls had images of various deities, no doubt there to berate and admonish any thief foolish enough to enter and fall into the deep pit. I was blown away to see the images included one of Osiris, with a green face! What did that mean? Why go to the trouble of representing him with a green face, unless he actually *had* a green face. So did the Annunaki have green skin, or was this a twisted reference to the Dracos? I was confused again.

The pit led via ever descending ramps through a small hall with no pillars or columns. Here again scenes from the 'Book of the Dead' adorned the walls, with images and cartouches of Tausert replaced by those of Setnakht. It would seem that Setnakht usurped her tomb, possibly trying to erase all mention or knowledge of her in the process. I wondered, 'If Pernille had been Tausert, who would be spiteful enough to try and wipe her name from history?' Within a microsecond I got my answer, 'Jacques'.

It wasn't Setnakht who defaced the tomb, but his son, Ramses III, who was Jacques. I couldn't believe how the pieces kept falling into place. That meant Setnakht could have been Bill. I was spinning, and I didn't have time to sit down and mull it all over, that could wait for later.

Conscious that Pieter and Yuko were waiting, I pressed onwards, the hall leading downwards in turn through a fourth corridor, with a small ante-chamber off to the left. Though access was blocked, I could still make out a beautiful relief of Anubis attending a mummy on a bier, while Isis and Nephthys stood at the foot and head of the bier as principal mourners.

The corridor continued through another doorway and into a second section, decorated with images of deities and scenes from the Opening of the Mouth ritual. In addition, there was more evidence of cartouches of Setnakht directly painted over erased figures of Tausert.

As I scanned the images, I contemplated the Opening of the Mouth ritual; an important ritual in both funerary and temple practice designed to re-animate the deceased pharaoh with the capacity to eat, breathe, see, hear and enjoy the offerings and provisions performed by the priests and officiants, thus supporting and sustaining the ka, or life force. There is speculation amongst some Egyptologists that the ritual may have been a symbolic re-enactment of the clearing of a baby's mouth at birth. For once I tended to agree.

Passing through the next doorway, I noticed beautiful reliefs of Hathor on the door jams. It led into a small antechamber filled with glorious images of all the major gods: a seated Osiris, Ptah being protected by a winged Ma'at, Geb, Horus, Isis, Nephthys, Thoth. Once again I noticed Osiris, and this time Ptah, had green skin. This was no small artistic license; this meant something. Other sections had images of Tausert plastered over and obscured by cartouches of Setnakht.

Across the lintel leading into the next chamber was yet another beautiful winged sun with two cobras; it had to have some special significance beyond that which the Egyptologists speculated.

Passing though the doorway I arrived in the first burial chamber, decorated with wall-to-wall reliefs. It was exquisite. No, it was breath-takingly beautiful. It comprised a sunken rectangular central floor surrounded by eight square pillars, each adorned with life-size (in human terms that is) depictions of the gods or pharaoh; Horus, Anubis, Thoth, Osiris, they were all there and more, including images of Setnakht painted over those of Tausert.

It was surrounded by a raised walkway forming the perimeter of the room containing four small incomplete niche-like annexes. Above the central floor spanned an arched ceiling with astronomical imagery. I stood in awe. It was magical. I wondered what all the images on the walls referred to.

'The first burial chamber has scenes from both the *Book of Gates;* a sophisticated text referencing the hours of the night, referred to as the twelve gates, and emphasizing the gates as barriers, and the closing scenes from the *Book of Caverns;* a vision of the underworld as a series of six pits, or caverns over which the sun god passes.

The *Book of Gates* deals with the problems of the underworld, such as justice, material blessings and time, symbolized by an apparently endless snake or doubly twisted rope being spun from the mouth of a deity originating in the depths of creation, and eventually falling back into the same depths.

In the *Book of Caverns*, most of the underworld is illustrated, while the text primarily praises Osiris. It emphasizes the destruction of the enemies of the sun god, and refers to afterlife rewards and punishments. The dead King, in order to complete his journey through the underworld, must know the secret names of the serpents and be able to identify his guardian deities.'

A shiver went up my spine: the Dracos. Here it was again, references to snakes, serpents, reptiles, and their direct connection to the underworld, to a place of danger. On the walls were images of huge fire-breathing or spitting snakes destroying the enemies of Osiris. Did that mean Osiris, Enki, the Annunaki, had forged an alliance with the Dracos? If so, an alliance against who? Perhaps against his half-brother, Set, Enlil; though I'm sure the Dracos would have played both off against each other.

Further along the wall was the image of the Sun/Creator God, Khnum, being pulled along on a barque, alongside images of Horus-headed sphinxes and multi-headed snakes with legs. Had the ancient Egyptians documented the true secrets behind their rituals; was it all about a journey from third dimensional existence through the 'underworld' of fourth dimensional consciousness to the 'nirvana' of fifth dimensional awareness, and have we been blind all along? It started to look that way.

And there, covering the entire end wall, the spread wings of the vulture. But a vulture that had a ram's head; Khnum, the creator juxtaposed with a symbol of death, the eternal cycle and illusion of life and death. And above it, the representation of the sun god, Ra, as a child, and Khepri, the scarab between not one, but two suns, one smaller than the other. Was this yet another cryptic reference to Nibiru?

Moving on quickly from the first chamber, as I exited it there were two more annexes on either side of the corridor, and then a further two corridors encroaching into the heart of the mountain.

'The following corridors are decorated with scenes from the *Amduat*, or the *Book of the Secret Chamber*. This is the earliest of the royal funerary texts, and documents the dangerous journey the deceased king must make in the boat of the sun. United with the sun god, and beginning on the western horizon, he must travel through the twelve divisions of the underworld, reappearing as Khepri, the scarab-god of the sun, creation and resurrection, in the guise of the newborn sun in the East.'

The corridors led straight to the second burial chamber, built in the exact same architecture style as the first burial chamber; eight pillars, raised perimeter walkway and arched astronomical ceiling, though on a slightly larger scale. This time the four small annexes in each corner were completed, however the walls were incompletely decorated, only the outer most wall containing the same scenes from the 'Book of Gates' on its walls, including the massive spitting serpent.

In the centre of the sunken floor was a reconstructed smashed sarcophagus of red granite. On the lid was the delicately carved image of the king, lying in state. However on the end of the lid and foot of the base of the sarcophagus, crude carvings and cartouches of Setnakht were cut into the surface, and it would seem across the top of some previous owner. Who that was, I could only speculate, but one thing was certain, this was more than likely the burial chamber of Setnakht. I scanned my notes.

'As was the normal custom, Setnakht had originally created his own tomb, KV11, but it was unfinished at the time of his death. However there appears to have been plenty of time for it to be completed prior to the Pharaoh's burial. Yet apparently against his final wishes, his son, Ramses III, decided at the last minute to have his father interred in the tomb of Tausert, rather than his own, and took his father's tomb as his own.'

The Egyptologists seemed to know nothing about the reasons for these clear departures from custom, but, as I entered the next corridor leading from the rear of the second burial chamber, I formulated a solution.

Setnakht, was possibly either the brother of Seti II, or one of the younger sons of Ramses II and thus an uncle of Seti II. It's possible that, some time after the death of Seti II and Siptah, Setnakht saw an opportunity to legitimately ascend the throne, and married Tausert: much as Ay had done with Ankhesenamun a hundred-and-thirty years earlier.

I also thought, that if Setnakht and Seti II were brothers, or uncle and nephew, that would totally be in keeping with the practices of the ancient Egyptian royal families, in this case Setnakht, marrying the *sang réal*, namely, Tausert. In any case, it legitimised Setnakht as pharaoh, the succession of his son, Ramses III, and the perpetuation of the Ramses name, thus forming the beginnings of the 20th Dynasty. That sorted in my mind, suddenly the corridor came to a dead end; it lead nowhere. Was this an indication the tomb was unfinished, or did it lead to some secret panel and a secret room? There were a few decorations but I could see no obvious signs of any secret chambers, so presumed that when Setnakht died, the tomb was left as is by the Amun priests.

I looked back up the corridor and through the burial chamber in the direction of the entrance. It was clear the tomb was carved out in a straight line from the entrance, and continued deep into the mountain for at least a hundred-and-twenty metres. That noted, I perused my iphone for any further morsels of information, without success, so stuffed it in my back pocket, and made a somewhat satiated and deliberate return to the outside world.

As I passed back through the second and then the first burial chamber, I extolled my gratitude for the secrets Tausert, and in some way Setnakht, had revealed. Then suddenly an idea dawned on me: perhaps the tomb was originally for Tausert and Siptah. But then I remembered Siptah had his own tomb here in the valley, just across the path, KV47, and if he was an illegitimate pharaoh, then it's unlikely he would be entombed with Tausert.

So maybe, just maybe, Setnakht actually wanted to be entombed with Tausert for eternity. Maybe he had the hots for her all along, and when his brother/uncle died, he made a move on her not just because she was the *sang réal*, but because he actually fancied her; he actually loved her. But, if that *was* the case, why would he have obliterated her name? Clearly he didn't, it was more than likely either Ramses III, or those pesky little Priests of Amun. In any case, as I emerged from the tomb I made a mental note to raise the topic of ancient Egyptian love with Crystal at a suitably appropriate moment.

It was starting to warm up outside and Pieter and Yuko were waiting just down from the entrance.

'Sorry I was a little longer than I thought, Tausert's tomb is about three times bigger than Thutmoses I's.'

'How was it?'

'Much more developed and decorated; more like what I expected a tomb to look like. The first burial chamber was beautiful.'

'In what way?'

'It's a pillared chamber with an arched ceiling and decorations similar to the tombs in the hills at El Kab, only better preserved and more extensive.'

Yuko was slightly disappointed.

'I hope we find something just as good as what you saw in Tausert's tomb, in the other tombs.'

'I'm sure we will.'

Pieter restored the enthusiasm.

'Then shall we go and explore Thutmoses III's tomb?'

'You're reading my mind.'

We made our way down passed the tomb of Siptah and took the other fork up to another part of the wadi. Pieter had been thinking.

'So Tausert's tomb didn't have any evidence of the sort of flooding or water damage in Thutmoses I's tomb?'

I thought for a second.

'No, no, I didn't.'

'Then Thutmoses's tomb must have been damaged before Tausert's tomb was dug.'

As we passed a number of unknown tombs, my mind started ticking over; Pieter was right, it must have, otherwise Tausert's tomb would have probably suffered the same fate. That got me thinking about the tsunami again. There was clearly one at the end of the 17th Dynasty with the eruption of Thera, but was there more than one?

It would make sense that the first tsunami was massive and wiped out Kamose, El Kab, etcetera, but then there would probably have been subsequent eruptions and earthquakes as Nibiru approached even closer, and possibly more tsunamis as well. Perhaps a second tsunami occurred after Thutmoses I was interred, flooding the tomb, but how long after, that's the question? The answers would probably be found somewhere amidst the subsequent tombs of Thutmoses II, Thutmoses III, Hatshepsut, Amenhotep II, Thutmoses IV and Amenhotep III.

Though no one had specifically found or identified the tomb of Thutmoses II, I was sure there was a tomb in the Valley of the Kings that must have fitted the bill. I rechecked my notes for confirmation.

'Although thought to be the tomb of Hatshepsut-Meryet Ra, wife of Thutmoses III, KV42 may well originally have been the tomb of Thutmoses II.'

So, the next spot to find clues was KV42, which, according to my reckoning, was around the bend to the right and straight ahead, and just before the tomb of Thutmoses III, which would make perfect geographical sense.

But, as we turned the corner, I got a massive surprise. Up ahead in the ravine, beside the entrance to KV42, a massive wedge of modern concrete steps led up to a long metal staircase which in total climbed the best part of thirty metres out of the valley floor. The tomb of Thutmoses III, KV 34, was apparently at the top of the ascent. Certain poignant questions came to mind; 'How the hell did the ancient Egyptians get up there?', and 'How on earth would they have transported all the contents to such an inaccessible location?'. It may well have been one of the earliest tombs cut in the valley, but I had to consult my notes to try and make some sense of why they dug it in such a bizarre place.

'The entrance to the tomb was located halfway up a cliff face, then, after the completion of the tomb, the stairway up to the tomb was hacked away to deter tomb robbers.'

I could see some logic in building a tomb in such an inaccessible place; it would supposedly make it harder for tomb robbers to get there. But then, if the tomb robbers were the Priests of Amun, that theory went out the window. So the question was simply, 'Why did they build it there?'. Then it hit me: unless of course it wasn't that high up when they built it. And that sparked a run of thoughts.

If there had been a second massive tsunami that washed everything away, it may have taken years for the water to fully recede. If that was the case, then the level of the tomb entrance for Thutmoses III's tomb may well have been just above the level of the river. A wild theory I know, but it did make sense. I just needed to find some collaborating evidence, and, though it wasn't on my list, that meant examining KV42.

'You guys go on ahead, I'm going to visit KV42.'

'Whose tomb is that?'

'I think it's Thutmoses II.'

'OK, we'll catch up with you later.'

Detour, water ahead

Yuko had already scaled the concrete steps and was starting the ascent of the steep narrow metal stairs. It reminded me of the vision I had seen whilst swimming earlier in the day; what an exquisite ass she had as well. Pieter followed on behind her and bizarrely I found myself checking out Pieter's bum as a matter of course. Whoa, that was weird! I best shift back to my objective, KV42.

There weren't many people around, and clearly none were visiting KV42, so I decided to save my tickets and try a little baksheesh bartering. I figured if an eighty-pound ticket covered three tombs then I could get in for ten, maybe twenty at the most, by slipping the guard cash.

As I descended into the modern entrance area he rose to take my ticket.

'Baksheesh?'

He looked around to confirm no one was looking, then held up three fingers.

'Thirty pound.'

OK, time to dance the barter tango.

'La, five.'

Backwards and forwards we volleyed, but the lowest he would go was twenty. I played my ace.

'La.'

And pulled out my ticket to hand him. He grimaced, realizing he was going to get nothing, then brought his price down to fifteen.

'La, ten.'

He shook his head, so I went to hand him the ticket again.

'Yes, ten.'

I was really getting the hang of this corruption and bribery game; all you had to do was hold the ace. I slipped him ten pounds and entered the tomb; I knew what I was looking for so wasn't going to waste any time.

A rectangular hole in the ground led down a set of steep steps, well cut out from the rock, to a steeply descending, mostly well-cut, but undecorated corridor. That led to another set of steep rough-cut steps with recesses to either side. Next was a large unfinished and rough cut square room, with a shallow pit in one corner and a bench running the length of one side, this was clearly an ante-chamber.

Turning left ninety degrees, another well cut but undecorated corridor led to what was the burial chamber. This gave the tomb an overall 'L' shape.

Like the tomb of Thutmoses I, the burial chamber was in the shape of a cartouche, though here there were the remnants of *two* damaged pillars, the rear one of which was severely eroded, having just the top and a pointed base remaining. I examined it closely. I couldn't be one-hundred percent, but it looked to me like water damage. Above, a star pattern on a blue background was still evident on several parts of the ceiling, and, to the right, was a small well cut but undecorated annex.

I focused on the walls of the chamber, which were plastered and painted, with a kheker-frieze, a colourful tight balustrade pattern that resembled close-knit papyrus plants, at the top of the walls, and a band of colour below the decorated area of the wall, though it appears the decoration was never finished. There was a clear line on the wall about six foot from the floor that circumnavigated the chamber, but it was hard to distinguish if this was a definite water mark as there had been considerable work done clearing and 'restoring' the tomb.

Then there was the neglected sarcophagus. Unlike Thutmoses I's splendidly carved sarcophagus, the sarcophagus here was simple; unpolished and undecorated, it was surprisingly offset and pushed against the back wall. The inner coffin, containing his mummy, was long gone; it had been found later within the mummy cache at Deir el-Bahri. It was all telling me something. I stood back and tried to put the pieces together; the damage to the plaster, the water mark, the damaged pillar, and the position of the sarcophagus. Then I got it.

Looking at the damage, it was not hard to reconstruct how water could have rushed in down the corridor, damaging the lower half of the walls, surged against the sarcophagus, thus accounting for its offset position against the back wall, and the damage to the rear wall. As for the severely damaged pillar, I could now see how the curved back wall would have acted like a parabolic mirror and focused the energy of the surging water to a focal point exact where the rear pillar once stood, thus causing rapid erosion of the central part of the pillar. I had my corroborative evidence; well part of it. It meant that this tomb suffered the same fate as KV38.

From all that, and not excluding the possibility it was appropriated later on by someone else, it was fair to assume that KV42 belonged first and foremost to Thutmoses II, and that it had been flooded by the same tsunami that inundated the tomb of his father. Totally pleased with my discovery I hurried to rejoin Pieter and Yuko in KV34.

Climbing the metal staircase was hardly exhausting, it was by no means Everest, but, with the humidity and sun starting to have an effect, it certainly seemed as long to scale. I realized that a trek even further into the desert hills to see the supposed tomb of Amenhotep, KV39, may not be my best option. But just to be sure I checked my notes.

'KV 39 is located at the head of a water course on the

plateau high above the valley, about a half a mile to the south of KV 34. It's a perplexing tomb, not just because of its location, about 200 metres north of an ancient Village, but because of its plan. The undecorated tomb descends in three different directions on three separate axes, each consisting of a series of corridors, two ending in rectangular chambers. The upper components of the tomb are cut in poor quality shale, while the lower corridors and chambers are cut in limestone; although several large cracks or fissures have led to structural damage and rock has fallen away, perhaps because the tomb was seriously damaged by flash flooding in 1994.'

The first thing I gleaned from the notes was that both KV39 and KV34 were dug along part of a water course, and that part of that water course was created by flood water flowing *down* in 1994, but was there an even greater flood, first up by the tsunami, then down, by the water retreating?

'The lower chambers to the east were partly filled with debris, although they are still accessible, while the southern corridors and chamber were completely filled.

Some have argued the tomb belongs to Amenhotep I, including Arthur Weigall, Chief Inspector of Antiquities for Upper Egypt from 1905-11. He based his belief on perceived similarities of position between KV 39 and the description of Amenhotep I's tomb in the tomb robbery papyri.'

To certain extent, I tended to agree with Arthur on some thing, but for totally different reasons, disagreed with him. Firstly, the location high up on the plateau would be consistent with the water level being much higher due to the first Thera tsunami. Secondly, the close proximity of the ancient village would support a rebuilding process soon after the tsunami.

Of course, there *is* the possibility the tomb was some time *after* Thutmoses IV, but that really didn't fit in with either Arthur's thinking, or mine, and I disagreed with the consensus of Egyptologists who said it belonged to Amenhotep, mainly based on the supposed 'robbery papyri', whatever they were. Seriously, someone made a hit list of what tombs they hit and what stash they nicked? If they did, then it could only have been the Amun Priests as they were they only scribes. But maybe it was an inventory list, and the tomb was prepared for Amenhotep, but he never occupied it?

You can see how easy it is to come up with any number of theories, but whether they hold up to scrutiny depends on the peripheral evidence. Anyway, I was now of the opinion Amenhotep left Egypt on a mission of worldwide rebuilding. But the high level of the tomb was a clue, and as far as I was concerned, given Kamose was washed away in the Red Sea chasing Moses, KV39 may well have been the actual tomb of Ahmose. It could even have been the tomb of Seqenenre Tao himself. That said, did I need to climb the mountain in the ever-increasing heat, to examine a damaged tomb with no decorations? No; if needs be I could check it out online when I got back to Australia.

The Tomb of Thutmoses III

The short path that led from the staircase weaved between the steep walls of an elevated gorge and led to the entrance of KV34, where I used my first ticket for the third time and entered the tomb.

A steep descending set of roughly carved steps led to a steep descending corridor, neatly hewn out of the rock but absent of any sort of decoration. That passed into and through an undecorated and roughly cut space comprising recesses on either side of a second set of steep rough-cut and poorly preserved steps. It was like rock-climbing more than tomb-exploring.

A second descending corridor, also lacking decorations, led to a well pit, or ritual shaft, nearly twenty feet deep. The ceiling was decorated with yellow stars on a blue sky-background; the same imagery as that in the burial chamber of KV42, while the walls were whitewashed and topped with the same type of kheker frieze as well. Time for a quick note check.

'The tomb of Thutmoses III was the first time a tomb was decorated by being plastered and then painted, and contained the first true well pit in any tomb in the Valley of the Kings. It's possible use was not just to stop tomb robbers, but to halt any flood waters that may enter the tomb.'

It was not quite true, KV42 was the first tomb with plastered and painted walls, but then if the Egyptologists all thought the tomb belonged to Hatshepsut Meryet-Ra, then it was a simple mistake. It was yet another confirmation that we shouldn't believe everything they tell us as being 'gospel'.

They may well have been right about the well pit being an innovation; though not as a booby trap to stop tomb robbers, but to prevent the flooding of the tomb. And that meant it was another piece of corroborative evidence for the flood. Of course the well pit may have evolved into a robber trap, but if the Priests were doing all the robbing, then it would have been an unnecessary structural device and damn inconvenient. However, if it *was* to protect the loot from water damage until they could get to it, then that made total sense as well.

The following doorway on the opposite side of the well would originally have been sealed and painted to conceal the rest of the tomb. It led to an antechamber set at ninety degrees to the left, just as in KV42, containing two square central pillars. Here is where the decoration really began, for, though the pillars were bare, the ceiling was covered in the same pattern as in the well shaft; yellow stars on a blue night sky. The walls were something different altogether; the overall pattern of the room reminding me of the walls of post boxes at the local post office. Maybe you had to pick the right message to send to the right god at the right time?

'Through the door you arrive into the antechamber, its walls decorated with lists of the seven-hundred-and-forty-one gods of the Underworld; the 1st to the 12th Divisions of the Amduat.'

Seven-hundred-and-forty-one gods? Isn't that a rather specific and particularly large number? 'Curiouser and curiouser', said Alice as she ventured further down the rabbit hole.

Painted on plaster were three distinct sections: at the top, the kheker pattern, below that were three rows of yellow boxes, each containing a white star and what looked like a plant shoot in a pot plant under it. Below that, three rows of black-on-white stick-figure gods in boxes: the figures sketched in a unique early manner much like the writings on papyrus.

At the end of the antechamber, in the left corner, a steep staircase descended to the burial chamber, which was again cartouche-shaped and contained two central pillars. That meant it had the same overall 'L-shaped' structure as that of KV42, as well as a cartouche-shaped burial chamber with two pillars. It confirmed for me that KV42 was a precursor to KV34, and that KV42 had to have belonged to Thutmoses II.

'How was it?'

Pieter and Yuko were at the far end of the tomb, tucked behind the pillars and examining the sarcophagus.

'KV42? It was very similar in structure to this, but not as big and not as developed. There was hardly any decoration, and it looked as it if the whole thing had been trashed in a flood.'

'So a waste of time then?'

'On the contrary, it totally convinced me it was the tomb of Thutmoses II, and that there'd been massive tsunami that flooded the valley and forced Thutmoses III to build his tomb higher up.'

'Wow, that's pretty amazing.'

I chuckled away.

'I'm starting to expect amazing revelations as par for the course.'

Pieter laughed as I moved to examine the pillars, which, unlike the ones in the previous room and tombs, were covered with images.

'On seven sides of the two square pillars of the burial chamber are passages from the "Litany of Re", an important funerary text of the New Kingdom reserved only for pharaohs or very favoured nobility, and written on the inside of the tomb for the deceased.

It's a two part composition; the first part invoking the sun, Ra, in 75 different forms, the second, a series of prayers in which the pharaoh is praised for his union with nature, the sun god, and other deities.

On the eighth side there is an abridged version of the *Amduat*, plus scenes showing the Pharaoh with his three wives and a daughter, as well as a unique scene showing the pharaoh being suckled by a divine tree goddess called "Isis".'

As in the ante-chamber, the walls of the burial chamber were similarly decorated; with a kheker frieze at the top, and three or four rows containing the 'Book of Amduat' below, designed like a huge ornamental scroll circling the room.

'Do you know what it means, Alex?'

'The ancient Egyptians called it the *Amduat*, the *Book of the Secret Chamber* or *that which there is in the afterlife*. It supposedly represents the twelve hours of night from dusk to dawn, and the journey of the pharaoh's soul towards his rebirth the afterlife.'

'Do you know where it starts?'

I looked around, not really having a clue, finally going to my notes hoping for some more about the *Amduat*.

'The 1st hour begins when the dying sun slips beneath the horizon. The pharaoh unites with the sun god Re and enters the netherworld on his solar boat, where he is greeted by gods, goddesses, baboons, and fire-breathing serpents.'

There were so many images of solar boats and serpents I didn't know where to start.

'Let's split up. Look for a scarab on a boat, that's the travelling sun, lots of baboons, and a boat with a ram-headed god on it next to lots of different gods.'

'Here it is.'

Yuko had found it straight away, on the side wall beside the door to one of four undecorated annexes to the chamber. There were serpents leading the boat, serpents underneath, there were serpents everywhere. Were these the reptilians in the fourth dimension?

'In the 2nd hour, guided by Hathor, the sun god journeys through the netherworld accompanied by other boats carrying other gods through the Field of Wernes, where the sun god grants lands to the blessed dead so as he can cultivate super sized crops.'

'That's here, next to it on the right.'

Pieter was right, clearly the text ran clockwise around the room.

'More boats accompany the sun god through the 3rd hour and the Waters of Osiris. In the upper row, baboons, Anubis, and other gods rejoice over the light the sun has brought them, whilst in the lower row, Osiris, lord of the underworld, is preceded by a cluster of bird-headed gods, knives in hand, ready to slay enemies of the sun god who lurk in the underworld and threaten to impede his progress.'

It was like reading the world's first comic book, plastered on the walls over thirty-four-hundred years ago. I was fascinated; we all were.

'In the 4th hour, obstacles begin to appear, as a zigzag path blocks Re's descent through the Land of Sokar. The waters have dried up, and the sun boat must be towed across a desert. The boat now has snake's head at the bow and stern as it has magically become a serpent that can slither across sand. In the middle row, ibis-headed Thoth, god of wisdom, hands the eye of the sun to falcon-headed Sokar for safekeeping, while other deities stand ready to thwart enemies of the sun god.'

I had to admit I was getting a little preoccupied with the imagery, and who could blame me as across the entrance, and on to the side wall, was a three-headed snake, a three-headed winged snake and the winged disc of Nibiru in the sky. Was there also a connection between the underworld, the Dracos, and Nibiru? Were there hidden clues within the text of the *Amduat*? We pressed on.

'Through the 5th hour, the sun-god's boat is towed around the secret cavern of Sokar, guarded by a double-headed sphinx, and sealed with the head of Isis. Inside, Sokar clutches the wings of a multi-headed serpent. Together they hold back the hidden chaos that threatens to block the sun-god's passage. In the centre of the top row is the burial mound of Osiris, from which a scarab beetle, symbol of the rejuvenated sun, emerges to help pull the tow rope.'

'That's not what's here.'

Pieter was right; the images were nothing like what was supposed to be in the fifth hour.

'Maybe it's wrong?'

Yuko had another thought.

'Maybe it's somewhere else?'

While Pieter and I scratched our heads trying to make the wall texts match up with my notes, Yuko went exploring.

'Here it is.'

It was almost directly on the opposite side of the room, back before where we had started. Why? None of us really had a clue, but Pieter threw an idea up for consideration.

'Do you think it might have something to do with gravity? I mean the sun, Khepri, is emerging from the mound of Osiris to help pull on the tow rope; the sun exerts a gravitational pull, so was there some relevance to the position of the sun relevant to the fifth hour of the evening?'

'It might; it's as good an answer as we'll find I guess. Maybe it will all become clearer in the sixth hour.'

'The 6th hour is the realm of Sobek, the crocodile god. At midnight, the soul of the sun god, Re, unites with his corpse, represented by the horizontal figure at far right, and protected by a five-headed serpent. This corpse was also understood to be the body of all those who had died. Thus, the union of Re's soul with his corpse brings light and eternal life to all of the blessed dead.'

The sixth hour spread up and over the side doorway, back to where we had started. What intrigued me most was the five-headed snake wrapped around the figure. Why five heads, and why protecting?

'Now where to; we're back where we started?'

As Yuko started exploring the rest of the room, I scanned my notes.

'In the 7th hour, the sun god, Re, confronts his archenemy, the serpent Apophis, who swallows the waters carrying the sun boat.'

It hit me like lighting.

'Whoa, Apophis, that's Apopi.'

'Who's he?'

'He was the Hyksos pharaoh responsible for the death of Seqenenre, and ultimately the beginning of the New Kingdom. The *Amduat* only came about in the 18th Dynasty, and must be a direct response to the murder and then resurrection of Seqenenre. It means the *Amduat* was probably created by his son, Ahmose, and passed on through Thumoses I and II.'

Meanwhile, Yuko was searching the opposite wall for the next part of the story.

'What does the seventh hour look like?'

'In the top row, Osiris sits on a throne, encircled by the protective Mehen snake-god, and watches as a god with cat ears decapitates and punish enemies. In the centre, the solar barque, containing several gods, including Isis holding her raised hand and hurling magical spells, approaches the snake god, Apophis, who has already been tied down indicating he is no longer a threat. In the bottom register, Horus presides over twelve gods and twelve goddesses, each crowned with stars, symbolizing the twelve hours of the night.'

'Here it is, back where the fourth hour finished?'

As we returned to the other side of the chamber, I let my mouth run off in Pieter's direction.

'If Apophis, or Apopi, was seen as the threat, then that would account for two different sets of snakes, one protective, the other dangerous.'

'Which is which?'

'The Hyksos must have been the threat, which meant the Dracos were the protectors.'

That sat strangely with me, and it did with Pieter as well.

'Why would the Dracos protect us?'

Then I got it.

'They would want to protect their investment in their genetic engineering program.'

'You may well be right.'

It seemed there was more in this *Amduat* than I had at first thought.

'What does the rest say?'

Yuko was just as curious as Pieter and I were to discover more, and continuing on from the seventh hour, beginning before the first of the two left side annexes, and spanning the first door, sat the next hour.

'The 8th hour signifies that the hours of greatest danger have passed. Re provides the deceased with shining white linen clothing to wear in the next life, whilst in the top and bottom rows, deities sit on hieroglyphs for cloth, derived from the shape of a loom.'

'Nothing special there.'

Or was there? Was the shining white linen cloth a direct reference to the white cloth used to wrap Jesus, the Shroud of Turin of Jacques de Molay, and used in the Templar rituals? We moved on, the texts leading directly onto the ninth hour, starting above the door into the second annex and continuing beyond it.

'At the 9th hour, Re, on his boat, and preceded by his crew of oarsmen, brings provisions of clothing and food for those in the afterworld. In the bottom row, three baskets topped by deities hold infinite supplies of bread and beer, while fire-spewing cobras protect the sun god and illuminate his path through the darkness.'

Pieter got it now.

'I can just see how the Dracos would keep providing food for the humans so that they would always be available as a gene pool from which to carry out their experiments.'

Curving around and into the back wall, was the tenth hour.

'In the upper row of the 10th hour, numerous deities protect and escort the solar disk, the eye of the sun. In the middle row, barques containing the souls of Osiris and Sokar appear in front of the sun boat, along with bodyguards whose heads are in the shape of sun disks. In the lowest row, the god Horus assures figures drifting in the primeval waters, those who have drowned in the Nile, that they will find bliss in the afterlife even though they had not received proper burial.'

That really got me thinking

'I wonder if that's a specific reference to all those who died in the tsunami; including Kamose?'

'Tsunami? You said that before, what tsunami?'

I forgot, that was a discussion I'd had with Bill and the others.

'I think the end of the 17th Dynasty was partly caused by the Thera eruption and a giant tsunami that surged across the Mediterranean, into the Nile Delta, and hundreds of miles up the Nile.'

Yuko got it straight away.

'That would have to be massive, but then again the Thera eruption was big enough to cause just that.'

'Do you think there's more about it in the *Amduat*?'

'There's one way to find out.'

As I read from my notes, Pieter and Yuko examined the back wall.

'At the 11th hour, in preparation for sunrise, the god Atum, upper left, holds a winged serpent who is about to devour ten stars symbolizing the ten hours of the night that have elapsed. The sun-god's boat in the middle row now bears a red sun disk on its bow. It is preceded by twelve men carrying the protective serpent believed to encircle the world. The semicircular shapes in the bottom row are pits, into which knife-wielding goddesses have tossed the dismembered bodies of the sun-god's enemies. This gruesome punishment was thought to explain the blood-red colour of the rising sun.'

They shook their heads.

'Nothing obvious, but I like the explanation for the colour of the rising sun.'

'But I think there's something in the winged serpent devouring ten stars, and the red disk on the boat's bow, that relates to Nibiru.'

'I think you're right. Any ideas?'

'Not yet. Perhaps the dawn will throw some light on things.'

It was a predictable quip, but Pieter and Yuko seemed to appreciate the spontaneity of it.

'The 12th hour is the hour of the sun-god's rebirth. In the upper and lower rows, gods raise their hands in jubilation, as in the middle row, the sun-god's boat is preceded by the snake known as the World Encircler, brought along in the previous hour. The towline held by gods and goddesses passes through the head of the snake to indicate that the sun god is pulled through the snake's body, from the tail to the mouth, and emerges rejuvenated as the scarab beetle, the sun-god's morning manifestation. Shu, god of air, will lift the sun out of the darkness while a mummified Osiris remains in the underworld.'

We all looked at each other, sharing a twinge of disappointment, before Yuko had a brainwave.

'Wait a minute. The World Encircler; do you think that could be some sort of force field, to protect the planet from the effects of Nibiru's passing?'

'It's possible, and it makes sense, but who put it there, how did it operate, and where is it now?'

'I guess we can't have all the answers handed to us on a platter.'

That was certainly the case, but it sparked Pieter's thinking as well.

'If it *was* a force field, do you think that being pulled through the snake's body, could be some sort of wormhole?'

'Could be, but *from*, or *to*, where, that's the question.

'I suppose we'd better move on, and see if we can find some answers elsewhere.'

'You go ahead; I haven't had a chance to examine the sarcophagus yet. It shouldn't take long and I'll be right behind you.'

'We can wait.'

'No, by the time you get down to the valley floor, I'll be biting at your heels like an over-enthusiastic kelpie pup harassing a herd of Poll Herefords.'

They laughed and headed off, as I turned my attention to the sarcophagus beside me. Though it had been partly damaged by the removal of its lid, the red granite sarcophagus was truly exquisite. Lavishly decorated, with numerous figures of Egyptian deities, it was probably the finest example of ancient Egyptian design and craftsmanship. The goddess, Nut, was carved on the outer surfaces of the lid, which was propped open with several blocks all round. Peering inside, I used the light from my iphone to illuminate the interior of the sarcophagus. On the inner surface of the lid, and also on the inside bottom of the sarcophagus, were more carvings of Nut.

I could make out some of the figures on the exterior of the sarcophagus, but, as I made a circle around it, deferred to my notes.

'Carved in the foot of the sarcophagus is an image of Isis kneeling on the symbol for gold. The right side contains images of Qebehsenuef, Anubis, and a pair of Wadjet-eyes up near the head to allow the mummy to look out. Moving round to the head of the sarcophagus, there is an image of a kneeling Nephthys, whilst the left side exhibits images of Anubis and Hapy, with another pair of Wadjet-eyes between them, again to allow the mummy to look out.

However, Thutmoses III's mummy was not found here, bur rather at Deir el-Bahri in tomb DB 320 in 1881. It is also possible that the tomb of Thutmoses III was used for a short while by Priests of the 21st Dynasty before being left empty.'

Well, if the Priests 'used' it in the 21st Dynasty, that fitted in exactly with my theory; the question was, 'what did they use it *for*?'. My guess was, that as the tomb was so remote and inaccessible, they used it to store the loot and coffins they had removed from the other tombs in the valley, until they could make arrangements to break down the stash, melt down the inner coffins of gold and silver, and shift the mummies across the hill top and into DB 320.

Hanging round here wasn't going to turn up any more clues, so I high-tailed back through the tomb and down the metal staircase, where I caught up with Pieter and Yuko just as they arrived at the valley floor.

'Done!'

'Where are you heading now?'

'I'm off to KV 35, the tomb of Amenhotep II, then Horemheb, KV20 which is Hatshepsut's tomb, and then KV43, the tomb of Thutmoses IV. What about you?'

'The tomb of Ramses VI, and then Tutankhamun.'

'Then let's pound the pavement.'

The Mysterious Smenkhkare

It was just passed 10:00 am and the thermometer was rapidly climbing. I was glad I wasn't doing the same, to KV39, but, all things considered, we were still making good time.

'Alex?'

'Yep'

'Pieter and I were just talking. Do you think Akhenaten left Egypt because Nefertiti died.'

'Nefertiti didn't die, not in Egypt anyway.'

'What do you mean?'

If there was one subject I knew inside and out, it was Akhenaten, his life, and his family.

'According to the Egyptologists, about three years before Akhenaten supposedly dies, Nefertiti disappears from the record, while at the same time Akhenaten's co-regent and probable immediate successor, Smenkhkare, appears.'

Pieter thought he had it worked out.

'So Nefertiti and Smenkhkare are one and the same person.'

'No, I don't think they were. Akhenaten's co-regent's name was Neferneferuaten; a name also bestowed on Nefertiti earlier in the Amarna period. Further evidence of her elevation to kingly status comes from the Coregency Stela; seven limestone stela-fragments found in a tomb at Amarna dating from late in the 18th Dynasty, which shows Akhenaten, Nefertiti and Meritaten.

Some time after the stela was made, Nefertiti's name had been chiselled out and replaced with Ankhkheperure Neferneferuaten, the name of Akhenaten's co-regent. At the same time Meritaten's name was replaced with that of Ankhesenpaaten, Akhenaten and Nefertiti's third daughter.'

'So who was Smenkhkare then, I thought Smenkhkare was a male?'

'I think he was as well.'

Pieter screwed up his face.

'I'm confused.'

So was Yuko.

The idea was still fairly new to me, so I tried to explain it as concisely as possible, not just for them, but for me as well.

'As you suggested, Akhenaten intended to leave Egypt, so he prepared the way by appointing Nefertiti co-regent, Then a few years later, when he actually left Egypt, he appointed Amenhotep IV to act as Nefertiti's co-regent in his place, anticipating Nefertiti would eventually join him. I think it's then that Amenhotep IV assumed the name Smenkhkare.'

'But wasn't Amenhotep IV, Akhenaten? Didn't they find his mummy?'

'No. Many of the so-called *experts* originally believed the mummy found in KV 55, in the tomb of Queen Tiye, is Smenkhkare, a younger son of Amenhotep III and Queen Tiye, and therefore must be a younger brother of Akhenaten. They believe he was Akhenaten's co-regent and immediate successor, and predecessor of Tutankhamun. And for the most part they were right.'

'But didn't they do some genetic tests on the mummies and confirmed the body found in the tomb was Tutankhamun's father?'

'Yes, they did, early in 2010, via DNA; they confirmed the body found in KV55 was the father of Tutankhamun, and the son of Amenhotep III and Queen Tiye. And that was the part they got correct. But then they *assumed,* and thus erroneously concluded, that the mummy was most likely that of Akhenaten, even though the mummy bore absolutely no likeness to any of Akhenaten's statues or images. The mummy was actually Amenhotep IV, who also chose the name of Smenkhkare when he became co-regent with Nefertiti.

You see that's where all the confusion comes about, because the *experts* think Amenhotep IV and Akhenaten were the same person, and they weren't. Akhenaten was Annunaki, one of the gods who came back to Egypt to rebuild it.'

'And what happened to Smenkhkare?'

'Smenkhkare, or Amenhotep IV, died soon after Nefertiti left Egypt, so his son Tutankhamun, as rightful heir, was chosen by the Amun Priests to marry the remaining *sang réal, Nefertiti's daughter,* Ankhesenaten, and ascended the throne.'

Yuko was putting it together.

'So, if Nefertiti was the *sang réal*, then when she left Egypt, she would have left the throne in the hands of her daughter, Ankhesenaten.'

'Yes, who was then married off to her cousin, Tutankhamun, because he was the son of Amenhotep IV; the one who the priests naturally appointed as pharaoh when Nefertiti departed. But the High Priest, Ay, conspired to reclaim the previous power of the Amun Priests and usurp the throne.

Firstly he convinced Ankhesenaten and Tutankhaten to change their names to Ankhesenamun and Tutankhamun, then he plotted and waited for the opportunity to seize the power of the throne for himself.'

Yuko was now one step ahead of me.

'And when Akhenaten discovered what had happened with the death of Tutankhamun, and Ankhesenamun's subsequent marriage to Ay, he didn't rush back to Egypt, he turned his back on the corruption nation and focused on establishing the philosophies and knowledge of the Tat Brotherhood in the Mycenaean civilization.'

'Brilliant!'

Brilliant? It was fucking awesomely history changing! And though I was sure there was much more to discuss, we'd stopped at the fork in the paths just outside Horemheb's tomb, and it was time to split once again.

'I'm off up this way.'

'And the tombs of Ramses VI and Tutankhamun are back in the main square.'

'OK then, if I don't see you by the time you are ready to leave, don't wait, I'll either catch up with you along the road at Hatshepsut's temple, at the Winter Palace for drinks with Bill and Pernille at 5:00, or later tonight at the hotel.'

'OK, have a great day.'

'Will do.'

Pieter and Yuko smiled, waved, then set off hand-in-hand down the hill while I headed up the path in the other direction; next stop, KV35.

The tomb of Amenhotep II

I did a quick check on my notes.

'Amenhotep II was the son of Thutmoses III. His tomb is cut into the bottom of the cliff face and is considered one of the best-completed tombs in the valley.'

Its position at the base of the cliff face, but still elevated, indicated that the flood waters must has subsided considerably in the twenty-four years since his father died.

'KV35 was the only tomb besides that of Tutankhamun where the mummy of the king was found intact in its sarcophagus. The mummies of Amenhotep II, his son Websenu, and probably his mother Hatshepsut Meryet-Ra were found, together with a cache of 11 mummies discovered in the annexes to the burial chamber including: Thutmoses IV, Amenhotep III,

Merenptah, Seti II, Siptah, Ramses IV, Ramses V, Ramses VI, an anonymous female called the "Elder Woman" (who some think is Tiy, the wife of Amenhetep III), and a further mummy, probably Setnakht. The mummies were placed there sometime in the 21st Dynasty and remained undisturbed until they were discovered by Victor Loret in 1898.'

There it was again, confirmation of the Amun Priests breaking into the temples. They could only have had one reason, to rob them. Some mummies were stashed in KV34, and then moved across the ridge later to DB320, others in KV35, who were either forgotten, or left in situ.

I headed down the modern metal steps into the mud-brick enclosure built to protect the tomb from water damage in 1994. The sign over the door was in French, *Tombeau d'Amenphis II decouvert et deblaye par le service des Antiquites MDCCCXCVIII* and said something about being discovered in 1898 for the Antiquities Service.

Not many visitors trekked up to the end of the path to visit KV35, so, as the guardian emerged from the entrance to greet me, I decided to once again roll the dice with my bribery skills. I was pleased with myself, as I was successful again, though this time it cost me fifteen pounds.

The entrance led to a well-cut but undecorated descending corridor, followed by an undecorated steep stairwell flanked by wide recesses. That led to another shorter descending corridor, well-cut, but still undecorated, which in turn ran into the well pit. The walls were plastered but still undecorated, and, looking down, it had an opening at the base that appeared to connect to another chamber or corridor. If it was important, I'm sure the Egyptians would have made it accessible, which they hadn't.

Across the pit, the doorway opened up into a two-pillared undecorated ante-chamber set at right angles to the left, with a modern wooden floor and a descending staircase in the back left corner; the tomb was appearing to be structurally just like those of Thutmoses II and III. The descending stairs in the corner were covered with a modern metal staircase leading to a short sloping corridor, and then to the burial chamber, also paved with a modern wooden floor.

This was the only part of the tomb that was decorated, and it was a step up from the burial chamber of his father. The ceiling had the similar starred ceiling, and the walls contained both the kheker frieze and 'Amduat', starting this time in the back left corner and moving continuously clockwise around the chamber. The difference was the artwork: it was beautiful: more refined and colourful than the 'Amduat' in the tomb of Thutmoses III.

The chamber itself was divided into two levels: an upper section with a double row of three pillars; and a lower 'sunken' section, reached by a central set of stairs, that covered about a third of the chamber and contained the sarcophagus. There were four side chambers, two to the left and two to the right, sealed and no longer accessible. Checking my notes, it was in these two right side annexes that the cache of mummies was found.

'Nine royal mummies, wrappings intact, laying in poorly preserved coffins arranged in two rows, were found in one, and the unwrapped mummies of two women and one young man in the other. Though the mummies have survived, many other artefacts found in the tomb have since disappeared, or rather been stolen, including a four-metre long, three-and-a-half-thousand year old boat made of cedar wood.'

How the hell does a four-metre boat just disappear? Maybe it was sealed in one of the annexes? And a boat! It gave support to my theory of the tsunami.

On the upper level, in the central part of the chamber, were the six pillars protected by glass panels. They were decorated with exquisite 'life-size' paintings of Amenhotep II receiving the ankh of life respectively from Osiris, Hathor and Anubis.

The fine art work continued on the sarcophagus; situated in the centre of the lower section of the chamber, on two large calcite blocks set in a pit in the floor. Made of yellow quartzite, the sarcophagus of Amenhotep II was decorated exactly the same as Thutmoses III's; kneeling images of Isis and Nephthys on either end, and, on one side, images of Imsety, Anubis, and Duamutef, with Qebensenuef, Anubis and Hapy on the other, both with the ever present pair of Wadjet-eyes.

I'd only spent about fifteen minutes in the tomb, but it was all I needed to confirm my ideas. As I retraced my steps I also retraced my thoughts; the imagery was more developed than in the earlier tombs of the 18th Dynasty, but not as elaborate as the decorations in the tomb of Tausert, from the end of the 19th Dynasty. Now it was time to move on, the question was, 'where to?'

Over the hill and far away

Exiting the tomb, I looked back at the shear cliff face behind me; somewhere over the hill in the next valley were the tombs of Amenhotep III and Ay. I had to make a decision; I really wanted to see them, but it was more than just a fair hike; at least half-an-hour there and half-an-hour back, and not only didn't I have the luxury of time to spare, there was a distinct possibility I wouldn't be able to get in to one or possibly both of them. I checked my notes again hoping to get an inkling of whether to go or not.

'The entrance to the tomb of Amenhotep III is cut in the side of the hill below a cliff face midway into the West Valley. Its plan is very similar to the tombs of Thutmoses III, KV34, Amenhotep II, KV35, and Thutmoses IV, KV 43, consisting of two descending undecorated corridors, separated by a stairwell, which leads to a well shaft with a side chamber dug off from the bottom.

The ceiling is painted with yellow stars on a blue background and a kheker frieze runs across the top of the walls, themselves almost completely decorated with scenes of Hathor, Anubis and Osiris with Amenhotep III on one wall, while Nut takes the place of Hathor on the other. Every representation of Amenhotep III has a vulture, representing the goddess Nekhbet and the *ka* of the king's father, Thutmoses IV, hovering over the king's head. Unfortunately the scenes are poor in quality; in several instances, the face of the king has been cut out.'

There was nothing new so far that inspired me to impersonate Lawrence of Arabia.

'The well shaft leads to a two-pillared chamber set at right angles to the left of the entrance with a staircase in the rear left corner that leads down to a corridor, another set of stairs to a small ante-chamber decorated with scenes of the king receiving life from Hathor, Nut, the Western Goddess, Anubis, Hathor and Osiris, several of them damaged, lost, or removed.

That leads into the burial chamber, set at ninety degrees to the right, which has six pillars in two rows on the upper level, and a short stairway between the rear rows leading down to the actual sunken burial crypt. Surrounding the chamber are five annexes, two on each side and one off the rear wall.'

Apart from the right-angled setting, it had the same basic structure as the tomb of Amenhotep II, so, unless there was some surprise in the chamber itself, I could forgo the safari.

'Most of the ceiling plaster has fallen away, but what remains shows it was once decorated with yellow stars on a blue background. The walls are plastered and decorated with a kheker frieze at the top, and the complete Amduat below; beginning on the left end of the front wall and proceeding clockwise around the chamber and rendered in a cursive style. However, much of the plaster has crumbled away from the lower parts of the walls because of salt leeching through the walls.

Decorated with images of the king before such deities as Hathor, Osiris, the Western Goddess, and Anubis, the pillars also have salt damage and are badly cracked, so in places have lost their painted plaster or have had the faces cut out by vandals.'

Nothing in the chamber so far convinced me to go. There was only the sarcophagus left.

'Decorated with images of Nephthys and Isis on either end, with Anubis and the four sons of Horus on the sides, the cartouche-shaped red granite sarcophagus and its lid had been vandalized in antiquity but reconstructed from the surviving pieces.

The king would have been placed inside the sarcophagus in a series of gilded and inlaid anthropoid wooden coffins, with the inner coffin and mask probably made of solid gold. The inner coffin is possibly evidenced by a superb cobra head of lapis lazuli, with inlaid eyes set in gold, found in the debris of the antechamber, which appears to come from a mask or coffin, and from wooden fragments of an inner coffin found at the base of the well shaft.

There is evidence of intrusive burials, probably of the Third Intermediate Period, with the mummy of the king being moved to the cache in KV 35 during the reign of Smendes, at the beginning of the 21st Dynasty.'

There again was proof that the 21st Dynasty Theban priests broke into the tombs of the previous dynasties and robbed them; I had everything I needed from Amenhotep III. I wondered if Ay would be similarly supportive.

The Tomb of Ay

'KV 23 has a fairly straight axis, though the burial chamber is offset. It is entered by a rock-cut stairway descending into two corridors separated by a badly damaged and steep stairwell The second corridor leads to a small chamber, usually the location of the well shaft, though here it was not cut into the floor.'

That made sense; if the priests were doing the robbing, it is more than likely Ay, as the first High Priest to become pharaoh, either would have left very little treasure in his tomb, or known it would be robbed, and thus didn't bother excavating a well shaft. Or perhaps he didn't have time, as the well shaft would have been the very last thing excavated.

Conversely, if the purpose of the shaft was to prevent water damage, building high up in the mountain would negate that aspect as well.

'The burial chamber is set ninety degrees to the right, and the only decorated chamber in the tomb.'

The offset chamber could mean the tomb was unfinished and the burial chamber originally would have been intended as the pillared chamber, but the annex off to the side sort of negated that theory somewhat, for if they added the annex after Ay's death, then surely they would have finished all the decorations.

'The decoration in the burial chamber is stylistically similar and thematically similar to that in KV62, the tomb of his predecessor Tutankhamun. It contains scenes from the first hour of the *Amduat*, the *Book of the Dead*, and representations of the king in unusual scenes such as fishing, hippopotamus hunting, and fowling, alone enough to justify a visit to the tomb.'

Not for me it wasn't.

'Other decorations include Nephthys standing behind a solar boat carrying the nine gods of the Ennead; Re-Horakhty, Atum, Shu, Tefnut, Geb, Nut, Osiris, Isis and Horus, plus the four sons of Horus flanking an offering table; Duamutef and Qebhsenuef wearing the crowns of Upper Egypt, and Imsety and Hapy wearing the crowns of Lower Egypt. Sadly, parts of the decoration have been lost; in some instances simply because the stone has fallen away, others as a result of deliberate damage to the figures and names of the king.'

That didn't tell me much: other than Ay was trying to cover all the bases and lick ass with all the gods.

'The king's red quartzite sarcophagus is very similar to Tutankhamun's, with two pairs of wadjet-eyes on the lid and carved images of Isis, Nephthys, Serqet and Neith at its corners protecting the deceased. It was found in large fragments, repaired and returned to the burial chamber in 1994, but Ay's mummy has never been found.

At an unknown date or dates in antiquity, the images and names of Ay were hacked out from the wall paintings, the southeast side of the sarcophagus was smashed and the lid overturned on the floor.'

That had to be the handiwork of someone who was either not too happy with the fact Ay was an Amun Priest and not a legitimate ruler, or someone acting in retaliation for being double-crossed. It might have been interesting, but it was hardly sufficient motivation to lure me across the desert hills on my own to some isolated tomb in a valley far away. But, it did spark my curiosity about who that certain 'someone' might have been, and the finger pointed straight at Horemheb.

So, with a desert trek now ruled out, I took a few deep swallows from the first bottle of water in my backpack and decided it was time to return to the end of the 18th Dynasty and visit KV57, the tomb of Horemheb.

The Military King

Arriving down the path, a modern shelter covered the tomb entrance, which sat at the base of a gently sloping hill. I realized I had no chance to bribe the guard, as there were too many people coming and going. So, it was out with ticket number two, and into the tomb, down the cut but undecorated stepped entry, and passing beneath a deep overhang, into the first corridor.

As I descended the finely-cut but bare and steep passage, I focused on Horemheb. He wasn't supposedly related to any of the earlier pharaohs of the 18th Dynasty, though he did supposedly serve in the court of Akhenaten as a royal scribe, and as a general of the armies during the reigns of Tutankhamun and Ay. Just the fact he made the massive jump from scribe to general of the armies said a hell of a lot about his drive, ambition, and dare I say it, opportunism.

A second descending stairway, with recesses in the walls had been covered with a modern stairwell that made life considerably easier. That negotiated, it led to a second corridor and a continuation of my thinking.

With Akhenaten out of Egypt, Horemheb must have seen the opportunity, with the boy king on the throne, of positioning himself as ruler of the armies. That in itself must have been quite a coup, as I doubt the military would have promoted a pen-pusher to such an auspicious position, and I doubt he could have made such a bold move without the support of someone important. Perhaps it was Ay and the Amun priests?

Perhaps Horemheb bribed someone, or blackmailed them, or maybe he murdered someone? All plausible theories, but perhaps the most logical reason was that Horemheb married into the lineage of the *sang réal.*

Horemheb's first wife was Armenia, a noble woman who died before Horemheb assumed the throne, no there was big deal there, however, his second wife, Mutnodjnet, was Nefertiti's younger sister, and that made her part of the *sang réal,* and that would be a perfect reason for why he was appointed to the throne.

I checked the files on my iphone for any information on Mutnodjnet. It seemed not every Egyptologist believed there was evidence to support the assertion Mutnodjnet and Nefertit were sisters, or, if they were, that it was even relevant. According to my notes, the Egyptologist Geoffrey Martin believes:

'... even if she were the sister of Nefertiti, her marriage to Horemheb would have had no effect on Horemheb's legitimacy or candidacy since Mutnodjmet (who is depicted in the private tombs at El-Amarna) was not herself of royal blood."

Well, Mr. Martin, I begged to differ. Sometimes I wondered where these guys got off when the evidence was right under their noses? One of Mutnodjnet's many titles was '*iryt-p't*' meaning 'Hereditary Princess'; if that wasn't direct evidence of a *sang réal* then I don't know what is. And it would totally explain why her image was on the wall of the tomb at Amarna, she was Akhenaten's sister-in-law. I wondered, was Pernille Mutnodjnet? If she was, who was Bill, surely not Horemheb?

Anyway, it perfectly explained why, with the death of Ay, and probably Ankhesenamun as she had refused to marry Horemheb because he was a commoner, that with Nefertiti and her remaining daughters having left Egypt for Greece, it left Mutnodjnet as the eldest, and possibly sole remaining female of the *sang réal.* And *that* explained why, as her husband, Horemheb was crowned first as '*iry-pat*', the Hereditary Prince, as Ankhesenamun first was not of childbearing age, then had not produced a live male offspring, as is evidenced by the foetal mummies found in Tutankhamun's tomb, and then, when Ay died, Horemheb was crowned as pharaoh.

Sang réal confirmed, although it did raise the question of Horemheb's successor, Paramesse, but I would jump that hurdle in due course, for now, I enthusiastically motored on.

At the end of the corridor was a now familiar well shaft, again decorated with a star pattern on the ceiling, kheker frieze around the top of the walls, and representations of various deities: on the left, Hathor, Isis, Osiris and Horus, with Horus presenting Horemheb to Isis, while to the right, Hathor, Anubis, Osiris and Horus, with Anubis seated on shrine, while Horemheb offers wine to Hathor.

The decorations were much more sophisticated and colourful than many of the earlier tombs, and more in keeping with those of Tausert. Obviously they had been created by more skillful artists, who had varied the stances, gestures, and clothing of the figures.

There was also a more extensive use of colour, with multicoloured hieroglyphs and blue-green backgrounds. In particular I noted the representation of Osiris, again with green skin, and of Hathor with yellow skin. This was in contrast to the brown skin of Horemheb, Horus and Anubis. Were they different races? Certainly. Were they from different planets? That was an entirely different question.

Looking down, the shaft had an opening in the base that appeared to connect to another chamber or corridor, as had the shaft in KV35. Again, if it was important, then the Egyptians would have made it accessible. But maybe it had some specific purpose. I checked my notes, but didn't find any reference to it other than its existence, so pushed on across the modern bridge that spanned the well shaft. It led to another familiar structure; a two-pillared hall.

The chamber was well cut, but undecorated, and the two pillars showed signs of extensive damage. There was even a staircase that descended from the back left corner. But the main difference to the previous tombs of the early 18th Dynasty was, that the chamber wasn't set at right angles to the preceding corridors; it continued straight on into the mountain. That surprised me, so I checked in with my 'bible'.

'The chamber following the well shaft exhibits an architectural innovation: its long axis is roughly parallel to the axis of the upper corridors.'

Supposedly this 'parallel axes concept' was an innovation. Come on guys, you really expect us to buy that? Wouldn't it seem the opposite were true? Wouldn't it seem the most logical structure, given suitable rock, was to keep digging in a straight line? Did you ever for one second consider there could have been something specific about the left turn? Maybe it had some special spiritual implication that the builders of Horemheb's tomb were unaware of?

So maybe it was an oversight. Or maybe, if the tombs were built and overseen by the Amun priests, they *were* aware of its significance, but because Horemheb wasn't a 'legitimate' ruler, they omitted it deliberately? Seriously, since when has a straight line been an 'innovation' over a right angle?

As I stepped down the next staircase, fitted with modern rails, and then travelled along the walkway through the following descending and undecorated corridor, the double-cross of Horemheb's tomb structure got me thinking about more possible conspiracies. Maybe, when Nefertiti left Egypt, Horemheb conspired with Ay to bring about the demise of the Amarna Period, and together they were responsible for the death of Smenkhkare (Amenhotep IV), most probably from poisoning? Had the Egyptologists done a toxicology examination on the mummy of Smenkhkare? I don't think so.

That led to another staircase and corridor, when I thought, 'Why wait a further eight years to eliminate Tutankhamun?'. No, it was more likely that Smenkhkare died naturally, and then, with Tutankhamun ascending the throne, that's when Horemheb would have conspired with Ay to remove Tutankhamun from the throne and end the Amarna period and the worship of the Aten.

Perhaps they did a deal; Ay was to be pharaoh for 'so' many years and he would then appoint Horemheb as his successor. Or maybe Horemheb was to be named pharaoh and Ay double-crossed him while he was away on military manoeuvres by seizing the opportunity to marry the *sang réal*; Tutankhamun's widow and Nefertiti's daughter, Ankhesenamun? Ankhesenamun's refusal to marry Horemheb may also have played a part, in that it pissed off Horemheb's ego.

Horemheb's common birth and embattled ego would all explain the defacing of Ay's tomb, the smashing of the sarcophagus, and why Ay's mummy has never been found. So many questions started running through my mind. One thing was certain; it was clearly a time of great political change in Egypt.

Eventually though, secure in his new position as leader of the armies, and as spouse to the sole remaining *sang réal*, Horemheb became the first 'military' man to ascend the throne, and that was to have massive impact through the 19th and 20th

Dynasties. I wondered what further tit-bits awaited in the burial chamber? But I had to wait a little longer to find out, as the corridor opened into a small ante-chamber, with images of Horemheb embraced by Hathor on the door jams.

The room itself was ablaze with colour; the star patterned ceiling, the kheker frieze, and wonderful full size images of Horemheb with numerous deities; Hathor, Horus, Anubis, Isis, Ptah, Osiris and one other god I couldn't identify. It was stunning. On the door jams exiting the small room were figures of Ma'at, again with yellow skin like Hathor. I couldn't wait to see what the burial chamber was like, but, when I stepped through the door, I couldn't believe my eyes; what an anti-climax, the burial chamber was virtually bereft of colour.

Like the burial chamber of Amenhotep II, the chamber here was also divided in two: the first section containing three pairs of pillars, some of which showed evidence of being restored, which means they were damaged in the past, and a lower section, reached by a gently sloping ramp between the three pairs of pillars and a subsequent central set of stairs. As I circled the room there were five side chambers, used to store funerary equipment; two in the left wall, the furthest one with a beautiful relief of Osiris painted over a thin wash directly on the wall surface, again with his green skin. A further annex led off from the right left corner of the back wall, and another two in the right wall.

There were decorations around the walls, but they looked unfinished, left in various stages of completion, from preliminary sketches in red, with black corrections over laid, to a finished painted relief in the near left corner. What was that all about?

'This is the first tomb in the Valley of the Kings that included the *Book of the Gates*, a text describing the nightly journey of the sun-god through the underworld. The decoration is of particular interest here not only for the innovative subject matter, but that its unfinished nature shows the different stages in the work of the artists.'

OK, here they were at it again, those 'experts'. Why on earth would the burial chamber be left undecorated, other chambers perhaps, but not the burial chamber? The clue was in the choice of text and the builders of the tombs.

This was the first time a military man had been pharaoh, so perhaps he chose the 'Book of Gates' as his text, rather than the 'Amduat', for a reason. Why? Clearly because he did not understand the symbolic spiritual references in the 'Amduat', so preferred the mortal battle-like aspects of the 'Book of Gates'. Or, alternatively, as it was the Amun Priests who excavated and decorated the tombs, they would have deemed the 'Amduat' too sacred, and unsuitable for a *commoner*, and so convinced Horemheb that the 'Book of Gates' was a more appropriate text.

As to the decorations being unfinished, Horemheb reigned for at least fourteen years, perhaps as long as twenty-eight years, so there would have been plenty of time to finish the most complex of tombs. So why weren't they finished? It was easy to explain. Once Horemheb was dead, the only people with access to the tomb would have been the priests. So why should they bother finishing the decorations for a 'usurper', and a commoner at that, and especially if they intended to rob it somewhere down the track.

I stood before the sarcophagus reflecting on how much crap the University-educated Egyptologists spewed out, expecting us to blindly swallow it holas-bolas. It seemed to me that anyone with even the slightest thread of common sense could see what was before them and piece together the bleeding obvious. But not so, it would seem the spoon fed 'intellectuals' just based their research, reputations, and lucrative book deals on the erroneous postulations of their forebears.

The large red-granite sarcophagus rested off-centre on a modern cement base and had the same figures on the side as the earlier sarcophagi of Thutmoses III and Amenhotep II, but lacking the wadjet-eyes. Instead, each corner contained the added winged figures of Isis, Nephthys, Neit or Serqet, protecting the interred mummy.

The gable-ended curved lid was unique and showed three cut slots for wooden cramps as part of ancient repairs to its diagonal split. Whilst not as ornately painted as the other sarcophagi, it was still an impressive chunk of rock.

I'd seen all I could, and found even more evidence to support my theory that the majority, if not all, of Egyptologists were a pack of pretentious, cerebrally misled and misdirected wankers. It was time to head for the sunlight, some fresh air, and another swig or two of aqua pura. It was now, 11:11 and I'd been able to visit or cover eight tombs: pretty good going even if I did say so myself. But I had a lot of ground still to cover, not just here, but before I had to be at Medinet Habu at 3pm.

I had a quick look for Pieter and Yuko in amongst the milling crowd hovering around the entrance to KV9 and KV62, but they were nowhere to be seen; I surmised they must still be in the tomb of Ramses VI. What I did see was a gaggle of Chinese tourists preparing to invade the tiny tomb of Tutankhamun. I didn't pause to witness the bun-fight, just pushed on, passed the resthouse and up the path on the opposite side of the valley, to the tomb of Hatshepsut and Thutmoses IV.

KV20

The daughter of the female Ahmose (daughter of Amenhotep I and Ahmose-Nefertari) and Thutmoses I, Hatshepsut married her half-brother, Thutmoses II, becoming both his senior royal wife and the most powerful woman at court. When Thutmoses II unexpectedly died young, Hatshepsut assumed the throne, and became one of ancient Egypt's most successful pharaohs, reigning longer than any other woman in Egyptian dynastic history.

Perhaps the oldest royal tomb in the Valley, there's some difference of opinion between Egyptologists over whether KV20 was constructed during the reign of Thutmoses I or Hatshepsut. Most Egyptologists went for the earlier construction and believe it was the original tomb of Thutmoses I; I believed a thorough exploration was sure to reveal some answers.

The entrance was cut into the hillside high above the valley floor and for me that instantly lent support to it being commenced *after* the tsunami, when the waters were still high. But which one? Either, it was just after the reign of Amenhotep I, while the waters were receding from the first flood, or, after the second tsunami that flooded KV38 and KV42, the tombs of Thutmoses I and II. I was sure the answer awaited within.

I knew from my research and notes that entrance to the tomb was generally not granted to visitors. However I was pretty confident that flashing a little baksheesh at the guardian would rectify that obstacle. I was wrong; not even a healthy bribe of forty pounds could turn his head. I stood there momentarily dejected, contemplating my next move. But, no time to sulk, just get on with it. Thankfully I had my notes, and as I consulted them, I made my way back and around the next fork to the tomb of

Thutmoses IV.

'KV20 descends at a steep angle of about 30 degrees for over 213 metres through a series of five corridors that curve to the right forming a wide U shape, finally turning back towards the direction of the entrance. Two of the corridors end in chambers with central descents, the final corridor ending at the burial chamber 97 metres below the surface.'

A key factor for me was that it lacked the 'L' shaped configuration of the later tombs of Thutmoses II & III and Amenhotep II and III, and *that* pushed it back to around the time of Thutmoses I.

'The burial chamber has three centrally aligned pillars, only one of which is still intact, with three annexes off the rear wall. The shale walls are unsuitable for decorations, so crude stick-figure scenes from the *Amduat*, written in red and black ink on limestone blocks like those found in the tomb of Thutmoses III, were probably meant to line the chamber's walls.

Two sarcophagi were discovered at the far end of the chamber, one on each side of the pillars. The sarcophagus intended for Thutmoses I, found lying on its side, was originally built and inscribed for Hatshepsut, but the inscriptions were changed and the interior enlarged to accommodate his coffin. It is now in the Museum of Fine Arts in Boston. The second sarcophagus, cartouche-shaped and made of quartzite, is inscribed for Hatshepsut and decorated with the four sons of Horus, Anubis, Isis, Nephthys, with Nut on the inside and the lid. It is in the Egyptian Museum in Cairo.'

I had to admit I wasn't disappointed at the thought of missing the chance to visit an empty tomb, but it was clearly evidence to support attributing a later date to it; which meant it was highly possible the tomb was started by Thutmoses I, with the pillared chamber and annexes finished by Hatshepsut, not only to allow for her own burial there, but also to house the relocated mummy from her father's original tomb, KV38, which had been flooded. The irony was, that though the mummy of Thutmoses I was discovered in the Deir el Bahri cache, Hatshepsut's body remains missing.

At the end of the path, high in the mountainside, sat the entrance to KV 43, one of the largest and deepest tombs constructed during the 18th Dynasty.

The Tomb of Thutmoses IV

I wasn't prepared to barter my way in, so handed my ticket to the guardian, who gave a corner a second punch, and invited me to journey within.

A roughly-cut unfinished stairway descended from the opening, leading directly to a long, narrow corridor. That connected to a stairwell, with narrow recesses on either side, leading down to a second sloping corridor and into the well shaft.

As in the other tombs, the ceiling was decorated with yellow stars on a dark blue background, and a kheker frieze spanned the top section of the walls. However, only the left side and remaining sides of the far wall were fully decorated; with representations of the pharaoh receiving ankhs from Osiris, Anubis, and Hathor. Again Osiris was depicted with his now all to familiar green skin.

The following undecorated two-pillared chamber echoed the pattern of KV35, the tomb of his father, Amenhotep II, similarly diverting off ninety degrees to the left, with a descending staircase in the back left corner. It was looking as if it had the same 'L' shaped structure as many of the other mid-Dynastic tombs.

The staircase led down the predictable long narrow corridors and stairways to an antechamber, again with a star patterned ceiling and, on two of the walls, a kheker frieze. Protected by glass panels, the walls were plastered and painted, but the decorations of the king before Osiris, Anubis and Hathor appeared to have been rushed. On the opposite wall were two texts I couldn't work out, but I was sure I had something about them.

'There are two Hieratic texts in the ante chamber detailing that the tomb was entered during the eighth year of Horemheb's reign. They refer to the robbery of the tomb, and record a tour of inspection and Horemheb's efforts to restore the damage.'

The mummy must have still been in situ when the tomb was 'robbed', as it was removed to KV 35 in the 21st Dynasty, most likely by the Amun priests. So, who was it that broke in and committed the robbery? There were three main suspects. Firstly, actual tomb robbers, which was highly unlikely, second, Horemheb himself, and he wrote on the walls to cover up the robbery. But then he would have had to have a prior reason for entering the tomb in the first place; so, possible, but not convincing. Perhaps he intended to rob it, but found it had already been robbed? Thirdly, Ay: he had the motive, the opportunity, he knew about the well shaft, and most importantly, the mummy was left behind in the burial chamber.

Moving into the chamber itself, I discovered that, like many of the other tombs, it was divided into an upper level with three pairs of pillars, a lower level with the sarcophagus, and four side annexes. Surprisingly the chamber was totally undecorated.

The enormous cartouche-shaped sarcophagus, made of yellow quartzite, was painted with the now familiar figures of the four sons of Horus, Anubis, Nephthys, and Isis, with Nut on the lid. And that was it.

I hadn't spent much time in the tomb; let's face it, there wasn't much to see, and, by the time I made my way back out to the surface, I was feeling a little disappointed and 'tombed-out'. It was 11.40 and I figured I could use my remaining ticket to see one more tomb before trying to bribe my way into the tomb of Ramses II.

Heading back down the path, I passed the tomb of Ramses X and stopped at the tomb of Seti I, KV17. At a hundred-and-twenty metres, it was the longest and deepest of all the tombs in the Valley and supposedly the best, but just my luck, it was closed to visitors; apparently they were excavating a tunnel, discovered beneath the alabaster sarcophagus at the rear of the burial chamber, that descended so far about two-hundred feet further underground, and they still hadn't reached the end.

I pushed the envelope as much as I could, but alas to no avail as the tomb was definitely off limits. Pity, because apparently the decorations were fantastic.

'The tomb of Seti I consists of seven corridors and ten chambers, including the first vaulted burial chamber in the valley. It is decorated almost completely with painted, raised relief of the highest quality and is the first tomb to contain a complete program of religious texts; the *Litany of Ra, Book of the Dead*, the *Amduat, Book of Gates*, Opening of the Mouth ritual, *Book of the Heavenly Cow*, as well as astronomical scenes, Seti I on his own, and also with numerous deities.'

I was pissed off. It was one thing to not be allowed into an empty undecorated hole in the ground, but to travel half way around the world and be locked out of the most beautiful tomb in the world was shit; it reminded me of the door bitches and Neanderthal bouncers who kept you waiting outside 'exclusive' nightclubs in the queue for over an hour, while they let in scantily clad bimbos who were supposedly on the guest list.

Then, after freezing your balls off for the best part of the evening, you make it to the front of the queue and, surprise surprise, they won't let you in because they don't like your shoes, tie, haircut ..... *fill in the blank as appropriate.*

I strutted off, much as I had then, vowing never to return. The truth was, I probably wouldn't be able to afford another overseas trip for years, let alone a return to Egypt and the Valley of the Kings just on the off chance KV17 will be open the day I turn up.

KV16, the tomb of Seti's father, and Horemheb's successor, Paramesse, Ramses I, got the flick, so did that of Amenmeses, KV10. I briefly contemplated Ramses VI, thinking I might run into Pieter and Yuko, but they were probably long gone by now, and those pesky Chinese were still scurrying around both there and Tutankhamun's tomb, so I strutted straight passed, or rather *through* them and headed out of the valley.

I paused briefly to see if I could get into KV7, the tomb of Ramses II. It was one of the larger tombs in the valley and they were still excavating it. Who knows, it may have up to two-hundred rooms and corridors, but it's position at such a low spot meant it would have been highly susceptible to flooding and therefore damage to the walls and decorations. I wondered if it was worth the effort.

'The tomb is decorated with scenes from the *Litany of Re,* the *Amduat* in the well shaft, an Osiris shrine, the *Book of Gates*, the Opening of the Mouth ceremony, the *Book of the Dead* in the antechamber, which was a new innovation future kings would follow, the weighing of the heart, and, in the right front annex of the burial chamber, scenes from the *Book of the Divine Cow.* However the tomb has also been the subject of numerous major floods, and the once magnificent paintings on the wall have mostly flaked off, and are now buried in different layers of flood strata.'

It didn't seem worth the effort, but since I was here I figured I might as well check it out. I shouldn't have bothered, I got knocked back again, and couldn't be stuffed arguing the point; besides I'd got far more from the Valley of the Kings than had even thought possible. I handed my partly used ticket to a little gray-haired lady coming in the other direction and made a beeline for the bicycle.

The 18th Dynasty

As I walked back down the path to the Visitors' Centre I was trying to get my head around the whole 18th Dynasty. But getting there was slightly convoluted to say the least; the lineage of the New Kingdom was about as straight as a dog's hind leg, and I'd always found it difficult to follow the paths of ascension as outlined by the 'experts'. However, as I examined my notes on the 18th Dynasty I suddenly realized the easiest way to follow the path of lineage might not just be through the pharaohs, but through the concept of the *sang réal*, and simple name association. So I set out to reconstruct the 18th Dynasty in a way that made sense.

Ahmose was about six years old when his father Seqenenre was killed, and ten when his half-brother, Kamose, died and he became the first ruler of the 18th Dynasty. However, many years later, after the eruptions of Santorini and the passing of Nibiru, Amenhotep, the Annunaki god, returned to Egypt and assumed the throne, relegating Ahmose to the position of Admiral of the Navy, and marrying Ahmose's sister, Ahmose Nefertari.

'Ahmose had four sons, Ahmose-ankh, Ramose, and Siamun, to his sister, Ahmose Meritamun, and the fourth, Thutmoses, to a commoner called Senseneb. However Ahmose and all his male heirs, except Thutmoses, died before Amenhotep left Egypt. So Ahmose's son, Thutmoses, was appointed pharaoh.'

But Thutmoses didn't directly have the *sang réal* matriarchy, so he married his two half-sisters, Ahmose, the daughter of Ahmose Nefertari and Amenhotep, and Mutnofret, the daughter of Ahmose Meritaten and Ahmose. In total they bore him four daughters, including Hatshepsut, the eldest, by Ahmose, and Iset, by Mutnofret, as well as a sole son, Thutmoses II, by Mutnofret.

As Thutmoses II was the direct male heir, he naturally assumed the throne upon the demise of his father and, as was the custom, married his half-sister, Hatshepsut, producing a daughter, Neferure; the next generation's *sang réal*.

But he also had another wife, Iset, and she bore him a son, Thutmoses III, who, as the sole male heir, assumed the throne upon the death of his father.

As for Hatshepsut, she was a real enigma. Rather than step aside for the secondary wife, Iset, who perhaps was Thutmoses II's full sister, and who had borne him an heir, Thutmoses III, Hatshepsut proclaimed herself co-regent of her young stepson, the young Thutmoses III, denying the old king's son, his inheritance, and soon assuming absolute power.

Clearly she must have had some clout around the court, more so than Thutmoses II's other wife, Iset. Hatshepsut claimed legitimacy through a divine birth, even calling herself a 'female Horus'. Perhaps it was because she was the granddaughter of Amenhotep I?

But perhaps it was because she had another relationship? I double-checked my notes on her.

'There was a key advisor and powerful official during Hatshepsut's reign called Senenmut, which translates as *Mother's brother*. He was the son of Ramose and Hatnofer; Ramose being a son of Ahmose and Ahmose Meritamun and half-brother of

Thutmoses I. Egyptologists debate whether the relationship existed at all, but he had unusual honours for just a palace official.'

What it meant, was that Senenmut was not just part of the royal family, but also Hatshepsut's first cousin.

In the meantime, after the early death of Thutmoses II, Hatshepsut, though officially unmarried, went on and gave birth to a second daughter, Merytre-Hatshepsut; no doubt in the hope of producing a future heir. A little detective work made it easy to put the pieces together; Hatshepsut obviously had a child by her cousin, Senenmut. How did I figure that? Simple association; the name Merytre was very similar to Meritamun, Senenmut's grandmother, and Ahmose's full sister.

Thutmoses III eventually became pharaoh in his own right, presumably when Hatshepsut died. He married his half-sister, Neferure, who bore him a son, Amenemhat, and a daughter, Neferity, but neither of them out-lived him.

However Thutmoses III also married Merytre-Hatshepsut, the daughter of his step-mother, Hatshepsut, also of the lineage of the *sang réal*, and, in addition to numerous daughters, including Tiaa, Iset and Meritamun, they produced a son, Amenhotep II.

'Keeping with tradition, Amenhotep II married his full sister, Tiaa, and they had ten sons, the eldest of whom was, or would have been, Amenhotep III, and a daughter. But the eldest son didn't assume the throne, possibly because he predeceased his father. In any case, the throne was assumed by Thutmoses IV, one of the younger sons.'

Thutmoses IV had two wives, one of whom, Nefertari, may have been the daughter of Nefertiry, and thus the *sang réal*, the other, Mutemwia, who, though a Mitanite princess, would have been considered a 'commoner'. But it was to Mutemwia that he had a son, whom he named Amenhotep III, probably in honour of his dead brother, but also as a way to legitimise his position as the heir apparent.

I scooted quickly through the Visitors' Centre and made for my bike, noticing Pieter and Yuko had obviously left, as their bikes were gone. I paused to quench my thirst, and sort out the rest of the 18th Dynasty.

Without a legitimate *sang réal* matriarchy, Amenhotep III's claim to the throne was tenuous, so he would need to address that 'weakness'. In doing so, he married Tiye, the daughter of Yuya, a wealthy land owner and priest, which, given the track history of the priesthood, was hardly surprising, and Tjuyu, a priestess, singer of Hathor, Amun and Min. Tiye also had a brother, Anen, who was a second Prophet of Amun. Clearly Tiye's mother Tjuyu was some relation to the *sang réal*, possibly she was Tiaa, or another sister of Amenhotep II. It would totally explain Amenhotep III's choice of her as a wife, more so when you consider his other wife, Tadukhipa, was a foreigner and not of the *sang réal*.

'Amenhotep III and Tiye had one son, Amenhotep IV, and four daughters, Sitamun, Henuttaneb, Iset and Nebetah.'

That's when I hit a little speed bump. Then I had an idea. I think that around the time of the demise of Amenhotep III, one of his daughters, either Iset or Nebetah, changed her name to Nefertiti, perhaps in celebration of the ascension of Amenhotep

IV to the throne, or perhaps in respect to her great Aunt, Nefertari; my preference went to Iset, as around that time she disappeared from the records. It meant that one of Amenhotep III's other daughters, possibly Nebetah as she was younger, changed her name to Mutnodjnet. As I repacked the bottle into my backpack, unlocked my bike, and got on, I wondered, was that such a big deal; women changing their names? Did it possibly have something to do with reaching pubity, or being married? Perhaps.

It was also interesting, given what I had learned, or rather remembered thanks to Crystal, that Iset was a combination of the names Aset and Isis. So, was Nefertiti an incarnation of Aset, of Isis? If so, it explained a lot of what was about to unfold.

Five years later the Annunaki returned and Akhenaten assumed the throne, forcing Amenhotep IV to abdicate. Akhenaten (Amenhotep/Imhotep) married Nefertiti (his reincarnated 'sister'), and produced six daughters, the first of which was Meritaten, the third, Ankhesenamun. Meanwhile Amenhotep IV took over his father's youngest wife, Tadukhipa, who changed her name to Khiya. Originally I thought Khiya was the mother of Tutankhamun, but then I remembered that recent DNA tests had shown that Tutankhamun was the result of a brother-sister pairing. That meant Amenhotep IV must have married one of his own sisters, possibly his youngest sister, Nebetah, which is when she may have changed her name to Mutnodjnet.

I set off down the road, contemplating that when Akhenaten left Egypt, he reappointed Amenhotep IV as a co-regent, knowing Nefertiti would soon leave Egypt. In becoming co-regent, Amenhotep IV assumed the name Smenkhkare, but, for some reason, Smenkhkare died just after Nefertiti left Egypt, possibly because of it, and, there being no other male heirs, Tutankhamun was crowned king. Meanwhile Mutnodjnet, now a widow but also, with Nefertiti and her daughters gone, the '*iryt-p't*', was married off to Horemheb, thus making him the '*iry-pat*'

In any case, Tutankhamun's claim to the throne was weak so he was married off as the 'rules' dictated to the *sang réal*, to his first cousin, Ankhesenamun, to secure his position. But that didn't last long as he died at the age of eighteen. It was then that Ay 'hijacked' the throne from Horemheb by marrying Tutankhamun's widow, Ankhesenamun, the *sang réal*, despite the fact Horemheb had originally been named 'Crown Prince' not by Tutankhamun, but by convention due to his marriage to Mutnodjnet. The interesting thing is that Ay was possibly a legitimate contender himself, and felt he was acting according to a higher power in avoiding the crown falling into the lap of a 'commoner'.

As the High Priest of Amun, Ay inherited all the titles of Tiye's father, Yuya, and was more than likely the full brother of Tiye, Tutankhamun's grandmother. Thus he was the only surviving male of the bloodline and moved quickly to secure the throne by marrying the *sang réal*, Ankhesenamun.

Probably furious at the double-cross, Horemheb, having been rejected by Ankhesenamun, but who had married Mutnodjnet, Nefertiti's sister, waited for his opportunity, and when Ay died, didn't seize the throne as many Egyptologists propose, rather he was 'rightfully' appointed pharaoh due to his marriage to Mutnodjnet. I couldn't go any further without knowing more, pulling over and checking my iphone for any more details on Mutnodjnet. I soon found some.

'Based on a wine-jar docket found in a burial chamber of Horemheb's tomb at Saqqara, Mutnodjnet died in her mid-40s, soon after Year 13 of her husband's rule. Her mummy shows she had given birth several times, and was found along with the mummy of a still-born, premature infant, suggesting that Mutnodjnet may have died in childbirth.'

It also suggests there may have been other children, not a son, as Horemheb had no living heir when he died, but, if there was a daughter, why wasn't she mentioned anywhere? Simple, the Amun priests, the scribes, would not have acknowledged her because even though she was the lineage of the *sang réal*, her father was not 'legitimate', meaning she was the daughter of a commoner.

And that raised the several big questions: first, as Horemheb had no heirs, did it end the matriarchal lineage of the *sang réal*, or, two, why did Horemheb appoint Paramesse as his '*iry-pat*', his Crown Prince? Was it as arbitrary as the Egyptologists would suggest, or was there more to it? Was Paramesse married to their daughter?

I could think of no other reason why the Amun priests would tolerate or permit Paramesse to assume the throne as Ramses I. But time was moving on, and I needed to as well; Paramesse would have to wait until later. And with that done and dusted, I took a final deep celebratory and self-congratulatory swig of water, repacked the iphone and bottle into my backpack, and bid the Valley of the Kings adieu.

CHAPTER 16 – THE QUEEN'S PALACE

I raised a hand and waved to the guards as I treddled off down the road and through the checkpoint.

'Shukran jazeelan. Maasalaamah, Assalaam Alaikum' - 'Thank you very much. Goodbye, peace be upon you.'

The great thing about riding *up* to the Valley of the Kings first thing in the morning was not that it was cooler, that we had a chance to experience the magical post-dawn awakenings of the Nile; it was now, when it was hotter and the sun approached its Zenith overhead, that it was downhill all the way.

I felt a sense of exhilaration and absolute liberation as I coasted down the curving road, warm air brushing my cheeks like velvet gloves. I WAS HERE. I was in Egypt, riding a god-damn bicycle, and had just visited the Valley of the Kings. Not only that, I had single-handedly rewritten the whole history of the 18th Dynasty of ancient Egypt, no, no, from earlier, from the beginning of time. I must have been the only person in the world who knew what I had just figured out. Now I knew how Archimedes felt.

'EUREKA!'

Heading back down the road towards el-Tarif I turned right and passed to the west of Dra Abu el-Naga. Occasionally I was passed in both directions by taxis and buses of tourists who looked out of their windows, like goldfish in a bowl, at the crazy cowboy riding a bike through the Egyptian desert and laughing his head off.

I'm sure some of them would have momentarily contemplated how liberating and adventurous it would have been, then, once I was out of sight, nestled back into the plush seat and luxury of their air-conditioned coach, and brushed me off as some sort of impoverished left-over from a hippie farm. The truth was I had never felt so alive; this had been the most extraordinary six-and-a-half days of my life. Hell, I still had over a week to go, could it get any better?

I rounded the turn off to the right and stopped beside the road about a hundred metres further on to check my notes; apparently, in addition to the tombs, there was once a temple to Amenhotep I and Ahmose Nefertari here.

'On the edge of the cultivation, at the southern end of Dra Abu el-Naga was once a tiny temple dedicated to Amenhotep I, second pharaoh of the 18th Dynasty. The southern part contained blocks with scenes of the king seated in a kiosk between standards of Horus and Set, while the northern section was dedicated to Ahmose-Nefertari.

Various blocks and statue fragments were found, including three of Ahmose-Nefertari, along with a sandstone stela, all probably dating to Dynasty XIX, discovered at the entrance to an antechamber. However the temple is now completely destroyed.'

I looked out over the shifting sands in the direction of the cultivated fields, hoping to spy some trace of the temple, but there was just sand. Who knows what might be awaiting discovery beneath?

Back on the bike, I pedalled passed an area to the south called El-Khokha; a hill with five Old Kingdom tombs and fifty-three numbered tombs from the 18th and 19th Dynasties. I had no time to stop and check them out.

Further on, towards the West Bank Necropolis, another turn to the right took me back up a slight slope towards Deir el Bahri and Hatshepsut's Temple. Just before the turn, on the left hand side of the road, I could see the scant ruins of several buildings.

'At the end of the causeway at Deir el-Bahri lies the site of two temples, the Valley Temple of Hatshepsut, and, just north, the Colonnaded Temple of Ramses IV. Both were destroyed in antiquity, though some blocks, inscribed with the names Hatshepsut, Thutmoses I, Amenhotep II, Princess Neferure, Ramses II and Thutmoses III, have survived and are in the Metropolitan Museum in New York and Cairo Museum.'

To me it was evidence that the whole area had been flattened by a tsunami. But that meant there had to be yet another flood sometime after the time of Ramses IV. That was possible, and it took me back to Crystal's comment about earthquakes around 224 BC.

What if that date was not exactly correct? All the dating prior to the BC/AD threshold is supposition, so what if the earthquake was about sixty years earlier? If it was, or if the dating of the Ptolemeic Dynasties was a little later, then it's highly likely that it was another earthquake and subsequent tsunami that wiped out all the temples along the Nile, which in turn led to the order to rebuild them during the Ptolemeic era. And that would perfectly account for the rebuilding of all the Ptolemeic temples.

A quick check of the time, 12:14, and it was back on the road again, passing el-Assasif, where there were supposedly forty tombs, mostly from the New Kingdom. I didn't even contemplate exploring them; the next stop was Hatshepsut's Temple at Deir el Bahri.

Hatshepsut was perhaps the first great woman in recorded history, though her rise to power went against all the conventions of her time. She claimed that the Oracle of Amun had proclaimed it was the will of Amun that Hatshepsut be her father's intended heir. Further, that following that divine decree, Thutmoses I made her the heir apparent of Egypt. However almost all the so-called 'experts' believe this was just historical revisionism on Hatshepsut's part. But what if it wasn't? Perhaps it was not her father's wish, but her grandfather, Amenhotep I's wish? And if he was Annunaki, what were the implications?

Perhaps the most famous legend about Hatshepsut is the myth about her birth, in which Amun-Ra (Amun-hotep perhaps) goes to Ahmose in the form of Thutmoses I, awakens her with pleasant odours, and places the ankh, the symbol of life, to Ahmose's nose, at which point Hatshepsut is conceived. Now, to me, that had the slightest resemblance to an anaesthetic. Further, Khnum, the god who forms the bodies of human children, is then instructed to create a body and ka, or corporal presence/life force, for Hatshepsut. That sounds very much like genetic engineering and artificial insemination. Finally, Khnum, along with Heket, the goddess of life and fertility, then lead Ahmose along to a lioness bed where she gives birth to Hatshepsut. I might have been pushing the limits of credibility, but, given that in the last five days that was the norm rather than the exception, I was willing to keep it as an option.

I navigated the fleet of tourist buses and taxis in the car park, locked the bike to the fence next to what I presumed was Pieter and Yuko's bikes, and paid the thirty pounds to enter the complex. As at the Valley of the Kings, there was another road train to take the tourists the two-hundred metres to and from the beginning of the temple, and, though it was now hot and steamy, and my shirt was swimming around on my back where it had been in contact with the backpack, I had just ridden the bike and was keen to stretch my legs again, so I decided to walk.

The temple stretched out before me in the distance; three wide terraces tucked into the base of the sheer cliffs that formed a horseshoe around it. Even with the hundreds of tourists crawling all over it, they still looked like a swarm of ants as they scurried over the massive structure. I took the backpack off, finished the contents of the first bottle of water, and set off to get a more personal perspective on this remarkable woman.

As co-regent, Hatshepsut gradually assumed the titles, powers, and, to further legitimise her position, even dressed as a king, wearing the ceremonial clothing and beard of a male Pharaoh. That included having herself depicted in reliefs with a Pharaoh's kilt and beard. The Egyptian people seem to have accepted this unprecedented behaviour; mind you, they had little choice in the matter.

She was formally crowned as king around the seventh year of her co-reign with Thutmoses III, and, once she became pharaoh, she further strengthened her position and assertion that she was her father's designated successor with inscriptions, and proclamations by the god Amun, carved on the walls of her monuments. And what a prolific builder she was, commissioning hundreds of projects throughout both Upper and Lower Egypt.

Under her reign, the Egyptian economy flourished as she rebuilt the trade networks disrupted by the Hyksos occupation and the Santorini eruption, thereby re-establishing the wealth of the 18th Dynasty. Amazing what a woman's leadership can accomplish.

The Mortuary Temple of Hatshepsut

The temple at Deir el-Bahri, known as Djeser-Djeseru, meaning the 'sacred of sacreds' or 'splendour of splendours', was designed and implemented by Hatshepsut's chief 'architect', Senenmut. Going by the sheer size of the temple, one thing was for sure; he certainly had designs on her. OK, it was a bad pun, but it had to be said. That made me wonder for a second how Crystal would have reacted to my witticism if she had been here, and what she was up to today with Pernille and Bill. But then it was time to refocus on the temple before me.

There was about a hundred foot long causeway leading up to the temple, which, in the past, more than likely would have been lined with sphinxes like those outside the temple at Luxor. What would have happened to them was easy to explain; any tsunami would have simply washed them away. That supported my theory about the 224BC earthquake and tsunami.

Beyond the causeway, Hatshepsut's Temple encompassed three massive terraces. Built out of limestone blocks rather than the usual sandstone, with the terraces connected by two long central ramps, it was barren and monochromatic. But, in Hatshepsut's time, the temple facades would have been ablaze with colour from the reliefs, and the terraces covered with green gardens and fountains; it must have looked truly spectacular and surpassed anything that had been built before.

I remembered they used to have massive outdoor productions of Verdi's *Aida* here back in the nineties. My folks used to play classical music at home, and one of the pieces that I didn't mind listening to was the 'Triumphal March' from *Aida*; for me, it sparked a real interest in theatre and music. The rest, as they say, was history. I could just picture how spectacular it must have been, sitting here under the Milky Way on a balmy night, the natural setting of the temple in its horseshoe theatre, and Verdi's exquisite score cascading through the air. Majestic!

I thought for a second about why they stopped? I vaguely remembered there was some sort of terrorist attack here years and years ago that put an end to any more productions. I couldn't really remember the details, but it seemed to me that it was safe enough now for them to start restaging them; I mean there were armed police and military everywhere you looked.

On either side of the ramp that led to the second court were two colonnades; I headed left, to the southern colonnade. The columns were square, plastered with modern concrete and didn't look at all like they belonged. They appeared to have been 'restored' to create an impressive façade more than to protect the wall and ceiling of the colonnade behind it. The ceiling had the now-familiar star pattern on a blue background, and the wall contained well-worn and often difficult to see reliefs. What I could make out was a barque transporting two obelisks, escorted by priests, soldiers, standard-bearers and musicians. I presumed they were being moved from the granite quarries at Aswan, though I found it had to comprehend that's how they actually did it.

But here was the poof; well, proof of how they moved them down the Nile, it didn't rule out how they actually got them to and from, and on and off, the barques. Further along the wall, but even harder to make out were reliefs of Hatshepsut offering the obelisks to Amun at Karnak.

I circled back around the ramp to the right colonnade. It had reliefs of two gods dragging a net full of waterfowl, as well as Hatshepsut in a boat, fowling and fishing. Further along were scenes of the queen offering statues and four calves to Amun, and Hatshepsut portrayed as a sphinx trampling her foes.

At the far end sat a colossal reconstructed statue of Hatshepsut. It was a bizarre place to put such an important statue; I could only assume that, once, similar statues stood in front of each of the thirteen columns.

Returning to the base of the first ramp, which was once flanked by crouching lions at the bottom and top, I started my ascent to the middle terrace. The ramp was about fifteen foot wide, with a central strip of shallow steps. Mindless inconsiderate tourists of all nationalities and ages seemed totally ignorant of anyone and everyone around them: you would think they might enact some intelligence and use one side to ascend and the other to descend, with the middle divided and allocated to the fleet of foot, but no, that would be too logical, better to push, shove, bustle and bundle all and sundry.

I tried considerately negotiating the mine field of morons, but, after several annoying collisions, decided that with my bulk and presence I would be best served to just forge forward in a straight line and plough my way through, and anyone in my path would just have to fare as best they could. It seemed to work, probably more because of my attitude rather than any actually bullying contact. In any case, having arrived, I stood at the top of the ramp and surveyed the lay of the land.

Christ, it was huge; the courtyard was at least the size of a football field, with a full colonnade across the rear, and a partial colonnade on the far right side. And hot, man, it was like walking on a hot-plate. The focusing effect of the cliff walls, the lack of breeze, and the massive stone surface, had turned the place into a giant cooker, so I cracked the top on my second bottle of water, and replenished my thirst.

Further up ahead on the next ramp I saw Diane, surrounded by her circle of women, all of them dressed in white. I remembered she'd been Hatshepsut in a previous life, so no doubt she felt perfectly at home here. They had obviously been doing some spiritual work on the upper level and were gliding down the ramp. It didn't feel right to get caught up in a conversation in the middle of a frying pan, so I pretended I hadn't seen them and wandered to the left.

Off to either side were about ten rows, forty metres long, of temple 'fragments'. I checked in with my notes.

'The 2nd terrace, now accessed by a ramp, originally would have had stairs. It once housed a temple dedicated to Amenhotep I and Ahmose-Nefertari, but was destroyed when Hatshepsut's architect, Senenmut, began construction of the new temple. A shrine built by Ptolemy III and dedicated to Asclepius that once stood in front of the southern side of the portico on the second terrace, was also destroyed.'

It may have accounted for the rows of 'rubble' on the sides, but, standing here at the site, I found it hard to believe that Hatshepsut would have permitted the destruction of her grandparent's temple. Also, the 'new' ramp, and the modern approach to restoration, once again indicated to me the haphazard approach of the present Egyptians and Egyptologists.

There had to be hundreds of rooms and chambers below the courtyard; I didn't see any entrances from the lower level, but you only had to look at the scale of the temple to realize that having a courtyard this large made no sense what so-ever unless, 1) there was a massive temple in the middle of it, which there was, and 2) there were rooms beneath the surface.

As I set off across the terrace, I surmised that it was more likely Senenmut designed the new temple *around* the existing temple to Amenhotep, as had been done at Luxor, and that it was destroyed by the actions of the tsunami. Though now, there had to be yet another tsunami, or earthquake, that post-dated Ptolemy III: perhaps the one in 1003 or 1303? Even more questions started popping up in my mind, but I didn't want to think about them right at that moment, so I moved on to the colonnade at the left of the second ramp.

Again the columns were square, with the heavy-handedness of the restorers still evident. The scenes on the wall behind, however, contained heaps of detail.

'The second terrace contains the famous "Punt" Colonnade; depicting the maritime expedition Hatshepsut sent, via the Red Sea, to Punt, around the 9th year of her reign.'

No one really knows the precise location of Punt, but it's thought to have probably been on the east coast of Africa, possibly Somalia.

'From the left, Amun commissions the journey, then the

161

Egyptian boats, headed by her high official, Pa-nahsy, sail from the Red Sea Coast. The end wall shows a village in the land of Punt, its dome-shaped houses on stilts with ladders to access them, where the expedition is welcomed by the king of Punt, Parahu, and his grotesquely fat wife, Ity.'

She wasn't hard to spot at all. I wondered if this was the world's first documented case of political incorrectness?

There were also wonderful images of birds and animals all around, and several different types of fish in the water below. Men were cutting trees and carrying off heaps of treasure to be taken back to Egypt.

'The Egyptians offer metal axes and other goods as trade, and, overseen by Nehsi the Nubian general, elaborately-rigged sailing boats get ready to bring the tribute back to Egypt, including myrrh trees, ebony, ivory, cinnamon wood, panther skins, incense trees in baskets, cattle, baboons and a panther.'

Further along, in the last relief, the incense trees were being planted in the gardens at Karnak, whilst the produce from the expedition was weighed and documented by officials, before being presented to Hatshepsut and then to Amun.

Heading back to the far left of the colonnade was the Chapel of Hathor, easily identifiable by its central columns with their goddess face capitals and sacred rattle. In the first chamber there were many reliefs of Hatshepsut being licked or suckled by the goddess in the form of a cow, as well as a portrait of Senenmut, but the next chamber, the inner sanctuary cut into the hillside at the back, was closed to visitors. Not fair! No matter, check the notes.

'On the northern wall in the Hypostyle of the Hathor Chapel are remarkably colourful scenes of boats, a parade of soldiers, a panther, and Libyans dancing in a festival of Hathor. When the sanctuary was first discovered, it contained stacks of baskets full of wooden penises, perhaps used in fertility rituals.'

It seems Hatshepsut was the Germaine Greer of the ancient world; 'A dildo a day keeps the doldrums away', and, though it didn't go any way to answering any of my questions, it at least put a wry smile on my face. I don't know why, perhaps because I had been on heat since I met Crystal and Candy had raised the Titanic, but, for a few moments, I wondered if Diane had something a little extra tucked away in her luggage.

I headed back across the courtyard, past the ramp, and on towards the northern, or Birth Colonnade; so called because it was here that the faded scenes of Hatshepsut declaring her right to rule by divine birth, were emblazoned.

The reliefs were not that well preserved, but they showed all the stages of the birth; Thutmoses I and Queen Ahmose sitting with their knees touching, the divine union of Ahmose with Amun, Khnum creating the queen and her ka on a potter's wheel, and Ahmose being led to the birth-room by the frog-headed goddess, Hekat.

Hatshepsut was then presented to Amun and a number of other deities, as the goddess Seshat recorded the details of Hatshepsut's reign. It made me think that this was possibly the first surviving example of self-promotion and billboard politicking;

nowhere near as prolific and exaggerated as Ramses II, but I guess someone had to start the ball rolling.

Down a few steps at the end of the colonnade, and mirroring the Chapel of Hathor, was the Chapel of Anubis, with fluted columns and colourful murals of Hatshepsut in the presence of the jackal-headed god. In some places Hatshepsut's image had been removed, but the figure of her stepson, Thutmose III, remained. Numerous gods were depicted receiving offerings from both Hatshepsut and Thutmoses III including Amun, Anubis, Sokar and Osiris.

Most of the Egyptologists believe it was Thutmoses III that chiselled out the images and references to his step-mother, out of revenge for her dominating him during his life, but I wasn't so quick to swallow that line of thinking. My suspects were, as always, the Amun Priests.

Venturing back into the direct sunlight, even my trusty akubra was feeling the bite of the suns rays; but thank god I had it. As I swallowed down a few more mouthfuls of water, a familiar voice avalanched down from the top of the second ramp.

'Hey, Alex, what are doing, Dude?'

I looked towards the heavens to discover the boisterous figures of Randy and Dwight.

'Hi guys; I'm just looking for a site to set up a hot-dog stand.'

We all met up at the bottom of the ramp, laughing as usual.

'Hell of a place to die, huh?'

'Sure is.'

'They wouldn't have had a chance.'

I had no idea what Randy was talking about.

'What? Who? What do you mean?'

'The massacre.'

'Sorry? What massacre?'

Thankfully Dwight brought things into focus.

'The Luxor Massacre; it took place in November 1997, right here on the Middle Terrace.'

I looked around again, this time with a different perspective.

'Jesus!'

The Luxor Massacre

'The attack was instigated by exiled leaders of Al-Gama'a al-Islamiyya, an Egyptian Islamic organization attempting to undermine the July 1997 "Nonviolence Initiative". Six terrorists from the Islamic Group and Jihad, Talaat al-Fath, the Holy War of the Vanguard of the Conquest, disguised themselves as members of the security forces, and, armed with automatic firearms and machetes, descended on the temple around 8:45 in the morning.

They ascended the first ramp, and then, with the tourists trapped inside the temple on the upper terraces, went on a systematic forty-five minute killing spree, murdering fifty-eight tourists, including over thirty Swiss, four Japanese couples on their honeymoons, and a five-year-old British kid. They also killed four Egyptians; three police officers and a tour guide, and during the slaughter, many of the women were mutilated with machetes; there was even a note found inside one of the disembowelled bodies, praising Islam.'

'Christ! But why?'

'Their aim was to devastate the Egyptian economy and force the government into policies that would strengthen support for the anti-government Islamic forces.'

I didn't know why, but something about that didn't add up. It sounded like rhetoric, and I couldn't see how murdering dozens of tourists in Luxor could destabilize the economy. Although tourism was a big slice of the countries income, it made more sense to attack the petrochemical industries.

'What happened next?'

'The terrorists hijacked a coach, but that's where the story diverges.'

'What does that mean?'

Randy was never going to be a Professor of English, that's for sure.

'It means the stories go in different directions. According to one story, the coach ran into a checkpoint of armed Egyptian tourist police and military forces and, in the ensuing shootout, one of the terrorists was wounded while the rest fled into the hills, where their bodies were later found in a cave, apparently having committed suicide. In the other version, the coach driver deliberately crashed the coach by the Valley of the Queens and the local villagers chased them down and killed them before the police arrived.'

Randy wasn't so fussed about the details.

'Well, whatever the outcome, now all the temples are heavily guarded with fences, security checkpoints and guards, and there hasn't been a terrorist attack on tourists at a temple in Egypt since; so I guess things are pretty safe.'

I wasn't so easily convinced.

'I don't know, both stories sound pretty dodgy to me. I mean firstly, how would they get off the bus at the checkpoint and escape into the hills, and if they did, why would they commit suicide? And secondly, if they crashed miles away at the Valley of the Queens, surely the villagers would have come to their aid; not chased them down and killed them. Think about it, firstly the villagers wouldn't have known about the attack, and secondly, how did the villagers, armed with just hoes and rakes, overpower six assassins armed with fully automatic weapons?'

'It's funny you should say that, because the Islamic organization supposedly responsible for the attack, reacted by denying any involvement, instead blaming the Israelis for the killings. Ayman Zawahiri even went as far as saying the attack was the work of the Egyptian police.'

'Who's Ayman Zawawhoosy?'

'Ayman Zawahiri was the last emir of Islamic Jihad in Egypt, and supposedly the real brains of al Qaeda.'

Randy had it pegged.

'Well if anyone would know, he would.'

I was scratching my head.

'But why would the Egyptians murder their own people; it would destroy their tourist industry?'

'Maybe that's what they wanted, to get all the tourists *out* of Egypt?'

'Why?'

'For the same reason they built the Aswan Dam, to rob the temples. Maybe when they were restoring the temple here they found stuff buried deep in the mountain?'

'Jesus, Randy, you've done it again.'

He looked like a stunned squirrel in a snowstorm.

'What? What?'

I checked my phone; it was 1:24 and I still had to get to Medinet Habu.

'Listen, guys, I'm running to a bit of a schedule, how long are you in Luxor for?'

'We fly out tomorrow afternoon back to Cairo, then Randy's heading straight back to the States later that night.'

'Cool, then can I catch up with you sometime tonight or tomorrow morning back at the hotel, and talk about this some more?'

'Sure, we're off to the Valley of the Kings next, but we'll catch you later, Dude; you know where to find us.'

'The rooftop bar, no doubt.'

'You got it.'

I stood there digesting the conversation as they disappeared across the terrace and down the ramp; it was one thing to build dams so you could rob temples, but to murder innocent bystanders was another matter. Surely it couldn't be true. But if it was, it meant that the Illuminati were not only still active, but that they must be active within the Egyptian Government, and also within the Supreme Council of Antiquities. The vulture! Could Saeed have been right? I was even more keen to meet Saeed's uncle; but, first, time to finish my visit to Hatshepsut's Temple.

I turned to face the second ramp, a pair of Horus falcons flanking the base, and strode up to the top terrace. There had been massive restoration work done, especially to the front row of columns, which would all originally have been fronted with floor to ceiling statues of Hatshepsut in the guise of the mummified form of Osiris; it was part of her extravagant and blatant expression of herself as Pharaoh.

Hatshepsut certainly not only had the balls to think of such a thing, but the chutzpah to pull it off. Hmm, that was an interesting image, and somewhat in keeping with a chamber filled with wooden willies and Germaine Greer's reputation as a communicative castrater of chauvinists.

Four out of thirteen of the statues had been reconstructed on the left side, and five on the right. Then I saw it, straight ahead, sticking out like an elephant's testicles, was a huge pink granite doorway.

Closer examination of the hieroglyphs revealed they were crudely made, which suggested to me they were a later addition to the stone. So, was there a much older temple here some time in the past? If my theory on the other temples was correct, then the answer was a resounding, YES!

As if on cue, Pieter and Yuko emerged from the doorway.

'Hey Alex.'

'Hi, guys, how was the Valley?'

'Fascinating. We looked for you after we finished at Tutankhamun's Tomb, but couldn't find you.'

'It's OK, I had a few more tombs to see.'

'Did it go well?'

'Brilliant, I'll fill you in on it all later at drinks.'

Pieter had his curiosity peaked.

'Sounds interesting.'

'It is.'

'OK then, well we'll leave you to it; we're off to the Valley of the Queens. '

'Safe peddling, see you later.'

They took off down the ramp and I entered the inner courtyard. To the right, the wall was covered with processional scenes of barques carrying statues of Hatshepsut, Thutmoses I, II, and III. Other scenes showed several gods on barques, carried by priests and preceded by dancers and musicians. Beyond the wall was again off limits to visitors, so I hit the iphone.

'To the right of the courtyard is the Sanctuary of the Sun, dedicated to the solar cult of Re-Horakhty; an open court with a huge central altar made of alabaster. Leading off from the courtyard are other niches and chapels, including another dedicated to Anubis and one to the parents of Hatshepsut. They contain numerous well-preserved and colourful paintings.'

Returning to the central courtyard, at the far back, cut deep into the rock of the mountain, was the sanctuary of Amun, the focus of the temple. It had a doorway of pink granite as well, but it was also closed to visitors. It made me wonder what lay within. That made me think of Abu Simbel, Philae, and all the other temples that had areas 'off-limits' to the general public.

'The Sanctuary of Amun was the resting place for the barque of Amun during the "Valley Festival".'

OK, apparently there was no profound secret. But then again, perhaps they didn't know what to look for. The southern side of the court, the Sanctuary of Hatshepsut, housed the cult chapels of Hatshepsut and her father Thutmoses I, also closed to visitors.

'Two chambers within the sanctuary show scenes of Hatshepsut, along with her daughter Neferure, and Thutmose III, all worshiping various gods. The wall shows scenes of processions of royal statues in boats with their attendants, as well as scenes of priests making offerings to various deities. The sanctuary was later expanded by Ptolemy VIII, who added a third chapel dedicated to Imhotep and Amenhotep.'

A Ptolemaic chapel dedicated to both Imhotep *and* Amenhotep? How interesting! I exited the courtyard through the pink granite door and for the first time truly appreciated the view looking back down the valley. You could see down through the whole valley all the way to the river and across it. In fact the temple lined up directly with the ruins of Hatshepsut's Valley Temple and, over the river, with Karnak on the east side of the Nile. I could see how the level of the Nile would have been much higher back then, making access to the Mortuary Temple so much easier.

I looked out to the right, over the rest of the Deir el Bahri. Somewhere here in the cliffs overlooking the temple was the tomb known as DB320, the tomb that contained an astounding cache of 17th to 21st Dynasty mummies. Many of Egypt's most famous pharaohs, supposedly including Ahmose, Amenhotep I, Thutmoses I, II and III, Ramses I, II and IV and Seti I, were discovered here, but in a great state of disorder, many placed in other people's coffins. Several of the mummies are still unidentified, and given my theories about the Annunaki and the lineage of the 18th Dynasty, mummies such as Amenhotep I are probably *mis*identified.

Now, I knew it was the Amun Priests that broke into the tombs at the beginning of the 21st Dynasty and relocated, or, to put it more succinctly, 'dumped', the mummies in DB320. However, the mummy of Hatshepsut was not found in DB320, or any of the other tombs, and has never been found. So what could that mean?

The fate of Hatshepsut

Hatshepsut was the granddaughter of Amenhotep, and that meant, if my theory about the Annunaki was correct, that Amenhotep was also Akhenaten. So, just like Akhenaten, Amenhotep would have been a thorn in the side of the Amun priests and, if Hatshepsut was anything like her grandfather, and her over twenty-year rule would suggest she was, then the Amun priests would have been overjoyed to see the end of her.

It's reasonable to assume that the Amun Priests 'groomed' the young co-regent, Thutmoses III, turning him against his step-mother, convincing him she was usurping his rightful position as pharaoh. Eventually Thutmoses III grew into a man and took his rightful place as pharaoh.

According to the Egyptologists, the circumstances of Hatshepsut's demise, and Thutmoses III's ascension, are unknown, and what became of Hatshepsut is a mystery. But, it's not beyond the realm of possibility that the Amun Priests poisoned Hatshepsut as soon as Thutmoses III was old enough and sufficiently 'conditioned' enough to rule.

The priests would have been responsible for the embalming and mummification of the body, but, given their 'dislike' of Hatshepsut, they probably faked the funeral, dismembered the body in mock irony of the way Osiris was dismembered, and disposed of the parts in various inconspicuous corners of ancient Egypt.

That said, according to the 'experts', it was Thutmoses III who was responsible for the destruction of many of Hatshepsut's statues and images; smashed or disfigured, then buried in a pit. Some of them say he did it because he was fearful of a challenge to his legitimacy as a successor. That didn't wash with me. According to my research the only male heirs were his own; Hatshepsut certainly had no sons, and even if Thutmoses III had a brother, he would be just as illegitimate as himself. So the thinking that Thutmoses III immediately went about chiseling out all the images of Hatshepsut off temples, monuments and obelisks, didn't hold water. Sure, he supposedly omitted her name from the Kings' List in the Chamber of Ancestors at Karnak, but that wasn't him, that would also have been the Amun Priests.

Other 'experts' believe Thutmoses III waited at least ten to twenty years after Hatshepsut had died, towards the end of his reign, that it was even into the reign of his son, Amenhotep III, and as late as the Amarna Period, before the evidence of her reign was removed. That didn't wash either, Thutmoses III became one of the greatest Pharaohs of all time, and how could he remove any references to her *after* he died. Again, the finger pointed straight at the Amun Priests. They had an agenda to obliterate any connection to Amenhotep, Akhenaten, ... no, ... I gazed out over the Nile, ... NO, it was an agenda to obliterate any reference to the Annunaki, to matriarchal rule, ... and the *sang réal*.

As I looked back around the cliffs, I noticed the ruins of another similar shaped temple alongside the Temple of Hatshepsut. I had to check my notes on that one, as it was a bit of a mystery to me.

The Temple of Montuhotep II

'The Temple of Hatshepsut is built on a site adjacent to that of Montuhotep Nebheptre, the founder of the 11th Dynasty.'

Oh, there he was again, Montuhotep, and here *it* was again: a temple dating back at least to the 11th Dynasty on the site of a more modern temple. Clearly Senenmut had modelled Hatshepsut's Temple on this earlier temple, just larger.

'The temple seems to have been built in three or four stages and was unique for the period, built on a multi-level platform combining the earlier saff-tombs and the Old Kingdom pyramids. The forecourt was walled with an avenue of colossal Osirid statues of Montuhotep. On the rear walls of the lower colonnade, fragments of reliefs were found of boat processions and foreign campaigns.

An avenue of colossal Osirid statues of Montuhotep: how in the hell did they know that? Had they found some statues, or even the remnants of them? There certainly didn't seem to be any lying around on the valley floor. But it was a powerful point - colossal statues of Montuhotep, to me that would imply he was Annunaki. And combining saff-tombs and Old Kingdom pyramids? Tell me more.

'A ramp, with a grove of sycamore and tamarisk trees on either side, led to the second terrace, surrounded on three sides by a double colonnade of pillars inscribed with scenes and texts of Montuhotep before various deities. Inside the colonnade was a walkway, which surrounded a forest of 140 octagonal pillars arranged in rows of two at the back and three on the other sides.'

I could see from my vantage point how impressive it must have been, and how Senenmut would have chosen to copy it, and the Osirid statues.

'In the centre of the platform was a large square structure clad in limestone blocks. Egyptologists originally thought it was the base of a pyramid, but now they interpret it as a mastaba-like structure.'

Clearly Senenmut couldn't build a similar mastaba at Hatshepsut's temple, as the temple of Amenhotep occupied the space, so he had modified his design accordingly.

'At the rear of the colonnade, six shaft tombs were discovered, each with its own chapel dedicated to individual female family members of Montuhotep. Montuhotep's own tomb was cut into the rock beneath the courtyard and contained an uninscribed alabaster shrine, though Egyptologists debate whether the king was ever buried here, as no sarcophagus was found.'

Beyond the tomb entrance was Egypt's largest Hypostyle hall to date, which contained 82 pillars, at the rear of which was a long rock-cut chamber with a vaulted ceiling, the sanctuary of the royal mortuary cult. In the centre of the sanctuary, a shallow ramp led up to a limestone altar with a statue of the king placed in a niche carved into the rock behind it.'

I would have loved to have been able to make my way back down and round to explore it, to see if it had any massive blocks of red granite, however the site was clearly off limits as it was still under excavation and restoration. Bummer! Who knows what lay under the pyramid, in the tomb, and inside the rock face?

But that wasn't the end of the ruins; there were the remnants of another structure between the Temple of Hatshepsut and Montuhotep's temple. The ruins were right under the cliff-face, directly behind the Chapel of Hathor abutting Hatshepsut's Temple, and consisted mostly of a pillared hall, with column bases and some of the round columns visible. Some of the paving in front of the hall was evident, and there were lots of scattered blocks and architectural fragments. Checking my notes, I discovered this once belonged to Hatshepsut's successor, Thutmoses III.

'High on the hill at Deir el-Bahri, squeezed between Montuhotep's temple and the Temple of Hatshepsut, sits the Temple of Thutmose III, originally named Djeser-Akhet, or Sacred Horizon, and dedicated to the god Amun.'

The Temple of Thutmoses III

The Temple of Thutmoses III took up about forty metres of the central part of the valley, above the level of the upper terrace of the Temple of Hatshepsut, and rested on a roughly square platform partially cut from the rock and partially supported by a stone barrier.

'It was discovered in 1961, while restoration and cleaning work was being carried out between the Temples of Hatshepsut and Montuhotep, and included a system of ramps and terraces, a large Hypostyle hall with 76 polygonal columns around the perimeter and 12 larger columns closer to the centre. This was followed by a hall for Amun's barque, and the inner sanctuary. Granite door jambs to the inner chamber were found, with the king's name inscribed, as well as several statues of Thutmoses III.'

Granite doorjambs! Now those I would love to see. I was betting they were much like the ones in Hatshepsut's sanctuary; possibly red granite, crudely carved, and belonging to a much earlier structure. Unfortunately, like the Temple of Montuhotep II, the site was still being excavated, and I didn't have the time to find out who was in charge, or snoop around. Double bummer!

'Beneath the Hypostyle Hall, they found a shaft tomb dating back to the Middle Kingdom, the 11th Dynasty, as well as a cache of papyri dating back to the 3rd Intermediate Period, the 21st Dynasty.'

The shaft tomb echoed the temple and tomb of Montuhotep II next door. Could this originally have been the tomb and temple of Montuhotep I? Or maybe it went back even further than that? What else was there to find?

'Today, only a small part of the western wall survives,

along with some chambers. There was a Kiosk of Thutmose III to the east of the temple, on the causeway, which replaced an original building by Thutmoses I, but there are no remains of the kiosk left today.'

OK, if Thutmoses I had built a kiosk in front of the space, then he must have built it in front of some older structure, otherwise he would have built it where Thutmoses III built his temple. It confirmed my theory there was a much older structure beneath the ruins. Everywhere I went, I found evidence to support my theory; it was blowing me away.

'Cult worship at Thutmoses III's temple lasted into the 21st Dynasty before being abandoned, probably because the Temple of Amun was largely destroyed and hidden by a landslide or rock fall from the mountain behind, resulting from an earthquake.'

There it was again, but not just an earthquake, there could also have been an accompanying tsunami. I looked back towards the river and could visualize the waters rushing in, swirling around the horseshoe shaped valley, much as they had in Thutmoses I's tomb. Focusing in the centre, they would have wiped out all the temples, doing the most damage to those centrally located: the Temple and Kiosk of Thutmoses III.

That was easy to figure out. But what was below that, what was underneath? There was certainly a temple or structure in the centre of Deir el Bahri, dating back to who knows when, at least the 11th Dynasty. Montuhotep built his temple beside it, as did Amenhotep. Then Hatshepsut built hers on top of the right side temple, incorporating Amenhotep's temple. That was followed by Thutmoses III, who built his temple on top of the original unknown temple.

I was digging deeper, and if I was, why the hell couldn't the Egyptologists? Was it because they were all conditioned into believing nothing else could be there?

I looked back over the luscious green fields of the West Bank; this is where there were more answers awaiting, under the silt and sediment of the floods, in the runs of the West Bank temples constantly being discovered and excavated. And in one of them awaited Saeed's uncle, with hopefully some answers to even more pertinent questions.

It was 2:13, so I hastened back down the ramps, courtyards and causeways to my bike, swallowed about a gallon of water, and took off down the road towards the temples of the West Bank.

CHAPTER 17 – A CITY IN RUINS

Back in the saddle and dodging seven-year-old hawkers, I slalomed out of the car park and back down the road to the turnoff; the asphalt surface hissing at me like one long black cobra. It was no wonder the Dracos loved Egypt; it was perfect for their cold-blooded asses.

Plotting my course through a myriad of tourist coaches, taxis, and several fully-laden donkeys, I executed one big sweeping turn to the right, passed el-Assasif, rejoined the road south, and peddled into the plethora of temples that dotted the West Bank.

Who knows how many temples there were originally? Collectively, they were known by the Egyptians as the 'Temples of Millions of Years'; each of the temples built by an individual Pharaoh so the masses could continually worship them, not simply through festivals, but even after death. This was hence why Egyptologists often erroneously called them funerary or mortuary temples, rather than, as was intended, to keep the king's cult alive, guaranteeing him eternal deification. I think if we were building them today we would call them Memorial or Testimonial Temples.

The first one I stopped at was the 'Mortuary' Temple of Thutmoses III, which was mostly destroyed, apart from the ruins of a mud-brick pylon. I was sure my notes would tell me if there was any reason to explore it.

'The Mortuary Temple of Thutmoses III consisted of a quay, pylon and court, which led to a façade dressed with Osirid columns.'

Did I read that correctly – a quay? That's a wharf or pier. It was a clear indication that the water level was much higher than at present and totally supported my tsunami theory.

'The sanctuary contained a vaulted ceiling decorated with goddesses of the hours of the day and night, and a false door with an image of the king on the rear wall. There was also a Chapel of Hathor built from blocks re-used from earlier structures.'

It amazed me how these Egyptologists could claim to know so much about a temple from a few scant ruins. But that last bit really got my attention – earlier structures. Again there was reference to temples from another time. Was there red granite here? Most possibly, but given the poor state of restoration of the site, and my ticking clock, I decided I already had what I wanted and peddled on.

Passing another poorly preserved site, which I presumed was the Temple of Siptah, penultimate pharaoh of the 19th Dynasty, I approached Sheikh 'Abd el-Qurna, a hill that contained a hundred-and-forty-six numbered tombs, most from the 18th Dynasty, including supposedly some of the most beautiful private tombs on the West Bank.

On the east side of the road was the site of the Ramesseum, the Memorial Temple of Ramses II. While I could choose to ride on passed many of the other 'unknown' temples, many of which were poorly restored, I wondered if I could pass the opportunity to visit the temple of one of the world's foremost megalomaniacs.

Despite Ramses II having been Egypt's longest serving pharaoh, reigning for sixty-seven years during the peak of the power and glory of ancient Egypt, and having left perhaps the most indelible mark on the country through the many monuments he built, modified or usurped, hardly anyone was visiting the Ramesseum; there were maybe a half-dozen tourists over the whole site. Perhaps it was because it was still undergoing restoration, perhaps because most tourists made a one-day trip to the West Bank, with the check-list headed by the Valley of the Kings, Tutankhamun's Tomb, Hatshepsut's Temple and the Colossi of Memnon. It seemed only the more freely adaptable travellers, like me on my bike, had the flexibility, time and perspicacity that coach tours didn't have.

I wondered if Jacques had bothered to come out here to gloat before he scurried off back to Zurich with his tail between his legs. That led me to wondering how Pernille was doing, and, in turn, that led me to thinking about Crystal. How could I ever get the image of her naked before me out of my mind?

When a large coach went passed and snapped me out of my fantasizing, I checked the time, 2:25, and realized I had plenty of time to daydream later on, and that the sooner I visited all the sites I needed to see, the sooner I would be back across the river, sitting by the bar with Crystal and the others.

I had thirty-five minutes until I was scheduled to meet Saeed's uncle, and, eager to get a move on, I contemplated my choices: I could explore the Ramesseum, then head on to Medinet, or skip the Ramesseum and take in the Valley of the Queens before heading to Medinet. There was so much to see on the West Bank; to really do it credit you needed two days. 'Why wasn't there more time?'

Then I thought; 'There is!' Well, if I went by Egyptian time that is. If I spent ten minutes skating around the Ramesseum, five minutes cycling to the Valley of the Queens, twenty minutes looking around maybe two or three tombs, then five minutes ride back to Medinet that would get me there around 3:05 and that was totally acceptable.

I pulled off the road and raced down to the entrance, soon discovering from the guardian that it was necessary to purchase a ticket at the office some distance further up the road. Stuff that for a lark! I didn't have the time to backtrack and, as he was surrounded by an army of white-uniformed machine-toting antiquities police, I couldn't resort to Plan B by pulling out a twenty-pound note from my pocket and waft it before his eyes. Nor did I relish the concept of having to pay them all. Time for Plan C.

Actually I didn't have a Plan C, not until that moment. I suddenly had an idea and took my wallet from my pocket and flashed my Victorian Drivers' License around the group, trying to focus on the guy with the most pips on his shoulders.

'Professor. I need to visit for ten minutes and take some photo for my book.'

It was a bluff, but I'd used fake ID's when I was a kid with some success and it seemed the akubra appeared to carry some magical clought, because soon they were all nodded and deferring and had bought it hook line and sinker. Hell, I'd out-scammed the unscammable. What I didn't plan on was that they would escort me all the way.

Treading the short dusty path towards the temple, my posse of palomino protectors hovering around like a litter of lap dogs, the first thing that caught my eye was a sole sphinx of Anubis on the grounds of the adjacent site. Like the dog sitting on the Tuckerbox, he seemed poised, looking to the north, waiting for the return of his master. Or maybe he was on guard to bark at the first sign of the next impending tsunami.

I wondered, was there a cult temple to Anubis in this part of the West bank, I didn't think so? No time to loiter and contemplate the ramifications; that could be done later. A quick snap, and it was on to the main temple.

Behind it, about a hundred or so metres further on, stretched the remains of the Ramesseum. I couldn't believe what I saw. Part of the excavation of the northern area had uncovered a wall that extended along the side of the temple *below* the ground level of the temple, and, more importantly, it had a huge doorway, or tunnel opening about twenty to thirty feet below the surface. This was no drainage system; this was an access tunnel, but what to?

I pointed enthusiastically to the subterranean gold mine.
'Yes, here, under the temple.'
'Sorry, no, Doctor, it is not permitted.'
'Yes, but for my book; very important.'

The head honcho was unmoved.
'I am sorry, Doctor; nothing to see, not safe.'

Suddenly I understood why all the armed guards were there; they weren't there to protect me, or the temple, from terrorists, they were there to stop anyone from 'straying' into unauthorized areas. And underground was about as unauthorized as you could get. There may have been a pack of them, but I pulled out my big guns.
'Baksheesh?'

I figured a tenner each would cost me sixty pounds and, though three times more than what I would have initially forked out, it would possibly be well worth it.

Their eyes lit up and darted around each other; the guardians were probably only paid one or two pounds a day at the most; and that for sitting out in the summer heat from 8:00 in the morning until after 6:00 at night, so my money would have been graciously received. The uniformed guys probably didn't get much more either, but, here was the dilemma, they either *all* had to take the bribe, or all decline it.

In the end they all looked to the boss, and, corruption as it was, he clearly didn't trust the others enough to risk his position. So it seemed the mysteries below the Ramesseum would go undiscovered, well, perhaps not so much undiscovered as unreported. Slightly dejected, I headed off into the main site.

The Ramesseum

The Memorial Temple of Ramses II derived its more popular name from Jean-François Champollion, the man supposedly responsible for translating the Rosetta Stone. Champollion coined the term after visiting the ruins in 1829 and identifying the hieroglyphs of the names and titles of Ramses on the walls.

The design followed the standard architecture of New Kingdom temples, and was largely cast in the same mould as Ramses III's Medinet Habu; two stone pylons around sixty metres wide, each followed by a courtyard, the second leading to a Hypostyle Hall and inner sanctuary. It was going to be a whirlwind visit, so thankfully the temple was not as complete as the one at Edfu, more like Kom Ombo; I was mainly looking for granite and further proof of the tsunamis. I knew I had to fly through so I planned to snap as many photos as I could.

The first pylon was incomplete, the outer face missing.

'The outer face was originally carved with scenes of Ramses before various gods, the inner face with reliefs of the Battle of Kadesh. The damage to the pylon is mostly due to its location at the edge of the Nile floodplain. With the annual waters of the inundation reaching almost to the temple's east-facing first pylon, they gradually undermined the foundations of the temple and contributed to the collapsed condition of the structure we see today.'

No way: no one is stupid enough to build a temple right on the edge of a floodplain. It had to be firstly that the level of the Nile was higher than today, and secondly, the damage was due to a tsunami. And how the hell did they know what was on the outer face, when it was long gone? Were they just guessing, like usual?

From the ruins I could see the first court originally had two colonnades, but these were basically gone. On the western side, fronting the second pylon, once sat a pair of gigantic seated colossi of Ramses II. One had fallen to the ground and now lies face down in fragments; were it still standing, it would tower maybe twenty metres above the ground. The other is nowhere to be seen.

Only the right tower remained of the second pylon; again decorated with the Battle of Kadesh on its inner face, Ramses II in his chariot, with his tame lion, attacking the Syrian fort. In front of that was a row of four Osirid pillars, decorated with scenes of Ramses offering to various gods. The court that followed was on a higher level than the first, and also surrounded on each side by a colonnade, now all gone. It looked like someone, or something had just swept through the whole place: there was my tsunami again. Only something that powerful could have swept away a massive statue and most of the colonnades. It was all probably buried somewhere further to the south under metres of sediment.

The rear of the courtyard similarly had four Osirid statues against the columns, and the base of one of another pair of colossal statues. Only the black granite head of one remained; set up in front of the ramps leading to the Hypostyle hall. I snapped a few extra shots and moved on.

Three doors led into the Hypostyle Hall, which once contained forty-eight colourfully decorated papyrus-like columns. On the walls were further reliefs of Ramses' military exploits, as well as his mother Tuya, his wife Nefertari, and some of his one-hundred-and-six children.

'Beneath the Hypostyle Hall, modern archaeologists found a shaft tomb from the Middle Kingdom, yielding a rich hoard of religious and funerary artefacts.'

Again the temple was built on top of another temple, not beside it, which could only mean one thing: the other temple had been washed away! Or, maybe it was still beneath the ground? Perhaps that's where the subterranean doorway led, just like at Elephantine?

The Hypostyle Hall led to a small room with an astronomical ceiling of constellations, with the pharaoh making offerings to the various lunar gods around the edges.

'The chamber behind the Hypostyle Hall was known as the "Astronomical Hall", and may have been used as a library as a large cache of papyri dating back to the 21st Dynasty were found here, indicating that the temple was also the site of an important scribal school.'

Sure they may have found scrolls here, and in the 21st Dynasty it may well have been a library, however during the 19th Dynasty it was more likely the room was used as a barque shrine, as there were lots of scenes of barques bearing the Theban Triad, Ramses and Ahmose Nefertari, each carried by priests.

Next was another small chamber, the 'Hall of Litanies', in which the king offered libations and incense to Re-Horakhty, Ptah, and many other deities. On one of the architraves I could see a relief with five planets and nine kneeling gods.

Five planets - Mercury, Venus, Mars, Jupiter and Saturn? Either that meant they had telescopes, but not powerful ones, or that they were referring to a different solar system, maybe the Nibiru system. Boy, I wished I could decipher the texts that accompanied these reliefs.

The inner sanctuary should have been next. I say 'should have', because everything after here was not just totally destroyed, it was gone! Swept away by the tsunami no doubt.

Surrounding the temple were the ruins of various mud-brick storerooms and granaries.

"The granaries were so large they were capable of storing enough grain for fifteen to twenty thousand people, as well as workshops, and other ancillary buildings, including several other chapels and the temple palace to the south of the first courtyard. In turn, the whole temple complex was surrounded by a mud-brick wall.'

And that was it, all for free, and totally explored in ...2:38, that was thirteen minutes. Shit I was behind schedule.

As my entourage escorted me back to my bike, the captain or whatever gave me the signal. Yes, folks, he wanted some baksheesh, not just for him, but for all the others as well. But not for admitting me for free, or any 'illegal' reason, but because they had escorted and protected me and pointed out specific rocks and reliefs of interest that I could quite easily see for myself. In the end it cost me ten for each of the three foot-soldiers, fifteen for each of the two guardians and twenty for the boss; I had been well and truly scammed by the 'unscammable'.

Eighty pound lighter, I was back on my bike within a minute and peddling my buns off towards the Valley of the Queens, passing a huge excavated area where you could see exactly how much sediment had been deposited in the area during the flooding; at least four to five metres.

It seemed that every hundred metres or so, I passed yet another temple; firstly the totally destroyed Temple of Thutmoses IV, which from the road appeared to have the same similar 18th Dynasty floor plan, then, the ruins of the Temple of Tausert, wife of Seti II, or, as I knew her, Pernille. There wasn't much to see there either; just another reminder of how the tsunami razed nearly everything as flat as a pancake.

I was just south of Sheikh Abd el-Qurna passing Qurnet Murai; a hill with seventeen numbered tombs, mostly dating to the Ramesside period. It was inconceivable that, though there are probably thousands of tombs on the west bank, Egyptologists have only explored and numbered a total of about eight-hundred of them. Zahi Hawass was obviously keeping them for a rainy day.

On the left hand side of the road, just before it forked, the ruins of another temple, the Temple of Merenptah, had been turned into an outdoor museum. Merenptah was a son of Ramses II and ultimately his successor. Though the structure of his temple was similar to that of the Ramesseum; two pylons and courts followed by the temple with two Hypostyle halls, side chambers, and the sanctuary area, it had suffered the same fate; obliterated by the tsunami. Nothing really for me to see, so I took the fork to the right and powered on towards the Valley of the Queens.

About fifty metres further on, the first turn up the road led to Deir el-Medina, the ruins of a village that housed the craftsmen and workers who dug and decorated the royal tombs and other Theban monuments of the New Kingdom. It was also the site of several temples dating up to the Ptolemaic Period. I wasn't sure if I should detour or not: perhaps there was something to be discovered. Best check the iphone. Pausing at the intersection, I quickly scanned my notes.

'There are the remains of several temples and chapels at Deir el-Medinal; including a mud-brick birth-house built by Ptolemy X Soter II and Cleopatra III, and a Roman Chapel of Isis, probably built by Caesar Augustus.'

Augustus; he was the adopted great nephew of Julius Caesar, who sent out the message to have Caesarion, Caesar's son by Cleopatra, killed because he was a threat to Augustus and his legitimacy as ruler of the Roman Empire. Nice guy ... NOT!

'The largest of the surviving temples at Deir el-Medina is the Temple of Hathor. It was built by Seti I on the site of several earlier temples; the first constructed by Thutmoses I and dedicated to Amenhotep I, who was thought to be the founder of the workmen's village, whilst the second temple was built by Ramses II,..'

Who else?

'... and dedicated to the Theban Triad of Amun, Mut and Khonsu. However they were both destroyed during the Ptolemaic Period, after which Ptolemy IV Philopator began the present Temple of Hathor.'

That would be consistent with an earthquake and/or tsunami around 224 BC; I didn't need a detour to see that.

'The gate was added by Ptolemy XIII, a narrow vestibule beyond, decorated by Ptolemy VI, contains very well-preserved and beautifully decorated columns and Hathor pillars, one of which depicts Imhotep with his mother and wife and the deified Amenhotep, son of Hapu.'

Did they mean the god Hapy? If so, it was further confirmation Amenhotep was from the gods, that he was Annunaki, and perhaps one and the same being as Imhotep. Or that maybe he was Imhotep's son?

Though a detour may have been interesting, I felt I could comfortably skip visiting Deir el-Medina. So I stashed my iphone away, made a healthy impact into the contents of my final bottle of water, and once more put the pedal to the metal. Four hundred metres down the road, the next turn off to the right led straight on to the Valley of the Queens.

'Move your asp, Cleopatra, here I come.'

Actually, as far as I knew, there were no Cleopatras buried in the Valley of the Queens, in fact I'm not sure if they've ever found any of the tombs of any of the Cleopatras, especially the famous one, number VII, and her suitor and husband, Marc Antony; that would probably be in Alexandria somewhere.

The Valley of the Queens

I made an athletic dismount from the bike, not all that dissimilar to batman leaping from the bat mobile, locked it to the side of the ticket office, and grabbed a ticket; thirty-five pounds to see three tombs. Then I realized that *didn't* include the Tomb of Nefertari, supposedly the most beautiful tomb in Egypt. I was quickly informed the tomb was closed to visitors but that I could arrange a visit through Cairo. Cairo! Were they serious?

'How much?'

'Twenty-thousand Egyptian pound, for ten minute.'

'What? Have you been out in the sun too long?'

I tried plan B.

'Baksheesh?'

He just smiled and shook his head. OK, if I couldn't justify a hundred to see Tutankhamun's tomb, then I definitely couldn't justify twenty-thousand, even if I had it, which I didn't, and even if it was the most beautiful tomb in Egypt. So, I had just three tombs to see.

'The Valley of the Queens, or by its local names, Biban al-Harim, Biban el-Sultanat, or Wadi el-Melikat, was known in ancient times as Ta-Set-Neferu, "The Place of the Children of the Pharaoh" and begun around the start of the 19th Dynasty; the time of Ramses I.'

It's modern title was actually a poor choice as the tombs didn't just belong to the wives of the pharaohs, but also other male and female family members of the royal family, as well as some high officials of the 18th, 19th and 20th Dynasties. Checking my list of tombs and supposed occupants, it was evident there were even tombs that harken back to the end of the 17th Dynasty.

The valley itself was less imposing than the Valley of the Kings; the cliffs weren't as high, as encroaching, and the valley floor was less undulated and more condensed. By that I mean the tombs were almost lined up in rows.

There were apparently about eighty numbered tombs in the area, but it seemed most weren't open to visitors, so it meant I didn't have to spend much time deciding which tombs to see.

I ran up a short-list, headed by QV 46, belonging to Imhotep, vizier under Thutmoses I, then QV 47, Princess Ahmose, daughter of Seqenenre Tao, QV 76, Merytre, whom, according to my new line of thinking, I presumed was the daughter of Hatshepsut and Senenmut, and wife of Thutmoses III, QV 82, Minemhat and Amenhotep, sons of an 18th Dynasty pharaoh, and finally QV 88, Ahmose, son of an 18th Dynasty pharaoh, but possibly another candidate for the real tomb of Ahmose, not that back at wadi Hillal.

That was five tombs, or a sixty percent chance of striking pay-dirt. Well, that's what I thought, until I checked out the map and couldn't find QV 82 or 88 anywhere on it. I didn't have the time to go hiking over hill and dale to find them, so I cut my losses and aimed for a hundred percent strike rate.

First tomb along the path was QV 76; closed, I could only guess what secrets Merytre had to tell about her mother and husband. I skirted up passed Nefertari's tomb, QV 66, just on the off chance it was open. No.

Nefertari Mery-en-Mut, '*most beautiful, beloved of the goddess Mut*', was the Great Royal Wife of Ramses II, and, according to some Egyptologists, a daughter of King Seti I, and thus sister or half-sister of Ramses II.

By the derivation of her name, I figured Nefertari may also have been the great granddaughter of Queen Ahmose-Nefertari of the 18th Dynasty. It would have been great to see the interior, but it was not to be. Still, I could check my notes and put them into some context.

'Restoration began in 1992 when it was realized the paintings were badly deteriorating due to the effects of dampness. The plaster was strengthened and the damaged areas were painstakingly repaired, and finally cleaned, so that the tomb looks like it was painted only yesterday. But in January 2003 the tomb was completely closed to visitors for an indefinite period as the painted walls were thought to be deteriorating again. Entry is now strictly limited by application to the Supreme Council of Antiquities and to visits of only ten minutes.'

Hence why they charge the ridiculous sum of twenty-thousand Egyptian pounds; they have to make a return on their investment, so, by making it exclusive, they can justify the amount.

'The ceilings are beautifully decorated with yellow stars against a deep blue background, and the walls are painted with mythological scenes concerning Nefertari's life in the Underworld; meetings with gods, genii and monsters, and her ultimate entry into the kingdom of Osiris.'

Pretty much exactly what I had seen in the other tombs, so there was nothing new to see; except perhaps the depictions of Nefertari herself.

'In these scenes, Nefertari is usually depicted wearing a golden crown with two feathers extending from the back of a vulture-like headdress, and clothed in a long, transparent white gossamer gown. She wears rich jewels, in addition to bracelets and a wide golden collar.'

Fortunately I had also downloaded an image or two into my files, so checked out the one of Nefertari. Wow, now those would have been great to see in the flesh; the exquisite restoration of the reliefs to a level where they looked as if they had been painted yesterday - which pretty much they had - but which left the tomb as it would have looked when Nefertari was interred.

But I didn't have the time or funds to pursue a visit into the tomb to see things in person, however I did make a mental note to explore the Internet when I got the chance, to view the interior and the restored images; they sounded divine, it was a pity they were not even moderately accessible to the general public.

'Nefertari's tomb was plundered in antiquity and left open, although several fragments of a gilded wooden coffin and rose granite sarcophagus lid were found.'

Enter the Amun Priests right on cue, and exit me, stage left. With Nefertari's tomb off the itinerary, I felt there was really nothing here that couldn't be seen in the Valley of the Kings, hence why most day-trippers gave it a miss. But I was here now, so best make the most of it.

A little further down the path I found myself outside the first open tomb, QV 55, the tomb of Amunherkhopchef, son of Ramses III, dating to the 20th Dynasty. Since I now had a tomb up my sleeve, I headed in.

'Amunherkhopchef was a son of Ramses III by the Great Royal Wife, Tyti. Although he probably died when he was young, somewhere around the age of fifteen, he held a number of important positions within the court, such as, the fan bearer to the right of the king, a royal scribe and a cavalry commander, probably more honorary than practical.'

Perhaps these were titles he was expected to grow into?

A short flight of steps led down to the entrance corridor and straight into an antechamber with an annex off to the right. On the walls were scenes of Amunherkhopchef's father, Ramses III, leading Amunherkhopchef, who is wearing the sidelocks of youth and carrying a large fan of feathers, to pay homage to various underworld gods. These include Ptah, with his now customary blue skin, the four sons of Horus (Duamutef, Imset, Qebhsenuef and Hapy, protectors of the canopic jars), Isis, Hathor, Shu and Thoth. Surprisingly the annex leading off from the corridor was undecorated.

On the door jambs into the next room were depictions of Isis and Nephthys, performing the purification rite, and through the door was a long corridor with a sarcophagus pit in the centre, and annexes to the right and rear; this must have been the original burial chamber for the young prince.

On either side of the inside of the doorjambs were scenes of Horus.

'On the walls were chapters from the 'Book of the Dead', with reliefs of Ramses III, followed by Amunherkhopchef, before the gates of the kingdom of Osiris and the genies of the underworld, including one with a ox's head, Qutgetef, one with a black dog's head, Heneb-reku, and one with a ram's head, Sematy.'

Throughout the tomb, the decorations were beautiful; well carved and delicately painted on a light blue-gray background in superb detail. The overall appearance gave the tomb a soft and calming feel, much like a modern nursery. In a case at the entrance to the side annex was a Perspex box containing the skeleton of a mummified foetus, which, according to my trusty notes ...

'... belonged to a potential sibling of Amunherkhopchef, an unborn child of his mother, Tyti, who miscarried through grief upon hearing of her son's death .'

The side annex behind it, and the rear annex, which now housed the prince's rose-granite sarcophagus, were both undecorated. However, the architrave over the rear annex leading to the last chamber really caught my attention; it was decorated with the winged solar disk above two uraeus serpents, representing the goddesses Wadjet and Nekhbet. Below it were two more red disks atop the heads of winged serpents. Was this more evidence of Nibiru, the red destroyer? And sitting atop the heads of winged serpents, was that a representation of the reptilians coming from the skies and somehow being associated with Nibiru? It made sense to me.

Done and dusted, I exited the tomb and headed passed QV52, the Tomb of Tyti, which was also open. A quick glance to check the time; 3:03, shit! My brain went into overdrive, I hated being late; five minutes to see the next tomb, then a few minutes to ride back down the hill and I could be there around 3:10. OK, allowing for Egyptian time, it wasn't too bad. But do I visit here, or press on?

'In the first corridor are reliefs of Tyti before numerous deities; Ptah, the four sons of Horus, Thoth, Isis, Nephthys, overseen by a winged Ma'at over the Lintel, and, on the doorjam leading into the burial chamber, the goddesses Neith on the left, and Serqet on the right.'

It sounded pretty much the same as the previous tomb.

'The burial chamber that follows is square, with a ceiling decorated with delicate white stars on a golden background, and three annexes, one off each side and one off the rear.'

An extra annex didn't warrant a visit, unless there was something specifically in it.

'The annexes are all decorated, but vary in their condition. The one to the left is in poor condition, with parts of the wall and floor collapsed, the ones to the right and rear much better preserved.'

Reading on, the scenes sounded similar to those in the other tomb; colourfully painted on lightly carved relief, the figures set against a background of white, grey, or yellow-gold. They covered the usual main gods, solar barques, double scenes of Tyti shaking a sistra, or cobra encircled papyrus scrolls, before the Four Sons of Horus, the queen making offerings to Hathor, Anubis and a lion as guardians, two baboons, a monkey with a bow, a vulture, a hippopotamus, and other supposedly mythological guardians from the Netherworld. The major point of interest seemed to be the different depictions of the queen.

'In some scenes, such as those on the front wall of one of the rear chambers, Tyti is portrayed with the braided sidelocks and clothing of a teenager. In contrast, on the left wall of the corridor, she is represented as a middle-aged woman, with elaborate hairstyle, plumed headdress and dressed more conservatively.'

I guess nothing much has changed in over three-thousand years; women still want to look younger than they actually are.

I decided to give Tyti's tomb a miss and headed down the next path. Unfortunately the tombs of Princess Ahmose, QV 47, and Imhotep, QV 46, were also closed. Bummer, especially the tomb of Imhotep; there wasn't even a guardian around that I could bribe. Imagine if I found some evidence that Imhotep was not only vizier to Thutmoses I, but perhaps even Annunaki? Maybe there would be an extra large sarcophagus, or maybe they built the tomb and he never used it because he lived way beyond the other pharaohs? I looked in my notes but there was nothing about the tomb; which to me meant either there was nothing of note, or the powers that be didn't want us knowing the truth.

There was a tomb just beyond it that was open, QV44, the Tomb of Khaemwaset, eldest son of Ramses III and Queen Tyti, not to be confused with Prince Khaemwaset, fourth eldest son of Ramses II. I decided to use my ticket up and give it a cursory explore.

The inside of the entrance contained reliefs of Khaemwaset depicted on each side of the doorway as a priest. The entrance led to a long corridor with an annex on either side. On the left wall was an image of Ptah, followed by an annex containing images of Khaemwaset before various deities including Anubis, Horus-Inmutef, Selkis and Neith in one scene, and Nephthys and Isis in the presence of Osiris in another.

The decorations were outstanding; elegant workmanship and vivid colours. Once again Osiris was his traditional green colour, whilst Isis and Nephthys were painted predominantly in yellow; a colour it seemed was typically used for these particular female deities.

The annex opening was followed by a scene on the corridor wall of Ramses III presenting his son, Khaemwaset, dressed in a robe and wearing a necklace and the side-locks of youth, making offerings to the guardians of the gates to the afterlife; Thoth, Anubis and Re-Horakhty. It made me consider whether Khaemwaset had died as a young teenager, much like his younger brother, Amunherkhopchef, who died when he was somewhere in his mid to late teens.

Across the corridor, on the right wall, Khaemwaset stood with his father, presenting offerings of incense to Ptah-Sokar, Geb, Shu and Atum. The annex leading off the right wall showed scenes of the prince before Hapi, Ptah, and the four Sons of Horus, while on the rear wall was a double scene of Isis before Osiris, and Nephthys before Ptah-Sokar. However this time the females had green skin; was it an oversight, or a true reflection of their origins?

The corridor led directly to the burial chamber, containing two opposing side niches and a rear annex. The tomb was in a straight axis, just like the later tombs of the Valley of the Kings, but on a smaller scale; the general layout being a long corridor with antechambers, with the burial chamber and annex at the end. On the side-walls were scenes of Khaemwaset being led by his father as they head towards the genies guarding various gates of the kingdom of Osiris. I had no idea who they were, but one had a bird-head. On the rear wall Ramses III presented his son to several other figures I was unfamiliar with, one of whom had a cat's head.

There was no sarcophagus in the tomb, but my notes revealed some answers.

'When the tomb was discovered, numerous sarcophagi were found piled up in the corridor. This was a clear sign that it had been used for common burial.'

'Common burial', are they serious?

'The sarcophagus of Khaemwaset was found in a various pieces, its lid engraved with an inscription dating to the reign of Ramses IV. Why his uncle, Ramses IV, ascended the throne after Ramses III's death, rather than Khaemwaset, is unknown.'

Even I could figure that out, you only had to look at the walls of the tomb. Clearly Khaemwaset had died as a child, and predeceased his father. Hence when Ramses III died, he had no male heir, so his brother, Ramses IV, assumed the throne. As to his damaged sarcophagus and the additional piled sarcophagi, the finger pointed straight back to the 21st Dynasty Amun Priests. Are the Egyptologists so stuck in their thinking that they can't see common sense? It would appear so.

Like the tomb of Amunherkhopchef, at the rear of the burial chamber, across the lintel into the annex, majestically sprawled the winged solar disk of Nibiru above two uraeus serpents, representing the goddesses Wadjet and Nekhbet. The annex itself was decorated with brightly coloured scenes of deities on a gold background. To the left was Anubis the Jackal and a lion, as guardians, then Ramses III offering to Thoth and Horus. The rear wall showed a double scene, of a seated Osiris, with his green skin, being worshiped by Neith and Isis on the left, and Nephthys and Selkis before Osiris on the right. Emerging from a blue lotus flower at Osiris feet were figures representing the four sons of Horus; Imsety, Duamutef, Qebhsenuef and Hapy. The right-hand wall depicted Ramses III offering incense to two deities, Horus and Sheps, then, by the entrance, two guardian genies; one lion-headed, the other a young naked boy wearing a white headdress.

What was interesting was, that in every scene within the burial chamber, it was Ramses III officiating in the offerings, rather than his son, Khaemwaset. In the rest of the tomb the pharaoh seemed to be introducing Khaemwaset to the various gods of the underworld. Talk about an overprotective father!

I hadn't farted around exploring the other tomb, and I wasn't about to start now. In a blink I'd exited QV 44 and was debating whether to visit one more tomb, or give a miss and head on to Medinet Habu. Given I could do a tomb in about two minutes I choose the next tomb up the path, QV 43, that of Sethherkhopchef, another son of Ramses III, but one who would later rule as Ramses VIII.

The second I entered I realised something was amiss; instead of the customary colourful reliefs, the entire tomb was grey and 'dark'. There were some traces of colour visible beneath the black, but most of the reliefs looked like they had no colour at all.

According to the guardian the black appearance was because someone had cooked in here in the past. That didn't wash with me; why would you cook inside a tomb? There were only three small rooms and the oxygen would quickly run out in the confined space; the smoke would be choking to say the least.

Then I entered the left annex and suddenly felt violently ill, dizzy and nauseous. The walls, and especially the ceiling, looked like they had been caramelised. This was no 'cooking' by-product, the stone looked like it had been melted and reformed into a shining black marble. That had to be from some localized intense outburst of heat within this room. I didn't like it at all, and snapped a few photos then got out of there as quick as I could.

As I left Sethherkhopchef's tomb and made my way back to the entrance of the valley, I wondered if he had upset the priests in some way. Sethherkhopchef was actually never buried in QV 43, he was buried in the Valley of the Kings, as he ascended the throne as Ramses VIII.

I sucked in a few deep breaths, and within a minute or two I'd quenched my ever-present thirst and was back on the bike, freewheeling it down the road to Medinet Habu and my meeting with Saeed's uncle.

The forgotten temple

Minutes later, when I pulled up to the West Bank ticket office, I was surprised to find Saeed standing there chatting with a man, whom I presumed was his uncle; both puffing away on their high-tar cigarettes. It was no surprise how the tobacco companies operated, addicting the poorer second and third-world countries with their noxious control rods.

In his usual manner, Saeed swaggered towards me, arms open wide and beaming a landscape of pearly whites from ear to ear.

'Mister Indy, what is it, you could not find it a camel?'

'Saeed, No. Although I did do the King Arthur thing and go on a search for the Holy Grail.'

'The Holy Grail?'

'Yes, I did find a used Camelot, but they didn't have one in Ferrari red, so I had to settle for the bike.'

He burst out laughing.

'Yes, very good. Still, it is good to see it that you have not been left sprawled beside the road with your eyes picked out by the vulture. Please, this it is my uncle, Kareem.'

'Marhabbah, Kareem. Assalaam Alaikum.' - 'Hello, Peace be upon you.'

'Masah al khair, Mister Indy. Wa Alaikum assalaam.' - 'Good afternoon. And peace be upon you.'

'Keef haluk?' - 'How are you?'

His reply was pretty stock standard....

'Al hamdu lillah, bi khair. Shukran.'

.... but I only understood the last word, - 'Thank you.' And that, apart from 'aywa', (yes), 'La' (no), a few choice words of hello, goodbye, and some select phrases to fend off the street vendors, was pretty much the extent of my conversational knowledge of the Arabic language.

Saeed had me pegged straight away and lingered for a second, wallowing in my self-inflicted torture as I pretended I could speak Arabic, before he took charge.

'Please, Indy, we are very impressed with your attempt to speak it Arabic, but my uncle he speaks very good English. Besides, we would not be want you to embarrass yourself any further by without knowing calling the daughter of Mohammad the offspring of it the rapid camel with leprosy.'

I locked up the bike and went to buy a ticket from the office.

'No, Indy, please, you are the guest of my uncle.'

I looked to Kareem and nodded in deference.

'Shukran.'

'Come then, Mister Indy, please to let me show it you Medinet Habu.'

We made our way along the road that led towards the outer wall of the main complex, and then on to the eastern entrance.

'I didn't expect you to be here, I thought I would just be meeting your uncle.'

'You can never know it what Allah he wishes.'

'Well, it's always good to see you.'

'I will be just here if you need me, it is my uncle who is it the expert.'

Saeed clearly respected his uncle and had no intention of treading on his toes or raining on his parade. Accepting that as his cue, Kareem began his guided tour.

'Medinet Habu, it mean "City of Habu", but in ancient time it was name, Djamet, which mean *the male and mother*.'

That didn't make any sense initially, but as I mulled it over I started making loose connections to the pharaohs and their mothers, who would have been the *sang réal*. OK, I might have been clutching at straws but it was all I could think of that made sense.

'This it is outside wall of courtyard of small temple that go back to Eighteen Dynasty, but we will be see more when inside.'

We turned the corner and approached the entrance to the complex. The main façade was asymmetrical, with the Ptolemaic Pylon of the 18th Dynasty temple jutting out to the right.

'Here, once there was it the harbour for the boat, yes? They come in to it temple by canal.'

I pointed to the outline of the quay and the river flat beyond it.

'Kareem, maybe the river was much higher than it is now and came right up to here.'

He looked around slightly bemused, then nodded.

'Yes, yes, maybe it is so.'

'OK, Indy, I will leave you now with my uncle, I must be go off to do it other thing.'

'Thanks again, Saeed, perhaps we can catch up for dinner tonight?'

'Yes, but of course, Inshallah. It is most likely I will be down around it the dock, just ask it as always for Captain Jack.'

'Will do.'

Kareem and Saeed exchanged a few words in Arabic, of which the only word I understood was the last, 'Maasalaamah'; 'Goodbye'.

Then Saeed wandered off into the village to the east, as Kareem took the reins and pointed back towards the entrance to the complex, which was through a pair of low stone buildings.

'This is house of keeper of gate house, yes?'

'Gatekeeper's house, yes.'

I guessed a complex this large must have had a number of gatekeepers who guarded the entrance and had beds in the building. Next was an impressive convoluted gateway covered in decorations of Ramses III trampling the enemies of Egypt, and standing atop the heads of his prisoners. Then, having got the nod from the temple guardian, we entered the complex.

'This it is Migdol Gate; name after fortress of Syria that impress-ed Ramses so much he copy it and use it as gate...'

Near it were two statues of Sekhmet.

'...Come I show it to you room of harem.'

He took us up a staircase and into a room above the gateway, which was decorated with images of the pharaoh relaxing with scantily-clad dancers.

'Here harem of Ramses and the wife they plotting to kill him, but they not have the success.'

'He must have been a real asshole.'

And then I thought, 'Actually, he *was*; that was Jacques, and I wondered if the woman who tried to assassinate him was Pernille?

We headed down the stairs and on to the next building; a smallish structure of a few rooms.

'This it is Chapel of Wife of Amun, from Twenty-five Dynasty; Nubian...'

Kareem pointed to the lintels above the entrances to the chapels.

'...This say, *Appeal to Living*, which it mean those who pass they are ask-ed to repeat Offering Formula for it the ka of these women.'

I guess that meant the priestesses somehow still had a little power and attraction; even as late as the 25th and 26th Dynasties. Moving inside, there were even better reliefs in the forecourt and sanctuary.

'This, Shrine of Amenirdis, sister of King Shabaka, Twenty-five Dynasty.'

She was probably also his wife, and if she was, then that meant that somehow the *sang réal*, or rather the concept of it, had survived at least until around 700 BC.

The guided tour was great, and I was surely appreciative of it, but what I really wanted to talk to Kareem about was the Aswan Dam and the looting of the temples. The question was, when was it diplomatically polite for me to raise the subject? It didn't feel right just yet, so we moved on towards the main temple.

The Mortuary Temple of Ramses III

We paused in the huge open courtyard that led to the first pylon.

'This Temple of Ramses III. It once called "Mansion of Million of Year of User-Maat-Re Meriamun". User-Maat-Re Meriamun was throne name of Ramses III. It one of largest temple in Egypt, it measure about seven hundred foot by one thousand foot, second only to Karnak, but much better preserve. Whole temple it have huge mud-brick wall around, with two gate, one we come in, and one on other side. Temple it have over seventy-five thousand square foot of relief and carving on walls.'

I could see how the huge mud-brick wall surrounding the complex in the background would have provided some protection from the tsunami, and probably accounted for why the temple was still relatively intact when compared to the temples around it on the rest of the West Bank; maybe he even anticipated the possibility of a tsunami.

In any case, Ramses III had modelled his temple exactly on that of his ancestor Ramses II, which made total sense when you thought about the fact he had reincarnated so as to continue his reign; now he had an excuse to build yet another temple. So, this temple would give a good overview of what the Ramesseum looked like before its destruction.

The First Pylon was about the same size as the one at Luxor and Edfu, but had lost the cornice and right corner. Both sides were decorated with battle scenes.

'On left is Ramses he defeat Nubian, on right he defeat Syrian'

On one tower the pharaoh was busy smiting his enemies in front of Re-Horakhty, while on the other tower, he was bashing the crap out of them in front of Amun Ra. The funny thing was, that from my research, Ramses III never fought either the Nubians or the Syrians; but far be it for Ramses to let a minor detail like that affect his self promotion.

As we walked through the pylon, on the left a larger-than-life Ramses scattered the Libyans with his chariot, while, on the right, scribes were busy tallying up the severed hands and genitals of his enemies.

Kareem unlocked a gateway within the tower of the pylon and took us to the top. The view was extraordinary, looking right over the silt flats down to the Nile and the Colossi of Memnon in one direction, to the Ramesseum, Deir el-Bahri and the other temples in another, and to the Valley of the Queens, and Deir el-Medina to the west. I was going to broach the topic of the Aswan Dam, but, before I could, Kareem took off down the staircase. I snapped a few photos for my memoirs and followed the leader; I would look for another opportunity to 'chew the fat'.

Back down the pylon, we emerged into the first inner courtyard. About forty metres long and thirty metres wide, it was flanked by colonnades; the right side of which had Osirid statues of Ramses III attended by knee-high queens. The battle scenes from the front of the pylon continued on the north wall of the court, predictably exaggerated, but also included, on the back of the pylon, a scene of Ramses III leading his chariot in a hunt for wild oxen.

The outside of the Second Pylon contained reliefs showing Ramses proclaiming his victories in Asia and leading rows of prisoners to Amun on the right, and Mut on the left.

'Here, Mister Indy, you will see it on the roof of the gateway between the pylon, it is paint with the wing-ed disc of the sun and cobras.'

There was Nibiru popping up again, but I wondered what Kareem's take on it was.

'Do you know what it means?'
'It is protector of the god.'

Protector? More like a sword of Damocles perhaps.

'In back of column on south side of court, in middle of wall, is "Window of Appearance", yes. This where Ramses he present gold collar to loyal general. It lead out to Royal Palace.'

We exited through a side door and out into what were the ruins of the palace. For some reason there was virtually nothing but foundations left. Whether it had been washed away, or harvested, who knows; I certainly didn't.

However dumbfounded I may have been, I exhibited all the outward signs of how suitably impressed and grateful I was for the guided tour, and chose the opportunity to open up a discussion with Kareem about Aswan.

'Kareem, Saeed tells me you worked on the building of the Aswan Dam at Philae.'

'Yes, Mister Indy, as it the boy.'

'You must have seen some pretty amazing things.'

'Oh, yes, many, many such thing.'

He seemed slow on the uptake, probably because his priority was to show me the temple first. Instead, he led us along the exterior of the temple, through a doorway, and back into the second court, about the same size as the first. There were beautiful colonnades on three sides, the tops of the columns and the ceilings still having their original colouring.

'This it is second courtyard, this relief it show festival of god, Min and Sokar.'

Kareem also showed me scenes of the pharaoh with priests, making offerings to various deities, and, on the rear wall, a procession of the numerous sons and daughters of Ramses III.

We were about to enter the main body of the temple and, for some bizarre reason, maybe the sudden presence of a Kalashnikov toting guard, I felt I couldn't bring up the topic of robbing temples while treading the paths of the inner sanctum. Alas, too late and Kareem was ushering me into the Hypostyle Hall.

'Now we are in it first Hypostyle Hall. As you can see it is badly damage, probably by earthquake in 27 B.C.'

Earthquake? Normally I would have gone for that, but you only had to look around to see that didn't add up. The roof was missing and almost all of the twenty-four pillars, apart from the six rows of hieroglyphic-covered bases, were missing. If there *had* been an earthquake, all the pieces would still be here, somewhere, and possibly even have been restored. But the missing pieces were *totally* missing. Where were they? That was a mystery even a tsunami couldn't quite answer. However it did give me another possible date for an earthquake and tsunami.

'To the right is eight chapel, include; Ramses III, Ptah, Ramses II, Sokar, Osiris and sacred boat of Amun Ra. Left side is again eight chapel, six for store and treasure, one for sacred boat of Ramses II, and one for boat of God, Montho.'

There were reliefs depicting the weighing of gold and other valuables such as sacks of precious stones. No sooner had I given them the once over, than Kareem drifted deeper into the temple.

'Second hall contain, on left, funeral chamber of Ramses III, with Thoth he write it name of king on sacred tree of Heliopolis.'

It was similarly roofless and had eight columns in two rows, also severely truncated.

'On other side, chapel with it the altar to Re.'

As usual the altar was granite, totally out of place, and had obviously been usurped from some earlier temple. The third hall that followed was similar to the second, although the central aisle was flanked by statues of Ramses with Maat or Thoth. That in turn led to three sanctuaries dedicated to the Theban Triad: Mut to the left, Amun in the centre, and Khonsu to the right.

'Here, is it chapel of Amun. The wall, they cover it in electrum, yes, with doorway of gold. The door it have copper and many rich stone. Behind is false door for Amun-Ra.'

We walked back out through the temple and, as we hit the second courtyard, I felt sufficiently comfortable to make a second attempt at raising the topic of Aswan.

'When I was talking to Saeed on the boat, I was telling him that I thought the building of the Aswan Dam was just an excuse to rob the temples.'

'Yes, many thing they are taken from temple.'

'You worked at Philae, right?'

'Yes.'

'I'd love it if I could ask you some questions.'

He glanced around, as I did, making note again of the ever-present military presence that hovered in the shadows.

'Yes, yes, please. Saeed he tell me this. Come, we go around.'

He led us back out the doorway through which we'd first entered the second courtyard, lit up a cigarette, and we continued viewing the exterior of the temple.

'When you worked on the temple at Philae, did they finish the move?'

'No, they are run out of time, and water from lake over run wall of coffin...'

By coffin I assumed he meant the walled reservoir that had been erected around the island to protect it from the rising waters.

'...They remove all the piece of temple and get down to ground. Then they start to take it away stone from ground, but find other temple under.'

'Another temple? This was on the original island; the island of P'aaleq?'

'Yes, they only plan time to remove what they see, temple above. Now they find it much older temple and they are having no time left.'

'What did they do?'

'This when they tell all to leave. But, maybe one week after they bring us back, this time there are many Russian, soldier, they tell us we get special pay but must keep quiet what we see.'

Russians; was this another part of Project Isis? And, if it was, then what did they *really* find under the temple.

'We move top temple but when we find it passage or statue we are all told to leave and Russian they take over. When we come back, it is all gone.'

'Do you think they got everything?'

'No, run out of time; water flood everything.'

'Did they move the temple underneath?'

'No, just take it everything inside.'

That meant that the original temple at P'aaleq was still there, under the waters between the first and second dams. Kareem continued his guided tour, pointing at the southern wall.

'Here it is carving of festival calendar.'

They were faint but discernible.

'Tell me, do you remember what this other temple was made out of?'

'Stone.'

'Yes, but was it sandstone, like the temple on top?'

'No, it made of granite, red granite.'

'And what was on the walls, what sort of paintings?'

'No painting.'

'Nothing? No reliefs, no hieroglyphs?'

'Very strange; no painting, no relief, just very smooth. Very large block, much bigger than block of temple on top.'

'So who do you think took all the treasure, the Russians?'

'Of course, and UNESCO, they both take it the treasure.'

It meant that somehow the Russians and UNESCO were connected, and the only way that could be was through the Illuminati. UNESCO was easy, but how did the Russians get connected to the Illuminati? I did a quick cerebral exploratory of joining the dots.

The Illuminati were the funders of all the wars since they discovered the scrolls in 1118. They funded and provided weapons for both sides for all the wars from the 13th Century onwards. And they had a vendetta, an agenda, to bring down both the aristocracy of the French royal family and the Roman Catholic Church.

So they funded the Spanish and English against the French in the 14th and 15th Centuries and into the 16th Centuries. Hell, they backed anyone who wanted to go to war, and slowly they infiltrated each and every government and religious organization on the planet. They brought about the French Revolution and backed Napoleon, and likewise they would have backed Lenin and the Bolshevik revolution in Russia in 1917, and Hitler and the Nazis in Germany.

These guys left no stone unturned in their quest to control the whole world; and they were patient, plotting and planning over decades, placing their people in control. So they must have accumulated treasure not just from ancient Egypt, but the royalties of all the European dynasties; France, Spain, Russia, and the accumulated treasure of the Nazis. I returned my focus to Kareem.

'Where do you think the ancient treasure is now?'

'In private collection of people like Mubarak and Hawass.'

'Mubarak? The former President?'

'Oh yes, he has been it the most corrupt.'

'He's supposed to be worth around seventy billion dollars US.'

'Seventy billion US dollar, where you think he get all this money?'

I thought for a second.

'Isn't it through military contracts?'

'Where you read it that fairy story?'

'But didn't it come from military contracts when Mubarak was an officer in the Egyptian Air Force.'

'Mubarak was officer in Egyptian Air Force 1959 to 1961; he train in Moscow in Soviet Union.'

1961? Russia? I wondered if Mubarak knew about Project Isis, hell, I wondered if he was *part* of Project Isis! Was he even part of the Illuminati itself? It opened up a Pandora's box of intrigue and conspiracy involving the Egyptian Government, the Russian Government, UNESCO, the United Nations, and at the apex of it all sat the Illuminati, pulling the strings of everyone like the grand hidden puppet-masters they are.

'Do you think Mubarak knew about the treasure in the temples?'

'Of course, Mubarak he cannot make it so much money from just military contract. But he could not rob temple as easy as he want. That is why he kill Sadat.'

'Mubarak killed President Sadat?'

Kareem glanced back over his shoulder and shivers went up my spine; the same armed guard was standing outside the temple looking in our direction. Kareem turned back and hastened his step.

'Not him in person, but it was military that kill President Sadat 1981; they suppose to be against the sign of it Egypt-Israel Peace Treaty. That when Mubarak he become President.'

As we turned the corner to the west end of the complex, my mind was ticking a million miles an hour. Of course they killed Sadat, the Illuminati would *never* want peace - anywhere. Peace is not profitable. The Egyptian military were just Illuminati puppets.

'You think Mubarak was part of the assassination plot?'

'Does camel spit?'

'If Mubarak was put in place by the Illuminati, it would have been to make sure there was no peace, because the Illuminati made most of their money through weapons sales, hence why they chose Mubarak, a military man, and someone they could easily bribe through military contracts.'

I guess I was really thinking out loud, in any case, Kareem had a different slant on things.

'And once President, Mubarak he free to sell ancient treasure from the tomb and the temple to anyone who will pay.'

'And who wants it most, and has the money to buy it, the Illuminati.'

Either he didn't fully understand what I was implying, or Kareem *didn't* want to fully understand what I was saying. Instead, he walked towards the external mud-brick wall, seemingly more preoccupied with his temple.

'This it is west gate. Was destroy-ed when temple was attack in time of Ramses XI.'

Basically there was nothing left to see, so we continued outside and around the temple complex.

'I see how Mubarak was involved, but what about Hawass?'

'Mubarak he can use army to keep western eye from seeing, and also he use army to move treasure, but he need someone inside to run for him, tell him when new thing they are discover-ed.'

'But why Hawass, isn't he the great protector of the ancient temples?'

Kareem's cynical laugh rattled along the outer wall of the temple.

'Oh yes, Zahi great protector; so he can pick it eyes out of carcass. Then all left for you to see is bare bones.'

'But why?

'Simple, baksheesh. Zahi Hawass he very greedy man. He want be famous, and be rich.'

'Well the man has a massive ego, that's for sure. But how? How does he do it?'

'Zahi he graduate from Alexandria University 1967, then he get it job as Inspector for Tuna el-Gebel, Mallawi, and also at Abydos with Mission from Yale-Pennsylvania...'

Pennsylvania, the Liberty Bell, it must have been this first contact with people within the Yale-Pennsylvania group that led to Hawass's first involvement with the Illuminati. I wondered what the special interest in Abydos was. I guessed I would find out in a few days when I visited the temple.

Meanwhile, Kareem continued his biographical exposé on Hawass.

'...From 1972 until 1974 he Inspector at Giza, then Abu Simbel. From 1974 to 1979 he become First Inspector for Giza pyramid, then 1980 he become Chief Inspector at Giza. It then that Zahi he discover many thing beneath Giza Plateau.'

'Such as?'

'He dig in front of the Sphinx temple, and, fifty feet down, what you think he find?'

'Limestone? Chambers?'

'He find it red granite.'

I was stunned.

'But red granite's not natural to the Giza Plateau; the only source is in Aswan. It proves there's something under the ground there.'

As my imagination went into overdrive of what lay beneath the Giza Plateau, we reached the outer corner of the temple complex. Kareem paused and pointed out over the ground.

'Here, outside of wall, is temple of Horemheb, which he take it over from Ay, and South Temple also, but very little remain.'

Very little remained of anything outside the temple wall, but then again there was probably less than ten percent of the ancient ruins of Egypt that had been identified and excavated, and most of that was superficial by my reckoning, so who knows what lay beneath the sand and mud-brick wall that stretched out before me.

We made our way through a break in the wall and back to the temple itself, and though I may have only been a pace or two behind, in reality I was still fifty feet underground in Giza. Having arrived at the temple wall, Kareem set off down the side, back towards the entrance.

'All over these wall is story of the battle of the Pharaoh.'

As we scanned the reliefs he tossed away a comment.

'You know of course Giza Plateau is special official military zone, yes?'

'What? I thought the whole country was a military zone. No, I didn't know that. Why? Why would Giza be a special military zone?...'

Before I knew it I started brainstorming out loud.

'...Unless it was connected to Project Isis and there were things beneath the surface of great interest to the military, like the famed Hall of Records, that's supposedly beneath the right paw of the Sphinx, or ancient technologies and possibly even ancient weapons.'

Kareem kept walking.

'It was next year, 1981, Sadat he was killed, he know too much, he going to tell rest of world about what is find under Giza. This why he is killed and Mubarak he take over as President.'

'All a little too much of a coincidence.'

'Then five year later, new room they are found in great pyramid.'

'I remember that, there was all sorts of excitement about possible rooms off the King's Chamber and the passage to the Queen's Chamber, but then everything went quiet.'

'Zahi he closed the pyramid for six month.'

'To find the rooms?'

He chuckled away sarcastically under his breath.

'Of course.'

'So how come we didn't hear anything about it?'

'Because it was just to do it the repair work, yes.'

'So it was all a cover up?'

'Of course. And soon after, 1987, as reward for his *repair* work, he become General Director at Giza and Saqqara and become professor from University of Pennsylvania.'

'That's right, he was a Fullbright Fellow there, but I seem to remember Edgar Cayce's son saying something about how he was the one who got Hawass a scholarship there through ARE, the Association for Research and Enlightenment, and a person on the Fullbright scholarship board, so that Hawass could get a Ph.D in Egyptology.'

'Yes.'

'And what it is they get from Hawass in return?'

'They get it to keep all the secret secret and to pick it the carcass clean before the body it is reveal-ed to public.'

'But there are many foreign archaeologists in Egypt, and there's been many foreign investigations on the Giza Plateau, surely they have found out the truth? What about the doors in the queen's shafts? John West, Bauval, Hancock, all those guys would have to know the truth.'

'Yes, but to tell it mean they will be it banned from more work in Egypt. Zahi he must have complete control of what it is reveal-ed to public.'

'So Hawass *is* withholding the truth?'

'No more than Aswan Dam hold back river Nile.'

I'd taken a liking to Kareem, I could see where Saeed got his sense of humour.

'But if Hawass is such an asshole, why don't the government or someone just get rid of him.'

I guess that was probably the dumbest question I had ever asked, and Kareem stopped dead in his tracks laughing.

'They try, several time. It 1993, Hawass he fired by his boss, Doctor Bakr, because valuable statue under custody of Zahi disappear from Giza. Zahi he fly to America and meet with CIA, then three month later Mubarak reinstate Zahi as Chief Inspector, and Doctor Bakr he fired instead. Doctor Bakr he then say to public that official *mafia* they have been involved with Pyramid for over twenty year, and block archaeologic work for their own purpose.'

'So Hawass is just a puppet put in place by foreign groups, like the American Research Centre in Egypt, who are probably themselves a front for the Illuminati.'

'Very good. Then two year after, 1996, Zahi he expel it all foreigner from Giza, and next year become Undersecretary of State for Giza.'

'Makes you wonder what they found, and whether the statue Hawass was in custody of was something to do with it?'

'Yes, but many foreigner they start to ask it many many question, cause many problem for Zahi, so he and Mubarak they come up with it idea of Luxor attack, to get rid of foreigner.'

'JESUS!...'

Kareem had stopped me dead in my tracks; I must have looked more like an osirid relic from an Indiana Jones movie.

'...You mean the terrorist attack at Hatshepsut's Temple; I thought that was done by Al Gamaa al-islamiyya.'

'This it is what they wish it the people to believe.'

'How did they do it?'

He looked around, half expecting that the walls had ears, and, as if on cue, the same military guard appeared from a doorway in the temple wall up ahead. Was I being watched? Was he keeping a protective eye on me? And then I thought, 'Or was he watching Kareem?' Kareem's response seemed to indicate the later.

'We not talk here. Come, this way.'

He led us away from the temple wall, across the scant foundations of outer structures and towards a small nilometer near the outer wall and the eastern corner. There was nothing out of the ordinary about it, though it confirmed that the level of the river must have been much higher around the time of Ramses III. But could it be true? Could Zahi Hawass, the "protector" of the ancient Egyptian culture, not only be corrupt, but directly responsible for the deaths of over sixty innocent people? It beggared disbelief. But then again so did so many other things that had unfolded on the trip so far.

'Wow, so the Luxor massacre *was* deliberately done; to get westerners out of Egypt.'

Kareem leaned in and lowered his voice.

'Yes, and in next year pyramid it all closed and Zahi he do more secret excavation. Then, for no reason, all of a sudden he halt it all research for ten year at Giza, and 2002 he become Secretary General of Egyptian Supreme Council of Antiquities and build it wall around Giza Plateau.'

'But wasn't that to protect the pyramids and Sphinx?'

My naivety was amusing Kareem, and he chuckled away.

'Hawass always say how foreigner want to steal it from the Egyptian people, and that antiquity they belong to all Egyptian; it make Zahi look like he fight for Egyptian people. But truth is, Zahi is one who do all the robbing.'

'Are you sure?'

'I have known him Zahi Hawass for many year, I very sure.'

As our police shadow approached from the temple, Kareem led the way into the southeast corner of the compound.

'This it is Sacred Lake, one time very much the garden. Here where childless women come to bathe at night and pray to Isis for to have it the baby.'

It wasn't fully excavated, as was the case with much of the site, but there was a squarish pool of stagnant water that gave an indication that things must have been much more tropical than they now were; perhaps a result of the shifting of the earth at the last pole shift around 1600 BC.

The King is dead, long live the King

I was now very aware of the tail we had acquired, so quickly reverted to our discussion on Hawass, fearful that Kareem may shut up shop.

'So what you are saying is, that having contrived to get all the foreigners out of Egypt by making it too dangerous for them, and building a huge wall around the Giza plateau, Zahi Hawass was free to do whatever he wanted?'

'Exactly this. It was 2003, Zahi he expel fourteen foreign expedition from Egypt and deny hundred more. He decide who can dig and where, and reserve it the exclusive right to tell the finding. Zahi he dig at Giza and many other place, and rob what he find. And for his effort, 2009, Zahi he promoted personally by Mubarak to Vice Minister of Culture.'

'But the Egyptian people finally had enough, right, and rose up last year and ousted Mubarak.'

'And who it was take it over Egypt?'

'Well, the military.'

Kareem just looked at me and raised an eyebrow. I got it straight away.

'So nothing has changed?'

'A jackal in sheep skin, still a jackal.'

'What about Hawass then?'

'Before he go, Mubarak personally appoint it Zahi as Minister of Antiquity.'

Our shadow drew uncomfortably near and Kareem sensed it was time to move on.

'Come, we see it small temple.'

We moved back towards the main entrance to the small temple fronted by the original Ptolemeic pylon.

'So what has Hawass done since the revolution?'

'First thing Zahi he do is say how many site they have been rob or damage by the looting. But, when revolution it begin in January, only a few report of looting, including museum in Cairo.'

'But he said the antiquities guards and security forces at the sites were unarmed and this made them easy targets for armed looters.'

'Zahi, also he say Egyptian police cannot protect every site in Egypt. Most site in Egypt are military site, so it all big lie. Since Mubarak he resign, the looting it have supposed to increase all over Egypt, and many antiquity in grave danger from criminal who try to take advantage of situation.'

'But didn't Hawass use the military to protect sites?'

Kareem could hardly contain his mirth.

'Like most western people you so blind. Of course Zahi he use military to protect, but not from looter; Zahi Hawass he use military to protect Zahi Hawass, to keep it the foreign press away so he can rob it all the site, then he report site have been robbed by looter. At Giza, near Sphinx, looter break into tomb of Impy. In Saqqara, part of false door it is stolen from tomb of Hetepka, and illegal excavation it have been report near pyramid of Merenre and Mastaba Fara'un.

Also in Dahshur and Abydos looter have attack every night with it illegal excavation, some five metre deep; that not simple overnight raid. Then, north of Edfu at Nekhen several supposed thief they have been caught.'

'Nekhen, that's el Kab, right?'

'Yes, very sacred place. Like this temple....'

The Small Temple

We had arrived at the rear side wall of the Small Temple. I compared it quickly to the Mortuary Temple of Ramses III. The larger temple sat almost perfectly facing southeast, and yet the Small Temple was slightly out of alignment, further to the south. Was this an indication of the shifting precession of the rising sun? It had to have some connection to it, there is no way the Egyptians would build something out of alignment and not have a logical reason for it.

'...It holy ground, one of most sacred spot in all of Egypt. This primeval mound from which first arise out of receding water of Chaos. This burial place of first four pair of primeval god, and birth place of creator god, Re-Atum.'

My attention was quickly drawn to the ground, or more correctly to what might lie beneath the floor. As we entered a side doorway, Kareem continued his narration.

'Temple it was start in Eighteen Dynasty by Hatshepsut and Thutmoses III, three hundred year before Ramses III. She build it small temple to Amun on site of temple from before then, but we not sure when.'

It was another reinforcement that Hatshepsut deliberately build her temples on the sites of pre-existing temples that dated back probably to the time of Montuhotep or even earlier, perhaps back to the burial of the primeval gods, the time of the Zep Tepi. Who knows what treasures lay under the ground here!

And, as we moved through and out of the temple, we moved forward in time. And so did I.

'So Hawass is still in charge, still pulling the strings?'

'On April 17, Zahi he sentence to one year jail for refuse to obey court rule. But next day National Council of Egypt Administrative Court issue decree that stop it court rule. They say Zahi not serve it the jail time, and him to remain in it position as Minister of Antiquities. Then again Zahi escape it the justice when on June 15 he clear-ed of all charge.'

'I guess it helps to have friends in high places.'

'All very corrupt, government all very big pack of jackal.'

'Or a flock of vultures.'

Kareem sniggered away.

'Vulture, yes, very good.'

As we passed through the outer parts of the temple, with it's additions by later dynasties, I found myself rummaging around in the vaults of my memory, which was all too crammed with numerous midnight challenges of trivial pursuit.

Actually a circling group of vultures is bizarrely called a kettle, though I could never figure out why, whilst on the ground they were called a venue. I wondered if the ground reference had its origins with the meeting and goings on of the Egyptian Government.

'This was original entrance to temple, but it is replace by pylon of Nubian King Shabaka which is then take over by nephew, Taharqa.'

There was then a small fronting gateway built during the 26th Dynasty, which was usurped during the 29th by Nectanebo I, and finally the Ptolemaic Pylon, the latest addition, built in the 3rd Century BC and decorated with the brightly coloured winged sun-disc.

We'd come full circle, but I certainly hadn't finished where I had started. Though I did feel the uncomfortable presence of the police bearing down on us. Kareem sensed it as well.

'OK, Mister Indy, that is it Medinet Habu.'

It wasn't on the visiting list of most tourists, but Medinet Habu certainly should be. I shook his hand firmly and full of not only gratitude, but a well concealed fifty pound note.

'Shukran, Shukran jazeelan.'

'Aafwaan. You good man.'

'Can you tell me more about Zahi Hawass's involvement in the Luxor massacre?'

He grew even more uneasy, looking back over his shoulder at our encroaching shadow.

'We not talk about this here, too dangerous, but I can speak it more tonight, at Abou Asraf, restaurant of my brother, 8:00pm.'

'I'll be there. I guess I can get the location from Saeed later.'

'Yes, very good.'

'I'll see you tonight, then?'

He looked back over his shoulder, then quickly and quietly concluded the tour.

'Yes, Inshallah.'

'Assalaam Alaikum.' - '*Peace be upon you.*'

'Wa Alaikum assalaam' - '*And peace be upon you.*'

Kareem disappeared back into the complex, shadowed by his military escort, who gave me enough of a parting scowling glare to send me scurrying back to my bike as fast, yet inconspicuously, as I could.

It was 4:25 by the time I arrived back at the bike, gulped down the remainder of my final bottle of water, and set off towards the river. What the hell was going on? This was supposed to be a fun two-week 'journey of a life-time', and in many ways it was, but suddenly I felt like James Bond uncovering some worldwide conspiracy. Any second I expected Blofeld, Dr. No, or Goldfinger to pop up amid his bevy of gorgeous women. Now that part I could handle; Jane Seymour, Britt Ekland, Ursula Andress, mmmm.

What if Crystal was a double agent like Pussy Galore, Elektra King or Octopussy. Hmmm, what a way to go. I loved those double-entendre names, Plenty O'Toole, Solitaire, Mary Goodnight, Holly Goodhead, and of course, Onatopp. There was even a Bond girl called Tracy Draco.

That got me thinking just how deep the connection of the screenplays really went into world control. What did the movie-makers really know? Hollywood and the Illuminati? It made perfect sense. Hell they may even have been the advertising and marketing departments of the Illuminati; what better way to influence and control the masses than via mass media.

What if Kareem had definite proof that Mubarak and Hawass were implicated in the Luxor massacres? Shit, that would be massive! It was clear Kareem had an issue or two with Hawass himself, but maybe that was just professional jealousy and rivalry. On the other hand, maybe, just maybe, it was based on factual evidence and experience.

The Temple of Amenhotep III

The trip back passed the excavation of Kom el-Hettan, the Temple of Amenhotep III. It was closed to the public because of ongoing excavations, but stopping along the road and looking through the fence, it was easy to see the current status and, checking my notes, what was going on.

'Dedicated to Amun-Re, the principal god of the New Kingdom, and covering a total of thirty-five hectares, in its day,

196

the temple complex was the largest and most opulent in Egypt. Even the later temple complexes such as the Ramesseum, Medinet Habu; and the Temple of Karnak, as it stood in Amenhotep's time, were unable to match it in area. However, very little remained today, supposedly either washed away by annual floods or pilfered for use in the adjacent temple of the early 19th Dynasty pharaoh, Merenptah.'

I had a different explanation; the whole temple had been blasted away by a massive tsunami that surged up the Nile. And my theory was supported by the metres of silt that had buried the site and in fact pieces of the temple had been found not only all over the West Bank, but on the East Bank as well.

Given the format for temple design and building that now seemed common for the period, it wasn't hard to project it onto the excavation before me. Fragments of architecture, traces of mud-brick pylons and the limestone bases of what I would presume were papyrus columns, were emerging from the ground giving a general outline of the temple, including a columned hall at the rear, which looked to have been built on higher ground.

Moving eastwards, towards the river, there was what would have been an avenue of sphinxes leading from the third pylon towards a solar court that would have been surrounded by colonnades of sandstone papyrus columns and Osirid statues of Amenhotep III.

At the south side of what would have been the entrance to the solar court, a huge quartzite stela had been re-erected. From the road I couldn't see what was on it, but checking my notes revealed the contents.

'The stela contained references to Amenhotep III, Queen Tiye and the god Ptah-Sokar-Osiris, with texts below describing the king's building accomplishments.'

According to symmetrical design, that meant the twin of the stela, with similar texts, should have been on the north side of the entrance, but it was absent, probably under the silt somewhere upriver due to the tidal surge.

Continuing along the road, there were two large courts between the three pylons, all of which would have contained seated statues of the king. Numerous statue pieces had been excavated, cleaned, restored and were placed on concrete pedestals around the site, creating the impression of an open-air museum much like at the Temple of Merenptah.

'A headless sphinx of Queen Tiye was found near the second mud-brick pylon and there were also jackal statues on high pedestals as well as Osirid statues of the king. Another headless sphinx with the body of a crocodile was found in 1957 in situ on the southern side of the temple site.

In 2002 archaeologists unearthed three large statue fragments at the site of the second pylon: the right half of a red granite colossal seated statue of Amenhotep III, the head of a queen wearing a pharaonic head-dress with uraeus, and an unidentified pair of legs on a rectangular pedestal. A further two statues were unearthed in 2009, a polished black-granite statue of the king seated on a throne, a quartzite sphinx, and a four-metre statue of Thoth.'

I couldn't see any of the later statues, though I would have loved to see the statue of Thoth, but, near the centre of the site, a colossal granite statue of Amenhotep III, wearing the red crown of Lower Egypt, had been reconstructed.

'The head of the statue was taken to the UK in the 19th Century by Henry Salt and ended up in the British Museum. An exact replica was made by Michael Neilsen of the British Museum and taken to Egypt to complete the statue.'

Originally it would have been one of a pair, its companion presumably wearing the white crown of Upper Egypt. I couldn't see it, but apparently the head had been discovered just over a year ago.

'One of the best preserved likenesses of Amenhotep III, although the royal beard is missing, it is in almost perfect condition; smoothly-polished with finely-carved features and traces of red paint still on the uraeus.'

The entrance to the temple, facing south-eastwards towards the Nile, was guarded by two gigantic statues of Amenhotep III, known as the Colossi of Memnon. The name was more than likely a hangover from the Ptolemeic era, as Memnon was a Greek, the hero of the Trojan War, which in turn made me start linking Memnon with Amenhotep and Akhenaten.

The statues depicted Amenhotep III seated with his hands resting on his knees, gazing eastward toward the river and, one would presume, the rising sun. At his feet, alongside his legs were two shorter figures carved into the front of the throne; his wife Tiye and mother Mutemwiya. On the side were panels depicting the Nile god, Hapy, as well a numerous Greek and Latin inscriptions of those who had visited in the past. And, wonder of wonders, the statues were not only accessible to the general public, but, could you believe it, could be viewed and examined for free!!!

I didn't waste a second, pulled up the bike, and zeroed in to take a closer look.

The Colossi of Memnon

Known to the locals as el-Colossat, or es-Salamat, the massive twin statues looked more like two rusting old battle-scarred warriors than revered Goliath kings. They were set about fifteen metres apart; one presumes the width of what would have been the pylon entrance. Each was around twenty metres high, two metres deep, and a metre wide, but both statues were extensively damaged, with the features above the waist virtually unrecognisable. Originally they'd been carved from two single blocks of quartzite sandstone quarried all the way from Gebel al Ahmur near Cairo. There were closer quarries at Edfu and Aswan, so one would wonder what the special significance of the Cairo stone was.

The left statue, though almost indistinguishable, was still intact, however the right one had an extensive crack in the lower half and, above the waist, consisted of five tiers of stone. At some time in the past it had clearly been damaged and then reconstructed.

'According to the Greek geographer Strabo, writing in the early years of the 1st Century, the statues were partially damaged by an earthquake in 27 B.C. that shattered the northern colossus, collapsing it from the waist up. The current upper levels consist of a different type of sandstone, and are the result of a later, Roman, reconstruction.'

The replacement stone was most likely from Aswan or possibly Edfu, but the question had to be asked: where was the original top?

It somehow didn't quite gel; it wasn't so much that earthquakes don't cause rocks to break, they do, but that an earthquake was in fact the sole cause of the damage didn't ring true. Strabo was writing perhaps fifty years after the quake, and if a quake did in fact cause the damage, then it must have been one of considerable size. That would have caused more than just rocks to fall apart, but also major tsunamis up and down the Nile. So had the top been washed away like so many of the other statues and was buried somewhere upstream?

And then there was the location of the temple; it was much closer to the Nile than all the others on the West Bank. Did that mean it was built when the Nile was lower? Well, obviously it must have, and it made some pretty good sense considering the locations of the tombs in the Valley of the Kings, especially Tutankhamun and Horemheb's tombs, although not the tombs of Amenhotep III himself, and Ay. However that could be explained by the tombs being commenced some time before the temple, or perhaps they built their tombs higher up as a precautionary measure, or perhaps they new another massive flood was just around the corner.

It was still strange that Amenhotep III built where he did, I mean he could have built back in alignment with all the other temples, Amenhotep II and Thutmoses IV. But he didn't. Was it just because the Nile was lower? I don't think so, he could have just built a long avenue of sphinxes leading up to it. Perhaps it had something to do with the sacred location at Medinet Habu, the burial place of the primeval gods, and birth-place of Re-Atum?

Sure they were excavating the temple itself, but maybe they should be digging down even deeper, beyond the era of Amenhotep III. Who knows what they would find, perhaps a temple dating back to Montuhotep? Or maybe even back to the time of the Zep Tepi, perhaps they would even find evidence of the burial of the primeval gods. Perhaps the Colossi themselves had hidden answers.

I moved closer to examine the stones, focusing on the northern figure. As I did I remembered reading somewhere that the quartzite on the northern side showed microscopic evidence of being subjected to incredible heat, consistent with intense heat such as a nuclear blast, that had formed tiny glass spheres within the stone. It wasn't my area of expertise but I certainly knew someone who would know; I made a mental note to pick Bill's brain when I got back.

So, was it blown over by an atomic explosion, or maybe the heat blast of a comet or meteorite strike? Or perhaps the jet exhaust of a rocket, or starship? I didn't know; I wasn't there. But the statues were. Time to call out the cavalry; time to call on Nemo.

I looked around and, as there was no one else in immediate site, decided to jump the small retaining rope surrounding the statues, hug the rock and try to tune in. I headed straight to the northern face of the right statue, spread my arms wide and pressed myself to the surface.

'La, la! No, please to come away.'

Hell, where did he come from? Like a desert fox, the local guardian had manifested out of nowhere, most likely the shade of a small shrub in the adjacent field.

'No, you come away.'

I hesitated, then decided the best path was to slip him a little baksheesh. But as I stepped back over the rope, a tourist bus pulled up. The main temples and valleys had all closed down about thirty minutes ago and the Colossi were on the way back to Luxor, so it was logical they stop now. It was going to make bribing the guardian almost impossible. Not that he wouldn't take the money, but that he *couldn't* take the money and allow me to step inside the barrier in full view of everyone else.

'Shit!'

I couldn't believe it, as the door of the bus opened, out poured a swarm of snap-happy camera-toting Asian tourists. I knew they would probably file up like a column of ants, take two or three photos of themselves standing before the Colossi, then scamper back on board and disappear as quickly as they arrived. So, for a moment I considered standing off to the side and waiting it out. That was until another, and then another bus-load arrived. No, stuff that for a lark, it was time to pull the plug and head back to the watering hole, the Colossi could keep their secrets.... for now.

It had been a full-on day and as I pedalled down the road back towards the river I was looking forward to meeting the others at Bill's hotel and downing a nice cold beer or three. Needless to say, I was passed by several tourist coaches along the way until I hit the crossroad where they had to head off right and cross via the bridge up river, whereas I simply popped the bike on the ferry and sat down to rest for the first time since I had awoken to the call to Allah. I half expect them to fire up again from the minarets atop the mosques at any second. A quick check of the phone, 4:56, no still a bit early for them.

I relaxed back into the seat, my wet shirt clinging to the wood like a drowning sailor to a passing piece of driftwood, and tipped my akubra back. The sun was beginning to descend towards the mountains in the west and the sky was taking on that beautiful red hue that only the Nile could conjure. A gentle zephyr wafted over the water and across my face as the Nile undulated in its ever-unfolding journey towards the Mediterranean. Man, a pina colada would go down well.

The West Bank finished up holding more treasures than I could have even imagined. It was great to be alive and I wondered if it could get any better than this. The answer to that waited across the river at Bill's hotel.

CHAPTER 18 - SECRETS OF THE NIGHT

Back on the east side of the Nile, the thought of a few cold beers impelled me up the steps from the ferry and onto the esplanade. The only problem was, I didn't know where to find the Winter Palace. I had several options; ride back to the Nubian Oasis, dump the bike, and ask Seleh for directions, ride around and hope I ran into it, or simply ask a local.

'Yes, Cowboy, you need tax?'

Trust the local taxi drivers to smell a foreigner. It didn't matter that I had a bike with me, they appeared out of nowhere at the slightest sniff of a fare.

'No thanks, Pal, I'm on the bike. But, do you know where I can find the Winter Palace?'

'Winter Palace, yes, put bicycle in back, and we go, ten pound.'

After several attempts to make it clear that I didn't need a taxi, that I was going to ride there, he finally indicated it was further down along the river. Mind you he still wanted a little baksheesh for his troubles. Somewhere along the way, I must have picked up a little of Bill's generous nature, because I caved in and gave him a few pounds.

Riding along the esplanade, I cast my gaze once again across the river to the sun as it sank in the west. Every sunset was different and it was a sight with which you could never get bored. As was the sight of Saeed's beaming pearly whites, which flashed like a neon sign up ahead.

'Indy, how was it your time with my uncle? Did you get it the answer you were looking for?'

'Yes, it was great. Thanks again. But it raised as many questions as it answered, and we barely got a chance to scratch the surface. Kareem said he'd meet us tonight at your uncle's restaurant; your other uncle, that is.

'Yes, yes, at Abou Ashraf.'

'What's the address? I'm just heading to have a few drinks with some of the others, then I'll drop the bike back at the hotel, have a quick shower, and meet you there.'

'Do not mind, I will meet you at your hotel just before 8:00 pm and take it you there.'

'Is that 8:00 pm Western time or Egyptian time?'

'8:00 pm Dinner time!'

'OK. Hey, why not join us for a drink at Bill's hotel; I'm sure you'd be more than welcome?

'Which hotel?'

'The Winter Palace.'

He chuckled away.

'Oh, I do not think they would be very happy with me gracing it their lounge and bar.'

'Why not?'

'The Winter Palace, it is very upmarket, even the water it is outside of my budget.'

'Are you sure?'

'Yes, yes. Go on, I will see you later. Where is it you are staying?'

'The Nubian Oasis.'

'Yes, I know it. I will meet you there.'

I pedalled on along the esplanade, passing the Luxor temple as the late afternoon rays of the sun illuminated its columns. I wondered if the work we had done last night had really made any difference, but, as it was now passed 5:00, I didn't have the time to stop and check it out.

A couple of hundred metres further down the river, or rather, back *up* the river, I stopped in awe. The 'Winter Palace.'

Shit! It was the sort of hotel you expected in an Agatha Christie murder mystery like 'Death on the Nile'. Clearly built some time in the Victorian era, its white exterior had the classic styling best described as 'opulent'. I could just see the royalty of Europe, Dukes and Duchesses, Lords and Ladies, sipping tea and quaffing scones as they discussed the latest discoveries in the Valley of the Kings.

This was the top end of the market in every way, 5 star, and then a few planets and comets thrown in for good measure.

How the hell could Bill afford to stay here? And how could he afford to pay for an extra room for Pernille? Maybe he won the Lotto?

I parked the bike; half expecting someone to come out and take it away for valet parking, then strolled inside. 'Bloody hell!' As I entered the lobby I entered a world I'd only ever seen on film and television, and in the 'lifestyles of the rich and famous'. Ornate furnishings, luxurious decorations and antiques adorned the lobby.

Suddenly I felt massively under-dressed, especially as I was as hot, sticky and sweaty as a middle-aged obese Italian pizza-maker on a hot muggy summer's night. I looked like a fish out of water; as out of place as lipstick on a great white shark.

The concierge spotted me straight away; this looked bad.

'Mister Alex?

'Yes, how did you know?'

'Mister Sullivan he has described you, but your hat, it was the give away. The others they are waiting for you on the Nile Terrace.'

'Which is where?'

'Please to follow me.'

He led me up the stately staircase, through a few large rooms that reeked of decadence, money, and more money, and finally out on to what was the Nile Terrace. It had a glorious elevated view over the Nile towards the West Bank: in a word, magnificent.

'Hey, Alex, you made it....'

Bill, Pernille, who it seemed hadn't taken the plane trip out of Luxor with Jacques, Pieter, Yuko and Crystal were all seated around two tables at the centre of the Terrace. Pernille had a new hair cut, short and very sexy. She looked like a new woman.

'...How was the West Bank?'

'Amazing; so much to talk about.'

'Then you'd better pull up a pew and get a cold beer into you.'

I accepted Bill's offer and, as Bill ordered another round of drinks, I planted myself in the chair left vacant between Crystal, who was calm and serene as usual, and Pernille, who was simply beaming. I took that as a signal to find out more about Napoleon's Waterloo.

'So, did Jacques make it to the airport?'

Pernille grabbed Bill's hand, gave it a squeeze and gave him a huge smile.

'Yes, he's gone and out of my life for good.'

'That's good to hear. Last time I saw him was on the dock last night. I was a bit concerned as he was on his way here to the hotel.'

'Was he drunk?'

'Not really; not when he left.'

'He was when he arrived.'

Bill joined in.

'We were having a delightful dinner when Jacques just burst in, demanded to see Pernille, then insisted she leave with him at once. I tried to explain to him that he was interrupting our meal, wasn't welcome, and that it would be best if he left immediately. Instead, he caused a scene and tried to drag her off.'

'That's when Bill intervened. Jacques took a swing at him, but Bill brushed him aside and restrained him until the police arrived and escorted him from the hotel.'

'So, that was the end of it?'

'No, he made one more try before lunch on his way to the airport.'

'What happened?'

Bill chuckled to himself.

'Let's just say he beat a hasty retreat with his tail between his legs.'

'Bill punched him in the nose.'

'Oh, you have all the luck! Still, can't say he didn't deserve it.'

We all had a bit of a laugh.

'How did you spend the rest of the day, Bill?'

'I spent most of the morning with Pernille, organizing massages, pedicures and manicures, a facial, hair cut.'

'Gee, Bill, I wouldn't have picked you for a SNAG.'

'A snag?'

'A Sensitive New Age Guy. Your skin looks as smooth as a baby's bum by the way.'

'That's good to know. Just so long as it doesn't smell like a baby's bum.'

We all had a good chuckle.

'What about *after* your make over, and after your pugilistic redecoration of Jacques' face?'

'This afternoon? Crystal and Pernille spent some time together while I made a few phone calls and caught up on some business matters.'

'And you ladies? Crystal?'

'I spent some time in a morning circle with Diane and the ladies at the Nefertiti, then came here to meet Pernille and have some quality time together....'

No matter what she said next, I instantly had images of the two of them frolicking around naked in the water.

'...As a result of that, we revisited the Luxor Temple once again, just to put a few lingering demons to rest.'

That surprised me enough to shift the images in my head.

'Oh, I thought we took care of them last night.'

'These were some personal demons.'

'And...?'

I looked at Pernille and she was glowing.

'No more demons in my life.'

The waiter placed the drinks on the table and I grasped the ice-cold beer with fervent glee. As I savoured that first thirst-quenching mouthful, Pernille inquired as to the happenings of my day.

'What about you, Alex, what's your news?'

Debrief

'Gosh, where do I start: Mubarak and Hawass, Saeed's uncle, Kareem, and the Luxor Massacre, the timing of the tsunamis and the 18th Dynasty, Ay and Horemheb and the lineage of the *sang réal*, lots of unanswered questions about Akhenaten, about the Minoans, Mayans, and Mycaeneans.'

'Why not start at the beginning?'

I took another life-saving mouthful, then let rip.

'Well, as Pieter, Yuko and I were riding to the Valley of the Kings, we were discussing how Amenhotep and Akhenaten probably left Egypt and set up civilizations in other parts of the world, particularly Greece.'

Pieter screwed up his face, crossed his arms and raised a hand to his chin.

'Yeh, Alex, Yuko and I have been thinking. I got what you were saying about Imhotep, Montuhotep, Amenhotep, Akhenaten, Apollo, and even Queztalcoatl, all possibly being the same being; the Annunaki god, Thoth. But if Akhenaten actually went to Greece, what was his connection, if any, to Alexander the Great?'

I thought out loud.

'Akhenaten would have instructed the new Mycaenean Civilization on how to rebuild after the destruction of the Minoan Civilization. Given that he lived so long, and that he was probably both Hermes and Apollo, he would have easily spanned the years from 1600 BC-300 BC and, along the way, was probably also the teacher of Socrates, Plato and Aristotle. And as Aristotle tutored Alexander the Great, then Akhenaten/Apollo may even have initiated Alexander the Great into the wisdom of the Tat Brotherhood, which would explain why Alexander *invaded* Egypt, but more why he was so quickly accepted and crowned as pharaoh.'

'But it doesn't really explain why his half-brother, Phillip III Arrhidaeus, succeeded him as pharaoh, and then how Alexander's son, Alexander IV, assumed the throne. That would just be because of natural succession to the throne.'

'Unless, they all married the *sang réal*. Maybe that's why Alexander and the Ptolemaic era had so many female pharaohs, so many Cleopatras; they were the true bloodline.'

I looked at Crystal who sat proudly beaming, sipping her drink. Though she did throw a spanner in the works.

'But they married Greek-Macedonian women.'

'Then the *sang réal* must have travelled with Akhenaten to Greece.'

Pieter was quick to pick it up.

'Yuko and I were discussing just that; that if Akhenaten left Egypt and went to Greece, and called himself Apollo, what happened to Nefertiti?'

I glanced at Crystal, looking for a response, which this time was not immediately forthcoming, finished my beer, then answered.

'I haven't really thought about that yet; Nefertiti was Apollo's wife I suppose.'

The chuckle and smirk on Crystal's face betrayed the fact she knew more than she was letting on.

'But Apollo didn't have a wife.'

Before I could mull it over, Yuko jumped right in.

'He did have over fifty consorts though.'

'Such as?'

'Artemis, Aphrodite, Cassandra.....'

'Who was Cassandra again?'

'She had the gift of prophecy, but no one would believe her.'

Crystal laughed.

'And so it has been for most women ever since.'

I declined the opening to indulge in a little sexist banter; that could wait until later when the alcohol had had a chance to take effect, preferring instead to focus on the current discussion.

'So Cassandra was one of the oracles at Delphi?'

Crystal took the lead.

'No, you are thinking of the Pythia.'

'The Pythia?'

'Located on the slopes of Mount Parnassus, and most commonly known as the Oracle of Delphi, the priestesses at the Temple of Apollo were the most important oracles of Greek antiquity.'

'When was that?'

Crystal deferred back to Yuko who was more than willing to respond.

'The Pythia was established some time in the 8th Century BC, with the last recorded response given in 393 AD, when emperor Theodosius I ordered pagan temples to cease operation.'

'Why *Pythia*? Is it related to snakes, to the python?'

'The name derives from Pytho, the original name of Delphi, which derived *its* name from the verb *pythein*, which described the decomposition of the body of the monstrous serpent Python after she was slain by Apollo. According to the earliest myths, probably dating back to the Minoan civilization, the office of the oracle was initially held by the goddesses Themis and Phoebe, and the site was sacred to Gaia, Mother Earth.

Sometime during the Dark Ages of Greece, from the 11th to the 9th century BC, the arrival of a new god of prophecy saw the temple seized by Apollo who expelled the twin guardian serpents of Gaia.'

'Wait a minute. Do you think it's possible the arrival of Apollo was before the 11th Century BC, and that the new god of prophecy was Apollo himself?'

'Or Nefertiti.'

Crystal had done it again, left us in awe; if anyone would know what happened to Nefertiti, it would be Nefertiti herself. Yuko shook her head.

'Anything is possible, after all, the 11th Century BC may just be when it was first recorded.'

I wasn't finished. Nor was the waiter, as Bill was ensuring we all had a fresh drink in front of us. I thanked them both, then returned to the topic.

'These monstrous pythons that protected a sacred space, do you think they could be the Dracos protecting some secret entrance to an underworld, perhaps an underground temple?'

Pieter was right with me.

'It's possible; the Dracos control everything, they're seen in so many cultures and civilizations, as both the protector snake and as the dangers.'

'The question is, what happened to Akhenaten/Apollo *after* he went to Greece?'

The Apollo mission

Yuko put forward an idea.

'I would suggest Apollo went to the Mayan Civilization around 250 AD, but disappeared in 1000 AD when Quetzalcoatl, feathered serpent creator-god of the Aztecs, attempted to take control back..'

'So what you're saying is that Quetzalcoatl was Dracos not Annunaki.'

'I think the evidence of blood sacrifices and rituals would support that.'

'So what happened to Apollo?'

'He went into a state of stasis.'

Crystal had dropped another bombshell.

'He what?'

'He went into a state of stasis; of suspended animation, hibernation, to regenerate.'

That intrigued Pieter.

'So, apart from living long, the Annunaki can also put their body into stasis?'

'And incarnate in a human form.'

'When?'

'At the same time; the soul can not only stay in one body, it can go into others.'

I couldn't comprehend it.

'What? At the same time?'

'Just as several souls can live one life, one soul can live several lives.'

'Yeh, that's reincarnation, right, but not one soul leading several lives at the same time?'

Crystal gave me a look of slight disappointment.

'There is no time; there is only this moment. All lives are simultaneous. Remember?'

'I get that. I get reincarnation and alternate lives, but I can't quite understand the concept that one soul could be conscious in more than one body at the same time.'

'Ah, that's the difference; it is a question of consciousness and awareness. Think of it like this: the body is just a vehicle, the soul is the driver. The driver parks one car in the garage for repairs and restoration, then gets in another, or a series of other cars, for each additional trip.'

Several seconds of stunned contemplative silence was broken by a pensive Bill.

'So, does this period of *in-stasis* the Annunaki gods go into have something to do with the ancient Egyptians' preoccupation with resurrecting the rejuvenated body? Was embalming the body an attempt to replicate the resurrective *in-stasis* abilities of the Annunaki?'

Crystal smiled.

'The Tat Brotherhood encoded the truth about resurrection into the texts.'

'So the whole *Book of the Dead* is really an Annunaki handbook of texts for the regeneration of the physical body?...'

Then it hit me.

'...No, not the *Book of the Dead*, but the original pyramid texts. They were written in old hieroglyphic text on papyrus scrolls and varied considerably. But basically it was all concerned with an afterlife in the sky. The spells include protecting the pharaohs remains, reanimating his body after death, helping the dead king ascend to heaven so that he can take his place amongst the gods, and reuniting him with his divine father, Ra; exactly what we would expect from someone coming out of suspended animation or other dimensional existences.'

The sun was setting in the west, spreading its golden rays over the mountains and across the Nile. It was majestic. I leaned back soaking it all in.

'Hey, Bill, do you think mono-atomic gold has anything to do with things? Isn't it supposedly essential in healing?'

'I think you might be on to something, Alex. It apparently neutralizes all negativity held in the cells, as well as protecting the cells from all disease. The healing benefits include strengthening the heart, toning and strengthening the pituitary gland and pineal gland, strengthening and revitalizing the thymus gland, thus boosting the immune system, enhancing the production of red blood cells, and causes all of the cells of the body to realign or regenerate, including brain cells.'

Yuko interjected.

'I thought brain cells didn't regenerate.'

'It's a lie. How can all the other cells of the body regenerate, but not the cells in the brain? If the cells in the feet can regenerate, so can the cells in the brain.'

Crystal took my hand in a concerned and sympathetic manner

'It seems there may be hope for you yet, Alex.'

So Crystal *did* have a sense of humour, I think.

'Bring it on I say; it can make up for all the brain cells I killed off drinking beer in my twenties at university. Anything else, Bill?'

'Well, consuming Mono-atomic Gold also effects the chakras, helping to increase the aura or biomagnetic sheath. It induces and enhances states of euphoria, spiritual bliss, and higher awareness; increases and enhances stamina, magnifies and sharpens insight, helps develop latent psychic ability, and allows subconsciously held beliefs, worries, concerns, and doubts to surface sequentially so they can be understood for the purposes of resolution and karmic cleansing.

Ultimately, consuming Mono-atomic Gold is an awesome aid for meditation purposes; inducing very deep states of meditation, helping you achieve super states of consciousness and mystical experiences, as well as astral travelling.'

'Astral travel? What's that again?'

'It's the ability of the soul to leave the physical or dense body behind and travel to different places and times.'

Pieter stretched the concept further...

'Or densities, and possibly even dimensions.'

...and Crystal blew it out of the water.

'Or to different bodies.'

'So that was the purpose of the Valley of the Kings, for the pharaohs to lay in state hoping they would rejuvenate just like the Annunaki?'

'It's a novel proposition, though I don't see you getting much support from the establishment; they've invested a lot of time and money in getting people to believe the rhetoric they trot out.'

'Your right, Bill, but I think I can give them a bit of a shake up.'

'In what way?'

'Well, take the end of the 17th Dynasty through to the beginning of the 19th Dynasty. I picked up on what we were saying the other day, about the death of Seqenenre, and followed it through.'

I looked around.

'Do you think we can get a pen and paper?'

Bill called the waiter over and within a minute not only did we have a pad of paper and a pen, but also another round of drinks. I started off recapping and bringing the others up to speed on Seqenenre and Ahmose, before spending a little time explaining my thoughts on Hatshepsut. As I did, I sketched out the family tree as I saw it.

'Rectangles are male and ovals are females. The fully coloured rectangles are the pharaohs, the coloured ovals are females who carry the *sang réal*.'

Finally, I explained the whole Amenhotep IV and Akhenaten misconception and how it ultimately led to the ascent to the throne of Ay and then Horemheb, and how the whole lineage and right to the throne was determined by the *sang réal*.

'Shit, Alex, you haven't just rattled the cage and upset the applecart, you've set the cat amongst the pigeons; it's brilliant.'

'Thanks, Bill.'

'Thing is though, can you prove it?'

'Probably better than the Egyptologists can prove the current beliefs. The point is not if *I* can prove it, but if the experts can *dis*prove it.'

Pieter was studying the paper and nodding his head.

'I like your thinking. And it explains so many things that currently seem forced or highly implausible. You've certainly had a busy day.'

'Oh, that's not the half of it. From the Valley of the Kings I headed off to Hatshepsut's Temple where I found more evidence of Red Granite, and at least three other temples dating back to at least the 11th Dynasty and supporting my tsunami, or rather tsunamis, theory.'

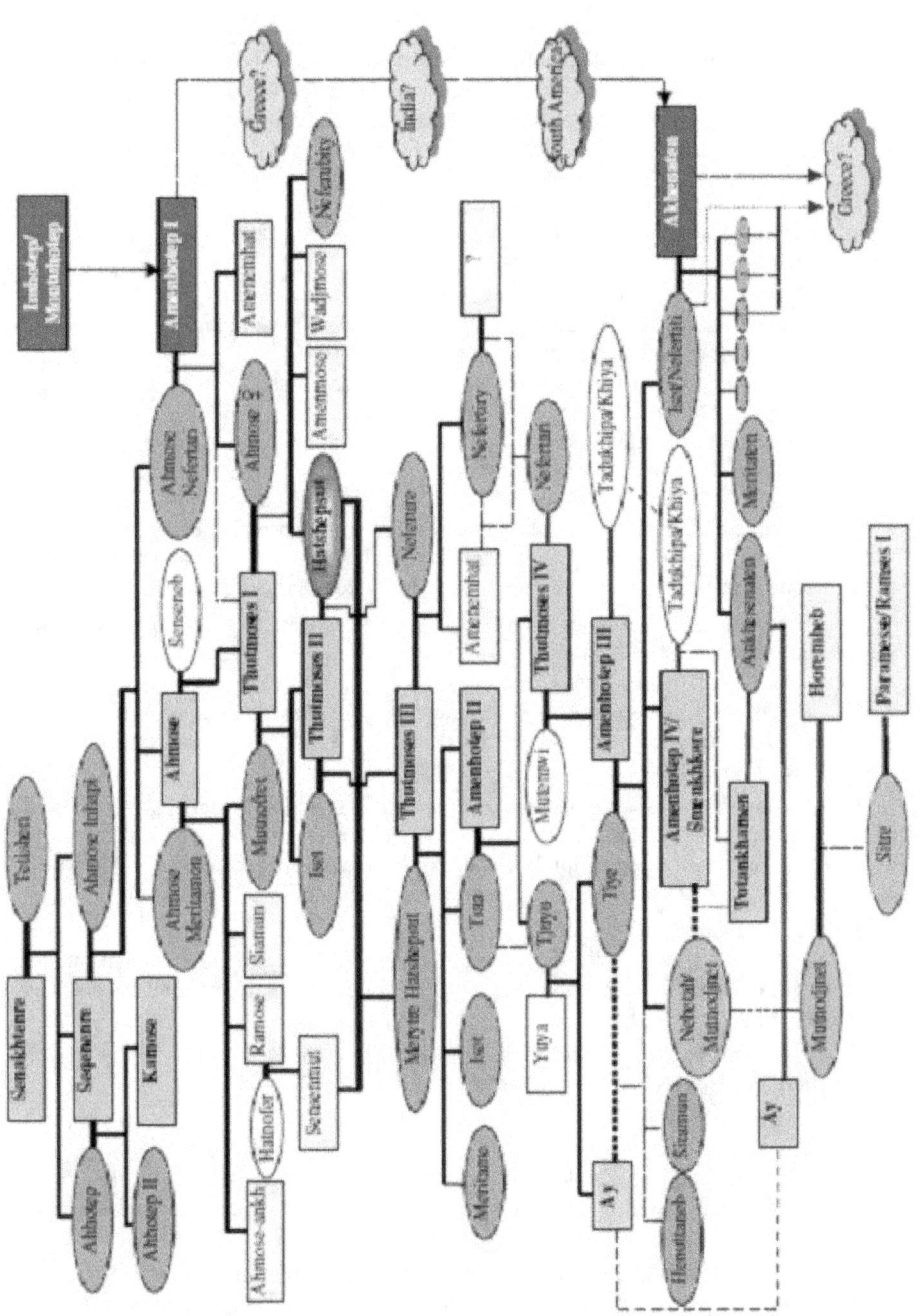

Bill was impressed.

'Man, you are on a roll.'

'That's nothing. I met up with Saeed's uncle and not only did he confirm there was another temple under the original temple which is now on Philae, but that there were no hieroglyphs on the walls, which were made of massive blocks of ....'

'Red Granite?'

'Exactly!'

'Now that's major.'

'Not compared to what he told me next.'

'Which was?'

'He said the Russians were involved in the whole Aswan Dam thing, including the relocation of Philae; their fingerprints were not only all over everything, but they were in it up to their armpits.'

'It seems Project Isis was not only real, but very busy.'

'And guess who's name popped to the surface?'

'Akhenaten? Amenhotep?'

'No, think more modern Egyptians.'

'Ah....Zahi Hawass? Mubarak? .... Omar Sherrif? I don't know.'

'Kareem suggested that, though he didn't so much pull the trigger, Mubarak was part of the assassination of President Sadat, and that Mubarak and Zahi Hawass were the ones really behind, and complicit in, the Luxor Massacre.'

That floored everyone, everyone it seemed except Crystal. However it was Pieter who was the first to respond.

'You mean the terrorist attack at Hatshepsut's Temple?'

'Yep. It seems Kareem's son, Saeed's cousin, was one of the supposed terrorists. Apparently he was part of the police, a fanatical Muslim, and had been brainwashed into doing it.'

I started going into the background and Hawass's career, as best I could remember them, when Crystal unexpectedly rose to her feet.

'I don't wish to interrupt, but you will have to excuse us. Pernille, Yuko and I must get going; we have been invited to join Diane's group for another circle.'

I checked my cell phone.

'Shit, 7:22, where did the time go, I have to get going as well. I'm meeting Saeed and Kareem tonight for dinner and I need to head back to my hotel for a shower and change of clothes first.'

Suddenly the thought of not seeing Crystal again flooded my mind, so, as the girls gathered themselves to leave, I tested the waters.

'So just the girls are invited?'

Crystal paused to answer me.

'It is a Goddess Circle focusing on the divinely creative and empowered feminine. I doubt if you're ready to handle *one* empowered woman, let alone a group of them.'

As she said it she sensuously and slowly shimmied her breasts and stroked her hips and backside as if adjusting her sarong. She was teasing me yet again, and I loved it!

'Will you be around later on tonight, or tomorrow?'

'We are all planning to meet outside Karnak in the morning at 8:30 am. Perhaps you would like to join us?'

'That'd be great, I'll see you then.'

As the girls disappeared into the hotel I breathed both a sigh of relief and a sigh of admiration at Crystal's perfect behind. I was starting to wonder if I would ever see it, and her, again. At least I had another day and another Temple to get closer to this mysterious German Goddess.

'So, Bill, how much do I owe you for the beers?'

Bill laughed and put on a quasi-pirate-come-vampire voice..

'A pint of blood and your first born child.'

I held up a hundred but Bill waived it off.

'Don't worry about it.'

'Then at least let me cover the tip.'

I threw it on the table then had an afterthought.

'Hey, Bill, do you know anything about the Collosi of Memnon?'

'A little. What do you want to know?'

'They're made of quartzite, right?'

'Yep. Each statue is an estimated three thousand tonnes of it.'

'Well, I read somewhere that the quartzite on the northern side had tiny glass spheres within the stone, and that was evidence of it being subjected to incredible heat consistent with the intense heat produced in a nuclear blast. Is there anything else that have caused that?'

'Interesting question. Quartzite is produced from sandstone when the sandstone is subject to the constant heat and pressure from tectonic activity. So it's highly unlikely the glass spheres were produced from tectonic activity as they're only on the northern side and not consistently through the stone. That implies the glass spheres must have been created by some sort of external directional extreme heat blast, like either a meteor explosion or nuclear blast. A mid-air meteor explosion creates glass spheres called impactite whereas the spheres formed by a nuclear explosion are called trinitite.'

'So what are the glass spheres in the Colossi from?'

'Alex, that's a damn good question and, no matter what the answer is, it certainly opens up a Pandora's box.'

Through the looking-glass

I bid my farewells, headed downstairs, jumped on the bike and hustled off back to the Nubian Oasis. All the way back my mind was tossing around two completely different images; the first, and most powerful, was a group of mainly twenty-five to forty-five year old sexy women all cavorting naked in the Nile or a steamy sweaty exotic hotel room. The second was the implications of the glass spheres in the statues, and though not as powerful as a room full of naked nymphs, soon compelled and captured my thinking.

I contemplated whether it was possible the stone had been blasted *before* it was quarried. It would mean the stone was more than likely horizontal and that it was the surface that was blasted. That made sense, and meant it could have been from a meteor explosion any time after the original rock was formed and became surface rock. In the end, I figured I would leave that one to the geologists, but the more I thought about that, the less it appealed to me. I mean, as far as I knew there was no other evidence of a meteor strike for thousands of miles, even a mid-air explosion. But, and it was a BIG BUT, if the rocks were analysed and it prove to be impactite, then that would all have to be considered. Then it would simply be a matter of *when*.

Of course if it had been blasted *after* being quarried, carved and put in place, it would give another possible reason for the damage to all the earlier temples. That would date it some time after 1600 BC, and that was plausible. If this second sun *did* pass around then, then it is possible there were also asteroids, meteors and comets being dragged in its wake, and that one of them hit the earth, or at least exploded in the atmosphere, somewhere in the vicinity of Egypt. But that would mean there would be other evidence of a comet or meteor, and that didn't seem all that apparent. But then again, as far as I knew, no one had really looked for that sort of evidence either.

But, if the glass spheres proved to be trinitite, then, no matter how you looked at it, the options would turn history on its head, because, if it was after the statues had been erected, then that meant there was a nuclear explosion some time after 1600 BC and before 332 BC. Why 332 BC? Because the temples were all rebuilt when Alexander the Great 'invaded' Egypt in 332 BC and, as far as I could ascertain from my observations so far, the rebuilt temples were all made from sandstone, meaning that any sort of nuclear blast after 332 BC would have turned the silica in the sandstone blocks to glass. But that wasn't the case, so, if it *was* trinitite, who was setting off nuclear bombs in ancient Egypt, and why?

There were the stories from the Indian texts, the Vedas, about nuclear wars, and also the Sumerian texts referred to the war between Enki and Enlil. Is it possible that when the Annunaki returned in 1600 BC that they were still squabbling; to them it would just be a few days? If so, it might give another reason for Akhenaten leaving Egypt. Maybe his city at el Amarna was blown away. Maybe it wasn't a nuclear bomb, but rather the crash of a nuclear powered spacecraft? I wonder if anyone has done radioactive tests of the remains at el Amarna? I couldn't wait to get there and see it for myself.

Of course the final option was the trinitite was formed from a nuclear blast that happened *before* the stone was quarried. If that was the case, then that pushed both the crash theory or bomb theory even further back into history, and that raised even more questions about the Annunaki.

A date for dinner

Arriving back at the hotel I returned the bike to Seleh and bolted upstairs for a quick shower. After a day of pedalling around the ancient temples in the Egyptian heat I felt like my skin was encased in at least three layers of sweat, dust and grime. I didn't even take my clothes off, just my hat and shoes, and walked straight in under the lukewarm yet refreshing water. Oh My God, that felt good.

Once soaked to the skin I picked up the soap and lathered up head to toe; head, shirt, trousers and socks. Working my way down I took off the shirt and washed it out, followed by my trousers, socks and finally my Calvins: that was the washing done for the day. Fully turning off the hot water tap, I let the cold water run over my head and down my body; I can't begin to describe how good it felt. I gave myself the luxury of standing there motionless for about a minute, before reluctantly turning the tap off and wiping myself down. Despite the humidity, the temperature of the air meant I was nearly dry before I even reached for my towel. Within a few minutes I had redressed and was heading out the door. I checked my watch, 7:57, brilliant.

Sometimes it's such an advantage to be a guy; in and out, shower and change, in under fifteen minutes, and that included doing my washing.

'Indy, I didn't recognize you without your hat.'

Saeed was leaning on the counter, chatting to Seleh, his beaming grin illuminating the lobby.

'I'm travelling incognito.'

'Did you meet up with the others?'

'Yes, thanks, and you'll be pleased to know that Jacques has flown the coop, and Miss Pernille has a new admirer.'

'Mister Bill, yes, very good.'

We left the lobby and strolled through the evening streets of Luxor. That was when the city really came to life. It made sense, why run around in the heat of the day, only westerners were crazy and stupid enough to do that.

The aromas of Egypt filled the air, restaurant after restaurant cascaded past, serving everything from falafels and sweet breads to fish stew, roast chicken and beef. Every step made my stomach yearn and churn, and saliva bubbled forth from my mouth like a ceremonial fountain to Pavlov's dogs.

About ten minutes later, after ducking, weaving and slaloming our way through the side streets of the city, we arrived at what I presumed was Abou Ashraf; our destination. The restaurant was larger than I expected and had a central dance floor with a small stage and band set up behind. The red carpet hadn't been rolled out, but it might as well have been, for upon arrival we were treated like royalty. Saeed's uncle, the owner uncle that is, graciously introduced himself; Mohammed. Yet another Mohammed, I was sure half the nation was named Mohammed. And the other half? You guessed it, Mohammed. Saeed's other uncle, Kareem, was also waiting, and collectively they all fussed over me as they escorted me to our table.

Before my bum had even warmed the seat, beer and appetizers adorned the table and I settled in to what looked like being a pleasant evening. I figured it was impolite to jump straight in and ask about the massacre, so I waited for the right opening. After more beer and food and brief inquiries about my days adventuring and perambulating through the desert sands on a bicycle, Saeed soon turned the topic to more pertinent subjects.

'Indy, I have been tell all your theory, and the talk you have on the felucca, to my uncle, and he has been it most interested in what it is you have to say.'

Kareem raised his index finger and wavered it knowingly in my direction.

'Mister Alex, there is inscription at Medinet Habu about War of Sea People, it supported by other inscription on wall at Kom Ombo which speak of Meshwesh, Shasu, and Tjeker - one of it People of the Sea....'

At first I wasn't sure what he was getting at.

'...These inscription suppose to refer to war one thousand year before temple it is built, which mean around 1400 BC.'

Maybe it was the beers but I was still drawing a blank.

'So why should some of these Peoples of the Sea be called by name, and referred to as enemies, on a temple from Ptolemaic times?'

Saeed was bridging the gap.

'Perhaps the Nile it and the ancient Egyptian people were more connected to the ocean back then, than it is now, because of your tsunami. Would it not support it your theory?'

'It would if I knew who these Meshwesh, Shasu and Tjeker were. Any ideas?'

Saeed shrugged and Kareem shook his head before picking up on another of my theories.

'I also have it the interest in your theory of ancient temple below modern temple, and also of building of it first Aswan Dam.'

'Yes, built to develop the cotton industry.'

'And to rob it the tomb.'

Kareem had taken me a little by surprise.

'The tombs?'

'Yes, many hundred of tomb in and around Valley of King and Valley of Queen.'

Of course! It hadn't dawned on me that not only would the building of the first dam cover up the robbing of P'aaleq, it would also have regulated the season flooding downstream of Aswan, in particular of the West Bank at Luxor, thus allowing the Aristocracy, AKA Illuminati, to completely plunder the tombs in and around the Valley of the Kings. No Aswan Dam means no Lord Canarvon, no Howard Carter and no Tutankhamun.

Meanwhile the band had fired up and, I have to admit, it was an aural assault to my western upbringing. Not only was the *music* lacking any sort of western structure, harmonic progressions or tonal complexity, but each instrument, especially the voice, was amplified with considerable volume and reverb. My brain felt like it was under siege from a mono-chordal rhythmically-repetitive microtonal melismatic plainchant from hell. But the Egyptians loved it. Maybe it was a sort of semi-hallucinogenic brainwashing or conditioning that left them in a quasi-zombified state.

In between 'songs', the food kept coming, course after course, as did the beverages. Throughout it all I related in detail, as best I could over the racket, the conversations about Imhotep, Amenhotep and Akhenaten, about the tsunami theory, and about the Annunaki and their relationship to the Zep Tepi. Kareem listened intently, often nodding and punctuating things with a 'Yes, yes this, it make much sense'. He was even prepared to accept my newly acquired religious perspectives of the origins of not only Judaism and Christianity, but also Islam. But it was the discussion of the Tat Brotherhood, the *sang réal*, and the lineage of sacred information through the ancient Egyptian priesthood, the Essenes, and the Knights Templar that captured his fully attention.

'The truth, it is sacred, and everyone they have it the right to this sacred truth.'

I could see in Kareem's time-worn and bloodshot eyes how passionate he was, and guessed this was the time to cut to the chase.

'Truths like the Luxor massacre?'

He reached under the table and lifted up a plain-looking bag, placing it before him. From within he pulled out a manila folder of papers, about two inches thick, and placed it on the table before me.

'Here, the eye of the world they are upon Egypt now, and at last we can be speak out without fear of it persecution and torture. I wish for you to take these paper to your western media and let them know the truth of what has been happen here in Egypt for the last fifty year.'

I opened the folder and started to flick through the papers.

'Why can't you do it yourself?'

'Despite it the people revolution, nothing it has changed; the old Jackal they still run the pack. Zahi Hawass and Mubarak they may be gone, but the army it is still in control; they are play the people like the puppet on string. I am get old and this, it is the battle of the young man.'

Saeed had another powerful reason.

'My uncle he has been told he has it the cancer, and he is not have much time left to live, or strength to fight it the battle.'

It was hard to be sympathetic to someone dying of self-inflicted lung cancer when they had inhaled the lethal constituents of cigarettes for over fifty years; we all have to suffer the consequences of our choices. Still, there was a sadness came over me thinking he would not be around to see the fruits of his labours.

As Kareem continued to explain his reasons, the will of Allah and that sort of thing, I kept flicking through the pages, all in Arabic and not a word of English anywhere. With reams of Arabic cursive, each page looked like an unsolved puzzle from Mr. Squiggle. I was like a ten-year-old looking at a complex mathematical and physics formula; it was impressive and I knew it meant something, but I didn't have a clue. As he wound up his explanation, Kareem grabbed my hand and squeezed it firmly.

'...But now the world it shall at least be know the truth.'

'I will make sure your work has not been in vain...'

It sounded a cliché, and I guess that's why clichés become clichés, but I wasn't sure exactly how I would go about it.

'...The only thing is, I don't speak Arabic, so how do I know what's in here.'

'Here there are many crime that go back to my time as a child, and to the build of the Aswan Dam. Mubarak, he have his claw in everything; from assassination of Sadat, and all corrupt thing through all of government in passed forty year, to real reason behind it the 'revolution'.'

'What about Hawass?'

'Dead body, it may rot from head down, but it will all rot.'

I looked to Saeed for some clarity and he didn't pull any punches.

'Like Mubarak, Zahi Hawass he is the egotistical power and money-hungry megalomaniac who would walk it over the dead body of his own mother to get to what he want. Zahi Hawass he has been systematic robbing of the temple and archaeological site all over Egypt since he was first appointed head of the Supreme Council of Antiquities.'

'These temple, they belong it to all mankind, not to handful of greedy hyena and crocodile.'

'And these papers contain the evidence that will condemn them?'

'These paper have detail of many excavation and discovery that have been covered up or denied by Hawass.'

'Such as?'

I mindlessly flicked through pages as if I was suddenly going to discover one in English.

'Here in Luxor they have thrown it many hundred of people out of their home, and demolish them because of Avenue of Sphinx.'

'In Australia we call that compulsory acquisition. The government offers landholders some token gesture of money, way below the current market value, not taking into consideration the sentimental and emotional connections to the property.

Then it's simply 'take it or leave it'.'

Saeed weighed in.

'At least in Australia, the people they are offered something. The people of Luxor they were simple told to get out. And this it is not the only place, Zahi Hawass he has done this all over Egypt.'

I rifled the pages.

'Where else?'

'Everywhere; even in Cairo.'

'Cairo? What happened there?'

Kareem looked to Saeed, who took up the mantle.

'About ten year ago, Zahi Hawass worked out the location of sacred temple site in the outskirt of Giza, close to the pyramid. The problem was that it was underneath part of the city, under the house. Hawass he seized the property then make the secret digging below the house. But, in the hurry to get to the treasure, the whole building it collapsed in on top of the excavation and ten men they are killed.'

'I don't remember hearing anything about that.'

'I am not surprised; Hawass and Mubarak they control everything, including the media. This is how they keep the people in the poverty and make for themself richer and richer.'

'That's all in here?'

'Yes, everything.'

'If that's the case, then villagers would never disclose discovering anything; they'd keep it quiet, rob the tombs themselves, then sell what they find on the black market.'

'And this it is exactly what happen.... Until Zahi Hawass he find it out this.'

'What happens then?'

'He move in with Antiquities Police, or sometime with the army, and close down the area. Then he either throw anyone who disagree or complain into prison for robbing of the antiquity of Egypt, or, in some case, they mysterious to disappear or suffer it the fatal accident.'

'Dead men tell no tales, hey.'

'You understand me.'

Before I could ask more questions, the leader of the band gave a huge welcome/introduction and the restaurant audience went crazy. It was the first time I noticed that the room was now chockers, packed to the rafters with mostly middle-aged Egyptian men. In fact there was not a woman in sight, only the belly dancer who appeared from the back and shimmied out onto the dance floor. In an optimistic light she was best described as well and truly on the healthy side of Rubinesque.

Kareem looked at me with raised eyebrows as if say, 'How risqué is this!'. I guess to fundamental Islamic Egyptians who were used to 'seeing' women fully clad in black regalia, it was equivalent to being taken to a 'Gentleman's' Club where a bevy of butt-naked beauties brazenly cavorted and openly displayed all their most-personal of alluring assets and the object of every teenage boys testosterone-imbibed desires. This was certainly no lap dance; to me, it was more like a muffin-topped contestant for Egypt's 'Biggest Loser' jiggling around the family restaurant to a cacophony of noise that masqueraded as music. However I didn't want Kareem and Saeed to know that, and I certainly didn't want to appear culturally ignorant or ungracious; especially if the talent turned out to be the boss's daughter.

I feigned aroused approval, watching as select members of the audience were invited up to become part of the floorshow: now *that* didn't happen at Spearmint Rhino, well not on the occasions I was there. The men may have danced *with* the woman, but it was still somewhat reserved, with them each holding opposing ends of a large handkerchief or table napkin; any sort of body contact was definitely taboo.

I should have guessed it, and I suppose on reflection it was inevitable, but, with Saeed and Kareem's encouragement, I was next candidate on her dance card. I did my best not only to entertain the locals, but more importantly to not make a complete asshole of myself. Then, having spent what I perceived to be an appropriate amount of time pretending to be the Egyptian John Travolta, I returned to the table, eager to follow up on the contents of the manila folder.

'Kareem, can I ask you more about the massacre at Hatshepsut's Temple?'

He cast a series of glances around the room then lowered his voice.
'But of course.'
'You were saying today they brainwashed young Islamic fundamentalists, convinced them to dress as police, and to kill as many tourists as they could, all in name of Allah.'
'But Mubarak he blame it Al Gamaa al-islamiyya. And when the protest it break out in Luxor against the terrorist, Mubarak he just replace Interior Minister, General Hassan al-Alfi, with General Habib al-Adly, and visit Luxor a few day later.'
'Are you Saying Hassan al-Alfi was aware of it, and Habib al-Adly was in on it?

He patted the folder.
'It is all in here?'
'Everything?'
'Everything.'

Not long after, the evening came to a close and it was time for me to express my gratitude and head back to the hotel. Kareem slipped the folio back into the bag as I tried to pay, but neither Saeed nor his two uncles would hear of it. To them, I was doing this in the name of their deceased cousin/son/nephew, and for the freedom of the Egyptian people; talk about no pressure.

'Come, I shall walk with you back to your hotel.'

Saeed handed me the bag, as we bid his two uncles farewell, then headed out into the night.

Pass the parcel

The broken chatter and hustle and bustle of the street noise were a welcome relief from the echo chamber I had just spent the past few hours in, and the warm yet refreshing evening breeze was at least reasonably smoke-free. As Saeed and I weaved our way through the street trade, I contemplated detouring via the Nefertiti Hotel on the off chance I might run into Crystal. But the truth was I was knackered, so, as I was hopefully seeing Crystal in the morning at Karnak, I pretty much decided to head straight back to the hotel and call it a night.

Enroute, we chuckled away at the dramatic differences in cultural attitudes towards women and sex between the Islamic culture and western civilization; they were like chalk and cheese. Suddenly Saeed grabbed my arm and dragged me into a shop.

'What's up?'

'I think we may have it the unwelcome company.'

I looked around and back out towards the street.

'Who?'

'The Secret Police.'

'I don't see anyone.'

'Would you know what to look for?'

'No, I guess not.'

'I cannot let you take it Kareem paper, it is too dangerous.'

As I walked back to the door and out into the alley, I couldn't help but think Saeed was being a little paranoid. There were the shop owners, a few old men sitting smoking a hookah, a dozen or so kids, several women looking through clothes at a stall, a half-dozen tourists being hassled and hustled, a mangy looking dog and a scrawny donkey on the brink of meeting its maker.

'I think you might be imagining things. I'll be fine with the papers. Besides, isn't this exactly what you're trying to fight? Isn't this what the whole revolution is about; truth and freedom?'

'Yes, for Egyptians, but not if it put your life in danger.'

I laughed it off.

'Saeed, I'll be fine. I'm a big boy; I can look after myself. Besides, danger is my middle name, and it goes with the hat.'

'But you are not wearing it your hat.'

He had a point. Then I spotted a naff tourist bag hanging on the wall; one with a typically hand painted or printed scene of Tutankhamun's death mask on it.

'How about we switch the papers in to this, then you head off back to the river with Kareem's bag and I'll go back to my hotel with this stunning piece of tourist apparel? That way anyone following us will think you still have the papers and I have typically appalling tourist taste in knick-knacks and souvenir paraphernalia.'

He wasn't convinced. Then he had an idea.

'Wait here.'

He said something in Arabic to the shop owner, who disappeared out the back, returned less than thirty seconds later with a handful of blank paper, and handed them to Saeed, who, in the meantime had taken the folio out of Kareem's bag.

'What are you doing?'

'I am create it the decoy.'

He put the contents of the folio into the tourist bag then wrapped the folio cover around the blank pages, putting them into Kareem's bag.

'When we get it to the end of the street we will say goodbye. I will go to give it to you the bag of Kareem, but you will refuse it. Then I will take it the paper out and offer them to you, but again you will refuse them as well. I will then put it them back into my bag, say goodbye, and head off back toward the river.'

'That way if anyone *is* following us, they will think you still have the papers and follow *you*.'

'Yes, this is good?.'

'Brilliant.'

The plan set, we left the shop, with me doing my best acting job to show my delight at my bargain buy. At the end of the street we executed the plan with pin-point precision and I headed back to the hotel. Every now and then I feigned interest in some trinket or food substance just so I could sneak a peek to see if I was being followed. All I could see was what I had grown to accept as a normal Egyptian street; Hell, I was becoming as paranoid as Saeed.

I arrived back at the Nubian Oasis, pausing at the entrance to look back down the street. Unless the Egyptian Secret Police were recruiting barefooted, runny-nosed street urchins kicking a makeshift soccer ball, or had disguised themselves as a marauding pride of scrawny alley cats, I had made it safely home, unnoticed. Seleh was still behind the reception counter: I wondered if he ever slept.

'Good evening, Mister Alex. Have you had it the good day?'

'Brilliant, thanks.'

'I have it a message for you from Mister Dwight and Mister Randy. They have gone to bed but said they will catch up with you at breakfast.'

'Thanks, Seleh.'

I hadn't even thought about the lads; I guess they got totally pickled over the day while chilling out in the hammocks beside the rooftop bar, and couldn't last into the night.

Up the stairs, I reached my room and contemplated firing up the laptop to bring my trip up to date. But, instead, as I sat on the bed, I took the papers from the tourist bag and slowly rifled through them. How could anyone read Arabic: it was ten times harder than trying to read a doctor's handwriting. Could there really be the evidence in here to support what Kareem had said?

I guess it could, because it tweaked my budding paranoia to such an extent that put down the papers, checked the door was locked and took one last stint of surveillance from my third floor balcony just to make sure I wasn't the object of a stakeout.

Convinced the coast was clear, and that it was highly unlikely a galabayeh-wearing 'spiderman' was poised to crawl his way up the exterior hotel wall and in through my window, I decided it could all wait until tomorrow and headed back inside to go to sleep. And yet, for some strange reason, I took the pile of papers off the bed and, rather than return them to the tourist bag, I stowed them in a plastic shopping bag I kept in my backpack for dirty clothes, and secreted them securely under my mattress next to my laptop; my thinking was, if someone *did* sneak into the room, they would go for the tourist bag.

That done, I stripped off to my Calvins, had a piss, brushed the fangs, and hit the sack. I was so knackered I probably went to sleep before my head had even hit the pillow.

CHAPTER 19 – THE ALABASTER KINGDOM

The next thing I remembered was running down a dimly lit tunnel, a man-made tunnel, with reliefs and hieroglyphs covering not only both walls, but also the ceiling. I was not so much running *to* something, as *from* something, or rather some*one*. And I wasn't alone. Beside me, a young Egyptian teen, dressed as a novice priest, was equally as concerned.

'Come on, they're right behind us.'

It was Saeed, but not as he was now, as he would have been as a sixteen-year-old, and it felt like we were related; like brothers, or cousins.

'Who? Who is it chasing us?'

'Are you crazy; the Amun Priests.'

'The Amun Priests? Why are they after us?'

'The scroll, Dummy.'

'What scroll?'

He pulled it from my hand and waved it before me like he had ripped out one of my own ribs and slapped me in the face with it.

'This one, Stupid, and if we get caught with it they'll probably tie us up out in the desert sun until we're ripped into a hundred pieces by a pack of ravenous jackals. Then they will feed the left over pieces to the crocodiles. All of that *after* they have first slowly drowned us in a pool of rancid camel spit.'

He ran ahead, urging me to 'get the lead out'. I looked behind, back down the passage, but couldn't see anything through the murky darkness. But I sure could feel it, sense it coming my way; a tsunami of intimidation and oppression. Saeed paused at a T-junction in the tunnel ahead.

'Come on!'

He disappeared around the corner to the right as I felt the bow-wave of hostility, surging from back down the tunnel, knock me off my feet. Time to get the hell out of there.

As I tried to clamber to my feet, I suddenly felt like I was trying to run through massive curtains of wet concrete: no matter how hard I tried, I could only move in slow motion. Behind me I heard the caws and shrieks of hungry vultures and saw their razor-sharp talons reaching out of the shadows towards me. Would I make the T-junction in time?

Then, just as I reached it, Saeed careered back around the bend, crashing into me and stuffing the scroll back into my hand, waving a second scroll in his other hand.

'Here, they're everywhere; even the walls have ears. I'll take this ordinary scroll and try to lead them in the other direction.'

And, with that, he took off down the left corridor of the T-junction, leaving me at the mercy of the impending attack of the vultures. I looked down at the scroll, crammed into my clammy fist, and slowly unrolled it.

'ALLAH U AKBAR, ALLAH U AKBAR.'

'What the fuck?!'

'ASH-HADU AL-LA ILAHA ILL ALLAH - ASH-HADU AL-LA ILAHA ILL ALLAH.'

Suddenly jolted back into the 'now', I manically tried to return to my quiescent cement sarcophagus back in Ancient Egypt, desperately trying to refocus on the contents of the scroll.

'ASH-HADU ANNA MUHAMMADAN RASULULLAAH.'

'No, not again!'

I buried my head under the pillow, deeper and deeper with each of the calls to prayer, but alas it was too late, I'd lost it; I'd lost my nocturnal connection to Ancient Egypt.

As I wrestled my bed linen, frustration, and the persistent thump of yet another dehydration-and-beer-induced hangover, the pre-dawn light crept in through the window announcing the impending continuation of my adventure. This was day..? I had to retrace my thoughts, eventually realizing this was Day Eight; Christ, I was into my second week already! But it was no good; my mind was racing a million miles an hour and, no matter what I tried, I couldn't get back to sleep.

So, surrendering to the inevitable, I staggered out of bed, had a quick shower to wake up, and decided to take my laptop up to the roof to bring my trip up to date before breakfast. I paused at the door and looked back at the bed. For some reason, perhaps residual paranoia from the previous evening, I couldn't leave the folio of papers behind. I picked up the plastic bag, stuffed them in the tourist bag, and took the documents with me, up the stairs to the rooftop.

Pieter and Yuko were already up, meditating in the large sand pit in the corner. I briefly contemplated reclining in one of the hammocks stretched across it, but decided that, rather than disturb them, instead I would sit at one of the tables and concentrate on writing my notes.

I placed the bag on the table beside my laptop and settled in, deciding the first thing to do once the laptop was fired up, was select some music to listen to. Classical, or Modern? Pick up where I left off with Aida, or something more suitable to start the day. Shirley Bassey perhaps, or Journey? All of them perhaps a little too much of a distraction for Pieter and Yuko. In the end I settled on Debussy's *Prélude a l'après-midi d'un faune*; it not only captured the feeling of the sunrise, but it sat calmly in the background, allowing me to process the events of the previous day.

Firstly there were those damned 'calls to prayers'. I just couldn't grasp how, if someone *was* truly connected to Allah, they needed to be reminded five times a day by someone calling out over a set of speakers perched atop a minaret. But I guess that was one of the many issues I had with religion – not only the dogma, but the conditioning and adherence to ritual. Still, while I was in a predominantly Islamic country I would just have to put up with it, that, or buy a set of earplugs.

If there *was* something good to come of it though, it was that it got me to an early breakfast with Pieter and Yuko and to learning a little about the 'Emerald Tablets'. I still don't know if they were made of emerald, or emerald in colour, or what they looked like, but if the tablets *were* in a sacred chamber beneath the Great Pyramid, waiting to be unearthed one day soon by reincarnated members of Ptah's ancient priesthood, then that discovery would surely turn the history of ancient Egypt, and dare I say it, the world, on its ear. It may even reveal the truth about the passing of Nibiru and the consequences of a partial or complete pole shift. Similarly, the discovery of the 'Lamp of Isis' at P'aaleq may shed some light on the spiritual aspects of the pure Goddess creative energy of the Universe and the true, higher-realm, function of the *sang réal*.

Christ, what had happened to me? I couldn't believe the thoughts and ideas that were now constantly cascading through my head. If someone had told me that a two-week holiday in Egypt would change me so much as a person I would have said they had some sort of dementia.

Having said that, the choice to hire a bike to explore the West Bank was a masterstroke. Not only was it *the* most economical way to do it, but also the most flexible and most fun. It was also an excellent way to spend time with Pieter and Yuko to find out all about Enki and Enlil and the history of Sumer. That led to an exploration of the whole history of man and to the Dracos agenda of wanting to conquer the higher realms; a topic that hardly fitted with the thinking of a plethora of university-educated professors.

But the Egyptologists were really only guessing about most things, and their 'educated guesses' were based on the limitations of their education, belief structures, and conditioning. Take for instance the fact there were no records of the actual dates of the pharaohs from the middle of the 13th Dynasty, supposedly around 1638 BC, through the 14th and 16th Dynasties, until the beginning of the 17th Dynasty. Was that because a massive tsunami had obliterated almost all evidence and reference to the period?

It didn't matter, as far as the Egyptologists are concerned it was all just a massive period of guesswork anyway, all done in an attempt to make sense of everything. In the end it was all based on their frame of thinking, and that made me just as 'qualified' as all of them. God knows what they would make of the truth of the Gods of the Zep Tepi. Could they contemplate the possibility that Imhotep, Montuhotep, Rahotep at start of 17th Dynasty, Djehuti, which translated as Thoth, as well as Amenhotep and Akhenaten, could all possibly be the same being; a Being that periodically set up civilizations not only in ancient Egypt, but the Minoan, Mayan and Harappon Civilizations?

And that this Being would periodically lay in some sort of stasis to rejuvenate its body; a process the ancient Egyptian priests tried to duplicate in mummifying the pharaoh, other members of royalty, high office, or perhaps all those of the lineage of the *sang réal*? And was this process of rejuvenation somehow connected to the use of red and black granite in the building of temples and sarcophagi?

Could the 'experts' stretch even further to consider the possibility this Being was possibly also Apollo, Hermes, Asclepius and Hermes, even perhaps Socrates, or Plato. It was all so radical it was bound to be laughed at. But then people often ridicule what they don't understand, hoping their laughter will hide their ignorance. They laughed at Copernicus, at Galileo, at many others.

The only difference was, that in the past, they usually burned them at the stake to keep them quiet; that was the usual method employed by the power-mongers of religions to keep the masses under control, as well as in fear, awe and divine separation.

'Would you like some breakfast, Mister Alex?'

Seleh had appeared from the stairwell and was obviously there in preparation for the breakfast rush.

'That would be great, thanks.'

He disappeared behind the bar and I returned to my notes. As I'd been exploring the tombs in the Valley of the Kings it became even more obvious to me who had robbed them: the Amun Priests - they knew the exact layout of each tomb, and the contents. And they had done it all, beginning with the vandalism of the Akhenaten era, through the rift between Ay and Horemheb at the end of the 18th Dynasty, to the final mass relocation of royal mummies and the final split in the 21st Dynasty.

It also became clearer and clearer from the condition and placement of the tombs, the West Bank temples and their quays, that there was considerable variation in the level of the Nile. In addition, the four-plus metres of 'sediment' covering the West Bank temples indicated there had not only been a major tsunami caused by the eruption of Thera around 1600 BC, that swept up the Nile and obliterated the 17th Dynasty and all before it, but that there were probably several subsequent eruptions and tsunamis as Nibiru approached even closer.

Inside the tombs provided even more extraordinary evidence; evidence that had been totally misunderstood or perhaps deliberately ignored by scholars. Firstly there were the images of the gods; Osiris and Ptah with green skin, Isis, Hathor and Nephthys with yellow skin, others, such as Anubis and Horus, with brown. Jack the blind minor could see they were at the very least from different races. And speaking of the Annunaki, there was the ever-present image of the winged-disk everywhere, especially over all the doorways.

Then there were the numerous serpents, some with three heads, some with five, some with wings, some breathing fire and destroying the enemies of Osiris, others protecting the pharaoh. There was clearly more to all this than met the eye, and somewhere behind the scenes were the Dracos and the Annunaki, beings that, in some way or another, *we* were all descended from. It made me pause to think what the future might hold; what the Dracos and their puppet-ruling servants, the Illuminati, and what our makers, the Annunaki have in store for us all when they return.

The more I thought back over the images on the walls of the tombs, the more I was convinced the Egyptologists had overlooked so much. To me, the 'Book of the Dead', the 'Book of Emerging Forth into the Light', the 'Book of the Path to Resurrection', was not just a development of the Coffin Texts of the Middle Kingdom, which in turn had evolved out of the Pyramid Texts of the 5th Dynasty, they were the representations and attempts of humans to explain the rejuvenation process of Imhotep, of Thoth, and the journey of consciousness through the 4th Dimension.

That also explained their preoccupation with gold, and the focus on mono-atomic gold now. And what about the ankh, what was it really? Sure Osiris held the ankh, it was the breath of life, but did it have something to do with resurrecting the rejuvenated body, awakening the sleeping giant. Was it some specific 'tool' that reactivated the pineal gland and led to an awaken consciousness?

It naturally led to discussions on Akhenaten, how he probably left Egypt in the hands of Amenhotep IV (who then changed his name to Smenkhkare), and how, when Smenkhkare died, his son Tutankhamun assumed the throne. And how that in turn instigated a battle for the crown between Ay, the head of the Amun priests, and Horemheb, head of the military.

Meanwhile, Akhenaten went firstly to Greece where he helped rebuild civilization as the god, Apollo/Hermes. Nefertiti followed and became the first of the oracles at Delphi. Sometime around 1000 BC Apollo disappeared, possibly because he went into a state of suspended animation, to regenerate.

That raised the issue that, though the body was in hibernation, the soul could astral travel and incarnate in another body, or series of bodies, and I have to admit that freaked me out a bit. Especially when I considered that Akhenaten was me, I was him, that his body was laying chilled out in some underground vault. The question was: where?

Eventually the *sang réal* travelled to Macedonia and later on the Tat Brotherhood returned to Egypt through Alexander the Great around 332 BC. But sometime around 250 AD 'Apollo' returned to the Mayan Civilization where he remained until 1000 AD when the Dracos, through Quetzalcoatl, feather serpent creator god of Aztecs, attempted to take control back. So what happened to Apollo/Akhenaten? Is he underground in Egypt, South America, Greece, or somewhere else on the planet?

In the end, the outcome of my trip to the Valley of the Kings and the West Bank was a totally revised lineage of the 18th Dynasty, based on the *sang réal* and the return of Nibiru and Amenhotep; a lineage that would set the supposed experts on me like a pack of .... well... a frenzied venue of rabid vultures.

In keeping with the feeding theme, Seleh popped my breakfast in front of me, the aroma of the freshly made omelette triggering my salivary glands into overdrive. At the same time Dwight appeared from the stairwell.

'Hey, Alex, I was hoping to catch up with you before we left.'
'Shhh!'

Realizing Pieter and Yuko were still meditating, Dwight lowered his voice to a whisper.

'I wanted to make sure I had your contact details.'
'Where's Randy?'
'Still in bed, sleeping it off. What are you doing?'
'Just making a few more notes on my trip.'

Dwight indicted to Seleh to bring him breakfast and sat down on the other side of the table.

'Yeah, it's certainly had me thinking about all sorts of things.'
'Oh, you ain't heard nothing yet.'
'What do you mean?'
'Well, you know how yesterday you were telling me about the Luxor massacre at Hapshetsut's Temple?'
'Yeah.'
'Well after meeting you guys, I headed off to meet Saeed's uncle, Kareem, at Medinet Habu? He told me the whole Luxor massacre was set up by Zahi Hawass.'
'No way! Why? Randy and I were talking about that all yesterday afternoon. We couldn't see the point in it just to rob the temples?'
'There's a lot more to it. Kareem said it went way back, to the building of the Aswan Dam.'
'Which one, the first one, or the one in the 60's?'
'The High Dam; he said the whole relocation project was a cover up for the robbing of the temples. And that when they moved the temple of Isis, they found another temple below it made of large blocks of red granite. And that the Russians suddenly arrived and took over.'
'So the Russians *were* connected to UNESCO?'

'Yep.'

'How?'

'Through the Illuminati; they've funded and provided weapons for both sides of all the wars from the 13th Century onwards. They systematically infiltrated each and every world government and religious organization on the planet, including the Russians.'

'I get it: and by the Russians supplying the money for the High Dam, in effect they made Egypt one of it's debtors; they owned it.'

'Yep.'

'It all makes sense; they lent them the money in 1956 and two years later Egypt becomes a semi-presidential republic under Emergency Law, and has been since the six-day war in 1967, except for an 18-month break in 1980s - which all ended with the assassination of Sadat in 1981.'

'And Sadat had to go because he was trying to bring peace to the Middle East.'

'The Illuminati would never allow the signing of the Egypt-Israel Peace Treaty.'

'So they simply assassinated Sadat.'

I'm the King of the castle

Dwight became pensive, scratching his chin.

'According to the official story, on the anniversary of Egypt's victory in the six-day war against Israel, as French Mirage jet fighters screeched overhead, several soldiers, riding in a truck which was part of the military parade, jumped to the ground and marched towards the reviewing stand. Most people watching believed the soldiers were part of the performance, but, instead, one soldier threw a grenade while others opened fire at Sadat and his entourage.

The attackers included four enlisted men, an army major, and a lieutenant. In the mayhem the major and two of the enlisted men were killed, while the other three were arrested and jailed. The attackers were eventually identified as Islamist nationalists associated with the Muslim Brotherhood under the name of Islamic Jihad.

Subsequently, the group was found to have hatched the assassination plot with Al Gamaa al-Islamiyya, the same Islamic Brotherhood offshoot that allegedly developed ties with al-Qaeda in the mid-1990s, and was supposedly responsible for the 1997 terrorist attack at Luxor.'

'The same group, the same number of 'terrorists'; it's all a bit of a coincidence, don't you think?'

'Even more so; one of the group's leaders, Ayman al-Zawahiri, subsequently al-Qaeda's Number 2, was tried and imprisoned for three years for his role in the plot, before being expelled from Egypt.'

'Zawahiri? Wasn't he the same guy who denied involvement in the Luxor massacre, saying it was the Egyptian police?'

'One and the same.'

'Me thinks something doth stink in Denmark.'

'Several years later the three soldiers escaped from prison; one was tracked down and killed by police, the second was wounded and returned to prison, but the fate of the third is unknown.'

'If he had any sense at all he would disappear; dead men tell no tales.'

'But how would they convince the soldiers to do it in the first place, money?'

'Brainwashing.'

'Brainwashing? But the Egyptians wouldn't know anything about ....oh, the Russians. I get it. The Illuminati use religions, ideology and fanaticism as the instruments and scapegoats for it's activities.'

'And everyone buys it; hook, line, and sinker.'

As we continued our political dissection, Seleh brought Dwight's breakfast over and set it out before him. I nearly had all the ducks, or rather vultures, lined up; all but one.

'There's one thing I'm not sure of, how did Mubarak go from being an army officer to become president?'

'He was Egypt's Vice President at the time of the assassination.'

'Oh, that was convenient. Given he had strong military and personal ties to Russia, I'm guessing he was probably put in place as the Illuminati's puppet master. Do you think he was part of the assassination as well?'

'Not directly, he wasn't on the podium at the time of the attack.'

'How fortunate!'

'Indeed. But I'm betting he was the ringleader and rubber stamp, because, within hours, he'd assumed power and used the assassination as an excuse to declare martial law, which has remained in effect ever since, even despite the recent people's revolution. And I guess that's how he got so rich; he's really just an arms merchant.'

'I think he must have been part of Project Isis as well.'

'Is that the secret Russian project you spoke about the other day, the one to discover alien artefacts?'

'Yep.'

'So you think Mubarak knew about the treasure in the temples?'

'He had to; surely he couldn't have made seventy billion US dollars from just military contracts. Sadat was probably getting in the way, but once President, Mubarak was free to sell the ancient treasures to anyone who would pay.'

'The Illuminati.'

'Precisely.'

'So how does Hawass fit in, he's not a military man, isn't he the great champion of the pharaohs?'

'Sure Mubarak could use the army to move and hide the treasure, but he needed an insider to not only run the whole racket for him, but to tell him where and when new things were discovered.'

'Hawass?'

'Yep. I think he was groomed for the job.'

'Who by?'

'Well, ultimately by the Illuminati, but through the CIA.'

'Oh, Randy would love all this: he believes the CIA have their grubby fingerprints all over everything; 9/11, the drug trade, he even thinks the Copenhagen summit in 2010, and all the G20 summits, are all just a front. That what they're really discussing is when to implement another global financial collapse and third world war, and how it lines up with the latest data on Nibiru, and their survival plans.

'That's heavy shit.'

'That's just the tip of the iceberg; he also thinks the plane crash that wiped out half of the Polish Government was caused by them as well.'

'How, why?'

'According to Randy, the Polish weren't a part of the 'inner circle', but somehow they found out about the Illuminati's plans and were going to tell the world, so the plane was shot down.'

'It didn't crash?'

'Who knows? Will we ever know the truth about 9/11 when the people who do the investigating are the very ones who are responsible in the first place?'

'I see your point.'

'So how is Hawass connected to the CIA?'

'Hawass got his PhD from Princeton, a stronghold of the 'Liberty Bell', and the forefathers of the United States. When he was fired in 1994, Hawass flew directly to Washington where the CIA intervened and somehow he was magically and instantaneously reinstated. And he's been there ever since. If that doesn't raise questions about who is pulling the strings in Egypt then I don't know what will.'

'Wow, I know the Supreme Council of Antiquities frequently receives satellite imagery from the US National Security Agency, the NSA, and that it contains information as to whether there are subterranean structures at certain sites.

Hawass's boss, Culture Minister, Farouk Hosni, even once announced satellite research had confirmed the existence of one-hundred-thirty-two archaeological sites in Egypt that *hadn't* been excavated. One-hundred- thirty-two!'

'And that's just what they're telling us. Saeed's uncle, Kareem, was telling me that there are things under the Giza Plateau, including objects or rooms made of red granite, and that, when new rooms were discovered in the great pyramid, Hawass closed it down for six months, supposedly for maintenance. He also said that the original revolution was a cover-up to remove large objects from under the Giza Plateau.'

'You know, if you could prove any of this, there'd be hell to pay.'

I took the plastic bag from its gaudy tourist sarcophagus and pushed it across the table.

'Maybe the answers are here?'

'What is it?'

'Supposedly the proof: Kareem gave them to me last night over dinner. But it's all in Arabic so as far as I know it could just be the rantings of a senile old man.'

'Do you mind if I take a look?'

'Go for it.'

As Dwight removed the papers from the plastic bag and started flicking through them, I looked up and realized the sun had not only dawned, it had been up for some time. I checked the time: gosh 7:52 already. I had become so preoccupied with the papers and the James Bond stuff I had forgotten Crystal and the others were meeting outside Karnak at 8:30. So, while Dwight was preoccupied with the papers, I took the opportunity to make a few extra notes. There was so much to get down: my conversations with Kareem about Zahi Hawass, the possibility there were pre-existing temples beneath Hatshepsut's Temple at Deir Bahri and her temple at Medinet Habu. I started to form the opinion there were probably long forgotten temples everywhere beneath the sands of Egypt.

Typing as fast as I could I still somehow noticed, over in the corner, Pieter and Yuko had surfaced from their meditation and were serenely strolling over to join us for breakfast. Seleh was right on to it, and in anticipation had their breakfast before them before they had time to warm their seats.

Apart from the usual morning greetings and pleasantries, no one was really saying anything; we were each in our own headspace. That was until, after few minutes rifling through the pages, Dwight suddenly paused.

'Where did you get these again?'

'Saeed's uncle, Kareem. Why?'

'This is dynamite. Most of these are official Egyptian government documents, some dating back to the 1960's.'

Instantly I took a more fervent interest in the ream of papers.

'You read Arabic? I thought you were Jewish?'

'My father is Jewish, my mother is Palestinian; he met her when he visited Israel.'

'Geez, it must be fun around your place at Christmas.'

He rolled his eyes.

'Well, as you can imagine, we don't have much to do with my Dad's side of the family; they are full-on Hasidic Jews and, when he married my mom, they pretty much disowned him like he had the black plague.'

'It must make the Hatfields and McCoys look like kissin' cousins.'

'Don't fret it, there's no love lost there.'

'The shame is that there was no love *found.*'

Yuko was right, and we all knew it. I'm sure we also all realized it was unfortunately indicative of the sort of problems and religious intolerance that infested the world. It was Dwight who confirmed it.

'The Jews aren't the only ones though; the Muslims are just as bad. I remember a few years ago Zahi Hawass wrote in Al-Sharq Al-Awsat that "the only thing that the Jews have learned from history is methods of tyranny and torment".'

'There's the kettle calling the pot black.'

'He tried to explain his way out of it saying he was not referring to the Jews' "original faith" but "*the faith that they forged and contaminated with their poison, which is aimed against all of mankind.*" Then a few months later, in an interview on Egyptian television, he had another stab, stating that "*although Jews are few in number, they control the entire world*" and commented on the control they have of the American economy and the media.'

'Given his ties to the CIA and the US secret societies, who were the beneficiaries of his light-fingered approach to Archaeology, he would know.'

'Yeah, but he back-pedalled again, saying he was just using rhetoric to explain the political fragmentation among the Arab world, and that he doesn't believe there's a "Jewish conspiracy to control the world".'

'I guess he must have upset his masters, the Occultist Zionist Wankers, er Bankers, of Europe. It's ridiculous; I mean the two religions are basically the same. Mohammed based Islam on Judaism.

'True, and he thought the Jews would immediately accept it. But, when the Jews didn't live up to his expectations and convert, he turned against them and many Jews subsequently died violently by the sword.'

'In the end, they're both based on the rantings of a megalomaniac, and are nothing more than collections of myths and superstitions, with a little twisted history thrown in for credibility.'

'That's a fair assessment, but at least one is compatible with the rest of humanity, whereas the other one is a barbaric blood-cult founded by a violent paedophile.'

'And that one would be?'

We both laughed at the obvious reference to the many religious wars over the years, each religion of course blaming the other. And as far as I was concerned, it was still happening.

'And then there was the people's revolution, and suddenly Mubarak and Hawass reached their use-by date.'

'But not before they put up a fight. Hawass called upon Egyptians not to believe the "lies and fabrications" of the Al Jazeera and Al Arabiya satellite television channels, and later said, "They should give us the opportunity to change things, and if nothing happens they can march again. But you can't bring in a new president now. We need Mubarak to stay and make the transition." Then, just after that, no doubt in an attempt to protect his interests, Mubarak appointed Hawass to a newly created post of Minister of Antiquities.'

'That's interesting because it shows they were not only covering each others asses, but that Hawass considered himself more of a member of the government than an archaeologist. Kareem even went as far as to suggest the whole revolution was a set-up to cover-up Hawass removing large objects from beneath the Giza Plateau.'

'I wouldn't put it passed them....'

Dwight dived back into the pages.

'...I wonder if there's something about it in here?'

'Seriously, you speak Arabic?'

'There's not much point studying Middle Eastern politics or wanting to be an Egyptologist if you can't.'

Pieter, who'd been sitting quietly, eating his breakfast, couldn't contain his curiosity any longer.

'What are the papers about?'

As Dwight continued to peruse the documents, I explained to Pieter and Yuko my meeting and subsequent dinner with Kareem and Saeed, and how Kareem had given me the papers to take out of Egypt.

'It sounds very cloak and dagger, they must be very important.'

'I guess we'll soon find out....'

I looked across at Dwight.

'...So what do they say?'

'Well this document is about the Luxor massacre, it talks about the date and time of the attack, the method of attack, the weapons, the placing of propaganda in mutilated bodies and the escape route.'

'Nothing unusual about that.'

'Except it's dated two weeks *before* the actual attack.'

We all looked at each other; we didn't need it spelled out to us to know what *that* meant. It was Pieter who eventually broke the moment, standing up as he spoke.

'It's all very interesting, but it's time we got going to join the others at Karnak.'

Standing to join him, Yuko inquired in my direction.

'Are you coming with us?'

I checked the time: 8:16.

'For sure, I'll meet you downstairs in a few minutes.'

'Dwight?'

He briefly looked up from the page.

'Randy and I have already been, besides we fly out for Cairo later this afternoon.'

'What time?'

'6:20.'

'We should be back around lunch so hopefully we'll see you before you go.'
'Cool.'

He wasn't really listening; he was too absorbed with Kareem's treasure trove of information. He didn't even notice Pieter and Yuko head off downstairs. I finished typing my paragraph; somehow managing to cover everything from the previous day in point form, then shut down the laptop, stuffing it into the tourist bag. Dwight sensed I was ready to go.

'Can you leave the papers with me for a while?'
'I was just thinking that, in fact why don't you take them with you, to Cairo?'
'I'd love to, but Kareem entrusted them to you to get them out of the country. I'd only be able to take them as far as Cairo, and that would be taking them right into the Dragon's Den. It's best you keep them.'
'But I don't know anyone else apart from you who speaks Arabic. And who else can I trust to get them translated, and more importantly, to keep quiet?'
'When will you be back from Karnak?'
'I'm not sure, how long do you think I'll need to look around there?'
'It's massive; Randy and I took four hours, and we still couldn't cover everything.'
'Ok, 8:30, 12:30, say 1:30, that's five hours. What time do you need to leave here to get to the airport?'
'Our flights at 6:20 so we'd need to leave here by 4:20 pm at the latest.'
'No problem then. You hang on to them until you go, make as many notes as you can, and I'll meet you back here say around four.'
'It's a date!'

As I picked up the tourist bag and headed downstairs, Dwight was already asking Seleh for a pen and paper, lots of paper. He certainly had an interesting day ahead of him, and hopefully, so did I.

I stopped off at my room, picked up my backpack, and for some reason decided to put my laptop in it rather than tuck it back under my bed. I guess the presence of the wad of documents had me a little on edge. It safely tucked away, I rendezvoused with Pieter and Yuko in the lobby. They were set to go, however, before jumping in the taxi, I called in at the little shop just down from the hotel and purchased a few bottles of water and some snacks to tide me over through the day. The shopkeeper was so nice, and surprisingly honest when it came to the prices, that I tipped her ten pounds, which brought a massive smile to her face; it seemed a little of Bill was rubbing off on me. I squeezed what I could into the backpack, and the rest into the tourist bag, which I brought with me, thinking it might make a nice gesture of good will to Diane, the leader of the ladies group.

Initially I thought of giving it to Crystal, but then thought *that* would be too obvious, and it would be much more strategic to give it to Diane in the presence of Crystal. I just had to pick my time so it didn't look ridiculous or insincere.

Stocked up for the duration, Pieter, Yuko and I climbed aboard the taxi and set off for Karnak. I would love to say the reasonably short trip from the hotel to Karnak was a pleasant one, but the truth was, the closer we got, the more uncomfortable I felt. I couldn't explain it at the time, but it was like a wave of impending foreboding was about to break on my head. I thought maybe we were going to have an accident, or that we were being followed by the police, which, as far as I could discern, we weren't, but when we arrived at Karnak, it all started to unfold.

The minute I stepped out of the taxi I felt a surge of energy, like a current pushing me away from the temple. I suddenly remembered it was the same feeling I'd had in my dream that morning. This was no illusion; it was a repelling *force* that didn't want me to go in to the complex. Spotting Diane and her group at the entrance to the visitors' centre, and then Crystal amongst them, gave me enough focus and intent to override the feeling and head towards them.

Bill and Pernille were there as well, rejoicing in each other's company, and soon we were all reconnecting and embracing as we had on board the White Rose. Bill took note of the tourist bag slung over my shoulder.

'I see the vultures in the bazaar finally wore you down: very kitsch. Though I have to admit I thought you would have gone for some little statuette or papyrus painting.'

'Saeed gave it to me last night. Along with a whole lot of official papers from his uncle.'

'Interesting! May I have a look?'

'No can do; I left them back with Dwight at the hotel. Besides, unless you speak Arabic it all looks like double-dutch.'

'Fair enough.'

'I thought I'd give the bag to Diane though, as a sort of thank you.'

'Nice touch.'

Diane had numerous small bags, no doubt containing all her tools of the trade, and I pictured how much easier it would be for her to carry them all in the one tourist bag. As I greeted her I took the one large bottle of water from within, and presented the tourist bag to her. She was extremely grateful, more-so for the thought than the actual bag, but never the less she made a fuss over the design and how she could now carry all her things with greater ease.

As Diane fussed and relayed everything to her new bag, I stole a glance in Crystal's direction to see if I'd racked up a few brownie points. Mission successful. Crystal looked, as usual, amazing; once again dressed in white, the flowing cloth still managing to betray the svelte form that simmered away underneath. It took me back several mornings earlier to where, on the river she had shed her sarong and stood naked before me.

That naturally led to me remembering the images of her intimately involved with Pernille and Yuko; how quickly the oppressive surge of energy that had haunted me en-route seemed to have disappeared, replaced by a more powerful surge of energy, namely good old-fashioned lust. Naturally, I wondered if similar episodes of fervid feminine intertwining were a part of the ladies' previous evenings' circle, so, as we all entered the visitors' centre, I innocently broached the subject.

'How was your night; your goddess circle?'

Crystal's look betrayed a wealth of information, though her words were far less revealing.

'It was most satisfactory.'

'What happened?'

'We were all re-initiated as High Priestesses and reclaimed our lineage.'

Cue my mind to go into overdrive.

'What does that involve?'

She smiled.

'Activities that are not wisely described for the vivid imaginations of men to cogitate, ruminate, and masticate over.'

I'm sure she knew exactly what she was doing: fuelling my imagination with a subsequent series of wry smiles and raised eyebrows, before abandoning me to my run-away fantasies. Of course it launched me into vivid scenes of the women that surrounded me, all naked and writhing over each other; a full-on lesbian free-for-all. Being the red-blooded male that I was, I casually probed for more details.

'Secret women's business I guess.'

'And best it stays that way, Alex.....At least for now.'

She knew exactly how to keep every part of me on tenterhooks. Meanwhile, Diane and her High Priestesses, along with Bill, Pieter, and ultimately myself, gathered around the massive model of the Karnak complex that took pride of place within the visitors' centre.

It was huge. I took out my notes, which included an annotated diagram, and tried to bring myself up to speed.

Hell, this model only covered the Precinct of Amun; that alone was sixty-one acres. Outside the north gate was the precinct of Montu, outside the south gate led to the Precinct of Mut, whilst outside the east gate was once the Precinct of Aten, built by Akhenaten. But none of these areas were open to the public.

I soon realized the reason why the model only included the Temple of Amun precinct was because it was the only precinct open to the public; the rest were in the hands of archaeologists from various universities around the globe.

As I stood there with the others comparing my diagram with the model that stretched out before me, I could think of only one thing - this place wasn't just big, it was massive. Who knows how vast it was back in the 26th or 30th Dynasty, or what lay beneath the dirt, dust and sand?

I checked my notes.

The Temples at Karnak

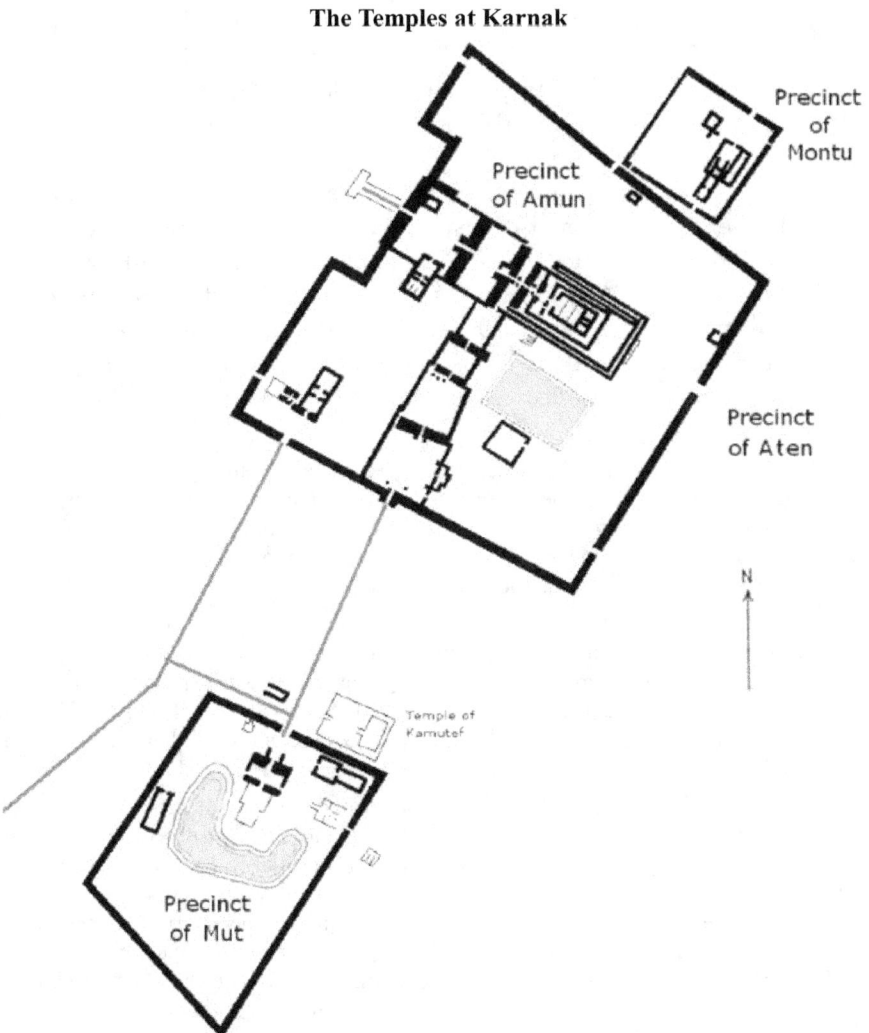

'The name Karnak derives from the Arabic for fortified village. Known as Ipet-isut (most select of places), it is the largest group of temples in the world, covering almost a mile by two miles, that's an area of 100 hectares. It's dedicated to the Theben triad of Amun, his wife Mut, and their son Khonsu, each of which has it's own precinct within the temple complex, the largest belonging to Amun. There is also a precinct dedicated to the falcon headed local god, Montu, an incarnation of Horus.

This vast complex dates back from as early as 2000 BC and was built and enlarged over a sixteen-hundred year time-frame by around 30 successive pharaohs, who added their own touches to the complex well into the Greco-Roman period.

All together, there are over 25 temples and chapels in the complex, including the Great Temple of Amun Ra, The Temple of Khonso, The Opet Temple, The Temple of Ptah, the Temple of Montu and the Temple of Osiris., with a 20 metre high, mud brick enclosure wall, surrounding all of these buildings.

At present the Akhenaten Temple Project, begun by the University Museum of Pennsylvania and carried on jointly by the Egyptian Department of Antiquities and the Smithsonian Institution in Washington, D.C., is using computer analysis to identify, date and classify architectural elements and relief bearing stones, making it possible to reconstruct earlier buildings which had been pulled down and reused in the structure of later ones. '

That in itself sounded suspect; I was already highly suspicious of Zahi Hawass and his connection to the University of Pennsylvania and the Illuminati, but I'd also read many articles of extraordinary archaeological finds disappearing once the Smithsonian Institute became involved. But that was another story. For the moment, I focused my attention on the area open to the public; the precinct of the Temple of Amun.

Before I could set a course of action of my own, Diane took the lead.

'We approach from the west, through an avenue of sphinxes, and once through the first pylon we'll head left into one of the small chapel and hold a little circle to honour the guardians of the temple. From there we'll head through the Hypostyle Hall and on to the inner sanctuary, the Temple of Amun. So, let's go.'

Like the Pied Piper of Hamlin, Diane led the way out of the visitors' centre; her devotees and disciples close in tow. Not far behind, the six sole survivors of the Minnow were seemingly being sucked along in her spiritual wake. And that's when I really started to feel it, or rather, feel *them*.

Something, or someone, didn't want me entering the temples. It wasn't the reptilians; I knew that, I'd felt their energy. But it was somehow similar, and, with each step forward, I felt like I was trying to drive against a hurricane of anger, resentment and malcontent. At first I wondered if I was just imagining it, but then, out of the blue, Crystal gently grabbed me by the arm.

'Remember who you are. When you do, no one can deny you.'

Akhenaten? Did she mean him? Or was she referring to the Annunaki? I wasn't sure, and it didn't really matter. But what it did do was give me the power and focus to shrug *them* off and forge forward, into their lair.

As we walked the modern entrance into the temple complex from the west, I remembered this entrance was once an ancient quay built by Ramses II to give access via a canal to the river Nile; more evidence of the much higher river level back in the 19th Dynasty. Stopping atop the small rectangular terrace that marked the beginning of our journey, I noticed a small obelisk, the remaining one of a pair that clearly marked the arrival from the Nile and the river entrance to the complex.

'The terrace contains one of a pair of obelisks erected by Seti II in the 19th Dynasty, Beyond it, to the right of the terrace, stands a small chapel built in the 29th Dynasty by the pharaoh,

Hakoris (392-380 BC), or his predecessor, Psammuthis (392-390 BC), which would have been used as a resting station to house the sacred barque on it's processional journeys of the gods up and down the Nile. '

From the terrace, two rows of twenty *'crio-sphinxes'* sphinxes, having the head of a ram with the curled horns of Amun, a nemes head-dress and the body of a lion, created an avenue that led towards the temple: not so imaginatively called 'The Way of the Rams' by the ancient Egyptians.

Each sphinx held a statue, supposedly of Ramses II, between its paws, though many of the experts suggest the sphinxes were the work of Amenhotep III, who inaugurated many of the processional ways associated with Karnak, and that Ramses II may have just claimed them as his own and carved his own cartouche over those of Amenhotep III: that wouldn't surprise me in the least.

As I walked between them I felt as if the eyes of all the rams and mini 'Ramses IIs' were watching me, testing me, challenging me. Was it Ramses II I was up against: Jacques? It couldn't be, could it? Jacques had been banished to the financial sewers of Paris; no, it wasn't Ramses II.

Nothing was going to stop me; I knew why I was here, and what I was looking for. I took my map from my pocket and scrutinized it closely.

Unlike most of the previous temples upriver, like Philae, Kalabsha, and Edfu, reconstructed during the Ptolemaic period, these temples were the real McCoy, more like Luxor. As far as I was aware, apart from a few minor repairs, renovations and additions, there were no Ptolemies here. In fact some parts of the complex definitely dated back at least as far as the Middle Kingdom.

That in itself said something I thought was quite profound. It meant the temples here were either not in need of major reconstruction, thus still relatively in tact, around 332-323 BC, which means they had not been damaged by any earthquake or tsunami, or that the Ptolemies never got around to fully repairing them.

The second point didn't make sense to me, as Karnak supposedly held much greater spiritual importance than most of the other locations, so much so that Thutmoses I made Thebes the capital of the New Kingdom. Therefore surely it would have been rebuilt first, or, at the very least, concurrently. But there was only the slightest indication the Ptolemies had even been here. I was no eminently qualified Egyptologist, but, to me, that needed further investigation.

I knew from visiting the previous temples that the further and deeper into the temple you went, the more you went back in time, and the more likely you were to encounter red granite. I was assuming the same would be the case here. Sure there might be some unexpected surprises along the way that had to be accounted for, but basically, as I looked closely at the floor plan, I knew my objective was the Sanctuary of Amun, beyond the sixth pylon, and possibly also the Middle Kingdom Courtyard beyond that. And so, beginning with the massive First Pylon, built during the 30th Dynasty of Nectanebo I, 380-362 BC, we started counting back the years.

Over a hundred metres wide, fifteen metres thick, and over forty metres high, the First Pylon is believed to have been left unfinished. As I looked at the uneven height of its upper regions I wasn't convinced it was deliberately left that way. It could just as easily have been part of the damage caused to all the temples by the actions of an earthquake or tsunami. But then I saw the unfinished blocks that projected from its undecorated surfaces, and, as we entered the subsequent courtyard, the remains of a mud-brick ramp that was clearly left over from the construction phase of the pylon. Adding two and two, I was thus prone to agree with the pylon's status as unfinished.

But that raised the question – What was it that caused the interruption to it's construction? Egypt wasn't invaded then. Was it a builders' strike? Not likely. Was there another quake and/or tsunami around 360 BC? Did some natural disaster initiate the demise of the 30th Dynasty, the last of the Egyptian rulers, and Egypt's ultimate 'occupation' by Alexander and the Greeks? Or did Alexander come to the rescue of his spiritual brethren and bloodline ancestors? Who knows, the answer might lie somewhere amidst the one hundred hectares of Karnak.

My notes said there was a magnificent view from the platform on the top of the pylon, reached by a staircase on the north tower. It would a perfect place to get an overview of the temples. But, alas, the access was locked, and it appeared there was no one readily around to open it. Besides, Diane was marching the troops with a real purpose, so much so that a few steps later we were fully in the open colonnaded courtyard.

'A hundred metres long and eighty wide, with colonnades along the sides, the first courtyard dates back to the 22nd Dynasty, 945-730 BC, and the rule of the Libyan Kings.'

That was around five to seven hundred years earlier. Initially I wasn't sure which one of the five Sheshonq pharaohs that reigned during the 22nd Dynasty built the courtyard, but I had my suspicions. It had to be either Sheshonq I or Sheshonq II because the Libyan Kings of Bubastis were responsible for reviving the traditions of the earlier pharaohs; traditions that were supposedly discounted and discarded by the military rulers of the 19th and 20th Dynasties and the Amun Priests of the 21st Dynasty.

'Welcome to Karnak everyone....'

On a wing and a prayer

Diane gathered her ardent devotees, most of whom were dressed in all white and looked more like a flock of doting doves.

'...On the right hand side is the Temple of Ramses III. It's of no significance to us and merely consists of the small pylon you see, which leads to an open court, a Hypostyle hall, and beyond that into the sanctuary. Next to it is the "Bubastite Portal", which leads to the south face of the main temple's side wall and the famous scenes of Sheshonq I, first of the Libyan pharaohs of the 22nd Dynasty, smiting his captives. He was the biblical figure, Shishak, from 1 Kings 14 in '*The Bible*', but we'll go over there in a minute for a look anyway....'

Diane confirmed my thoughts it must have been Sheshonq I who built the courtyard walls, but, to be honest, I was with Diane; Ramses III, Sheshonq I and the 22nd Dynasty held no significance or interest for me either. But just to be sure, I checked my papers.

'The Temple of Ramses III at Karnak was actually an elaborate barque shrine designed as a miniature version of the king's mortuary temple at Medinet Habu. The first court is lined with Osirid statues of Ramses III, while the walls are decorated with various festival scenes and texts. Beyond is a portico and small hypostyle hall, as well as an inner area for the members of the Karnak Triad.'

No, I'd seen the bigger version and was happy to give the mini version of Medinet Habu a miss.

'...In the centre are the remains of the giant Kiosk of Taharqa, who ruled during the 25th Dynasty. That leads through the temple to the Sanctuary of Amun....'

I guessed the Kiosk must've originally looked much like the one on Philae, although there was only one of the original ten huge columns remaining here; over twenty metres high, with a budding papyrus capital.

'...To the left is what is referred to as the Temple of Seti II, or rather, three chapels built for the Triad of Thebes; Mut, Amun in the centre, and Khonsu. It's thought the three separate shrines were for the three separate boats that took the statues of the gods on their annual trip on the flooding Nile. Come, we shall hold our prayer in there.'

That said, she led the others, like sheep, into the central shrine.

I'd never been into religion, so prayer wasn't a part of my daily activities, however I wasn't deliberately lagging behind because of any religious resistance, *they* had returned: the oppressive entities that were non-too-happy about my being here.

The chapels had been reconstructed, seemingly ad-hoc, from sandstone, modern concrete and granite. To me, each represented a different time; the sandstone to the time of Seti II, the concrete to the modern restoration, and the granite to some far distant past as I was firmly of the opinion that Seti II had usurped the granite from another earlier structure.

As I approached the entrance, the women had all entered and formed a circle within the space, with Bill and Pieter standing just inside the doorway, though outside the women's circle. There was only about a four or five inch step up to enter the chapel, and yet I couldn't take it; it was like a force field had been put in place across the entrance. Crystal saw me struggling and fixed her gaze on mine.

'*Remember who you are. When you do, no one can deny you.*'

I took a deep breath, I was Akhenaten, no one could defy me, and powered into the chapel. Once there, I stood between Bill and Pieter, forming a fourth wall that covered the entrance and made it difficult for anyone else to enter the chapel. Before us, the circle of women joined hands and softly started toning. It began as a unison sound; all on just one note, 'Ah'. But soon it added a fifth and then became a whole chord, a major chord in fact. Then they added a seventh and a ninth, it was trippy the way it resonated around the chapel.

Diane had barely begun her prayer to the guardians of the temple when all of a sudden some Egyptian guy dressed in normal attire burst between Bill and I and into the shrine.

'No, no, you must stop this. No praying in the temple.....'

Was he serious? This was a temple of worship for Christ's sake.

'...You must not do this, it is not permitted.'

I have no idea who he was; he certainly wasn't an official of any sort. Perhaps he was secret police, or more than likely one of the local tour guides who objected to any groups doing their own thing without coughing up a suitable amount of baksheesh. The others stopped toning and, as I stared at him in angered and incredulous consternation, a sudden surge went through me, no, came *from* me, and I felt my consciousness expanding in all directions, particularly upwards. It was like I was twelve foot tall, that I *was* Akhenaten.

I turned to the interloper and felt myself raise a hand directly towards his chest, almost feeling his pulsing heart in my claw-like grip. In that moment I truly believed that if I wished it, I could kill him just with my thoughts. That was freaky, and to be honest, the power-rush scared the shit out of me. A part of him must have felt it as well as he froze on the spot, his eyes fixed on mine like those of a deer in the headlights of fully loaded and speeding Mack truck seconds before impact.

'You are not to be praying in the temple.'

This was MY temple, Akhenaten, ruler of Egypt! No one could stop me from worshiping here, no one!.

'*You shall die for your insolence!*'

It was what I was thinking, but before I could do or say anything Diane asserted her position as leader of the group.

'No praying? Oh what a shame...'

I turned around. At the other end of the chapel, Diane was calm and unflustered, with everyone looking to her to see how she would react.

'...Never mind, we shall move on....'

Diane silently led the group out of the chapel and towards the centre of the square.

'...Nothing to be concerned about, we were able to let the guardians know we were here. We'll have a quick look at the Temple of Ramses III and then we'll head out to the Temple of Ptah, where I think we might get a little more privacy.'

In contrast to her serene disposition, I was furious, and, to compound things, as soon as I'd exited the chapel, *they* returned to harass me. Without any further ado, Diane led the group off to explore the Temple of Ramses III, but I wasn't interested; I was still fuming. I held my ground beside a small sphinx with the head and face of Tutankhamun, struggling to shrug off my uninvited and undesired guests.

'You ok, mate?'

Bill could tell I wasn't my usual self. He, Pernille and Crystal had remained with me.

'I feel like I'm being drawn and quartered both physically and spiritually.'

Pernille seemed very concerned.

'Is it the reptilians?'

'No, it's not them, but it's just as oppressive.'

'You need to reconnect.'

Crystal stood there majestically, an air of knowingness radiating from her.

'Reconnect to what?'

She raised an eyebrow and pointed behind me.

'Time to rock the Kasbah.'

I hadn't noticed it before, but stuck right in the middle of the courtyard, in the middle of the Kiosk of Taharqa, was a massive square block about four foot high and six foot on each side, and that's just what was visible above ground.

'Jesus!...'

What the hell was *that* doing here; not so much here in the temple complex, I was used to seeing large blocks of stone in temples, the question was, what was it doing here in the middle of the courtyard, the middle of the remains of the Kiosk? It was a massive worn piece of stone; I had no idea what sort.

'Hey, Bill, do you know what this is?'

He ran his hand lightly over the surface.

'Alabaster, crystalline calcite alabaster actually.'

'What's so special about it?'

'Nothing really, it's basically calcium carbonate, one of most common minerals on earth.'

'So why did the ancient Egyptians choose it; there must be some significance?'

He inspected it more closely, with a sense of personal involvement.

'Well, if I remember correctly, calcite has an interesting optical property; that of double refraction.'

'What's that?'

'If a ray of light enters the crystal, the crystal splits the ray into distinct beams, one fast and one slow.'

'I thought the speed of light was constant?'

Surprisingly, it was Crystal who answered *that* question.

'The speed of light is relative to two things, the time frame in which it is perceived and the medium through which it travels.'

Then she walked off encircling the altar. I turned to Bill.

'In layman's terms?'

'I guess it's like when white light enters a prism and it breaks up into the colours of the rainbow.'

I looked again at the massive rock before me.

'And how does that relate to the stone?'

'I guess that maybe when an observer looks through the calcite they'll see two images of everything behind it.'

'But I can't see through it, it's solid rock.'

Crystal completed her circuit.

'That is because you are looking with your eyes. Light is only a small fragment of the spectrum of energy.'

'You mean it's like a hologram?'

'That's one perspective.'

'And another?'

'Think of it as a complex and expansive dimensional Doppler effect?'

'Now you've lost me. So this is like some sort of massive prism of diffraction that splits beams of energy up into it's visible components?'

'Perhaps you should find out for yourself.'

'Huh?'

'Feel the stone.'

The last time I'd done that, at Edfu, I found myself drawn into the very sub-atomic structure of the rock. But this time I was not so arrogant as to *think* I was more conscious and intelligent than the stone. I addressed the massive altar before me, the top weather-worn and showing the effects of what was probably water erosion. Closing my eyes, I placed my hands purposefully on top and waited to connect.

Within a few breaths, my faithful piscatorial companion, Nemo, had appeared before me, leading me into the flow of the river, the flow of light, the flow of energy into the stone. Suddenly I was caught up in visions, flashbacks, whatever you want to call them, and they flowed through my mind faster than a striking cobra. The visions before me became a myriad of not just colours, but universal probabilities. It was indescribable, the most profound, prophetic and poetic words paling into insignificance.

I was soaking it all in; feeling I was not who I appeared today, feeling again the name Akhenaten resonating through me. The power was extraordinary. And then I became aware of *them*; the same entities that had tried to prevent me entering both the complex and then the chapel within the Temple of Seti II.

I opened my eyes, thinking the images would disappear. But, no, wispy dark shadows scurried around the periphery of my vision, loitering beyond the kaleidoscope of energies that continued to emanate from the calcite altar. I scanned the courtyard, trying to pin them down.

They were skulking behind two rows of sphinxes, each lined up shoulder to shoulder, on either side of the courtyard. Then it hit me: Christ, they'd done it again; the courtyard looked like a jumble store, bits and pieces from hundreds of years of history were juxtaposed against one another masquerading as contemporaneous. And it was so obvious.

The ancient Egyptians would never have lined up sphinxes shoulder to shoulder, they would have spaced them ceremoniously apart, as they had with the avenue of sphinxes leading from the Luxor Temple. They had to have originally been somewhere else, but where?

The most logical place was where the Kiosk of Taharqa now sat? To me they would have once formed an avenue leading from the river, from the quay, through the space that is now occupied by the First Pylon, through the courtyard, which at the time would have been some sort of forecourt to the temple, to what is now the Second Pylon? That made sense, as the Second Pylon was commenced by Horemheb at the end of the 18th Dynasty, and completed by Ramses I, the founder of the 19th Dynasty. Ramses II would most certainly have added an avenue of sphinxes leading from the river into what then would have been the start of the complex. Could the experts work that out? It seemed not! Or rather, they did, but they just ignored it. To be certain, I check my iphone.

'The sphinxes forming the temple approach in front of the First Pylon were moved there by Pinedjem I, third pharaoh of the Theban 21st Dynasty, and each of the sphinxes consequently has his name carved on the base. The sphinxes in the forecourt were moved to each side to make way for the monuments of Taharqa and Sheshonq I .'

The Amun Priests strike again: Pinedjem I would have reclaimed the complex for the priesthood from the previous military pharaohs of the 19th and 20th Dynasties.

In addition to the rows of sphinxes, the temples of Seti II and Ramses III would all once have originally been independent structures outside the main temple. And what about the sole sphinx to Tutankhamun that sat on its lonesome, all-forlorn in the central part of the courtyard: were there originally heaps more that had been disposed of by Ay or Horemheb, with only this *one* somehow surviving? Just one didn't make sense, nor did where the modern Egyptologist have it displayed; it stuck out like dog's balls.

It didn't take long before I'd had enough of the slapdash approach to temple restoration and turned my attention back to the ethereal entities lurking behind the rows of sphinxes. But the more I tried to focus on the shadowy figures, the more they retreated further into the depths of the temple complex: into the Hypostyle hall.

'Are you alright, Bill?'

He was standing further along from me; eyes closed and his hands on the altar, as mine had been. Pernille's concerned tone had snapped him out of it.

'Yeah, yeah, I'm fine.'

But he wasn't. His eyes were glassy, with a disconnected aspect. Had he seen what I'd seen, what I was seeing now? Pernille took his hands and held them tightly.

'Bill?'

'No, really, I'm fine, just doing a little day dreaming.'

As he shook it off, Diane and her entourage of pallid priestesses returned from the Temple of Ramses III. Strangely enough she seemed totally disinterested in the altar of alabaster before us.

'Right then, next we'll take ten minutes or so going through the Hypostyle hall, and after that we'll make a little detour and head out to the Temple of Ptah.

She led the way passed an osirid statue of Ramses II that faced inwards towards the path just in front of the doorway of the badly damaged Second Pylon. That seemed wrong; firstly the statue hardly seemed big enough for Ramses II and secondly I doubted he would have set it here like this. Surely there would have been a row of them, set facing outwards, against the façade of the pylon, much as they were at Abu Simbel, to greet arrivals and mark the entrance into the Great Hypostyle Hall, which would then have been the first part of the temple. Where were the others and what happened to them?

Checking my notes, I discovered that the diminutive figure standing between the pharaoh's legs was princess Bentanath, most probably one of his daughters, and later one of his queens. It was additional testimony of the practice of keeping it all in the family.

Further ...

'The statue of Ramses II at the entrance to the Hypostyle hall was usurped by Ramses VI and later by the Pinedjem I, southern pharaoh and High Priest of the 21st Dynasty. '

That was pretty indicative of, and reinforced my understanding of, the split between the 'church' and 'state' that existed in the 21st Dynasty; apart from robbing all the tombs, the Amun Priests even appropriated the statues of their predecessors.

They might have usurped some of his statues, but Ramses II was not going down without a fight. Further evidence of the grand statements made by him was the pedicular remnant of one of what would have been a pair of colossi of Ramses II just to one side of the pylon doorway. Just the base of one colossus remained. Where the hell were the rest of the pieces and the other colossus? It's not as if they could just be picked up and whisked away.

The Second Pylon itself was a mess. My notes indicated that, though it is attributed to Ramses II, ...

'Construction apparently began during the reign of Horemheb, using sandstone talatat blocks from an earlier temple belonging to Akhenaten'.

That made sense, though it was probably the Amun Priests responsible for destroying all the evidence of Akhenaten, and not necessarily Horemheb as the Egyptologists would have us all believe.

It got me thinking - if construction began in the reign of Horemheb, who ruled for fifteen years, and continued through the reigns of Ramses I and Seti I, two and twelve years respectively, then that meant that if the pylon really belonged to Ramses II, then it took over twenty eight years to finish the pylon; which I found highly unlikely. What was more likely was that the pylon was finished in the reign of Horemheb, Ramses I, or even Seti I, and that when Ramses II assumed the throne he simply claimed it as his own - as he was prone to do with anything and everything. My interest was naturally with the talatats of Akhenaten, however these had been removed.

According to my notes, the towers of the pylon had been freed from the ruins of later buildings erected in front of them. Running my eyes over them, the pylons had the usual four vertical grooves, supposedly for flagstaffs, though they may have just been to lift up supplies.

The huge doorway into the hall through the pylon contained a vestibule in which Ramses II was depicted, surprise surprise, smiting his enemies before Amun. The doorway also contained the cartouches and/or reliefs of Ramses I, Seti I, Ramses III, Ptolemy VI Philometor and Ptolemy IX Euergetes II before Amun, Mut, Khonsu and Seshat: no surprises there, that was totally consistent with the reliefs in other reconstructed temples.

The Hall of Shadows

The Hypostyle hall that followed measured about a hundred metres long by fifty metres wide, making it the largest room of any religious building in the world. It was filled with one hundred and thirty four enormous papyrus columns; the highest being twelve 'open' topped columns seventy feet tall, ten foot in diameter, and about forty-five feet around. These twelve were erected by Amenhotep III and formed two rows down the centre of the hall. They were later decorated by Ramses I, Seti I, and, surprise of surprises, Ramses II, however the decorations of Seti I were far superior to those of his son, Ramses II.

The other one-hundred-and-twenty-two 'shorter', 'closed-capital' columns flanking them were erected over fifty years later by Seti I and arranged in fourteen rows along side their taller predecessors. They contained scenes of Seti I making offerings to the gods.

At one time, the columns would have supported a roof, with small windows allowing light into the central avenue; used for the procession of the Triad during the festival of the Opet. It would have provided a muted illumination for the interior, thus symbolizing the primeval papyrus swamp. Alas, the roof was gone, though some of the windows remained. Yes it was big, yes it was grand, yes it was impressive; the sheer size of it was overwhelming. But, there was more, much more.

As I meandered, snaked and weaved my way through the hall, to me it appeared vibrantly alive with colour and exactly as it would have been in its prime. And yet behind every column lurked the etheric shadow of the spirit of an Amun priest. They waited until I had passed, then lunged out at me from behind, pawing at me, tearing at my shoulders. It took me back to the dream I'd been having that morning, the same sense of foreboding from me, and loathing by them.

I felt like I was being attacked by a pack of ravenous hyenas and quickly lagged behind the rest of the group, wrestling with my uninvited and unwanted adversaries.

'*Trespasser.*'
'*Pariah.*'
'*Heretic.*'

Their incessant attacks made me feel like I had jumped into the ring with Mike Tyson. In fact, by the time I'd reached the Third Pylon at the far end of the hall, I felt like I'd just done fifteen rounds with not only him, but every Heavy Weight Champion of the world since Jack Dempsey – AT THE SAME TIME!

Reaching the far side of the hall, I noticed the southern wall of the hall was covered with scenes of Ramses II worshiping the Triad of Thebes and making offerings to numerous deities. Against the southern pylon wall was a low alabaster block, termed the 'nine bows', decorated with the enemies of Egypt. But overall the scenes on the southern side lacked the level of artistic quality of the others in the northern half of the hall.

'Come on, everyone, this way.'

Diane was standing at the centre of the space and led the others out of the hall through a side door to the north. Most of the group having exited, Crystal, who had lingered towards the rear of the group with Pernille and Yuko, turned to see me once again struggling to keep it together.

'*Remember who you are. When you do, no one can deny you.*'

Within one breath Akhenaten burst to the surface and the priests were withdrawing to form a perimeter in the far corners of the Hypostyle hall. I felt they were circling like vultures, waiting for the breath and presence of Akhenaten to leave the body, so that they could once again move in to pick the eyes out of the carcass and the flesh from the bones. But Akhenaten wasn't going anywhere, other than briefly outside the temple with a flock of doves.

Exiting the main temple, I tagged on to the others as they walked an ancient paved road that led northeast towards the Precinct of Montu. Thankfully both Akhenaten and the Amun priests had remained in the hall and, though spiritually battered and bruised from pillar to post, I felt somewhat liberated. Taking a deep breath, I pulled myself together and set off after the others.

The dirt on the paths outside the temple was finer than a sunny day in the Sahara Desert; a powder that fluffed around your ankles as you walked on it. Beside it, to the right, rows and rows of hundreds of temple fragments, all covered in hieroglyphs, were lined up, much as they had been alongside the Temple of Luxor. You would think, given today's technology, they could all be scanned, and the data downloaded, so that some archaeologist who specialized in jigsaw puzzles could sit at his or her computer for hour upon hour, day after day, and figure out what they were, what they belonged to, and how to put the damn things back together again. Maybe they're actually doing that with the Akhenaten Temple Project, and some square-eyed professor is drawing a huge salary while he or she plays some sort of ancient Lego game, but then again, maybe not.

To the left of the path were the ruins of several small buildings.

'Outside the main Temple of Amun, to the north, are the remains of several buildings; a small brick-built fortress and three small chapels, or shrines, to the Divine Adoratrix, dating to the Late Period (672-332 BC). The first, and largest, of these chapels, was built towards the end of the 26th Dynasty by Pedeneit, a Majordomo in the royal household. On the doorway are reliefs of Psamtek III, last pharaoh of the 26th Dynasty, and his queen, Enkhnesneferebre, before Amun and other gods. Beyond this is the brick-built hall, with four stone columns. On the doorway into the sanctuary are reliefs of Nitocris, wife of Psamtek II, and Amasis.'

The name 'Amasis' was unfamiliar to me, but a quick check of my list of pharaohs from the 26th Dynasty made me think this must have been a Greek version of Ahmose II. To me the ruins looked like a pile of rubble, but Crystal paused for a short time, seemingly contemplating the past occupants, so there must have been something interesting about the building. Maybe it had something to do with the 'Divine Adoratrix'?

'The title of Divine Adoratrice, or "God's Wife of Amun" had been held by royal females since the Middle Kingdom, these women became supremely important during the Late Period, acting as the pharaoh's surrogate in Upper Egypt. The power and wealth of the reigning Divine Adoratrix is said to have exceeded even that of the High Priest of Thebes.'

That was significant; I figured the only way the Amun Priests would have tolerated that, was if the Divine Adoratrix was of the lineage of the *sang réal*, and they had no choice in the matter.

'By the Late Period the God's Wife was usually a daughter or sister of the reigning monarch, unmarried, but with the power to "adopt" her successor from within the royal family. Their names were written in a cartouche and the ladies wore regal iconography, crowns with a uraeus and a feathered headdress.'

That to me was even more proof of keeping it in the family, and that the *sang réal* lineage was through the matriarchal line. After ten to fifteen seconds Crystal moved on, passing the next building and gliding along through the ruins like a hot knife through butter. One thing Crystal sure wasn't doing was collecting dust.

'The central chapel was built by a Court official named Sheshonq in the reign of Amasis of sun-dried bricks with only the doorways, columns, and sanctuary made of stone. On the left hand jamb is a relief of the King, on the right hand one, Enkhnesneferebre, to whose household Sheshonq belonged.

The third chapel, the most northerly, is the oldest of the three and least well preserved. Built in the reign of Taharqa, in the 25th Dynasty, it is decorated with reliefs of Princess Shepenwepet II and the King.'

There was so much to excavate and develop, and so much poverty and unemployment in Egypt, it beggared disbelief to think that there were so many ruins still awaiting attention. I guess the wheels of administration go slow in all parts of the globe. In the meantime, the stones and buildings all sat there like medusa's minions collecting dust on the shelves of history.

Ahead, Crystal's svelte form oozed it way through the fabric of her white blouse and skirt; the carrot was well and truly dangled. I decided I wasn't going to die wondering, or get left on the shelf, and lengthened my stride to pull up beside her and take my chances.

'Crystal?'

'Yes.'

'Who are you?'

She smiled.

'If I were you, I'd be more focused on who *you* are.'

'Ok, I get that, and I am. I know now that I was Akhenaten and that you were Nefertiti, but I was just wondering who else you've been.'

'Do you mean all of my lives, or just ancient Egypt?'

'Let's just start with ancient Egypt.'

'I have had several lives as a peasant, as a novice priestess, none of which you, nor anyone, would have heard of.'

'What about those we do know?'

'Ahmose-Nefertari, daughter of Seqenenre, and wife of Amenhotep I.'

'You were Amenhotep's wife; so we've had several lives together?'

'Oh, yes!'

'And Pernille has been your daughter?'

'Yes, and I hers.'

'Anyone else?'

'Further back I was Nefrusobek, daughter of Amenemhat III, and the last pharaoh of the 12th Dynasty. Before that, Nitocris, daughter of Pepi II and Queen Neith, and the last pharaoh of the 6th Dynasty. Then, all the way back to my first time as Egyptian Queen, as Neithhotep, wife of Narmer in the 1st Dynasty. Before that, I was the being known as Nephthys, and, well, before that, is a whole other story.'

Initially I was stumped for words; boy, did this girl have some pedigree behind her. Then I started to join the dots; so did I, hell, I was Akhenaten! But, before I could explore it further, we'd arrived at the northern wall and joined with the others.

'This is the Temple of Ptah...'

The Temple of Ptah

It ran just inside the outer wall near the northern gate to the precinct of Montu. To be honest, compared to the grandeur of the rest of Karnak this looked more like a garden shed tucked in the back corner of the paddock. In fact, it reminded me a bit of some of the toilet blocks erected by the local councils back home, especially with all the ladies queuing up outside to enter.

'...Back in 1900 this wasn't the easiest temple to excavate here at Karnak. To the locals, it was known as the "infants grave". Apparently seven small children were swallowed up by a cave-in, and, because their bodies were never recovered, the Egyptian labourers were reluctant to come near it because they thought it was the underworld lair of a ghoul that had eaten the children. But when an explorer by the name of Legrain unearthed a black granite statue of Djehuty, or Thoth, in the northern corner of the location, and shipped it off to Cairo, confidence was restored, and the excavation and restoration of the temple site commenced....'

A cave in! Were there chambers underneath here? Was it possible the children had fallen into part of a temple that existed before this one was built? Had they wandered away, down dark corridors, trying to find a way out, eventually starving to death in some underground vault?

'...The core of the temple was built by Thutmoses III on the site of an earlier Middle Kingdom temple, and it was later restored by the pharaoh, Shabaka, during the 25th Dynasty. Further restoration and expansion took place during the reign of the Greeks, the Ptolemies, and after that by the Romans. Interestingly, the Ptolemies didn't replace the earlier royal cartouches with their own, but actually repaired damaged and missing sections, retaining the names of the original builders... '

There was my proof. The earlier Middle Kingdom temple would have been covered by the Thera tsunami, thus creating sinkholes and underground chambers for the children to fall into and disappear. Thutmoses III was possibly the first to access the site once the waters receded, and he naturally built on top of the existing site: the core of the building that exists today.

But there must have been some cause for the damage between his reign, around 1412 BC, and that of Shabaka, seven hundred years later: perhaps another tsunami, or maybe just an earthquake? Then the Ptolemies did further repair work four hundred years after that. But it wasn't so much the cause of the disasters any more that interested me, but rather the older temple that clearly must lie underneath, awaiting discovery. In the meantime, Diane continued as tour guide.

'...All together, the temple consists of five gateways leading to a small portico of two columns and a pylon in the name of Thutmoses III, who, as I said, built the core of the temple. That leads into the inner sanctuaries, comprising three interconnecting rooms that are dedicated to the Memphite triad of Ptah, his wife, Sekhmet, and their daughter, Nefertum. Our objective is within the sanctuaries, so let's go.'

Diane led the way through the first gateway. The exterior and interior façades exhibited the cartouches of Ptolemy VI, while on the interior façades of the passage there were those of Ptolemys XI and XIII. I noticed Crystal paused in admiration at a depiction of Nefertum with two long feathers on her head and bearing a lotus feather.

'Someone familiar; a distant relative perhaps?'

She smiled.

'You would know.'

She'd done it to me again. Who was Nefertum again? The daughter of Ptah and Sekhmet. Who else did Crystal say she had been? Nephthys, that's right. So was Nephthys also Nefertum? And was the prefix *Nefer* a common usage for women of the *sang réal*: Nefertiti, Nefertari, Nefertum. Was it some secret code, only to be used by the descendants of the Annunaki?

Moving on, the second gateway apparently belonged to Shabaka, although his cartouches had been chiselled out; what he'd done to piss people off, who knows. The third gateway supposedly belonged to Ptolemy XIII and consisted of two engaged columns, while the fourth gateway once again belonged to Shabaka. That didn't make sense to me as it was inconsistent with the idea that the further you went further from the sanctuary, the addition of pylons systematically and chronologically followed the arrow of time.

I pause briefly to contemplate it: if this temple was augmented and altered in line with the rest of Karnak, then the original rebuilt temple constructed by Thutmoses III was probably augmented in turn by Hatshepsut, Seti II, Ramses II and Ramses III before further modifications were done by Sheshonq, Shabaka and then the Ptolemies. Someone needed to dig deeper to find the truth: a *lot* deeper.

Moving on, the fifth gateway, a portico of four composite columns about two and a half metres apart, belonged to Ptolemy III. The columns were just over five metres high and very elegant. On the first pair, as well as the doorpost of the pylon doorway beyond, were images of the pharaoh wearing the white crown to one side, and to the north, the red crown. The sixth gateway, bearing the cartouches of Thutmoses III, crossed through the pylon and led to the ante-chamber.

As the others slowly entered the inner sanctuary, I took the time to look around. Turning right and to the south, a door led to a small chamber with another door leading outside. On the lintel of the first door, Ptolemy IV was making offerings to a seated Ptah. Further right was a large scene of Ptolemy IV before Hathor. Past the doorway, on the south wall of the main chamber, Ptah, his body wrapped and head tightly bound in a blue lapis lazuli headdress, stood behind Amun, and on the pedestal of Ma'at. He held the djed pillar, the *was* sceptre of power emerging from it. Behind Ptah stood Khonsu, wearing the crown-prince's braid and holding a number of different sceptres, including the djed pillar, the *was* sceptre, the ankh, the hek crosier and the nekhakha sceptre.

Further east, along the south wall, another scene depicted the pharaoh wearing a blue helmet and making an offering of wine. Following him was his ka, in the form of a falcon, holding a long cane topped by a bust of the pharaoh in his right hand, and, in his left, the key of life and the feather of Ma'at.

On the northern side of the chamber the interior façade of the doorway was sloped, with cartouches of Thutmoses III, whereas the wall of the north wing of the pylon was vertical and carved with the cartouches of Ptolemys III and IV. Like the south side, the north also had a small door that led to a tiny chamber containing scenes of Ptolemy IV. Other scenes on the north side included scenes of Ptolemy with Ptah, Hathor, Ma'at, Amun, Mut, Konsu and Imhotep.

By now, most of the others had entered the sanctuary, through two large sixteen-sided columns about a metre wide and three-and-a-half metres tall, and passed a small altar that was framed by the seventh doorway. Unlike the others, who passed by without even noticing it, Bill had paused at the altar.

'Red Granite, Alex.'

I nodded.
'Mmmm.'

It was well worn and far older than any of the rocks that surrounded it.
'Who knows what we'll find inside?'

Maybe it was just me, but as he'd said it Bill seemed sort of detached and preoccupied. As he entered the sanctuary with Pernille, I shrugged it off and focused on the altar. Doing so, Crystal stood to face me on the opposite side and I seized the moment.

'Before we go in, I'd love to talk to you more about all this, and about your visits to the temples; you said something about it having to do with your chakras. How is that relevant to why we're here?'

'If you are lucky, you may be able to resolve issues from this life by looking in the mirror. But the reality is, most of the time you can't just *wish* your blockages away with well-intentioned meditations and shallow rituals. Sometimes you need to go back to the scene of the crime, so to speak, and if that was in another life, in another country, then going back to that location and reconnecting to objects that were there then, that hold the history of that time and place, is sometimes the best, and only, real option.'

'Wow, so I guess that's why we're all here; you, me, Bill, Pernille, Pieter and Yuko; everyone is always exactly where they're meant to be.'

She shook her head in mild disappointment

'That is about as useful as saying; "*My keys were in the last place I looked.*" It is more congruent to say; "Where I am has meaning".'

That said; she turned away and followed the others into the temple. What she had said hit me like a sledgehammer: I was dazed and confused, but I knew it sure had impact. I decided to mull it over and ask her for more details later on, and headed right after her into the sanctuary.

The mouse that roared

If the temple looked small from the outside, by the time we were all crammed into the central of the three rooms, it looked downright claustrophobic. I stuck my head briefly into the room to the left: nothing to see. I guess that was why everyone was squeezed into the middle chamber, arranged in a semi circle around something occupying the centre of the room. Even though I was over six foot tall, I couldn't quite make out what it was. Thankfully Diane went into Guru mode.

'Here we are, in the inner sanctum of the Temple of Ptah: Ptah; god of creation, who, having dreamed creation in his heart, called all things into being by thinking of them with his mind and saying their names with his tongue. Mighty Ptah: who fashioned the whole universe and all that is in it through thought and harmonics…'

It sounded exactly like in *'The Bible'* where God spoke the word and everything came into being. Hell, Moses just stole Genesis from the Egyptians, changed Ptah's name to Yahweh, and tweaked it to suit his objectives: what a plagiarist! I shuffled around to get a better view.

Holding centre stage was a headless statue seated on a throne. Made of black granite it had been tactlessly and tastelessly deposited upon a plain rectangular concrete plinth about a metre high, making it about six foot tall in total: good one Zahi - NOT. I wondered if the decapitated state was the result of some natural disaster, a roof collapse perhaps, or rather if it was due to the actions of some moronic religious fanatic who was blinded by ignorance and had no concept or appreciation of artistic expression. Given the wanton defacing of most of ancient Egypt's buildings, reliefs, and statues, my leaning was towards the latter.

'…Ptah's importance is best understood when you know that "Egypt" is a Greek corruption of the phrase "Het-Ka-Ptah," or "House of the Spirit of Ptah"…'

As Diane continued her homage I somewhat tuned out, as it began to sound like the sort of typical New-Age holier-than-thou esoteric waffle I had run into numerous times in my life. Instead I focused on examining the statue itself.

In his hands, Ptah held the same sceptres I'd seen in his representation in the reliefs: an ankh, the *was* sceptre, and a Djed; respectively the symbols of life, power and stability. The massive feet were wrapped in a cloth, consistent with the usual depiction of Ptah shrouded as a mummy, and before them were the legs of a kneeling figure, which had not just been decapitated, but majorly dismembered. The other part of the statue worth mentioning was the extent of the detail in what's known as the *user* necklace; it was quite divine. I could only assume that the head upon which the necklace was once perched would have depicted Ptah skull-capped and with a beard.

'…To the ancient Egyptians, Ptah was the primal creator, the deification of the primordial mound, though Ptah himself was not created, but simply is. As such, he was considered the god of architects, skilled craftsmen such as blacksmiths and boat builders, and, in particular, the stone-based crafts of stonecutters and sculptors…'

I tuned back in. What did she say? "*Ptah was the god of architects, stonecutters and sculptors*". Of course he was; the ancient Egyptians built the pyramids and fashioned massive statues and blocks out of red and black granite. But what I hadn't connected until that moment was that my dad was a Freemason, and they called the creator the Great Architect. Not only that, but the masons were traditionally stone-based craftsmen. To me, it was all just further confirmation of the connections between the Illuminati, the Freemasons, and the teachings of ancient Egypt.

'…The origin of Ptah's name is unclear, though some believe it's related to the "Opening of the Mouth" ceremony performed by priests at funerals to release souls from their corpses. It was an important ritual in both funerary and temple practice and said to have been created by Ptah as a ritual to endow statues with the capacity to support the living ka, and to receive offerings…'

Beside me, Bill started slowly and softly grunting in a deep voice, his eyes closed and his body gently swaying back and fro. I guessed he was just in deep contemplation of what Diane was saying and didn't pay it much heed. Meanwhile Diane continued.

'…The Opening of the Mouth Ceremony was performed on the cult statues of gods, kings, and private individuals, as well as on the mummies of both humans and Apis bulls. It was even performed on the individual rooms of temples and on the entire temple structure.

The ancient Egyptians believed that the effect of the ritual was to animate the recipient or, in the case of a deceased individual, to re-animate it. The ritual would bring life back to the mummy, statue, or temple, enabling it to see, smell, breathe, hear, and eat, and enjoy the offerings of food and drinks brought to the tomb each day by the priests and officials, thus sustaining the ka or spirit.'

I got a flash: was the Opening of the Mouth ceremony really about part of the regenerative process of the Annunaki; that they breathed "life" into not only the body, but also the very stone in which the body was surrounded? Was the "breath" not so much a "breath" but rather a vibration, a sympathetic vibration that triggered not only the atomic structure of the stone, in particular red and black granite, but also the sub-atomic spin resonances of DNA itself? The mere contemplation of that began to blow my mind.

'Itanaa, öveqatsit ep qátuhqa, nam uhnatngwani pas kyaptsi'tiwaa...'

The true origins and meanings of the Opening of the Mouth ceremony instantly got put on the backburner as Bill suddenly erupted in fervent adulation; his arms raised, eyes closed, as he was nodding and swaying energetically towards the statue. Hell, Bill was possessed!

'...Itanaa, öveqatsit ep qátuhqa, nu' umi unangwa'ta. Pu um okiw itahpöiy itamuhpiy ayo yúkuni...'

I looked around to see the reaction of the others. To my surprise they were not only unfazed, but in many cases the women, including Pernille, were sobbing in sympathetic fervour. Shit, Bill wasn't possessed, he was in some sort of trance. No, he was channelling someone.

'...Itanaa, pu okiw um itamuy unaheppit qa ang tsâmi'mat, hakiy qalolmat angqw itamuy ayo ôoyhtimani...'

Like the others, I focused my attention on him, much as I had with the stones and Nemo in the water. As I did, Bill changed, morphed. Well not literally, but in my mind's eye. His suntanned features grew even darker and redder and he aged about twenty years. Crowning his head and flowing the full length of his body and down onto the ground was a massive headdress of white eagle feathers; Bill was an American Indian chief, and obviously an important one. Well, who'd have thought it?

The language was clearly American Indian, but I had no idea what tribe; the only names I could think of were Crow, Sioux, Cherokee, Apache, Mohican and Hopi, but there must have been heaps more. Oh, and of course there was the Hekawi tribe from F Troop. Suddenly my images of Bill orating majestically in a large tee pee to a group of elders were replaced with childhood recollections of Cpl. Agarn, Sgt. O'Rourke, Chief Wild Eagle and Crazy Horse.

'...Itanaa, nu' umi unangwa'ta. Askwali, askwali!...'

Bill was on a roll; obviously he'd been waiting a long time to say what he had to say and it wasn't looking like settling up.

'...Itanaa, öveqatsit ep qátuhqa, nu' umi unangwa'ta. Pu um okiw itahpöiy itamuhpiy ayo yúkuni.'

He prattled on like a rabid Billy Graham or Jimmy Swaggart on speed, but no one seemed to mind, on the contrary they were all absorbed by it and resonated with every gesture and word. I had to admit it was incredibly powerful. Eventually, after what seemed like an eternity, but was probably ten minutes or so, Diane gently moved behind him and placed her hands on his shoulders.

'Thank you; your words are most venerated. We thank you for your presence and your wisdom, however this one must rejoin the group as we have more work to do.'

'Itanaa, nu' umi unangwa'ta. Askwali, askwali!'

Diane gently persisted, reiterating her gratitude, and slowly quieting down Sitting Bull so that Aussie Bill could return. And eventually he did; the passionate proliferations of the Indian Chief mumbling into the Otherworld as Bill rejoined the present; though he wasn't completely himself, but rather more like a heavily-sedated psych patient after a Valium bender.

As he slowly regained his awareness in the now, Pernille, in a sign of their new-founded connection, wrapped her arms around him, comforting and reassuring him that all was right with the world. Meanwhile, Diane motioned for us all to follow into the next chamber.

This was all getting a bit full-on, after all, I was supposed to be here on a holiday, wasn't I; a sabbatical from the weird world of the worries of western civilization? Wasn't I? Or was I really here to find myself, my true self that is, and to find my true purpose and a new direction in my life? As the others followed Diane into the next chamber, I tried to catch Crystal's eye to get an insight on what had just happened and what she was feeling about it, but she was in her own zone, and that left me in mine.

The others all having filed into the adjoining sanctuary and along the side walls, I tagged on at the rear and finished up smack bang centre of the nearside wall, facing an effigy of Ptah's consort, Sekhmet.

The lion's den

'This is Sekhmet, lioness-goddess and Ptah's wife, one of the oldest known Egyptian deities. Often depicted as we see her here, with the sun-disc on her head, her name derives from the Egyptian word *Sekhem,* which means "power" or "might".

Less commonly known as Bast, or, in later times Bastet when the Greeks tinkered with her name to mean "soul of Isis" (ba-Aset), some Egyptologists have suggested the name Bastet actually comes from bast meaning 'ointment jar', while others are of the opinion that the name Bast means 'Devouring Lady', from bas, which translates as devour, with a feminine 't' added...'

Well that was no-brainer, how could you even contemplate associating a lion goddess with an ointment jar? It was *san greal* and *sang réal* all over again.

'...The earliest inscriptions with the name of Bast were found in the step-pyramid complex at Saqqara and date from the early 2nd Dynasty, (c 2890 BC); there's even some evidence pointing to an earlier date, but it's unreliable.

By the 4th and 5th Dynasties, Bast was a protector of the Pharaoh, and, by the Middle Kingdom Coffin Texts, Bast is ascribed great importance as the first-born daughter of Atum, or 'Daughter of Ra', therefore confirming her great protective abilities...'

I already had ideas about the evolution of the Book of the Dead from the Coffin Texts, and those in turn from the Pyramid Texts at Saqqara, this got me contemplating the true origins of who Sekhemt, or Bastet, really was. Was she Annunaki? Or was she from somewhere else all together; even another star system?

'...Bastet was originally shown with a lion's head or as a desert sand-cat headed goddess, that is until around 1000 BC and the end of the New Kingdom, when she also became associated with the cat, and a more friendly appearance developed...'

That meant this statue most probably predated the New Kingdom, which, according to my theory about the tsunamis at the end of the 17th Dynasty, along with a pre-existing temple below where we now stood, made total sense.

'...Because of the influence of the Greeks, the Ptolemaic pharaohs, Bast became not just the protector of the pharaoh, but also of pregnant women, children, musicians and the goddess of all kinds of excess, especially those of a sexual nature. It was probably here, with Bastet, that the concept of the cat as a form of female sexuality first developed. She was also considered the earliest form of Hathor...'

Huh? That didn't make any sense to me at all; every image I'd seen of Hathor depicted her as a cow-eared god, totally different in appearance to what was before me. How anyone could confuse a lion or cat with a cow was beyond reckoning.

'...But it was here at Karnak, in the Precinct of Mut where there was a cult centre to Bast during the New Kingdom, that it all came together. Because Mut, the spouse of Amun, claimed both the lion and the cat as sacred animals and was depicted as a lion-headed goddess...'

It was all coming together; Amun, Atum, Ptah, Ra, all the creator god; they were all the same entity. Similarly, possibly so was Mut, Sekhmet, Bast and Bastet. As differing invaders occupied the land and successive dynasties shifted their language and cultural backgrounds, so did the naming and identities of the gods. What may have started in the 1st Dynasty as perhaps half-a-dozen beings had morphed by the 30th Dynasty into a myriad of fragments of that initial set of gods.

'...The statue was found in numerous pieces by Legrain when he was excavating. He pieced it back together and re-erected it here in its original site in the south chapel below a small opening in the roof, through which, on certain nights, the moonlight shines directly on to the statue's head...'

Excavated from below, in pieces? It confirmed my thoughts on its pre-'New Kingdom' origin. The only question was how far back it really went. I examined it more closely. Like the statue of Ptah in the previous chamber, Sekhmet's statue was also made of black granite. She was beautiful; her long slender body, narrow hips and thighs, and pert, perfectly rounded breasts echoed the catwalks of Paris and Milan; maybe that's where they got the term from in the first place? In her left hand she held the 'was' sceptre with the flowering lotus, and, in her right, the ankh of life. In contrast to the lithe and graceful body, the massive lion head was crowned with a large flattened disk sprouting a single raised cobra. If she was so important, that meant everything she carried was significant, including the disk on her head and the lotus flower, which must have held as equal importance as the ankh and *was* sceptre.

'...Use this time to connect to Sekhmet, to the mighty ancient Egyptian defender of Ma'at, of truth and justice. Feel free and welcome to show your gratitude for her protection.'

While some of the group prayed or meditated, others cried, knelt at Sekhmet's feet or hugged her body in a reverent embrace. As for me, I imagined a far distant time, a time of pollution-free skies, of a Nile river flowing free from the strangling yoke of discarded soft-drink bottles and plastic bags, of nights free from the rattling sounds of ramshackle car engines and omnipresent taxi horns, free from the encroaching lights of street lamps and neon signs, the silvery stream of moonlight filtering through the ancient skylight above, illuminating the image of Sekhmet in the darkness.

It must have been quite an experience for a young initiate, male or female, prepared and primed with powerful stories and legends; to be led into the darkness of the inner sanctum, probably blindfolded, to stand before the statue of Sekhmet on the full moon of a key festival. Their imagination would have been firing up like a lightning pole atop the Empire State building during a category-five hurricane. And then the blindfold would have been removed; the veil would have been lifted.

Before them, the moonlight cascading over her black granite face, stood the ghostly spectre of the feared and revered goddess, Sekhmet, consort of the creator and the satiated devourer of blood, who, given half a chance, would destroy all humanity in her dispassionate fury. I guess it would have looked like a black and white hologram and filled the young initiate with fear and reverence. But that's not what I saw, and certainly not what I felt.

To me, the eyes came alive; brown and friendly with the depth of not just strength, but compassion. The breath of life spread from the eyes and soon the whole face was alive. It was as if the ka stored within the granite of the statue had breathed life into its very body. Was this what the Egyptians were talking about?

Before I knew it I found myself scratching her whiskers as if she were an old and dear companion; like I had with my pet cat, Crotchet, when I was eleven years old. I could even hear and feel her purring away in ecstatic contentment. Okay, now I was convinced I'd definitely lost my marbles; there I was scratching the whiskers of an ancient granite statue. Thank God the room was dimly lit and the only other people in it were clearly also as batty as I was.

Several minutes later Diane indicated it was time for us to leave and I took a step back from the statue, the head of which continued to appear fully alive and purring. I allowed all of the others to exit first, then, sure I was alone, stepped back to the statue and scratched it under the chin.

'It was good to see you old friend.'

As the others were exiting slowly back through the gateways, I paused to take a few deep gulps of water, then decided to do a quick lap of the exterior of the temple. What I saw got me scratching my own chin. Going from left to right, at two different levels on the back wall of the temple were representations in light relief of Ptah, the head carved on an a stone that is now missing, and Hathor, with a very small child, Horus in front of her.

That was nothing out of the ordinary, or that each was followed by a scribe, it was that one was from the Old Kingdom, Imhotep, wearing only a loincloth and a pectoral necklace and holding the *was* of the gods, the other scribe from the New Kingdom, Amenhotep, dressed in a long robe and carrying a palette and scroll. Was this link between the Old and New Kingdoms confirmation that Imhotep and Amenhotep were one and the same being? And was the fact they were both recording the actions of the gods a direct link to Thoth? It seemed more cut and dry to me than the very stones they were adorning.

Deep in thought, I rounded the temple and saw Crystal waiting for me outside the first gateway. She smiled, nodded her head slightly, then turned and followed the others. Naturally I picked up the pace, and by the time I reached her, the rest of the group was re-entering the main temple beyond the Third Pylon and the Hypostyle hall.

'What happened to Bill back there? Was he channelling?'

'Of course.'

'Who?'

'A part of himself.'

'I saw him with this massive Indian headdress on.'

'Very good.'

'Who was he?'

'Who *was* he, or who IS he?'

'I know who he is, he's Bill, Aussie bloke and miner from the west.'

She lifted both hands indicating quotation marks.

'"Bill" is no more Bill than an actor is just one of the hundreds of roles they have played.'

I was confused, I mean I'd sort of grasped the concept of time only being linear if I chose to perceive it that way, but to actually experience the reality of 'no' time, or rather 'all' time was a different matter, especially when it related to who someone was.

'You must think I'm crazy.'

'Must I? I do not have to *do* anything, especially involve my mind in the actions of others. But, since you asked, no, I do not think you are crazy, you are just remembering what it is to be out of your mind.'

I got it straight away, yes, I *was* 'out of my mind': not thinking, just being. And I guess that's what happened to Bill, though I doubt he knew what was coming, or when it happened, what hit him. But I was sure Crystal did.

'I was just curious to know which Indian Chief Bill was.'

'Then perhaps you had better ask him.'

Crystal was right, but, as he disappeared back into the main temple, I thought, 'what if he doesn't remember anything?'

Ground Control to Major Tom

As we approached the temple and the Courtyard of Thutmoses I, I was surprised to see the rear wall of the Hypostyle hall was not part of the Third Pylon, in fact, the third pylon didn't abut against the rear wall of the Hypostyle hall at all; there was a small gap of about a metre between them.

I wandered down the alleyway to check out the hieroglyphs, as this would have been the original façade of the temple at the time of Amenhotep III. The depiction was the same as the one in Tutankhamun's Opet reliefs at Luxor Temple. Returning to the courtyard of Thutmoses I, the eastern face contained a beautiful image of the Userhet Barque of Amun. But it was something else about looking back at the Third Pylon that triggered me to check my notes.

'The Third Pylon once contained marble alabaster stones, from the period of Amenhotep I, embedded in its structure, whilst the adjoining court outside contained the famous wall of Amenhotep IV, which is now in the Open-air Museum.'

Several questions arose, firstly, where are the alabaster stones now? Are they also in the open museum? Secondly, why were they removed from some structure belonging to Amenhotep I, by whom, and when? And thirdly, why were the pylons numbered the way they were, the way you enter the complex, when surely it would make more sense that they should be identified in the order they were built, chronologically? I presumed the Amenhotep I stones had most recently been removed by Zahi Hawass, or some other over-zealous Egyptologist and, if they weren't in the Open Museum, were now tucked away in the bowels of the Cairo Museum or some private collection. Why? Because they referred directly to Amenhotep I and probably referred to his being Annunaki.

As to why they had been removed from their original site, wherever that was, and incorporated into the Third Pylon, that made me contemplate the tsunamis again. There was a period of around one-hundred-and-twenty years between Amenhotep I and Amenhotep III, it's highly possible the original structure was destroyed by a subsequent earthquake or tsunami, just like the Temple of Amenhotep I at Hatshepsut's Temple, and the stones were used by Amenhotep III to rebuild parts of the temple at Karnak in deference to his great great great great grandfather, Amenhotep I, in my opinion the true founder of the '18th Dynasty'.

The naming of the pylons was another issue. The name 'First Pylon' should refer to that built first, namely the one before the inner sanctuary, and subsequent names allocated chronologically. And they should have used the same process at Kalabsha, Philae, Edfu and all the temples. Perhaps the term 'Pylon number 1', 'Pylon number 2', etcetera, would be more appropriate in referring to the pylons as you encountered them, or naming them after who built them, namely 'The Amenhotep III Pylon', or 'The Pylon of Nectanebo I'. It may have seemed a minor point to most people, but it reflected to me the lack of awareness of the Egyptologists.

While I was pedantically preoccupied with the naming rights of the pylons, the others were standing around an obelisk that stretched towards the heavens. Diane explained that it was one of only four original obelisks still standing. It belonged to Thutmoses I and was one of a pair that would have sat outside what would have been the entrance to the Temple of Karnak at an earlier time.

Carved from a solid piece of red granite it reached over twenty metres into the air and probably weighed well over three hundred tons. It, and its now missing partner, were further markers of the beginning of what I called the 'build-it-big' era, and probably the first obelisks raised in ancient Egypt. Perhaps they were just built in homage to Thutmoses I, or more likely to his Annunaki father, Amenhotep I. Just because his name was on it, didn't necessarily mean Thutmoses I actually built it. Or maybe there was even more to it?

The obelisk looked like a giant aerial, and if my emerging theory about red granite had a basis in truth, then that's exactly how it may have behaved. But was it a receiver or transmitter, or both? And what exactly did it receive or transmit? There was one way to find out; feel the stone.

Before placing my hands on the stone, I took a long swig of water then circled the obelisk and examine it closely. The hieroglyphs started at the base and rose fully to the pyramid-shaped apex. Were they original to the stone, or had they been added during the time of Thutmoses I?

There were large chunks missing, mainly from the edges, and it sent me into speculation as to the cause. My first thought was, that because other obelisks had fallen and fragmented, it was the debris churned along by a tsunami that had knocked chunks out of the edges. But I quickly concluded that the sheer size and quantity of blocks, and the water tumbling them along, would have surely levelled all the obelisks, so it had to be something else other than contact.

Earthquake perhaps? No, that didn't float my boat; I surmised that an earthquake would be more likely to cause cracks that would fracture or topple the whole obelisk. I quickly ruled out human intervention, as the damage was not aimed at the hieroglyphs and it didn't commence at the bottom of the spike and work its way up. A bolt of lightning? Hmmmm, possible, I'm sure the obelisks would have acted as lightning rods, that is, if there were ever any major storms in Egypt to speak of. Wait a minute, what did Crystal say before?

'*Light is only a small fragment of the spectrum of energy.*'

So is lightning. Well, it's not so small; it's a massive discharge of energy. But what if it wasn't lightning? What if it was some other form of energy, some oscillating pulse that caused the granite to vibrate in such a way it literally fell apart at the seems? I guessed it was time to find out. So, as Diane led the others further into the temple, through the Fourth Pylon, I closed my eyes and placed my hands on the obelisk.

At first I heard, and became aware of, a low-pitched grumbling hum. It started under the ground and slowly crawled its way up and inside the very core of the obelisk. It was as if the earth was plugging in to the obelisk, or rather the other way around. That connection fully established, the stone started to hum and I felt it sucking in energy from all around it, like a black hole sucking everything into it from the surrounding cosmos. I felt like the stone contained the complete history of every event in ancient Egypt and every person who'd come within a hundred miles of it. It got me wondering if obelisks were some sort of download stations, or energy collectors?

Momentarily I had visions of crystal skulls, that they somehow did the same sort of thing. But, before I could focus on them and go deeper into the sensation, all of a sudden the obelisk fired a jet stream of energy up into the sky, just like quasars and the centre of galaxies. Where to? I had no idea!

'Stay grounded, Alex, there's plenty of time to go back there in due course.'

Crystal's voice and her hand on my shoulder instantly pulled me back to earth.

'Shit, what the hell was that all about? What's happening to me?'

'Your awareness is expanding far beyond your present conscious perceptions of life and who you are. Don't worry, it's all good. Come on, let's catch up with the others.'

What did she mean, *"far beyond my present conscious perceptions of life and who I am"*? And what was that about *"there's plenty of time to go back there in due course"*? Where is *"there"*?

As she took me by the arm and led me from the courtyard and after the others, I gathered my thoughts and starting thinking of the significance of all the obelisks that were once in Egypt and that had been hijack to significant sites around the world.

From memory, there were three in Rome: one in the Vatican City, one in St. Peter's Square, and one in the Piazza del Popolo. Then there was one in the Place de Concorde in Paris, and of course there was Cleopatra's needle in London, and another Cleopatra's needle in New York. Rome, Paris, London, New York; they were all major influential cities dominated by the influence of the Illuminati. I suddenly truly believed the obelisks weren't just removed as trophies; whoever removed them knew exactly what they were doing, and where they were placing them.

Then I remembered there was one more, in Istanbul. Istanbul? Was it there because it was somehow pivotal in the politics of the Middle East and the link between East and West? Istanbul, or Constantinople as it was once called, was certainly pivotal in the past, before the relocation of the obelisk. So, given it must have some significance, I wondered what the future held in store.

There wasn't much of interest about the damaged Fourth Pylon, built by Thutmoses I, other than the doorway that, according to the relief inscription, was restored by Alexander the Great. Beyond the pylon was a colonnade, also ruined.

'The colonnade originally contained huge statues of Osiris set in niches and two obelisks of Aswan granite erected by Queen Hatshepsut, the tips of which were covered with electrum.'

Wow, electrum! I knew electrum was is an alloy of gold and silver, and would make a perfect conductor of electricity. Was this proof the obelisks really were part of some giant energetic circuit? The statues of Osiris were gone, however the two obelisks, originally erected by Hatshepsut's on the occasion of her Jubilee in the sixteenth year of her reign, remained.

The right hand obelisk lay in pieces on the ground so I was able to examine it; the upper part lying horizontal on a few rails of concrete. Unfortunately none of the electrum remained on the tip; obviously removed at some time in the past for its monetary value. The bottom part of the obelisk contained long inscriptions that, according to my notes, 'celebrated the power of the Queen'.

Against the wall to the left was a granite statue of Thutmoses kneeling and holding an altar. Before it, the other obelisk, also of red granite, around thirty metres high, with a diameter at the base of over two-and-a-half metres and weighing over three-hundred tons, still stood proudly in place.

'On each of the four faces is a vertical inscription recording the dedication of the obelisks and the fact that they were constructed in only seven months. On the upper part are reliefs depicting Hatshepsut, Thutmoses I and Thutmoses III making offerings to Amun; the names and figures of Amun were defaced by Amenhotep IV but restored by Sethos I.'

That part I didn't believe. I might have if I'd read it before I visited Egypt, but having been here in the flesh and seen the evidence, I doubted if either Amenhotep IV or Akhenaten would have defaced the obelisk; the Amun Priests, yes, the lineage of Amenhotep I, no.

Bill and I were both tempted to place our hands on it, but, given the mood of the ladies to press on, and what we had both been through already, I think we both felt discretion was the better form of valour and gave it a miss. There was always the chance to do it later, on the way back, time and nerves permitting.

After Hatshepsut's death, Thutmoses III was supposedly responsible for building a long twenty-five-metre-high sandstone wall around the two obelisks to hide them. Parts of the wall were still visible, along with the remains of several papyrus columns that once formed part of the colonnades running on the north and south sides. Looking at it all, I somehow thought the work to 'conceal' the obelisks, or rather restrict access to them as they towered into the sky and would still have been visible, was more likely the handiwork of the Amun priests rather than Thutmoses III.

Beyond the damaged Fifth Pylon, also built by Thutmoses I, were the ruins of two small antechambers, built by Thutmoses III, in front of the Sixth Pylon.

'To the right and left were once courts with colonnades of sixteen-sided columns and statues of Osiris - remnants of the large court built by Thutmoses I round the temple of the Middle Kingdom.'

In the passage leading to the north court was a colossal seated figure of Amenhotep II made of red granite. In fact there were statues tucked into corners everywhere.

But something was changing; the further we went into the older parts of the temple, the more frequent I discovered red, and sometimes black, granite. A lintel here, a doorjamb there, a section of pylon or wall, a statue; it was a clear sign to me that I was approaching pay dirt.

Moving on to what remained of the Sixth Pylon, something took my eye: a black granite doorjamb; it was totally out of place.

'On the walls to right and left of the granite central doorway are lists of the cities and tribes subdued by Thutmoses III: to the right the peoples of the southern lands, to the left "the lands of the Upper Retenu [i.e. Syria] which his majesty took in the miserable city of Meggido."'

It may have been covered in hieroglyphs, but this was old: *way* older than the surrounding sandstone of the pylon. A quick check of my notes revealed the Sixth Pylon, the last and smallest of all the pylons in the Amun Temple, was built by Thutmoses III. That was at odds with my observation that, the further into the temple complex you went the further back in time you went; this was actually a jump forward about thirty years.

So, if Thutmoses I had built his Fifth Pylon outside of some pre-existing smaller temple, what happened that, thirty-odd years later and after the death of Hatshepsut in 1444 BC, Thutmoses III built a Sixth Pylon within, using black granite rather than the conventional sandstone? Did some event cause the destruction of what was previously there, or, did Thutmoses III, or maybe the Amun priests, seize the opportunity to deconstruct a temple, or some structure, dedicated to the lineage of Amenhotep I?

As we all passed through the doorway, I paused and ran my hand slowly over the granite. Again I examined the hieroglyphs closely; they seemed to belong, of course they did, but I still wondered if they were contemporary with the first use of the blocks or a later addition by Thutmoses III. What ever, there was something incredibly powerful about this place that was for sure. What was it about black granite? Did it have some special attribute, some frequency of vibration that had some extraordinary function? Just touching it seemed to cause a deep spiritual connection, to what, now *that* was the question? But, before I could let Nemo loose, I felt a hand gently grasp my other arm.

'Save yourself, we are nearly there.'

It was Crystal, and right before us, the pylon led to a court with two magnificent granite pillars bearing the floral emblems of Upper and Lower Egypt on the respective northern and southern sides. On the court's north side were two large statues of Amun and Amaunet, dedicated by Tutankhamun. Beyond that, in the heart of the complex, was our destination, the inner sanctuary, the Temple of Amun.

The Heart of Amun

More impressive than the previous gateway, the entrance to the sanctuary itself was a magnificent granite doorway about a foot thick, with the jamb itself over eighteen inches wide at the sides and a three-foot-high lintel above. It was in better condition than the previous doorway, almost too good a condition. As the others entered, I quickly checked my notes.

'The sanctuary of Amun was originally built by Thutmoses III, but later rebuilt by Alexander the Great's short-lived half-brother, Philip Arrhidaeus.'

Standing before the chamber and seeing it for myself, the only part of that load of waffle that rang true was, that like many of the other temples in Upper Egypt, it was probably rebuilt by the Greeks. And even that was distorted, as it'd clearly had some modern 'restoration', especially as regards the surrounding supporting wall.

The main problem I had with it being 'built' by Thutmoses III was that the sanctuary was the centre of the whole complex and the usual process would have been that things were subsequently built *around* the sanctuary. There is no reason to believe that wouldn't have been the case here.

Also, how the hell would they have brought all the granite in through the rest of the complex? So obviously either Thutmoses III rebuilt the doorway from some previous structure constructed of granite, or he just claimed it as his own by scrawling his cartouche all over it.

The other thing that suddenly hit me was the importance of Alexander the Great's involvement in its rebuilding.

Given Alexander was probably an initiate of the Tat Brotherhood and returning to Egypt to claim the throne and reinstate the spiritual direction of Egypt, it made sense to me that Alexander entrusted his half-brother to rebuild the sanctuary.

That raised two further issues: firstly, who, or rather what, caused the damage prior to each of the reconstructions, and secondly, what was the importance of this chamber that it received Philip's personal attention ahead of all the other temples in Upper Egypt reconstructed by the Ptolemaic pharaohs? With the others all inside, it was time for me to join them and find out.

Stepping through the door, I couldn't believe what I saw; the entire room was made from red granite. Clearly the floor was a modern addition, but everything else, the ceiling *and* the walls, was red granite. The walls in particular were way past well worn: yes, they had hieroglyphs, adorned with scenes of offering rites, with Amun appearing in both his usual anthropomorphic and his alternative ithyphallic forms, but in no way did they look part of the original stone; I was convinced the decorations were a later addition attributable to Thutmoses III. This place was ancient, dare I say it pre-historic, at least pre-Egyptologist-defined ancient Egypt.

The others were all gathered in a circle around a central granite altar that had been pieced together in such a way it looked like a battle-scarred relic from an explosion. I wondered what 'thing' or 'event' had the force to cleave solid granite blocks apart like splitting slate or mica?

Meanwhile, Diane, having finished her opening address, and standing eyes-closed with hands raised towards the stone in a sort of homage, led the others in their usual toning process. The group quickly followed suit and soon they were all toning a low 'Ooh'.

Having started in unison, Diane soon added a fifth above it on 'Aw', with others joining her. Next was added an octave above, and then a third above that on 'Ah'. The resulting chord, a major chord, was bouncing off the walls and roof, resonating around the room.

Looking around, I took extra note of the structure of the chamber, particularly its dimensions; it seemed 'perfect'. The height was about 1.6 times that of the width, and the length about 1.6 times longer than the height. Was this whole room, just like the shrines at Elephantine and Edfu, designed around the ratio of phi? Was that why the harmonics were so resonant, or was there more to it?

Still higher notes were added on the vowel 'Air', and then a seventh on 'Eee'. Before I knew it they were producing complex cluster chords that shifted with the dovetailing of each person's new breath and new note; it was like they were 'feeling' there way around the room using sound as their fingers. I don't know what it was they did next, or what chord they made, but suddenly, as one, they intuitively settled on one particular chord, and the whole room felt like it was 'alive', as if it were oscillating in sympathetic vibration to the chord. It felt like the room itself was breathing. Was this the 'ka' referred to by the ancient Egyptians, a breath that brought statues, temples and deceased pharaohs to life? With all the others preoccupied with the experience, it was time for me to call on Nemo.

I closed my eyes and placed my hands on the altar. Within a breath, a rush of energy surged through my body; not just through my body, but it felt like each and every cell was getting a jump-start. Images started to run through my mind, as if I was in the room, but not in my body, as if I was lying flat in the centre of the room facing the ceiling. An image came to mind of lying in a booth in a sun-tanning saloon and I wondered if the sanctuary was once a chamber for a much taller individual. Perhaps it was a chamber of rejuvenation for an Annunaki god, perhaps Amenhotep, or perhaps someone even earlier, Montuhotep or even Imhotep. Then, after the passing of Nibiru and the tsunami in 1600 BC, the ruins of the chamber were reconstructed and modified by Thutmoses III for use by the humans, the servants of the gods.

Upon opening my eyes I saw that Crystal and Diane also had their hands on the altar. Why them? Why *just* them? Why not any of the others? Did Crystal and Diane have some spiritual connection to this chamber? Well, of course they did, Crystal was Nefertiti and Diane was Hatshepsut. Well, that was all that I could figure at the time.

Almost as quickly as it started, it was all over, and everyone stopped toning. Strangely enough, I could still hear and feel the chord resonating not only through the chamber but also through my body.

'Right, done!...'

Diane had resorted to her cheery, 'normal' self.

'...Everyone's free to explore the rest of Karnak at your leisure, and I'll see at 7:30 tonight back at the hotel for a circle.'

Silently they filed out of the sanctuary, through a small gathering of onlookers who had assembled outside the chamber gawking in stunned disbelief, and dispersed to all corners of the complex. I stood there somewhat gob-smacked – What the fuck was that all about? *'Done'?* What did she mean by *'done'*?

I thought Crystal would have taken off with Bill and Pernille, but instead, she walked off silently on her own and headed to the rear of the complex. That was a no-brainer. At the risk of being accused of stalking, I followed in her footsteps.

We passed the outer walls of the inner chamber, depicting various festival scenes, some still retaining much of their original brightly coloured paint. The chambers that surrounded the granite shrine were made of sandstone, and supposedly built by Hatshepsut, though the walls closest to the sanctuary were apparently built by Thutmoses III, who decorated them with the 'annals' of his military campaigns and dedication to the temple, including a scene in which the pharaoh presents his two obelisks.

It wasn't really making sense. What did make sense was that some previous structure, perhaps built by, or restored by Hatshepsut, had been replaced or claimed by Thutmoses III. It would certainly account for the sudden use of sandstone.

The walls preceded a badly-damaged, wide, open court to the east, towards the back of the temple. It appeared the modern Egyptologists had constructed a 'staircase' leading from the inner sanctuary out into the courtyard. But what a shamozzle it was; long red granite blocks mixed with more modern sandstone. These guys really didn't have a clue. Did they add the sandstone to the already present granite block? And was the granite block a lintel of some structure beneath the sand?

As Crystal slowly made her way across it, I felt the need to check my notes.

'The court was probably the site of the original Karnak Temple, dating to at least the Middle Kingdom. Unfortunately, the building was plundered for its stone during antiquity, and there is little left other than the large calcite (alabaster) slab on which a shrine once stood.'

Yes, it proved my theory! Just like on the western bank with the Montuhotep temple, there was a temple here dating at least as far back as the Middle Kingdom, probably further. It's highly likely that temple was made of red granite and destroyed or badly damaged by the Thera tsunami around 1600 BC. Then, around the time of Thutmoses I, the temple was rebuilt, with Thutmoses III either completing the inner sanctum using the remnants of the damaged temple as the basis of the 'new' Temple of Amun, or claiming it as his own.

I wanted to share my thoughts with Crystal and get her views on it, but she seemed to be deeply processing what had just happened in the chamber, veering off towards the back right corner of the courtyard, so I hung back, leaving her to her business. The last thing I wanted to do was to piss her off and seem inconsiderate and self-absorbed.

Running down the centre of the courtyard was a series of red granite blocks; clearly there were part of some previous structure. And they weren't just old, these were ancient, weathered like the blocks at El Kab, rounded and crumbling. Beyond them, in alignment was another massive alabaster block, just like the one in the first courtyard, but again, showing far greater effects from the elements.

Further off to the right were a series of ancient altars set in a row along the edge of the courtyard; perhaps the oldest I'd seen so far, three red ones and a black one. They had obviously been found when the courtyard area was excavated and put to one side.

The black one in particular caught my attention as it had defined grooving it the top and appeared a different style to all the others. Either this was more Greco-Roman, or it was bloody ancient. Given where it had been discovered my thoughts went to the latter.

Wandering out of the courtyard, Crystal continued on into the next part of the temple, the relatively complete and intact Festival Hall of Thutmoses III, or Akh-Menu, meaning "Most Splendid of Monuments". She entered the hall from the southwest, what I presumed was the original entrance, apparently once flanked by two statues of the king in festival attire, although only one remained.

I shadowed her as she headed north into an antechamber with storage magazines and other rooms on the right and left of the temple's great columned hall, dedicated to Sokar, the sun god in his morning manifestation, and to Amun himself.

Around the perimeter, the roof was supported by square pillars, though in the central section there were curiously shaped columns more like ancient tent poles. The walls had carved reliefs of Thutmoses III in some very interesting scenes, including a hippopotamus hunt.

As opposed to the rest of the complex, which so far had been oriented west-east, this was the first building I had encountered that lay south-north. It felt weird; actually it felt totally wrong.

It didn't seem to affect Crystal though; in fact she seemed totally oblivious of her surrounds, strolling through the temple as if she'd once owned the place. But she hadn't, had she? No, Diane was Hatshepsut, maybe it was more to do with what had been there *before* the Akh-Menu.

I kept a close but respectable distance as she paused, at what would have been the inner sanctum, looking at the decapitated remains of a red stone statue that sat at the end of the room. To the side of the entrance, the placement of a seated alabaster statue felt a total mismatch of periods, especially when compared to the kneeling granite statue four feet to the left on the other side of the door.

I was getting angry, really pissed off; nothing was where it should be and everything was a bullshit façade set up to attract tourists and divert them from the truth.

After ten to fifteen seconds she shook her head, then turned and walked away with a wry grin on her face. I guess she didn't have much time for Thutmoses III.

Apart from that, Crystal was on another planet and took no notice of anything in the hall, or the area behind it, making her way straight back through the main hall, passed the rooms and corridors until she left the ruins of the temple and headed left towards the eastern gate.

'You might find this room of interest.'

Suddenly she'd stopped outside a small chamber just to the south east of the Akh-Menu.

'Thanks.'

She smiled and watched as I entered the room. It was tiny, about twelve feet long and maybe eight feet wide, with an unrecognisable remnant of a statue against the far wall. At first I didn't know what she was referring to, perhaps the walls, so I searched the walls looking for things of interest.

There were the predictable cartouches of Thutmoses III, which connected the room to the Akh Menu temple beside it. And then there were the even more predictable cartouches, of, whom I assumed to be, Ramses II claiming it for him self.

But it was the cartouche of whom I could only conclude was Amenemhat II, or related to one of the Amenemhat's of the 12th Dynasty that peaked my interest; it confirmed my beliefs about a Middle Kingdom origin to this part of the complex.

And that was it; no wonderful relief that had any major significance, no beautiful colour, nothing on the ceiling of any note. Perhaps Crystal had realized I was shadowing her, stalking her more like it, and sent me on a wild goose chase to throw me off her tail?

The only other thing in the room was the rock, and it couldn't have been that, could it? I mean it was so badly damaged you couldn't even tell what it originally would have been. Initially I didn't recognize the rock, I knew what it *wasn't*: it wasn't alabaster, sandstone, red or black granite. Where was Bill when you needed him?

I was just about to place my hands on the rock and let Nemo loose when I noticed a small section of decoration that had somehow survived the damage. Was that what I thought it was?

It certainly looked like it. I trawled my brain to see if there was anything else that it *could* have been, but in the end there was only one thing it could have been; a reptilian claw.

There was one in exactly the same place on the other side of the rock, but this one was even clearer. Did that explain why the statue had been destroyed; as a reaction to the reptilians? Perhaps. But did it explain why the statue had been made? Or *when* it had been made? No, this little beauty raised a hell of a lot more questions than it answered. And it seemed the Egyptologists hadn't even taken up the task of answering any questions on it, not that they would have been anywhere in the ballpark anyway.

I gingerly placed my hands on the stone and was suddenly hit by images of them walking in amongst us like ... well like cattle herders; these guys had absolutely no respect or regard for us at all, we were simply a commodity. I pulled my hands quickly away; 'that' was more than enough thank you very much.

I left the room half-expecting, half-hoping Crystal would be waiting, but no, she had moved on. Given she was originally heading east, like a lovesick bloodhound, I decided to follow her scent. It led through a series of rooms adjacent or behind the Akh-Menu. I quickened the pace, though took the time to note the closed papyrus topped columns behind the hall, and the extraordinary scenes of plants, animals and birds, that Thutmoses III had encountered on his military campaigns and carved into the remaining walls of the vestibule.

The path led over some makeshift bridges that scaled and spanned the half-ruined walls, and out past what I believe at some time would have been the rear outer corridor of the main complex: it sort of looked like an old medieval moat and who knows it may even have formed a similar function of keeping out undesirables.

One of the advantages for me was that from that vantage point I spotted Crystal heading further east towards the outer wall. I was back on her tail and would have continued to shadow her, every ready to step into the fold the moment she either needed help or gave the signal she was ready to rejoin 'the now' and communicate, but something unusual caught my attention.

Tucked into a nook outside the back, or rather eastern side, of the Festival Hall, were several niche shrines built against the temple. In one, was an alabaster statue of two seated figures, the upper part above the waist missing. I presumed it was a king and queen, though I couldn't discern whom.

It was badly damaged but it felt like it should have held pride of place somewhere, not stuck against the back wall of the Festival Hall of Thutmoses III. I snapped a photo then stood transfixed. Alabaster? Why wasn't it made of granite? I checked my notes.

'It was here that the ancient Egyptians brought their petitions for Amun's consideration.'

What a load of bollocks! Who the hell cam up with that? I bet it was some old theory put forward by a toffy-nosed turn-of-the-twentieth-century Egyptologist, who put two and two together and came up with diddly-squat, and every academic sheep ever since has just quoted it verbatim as if it were so.

But it got me thinking, that if it *was* from the New Kingdom, the 18th Dynasty or later, then surely it should have been made of granite. But it wasn't; it was alabaster, just like the massive block we encountered when we first entered the complex, and the calcite slab in the centre of the Middle Kingdom Courtyard. It had to have been part of the original temple from the Middle Kingdom, or even earlier. And that got me wondering if the use of alabaster was a signpost of the Middle Kingdom, or maybe of an even earlier period? If it was, then there would no doubt be lots of alabaster statues back at the ruins of the Temple of Montuhotep on the west bank at Deir el Bahri.

'It was also here, on either side of the shrines, that the two long lost obelisks of Hatshepsut were located.'

The bases could still be seen. More granite, more obelisks, no, I was convinced the alabaster statue was total incongruent with the 18th Dynasty.

I took a drink as I stood there contemplating if the chronology of ancient Egypt was somehow directly linked to the rock used to construct the temples? If that were so, then the oldest temples, possibly dating back tens or even hundreds of thousands of years, were made of red granite, that Alabaster was indicative of the Middle or possibly also the Old Kingdom, and sandstone attributable to the New Kingdom through to, and primarily including, the Ptolemaic reconstructions? It didn't quite gel with the red and black granite statues, and red granite obelisks of the New Kingdom, but maybe there was a good reason for that? I thought of spending a little time connecting to the stone and seeing if Nemo would uncover any clues, but, when I turned around, Crystal was continuing eastwards.

I fell in behind her as she headed towards the ruins of yet another temple, this one stretching almost to the eastern gate of the complex: the Eastern temple of Ramses II. Meandering towards it, I pulled out my iphone to check my notes and mull it all over.

'A little further to the east, are the remains of a small "temple of the hearing ear" that allowed common Egyptians, not usually allowed within the temple proper, access to their state god, Amun.'

This is most likely where Dr. Diddly-Squat got confused, connecting this temple to the 'shrines' behind it. I returned to my examination of the dynasties.

Time for a rethink

Noticing again that the groupings of the dynasties were into numerous periods, including the Old, Middle and New Kingdoms and the three Intermediate Periods, I suddenly realized yet another flaw in the Egyptologist's dating of the ancient Egyptian Dynasties; they hadn't taken into account the *sang réal*.

I have to reiterate that all the dates of the periods and reigns of the pharaohs 'given' by the Egyptologists are guesses: ALL OF THEM, and flawed ones at that, as I explained earlier, they all stemmed from the false premise of Manetho. But I had to use some 'guide' and the accepted Academic one was really the only one available. Maybe it was time to rewrite the record books?

Up until the end of the 6th Dynasty, 2176 BC, everything seemed kosher and logical, but, to my eye, problems started appearing around the 7th Dynasty: the supposed beginning of the First Intermediate Period, which incorporated the 7th to 10th Dynasties. To me, the 7th, 8th and 9th Dynasties didn't appear part of an 'Intermediate' period at all, they seemed a local progression from the 6th Dynasty. Why? Firstly because the names in the 7th and 8th Dynasties were still clearly Egyptian; Menkara, Djedkara, Neferkara, Neferkarnin, Neferkahor, Imhotep, Hotep, etcetera.

Further, according to the 'learned scholars', the 8th Dynasty supposedly ended in 2140 BC and then the 9th Dynasty began, having a succession of pharaohs named Kheti in both the 9th and the following 10th Dynasties. However, the Middle Kingdom, supposedly starting with the 11th Dynasty, but having only seven pharaohs (Montuhoteps I-IV and Intefs I-III), the first being Montuhotep I, had also begun around the same time, in fact only ten years later in 2130 BC. Something didn't gel, the names didn't sound foreign: so I ruled out an invasion; it had to be some sort of internal squabble. Therefore I concluded the 9th and 10th Dynasties may well just have been a 'breakaway' or parallel branch of the *sang réal*, like a disgruntled brother or nephew who represented a minor bloodline asserting his claim to the throne.

With Montuhotep I, who I believed was probably Annunaki, possibly even Imhotep, establishing the 11th Dynasty and the 'Middle Kingdom', I saw a logical progression from the Imhotep and Hotep of the 9th Dynasty, and things not just getting back on track, but continuing 'business as usual', much as they had with the return of Amenhotep at the start of the 18th Dynasty.

Thus there was no 'Intermediate Period'; the 'breakaway' bloodline of the 9th and 10th Dynasties may have simply been a minor bloodline who believed they had the right to rule. They were hardly 'Intermediate', more opportunistic. But all questions as to who was the rightful ruler were clearly settled when Montuhotep 'returned' to take the throne and 'unite' the family.

Following that, the 11th, 12th and first sixty-eight years of the 13th Dynasties seemed totally in keeping with the concept of the *sang réal* and to motor along without a hitch. But then, in the middle of the 13th Dynasty, from around the reign of Seth I in 1708 BC, things started to get interesting.

Now I may have been doing a little creative conjecture, but historically Seth was Osiris's twin brother, who supposedly killed him and seized the throne. Did this Seth try and do the same thing? Perhaps he did. Why did I think that? Because the 14th Dynasty started in 1710 BC, around the arrival of Seth I, right smack-bang in the middle of the 13th Dynasty, even though the 13th Dynasty continued, and did so way *beyond* 1638 BC, in fact for another twenty-three pharaohs of unknown reign. Did Seth spark a rift in the bloodline? It certainly looked that way. Was he also Annunaki, perhaps Enlil returning early, an advanced guard so to speak, who challenged the bloodline of his brother Enki/Osiris?

The theory was unsupported, but so was the current rhetoric of the Egyptologists. On only fact *was*, that little was known of the 14th Dynasty other than a list of thirty-eight pharaohs of unknown dates and length of reign. In seemed the entire 'knowledge' of the whole 14th Dynasty consisted of 'educated' guesses by the 'experts' about a list of names.

Further to that, there were at least three other lineages claiming the throne around the same time: the invading Hyksos pharaohs of the 15th Dynasty (1624-1514 BC) and 16th Dynasty (1620-1540 BC), as well as the Theban pharaohs of the 17th Dynasty (1619-1534). Perhaps the Hyksos, aware of the rift between the ruling families, seized the opportunity and invaded from the East? It sounded not only plausible, but highly likely.

At the other end of the scale, and probably further south in the real seat of power in Egypt, the Theban pharaohs logically followed on from the 13th Dynasty and the lineage of the *sang réal*. So, according to me, that left the lineage of the bloodline as; the 1st - 8th Dynasties followed by the 11th - 13th Dynasties, followed by the 17th and

18th Dynasties. Then it headed to Greece for nearly a thousand years, before returning after the 31st Dynasty with Alexander the Great and the Macedonian and Ptolemaic Kings. I'm not sure where it went after that, or how, but according to the Jews they were the chosen ones, so maybe it followed the lineage of David as they believe. Maybe Jesus *was* the son of God after all, or rather *a* 'son' *of* the gods.

In between the direct lineage dynasties there were several internal and external attempts to take over sovereignty from the *sang réal*; the 9th – 10th Dynasties (internal), the 14th – 16th Dynasties (external), the military pharaohs of the 19th and 20th Dynasties (internal), the Amun Priests of the 21st, 25th, 26th, 29th and 30th Dynasties (internal), and the northern invaders of the 21st- 24th, 27th, 28th and 31st Dynasties such as the Libyans and Persians (external). That sorted, the whole structure of ancient Egyptian history suddenly became a hell of a lot clearer, at least to me it did. Not only that, it made sense.

That sorted in my mind, I looked around for Crystal, but she was nowhere to be seen; it seems I had become so preoccupied with sorting out the history of ancient Egypt, that, in weaving in and out of the columns of the eastern temple, I'd lost sight of not only the future I desired, but the past I'd been pursuing. I'd been so preoccupied with my reworking of the past that I hadn't even noticed the red granite 'cobblestone' path I had been walking. The temple around and on top was all made of sandstone, and yet here, the very foundation seemed to consist of red granite.

A galabeyan-clad Egyptian suddenly grabbed my attention and beckoned me off left towards a small building against the eastern wall seemingly guarded by a machine-gun-toting member of the Tourist Police who was perched atop the outer wall. I wondered what threats he was there to defend tourists from, or was he there to stop tourists from going where they weren't welcome?

In any case, naively thinking Crystal must have headed there, I responded to the guardians gestures and followed the path to what I confirmed by my map was the Temple of Osiris Heka-djet, 'Ruler of Eternity', supposedly built by Osorkon IV in the 22nd Dynasty. That now didn't make sense; why would a Libyan Pharaoh build a temple here? It made more sense it was built by the Theban pharaoh, Osorkon during the 21st Dynasty and completed or augmented in the 25th Dynasty.

Traipsing across the dusty ground, I returned to the issue of which stone was employed for which periods of construction. I realized ages ago that the red and black granite altars and statues of the gods could possibly have survived for thousands of years until the tsunami hit. Now I added to that, for if, by the time of the 13th or even 17th Dynasty, the temples were constructed of alabaster, then it would explain how easily they were obliterated by the Thera/Santorini eruption and subsequent tsunami; all I had to do was find the ruins of a temple made of alabaster.

After the passing of Nibiru, Amenhotep, or Thoth/Imhotep as he may also have been known, returned, and, with him, the technology to not only sculpture red and black granite into the new massive statues of the 18th Dynasty, but also transport them hundreds of miles and erect them where most were found today.

However, with the exit of Akhenaten, the remaining knowledge and technical capabilities would possibly have been restricted to a chosen few, perhaps some hybrid offspring who had become one of the High Priests of Amun. It's highly plausible Ay fell into that category, though, as far as I knew, there were no such massive granite statues made of him. It is of course possible they did exist, but, that they were destroyed by Horemheb in a revengeful spree. In any case, until some remnants of a massive red granite statue of Ay are discovered, it could only be conjecture.

But someone must have passed on the knowledge of how to do it: perhaps Ay, maybe one of the other High Priests of Amun. If, as I suspected, Ay was a minor part of the lineage of the Annunaki *and* a High Priest of Amun, he would not only have known how to chisel the statues out of granite, but had the ability to do so, and thus he was the logical candidate. But after his death, who would have been able to carry the knowledge into the 19th and 20th Dynasties? The key had to lie with the relationship between Ay, Horemheb and the Amun Priests, and then Ramses I & II.

Lured into the small temple by the guardian, I quickly discovered Crystal was not inside and that I had been led astray. He pointed to several images on the wall.

'Isis. Osiris.'

According to my notes, the unusual reliefs contained images of the Divine Adoratrix, Shepenwepet and Amenirdis, depicted before the deities. They were nothing really to write home about, especially in comparison to what I'd seen at all the other temples, and in the tombs.

Suddenly the guardian was thrusting his hand out for a little baksheesh. I was pissed off to say the least, and at first I refused to cough up any moula. But he persisted, and eventually I took a leaf out of Bill's book, gave him ten pound, and headed out and back towards the eastern gate looking for Crystal.

As I strode along, my galabeyan pirate in my wake, I returned to my notes. They indicated:

'Ay was Horemheb's father-in-law; the father of Mutnodjnet, Horemheb's wife.'

Nice one Horemheb, marry the boss's daughter, then do in your father-in-law and take the throne. Now, to do in the mother-in-law, *that* I could totally understand, perhaps even contemplate as my ex mother-in-law was the bitch-queen psycho-harpie from Hell, but I could hardly see the point in disposing of the father-in-law, perhaps because my ex-father-in-law was a wimpy pussy-whipped doormat. Mind you, I don't think bumping off one's in-law to ascend the throne is unusual, and Horemheb topping Ay was not the only time it's been done in history: one of the first perhaps, but definitely not the only time.

The problem, as far as the *sang réal* went, was Horemheb and Mutnodjnet supposedly had no children, so Horemheb appointed the military leader Ramses I as his successor, and thus the *sang réal* chain was truly broken. Unless, of course, there *was* a link connecting Mutnodjnet to Ramses I, like if he married her, then that would confirm the lineage. But that did not seem to be the case, so I had nothing to confirm my theory. Mind you, not having any concrete evidence never stopped the Egyptologists from not only guessing, but continually putting their theories forward as fact. So, if it was good enough for them, why not for me?

What of this supposed daughter of Mutnodjnet and Horemheb, did she exist, and did she marry Paramesse? Time to do some digging.

'Originally called Paramesse, Ramses I was the son of a troop commander called Seti, born into a noble military family from the Nile delta region.'

Horemheb clearly frequented Northern Egypt as his 'tomb' there would attest. Was it here, in and around Saqqara and Memphis, that as a military general he was acquainted with Seti, a military troop commander and father of Paramesse? Surely this is how Paramesse gained such favour with Seti, or was it?.

'Horemheb remained childless, he appointed his Vizier, Paramesse, to succeed him upon his death, both to reward Paramesse's loyalty and because the latter had both a son and grandson to secure Egypt's royal succession.'

The 'experts' say Horemheb was childless, I begged to differ, I think they had a daughter.

'Seti I was born of Paramesse and Tia before Paramesse became king.'

The name Tia was a direct lineage to the Mutnodjnet's mother and Ay's sister and wife. Tia, who had been married to Seti's son Paramesse, probably when Horemheb was still just a general in the army. When Tutankhamun, then Ay and Ankhensenaten all died, and Horemheb was catapulted in the throne because of his marriage to Mutnodjnet, Paramesse was named Crown Prince because he was married to their daughter, Tia.

So, did Tia, as Paramesse did, change her name when they ascended to the throne, Tia becoming Sitre? It would appear so, and is reinforced by the fact that one of the daughters of Ramses II was named Tia-Sitre makes it even more likely. That was simple, it was in accordance with the *san real*, it linked the 18th and 19th Dynasties and totally explain everything.

Any way, without the Mutnodjnet-Ramses link, it would still have been left to the Amun Priests to solely hold the knowledge, and by 1118 BC, the knowledge was apparently lost, perhaps before it could be passed on, and no further massive statues were either made or transported.

I stood by the imposing twenty-metre-high eastern gate, constructed by Nectanebo I, looking around for where Crystal had gone. Then I spotted her through the gate, outside the complex, in what was the Precinct of Aten. I thought the area was closed, off limits to the public, but somehow Crystal had finagled her way through. But, you guessed it, the minute I went to go through the gate and join her, the machine-gun-toting sniper from the heavens sprang into action.

'No, please, closed. Not allowed. Nothing to see, only snakes.'

I pointed towards Crystal, obviously there was some reason to be there.

'I am with the lady.'

He nodded ...

'Oh, yes, the madam. Please, to wait.'

...and then he was down from the wall quicker than you could say 'Jack Robinson', holding out the mandatory claw for compensation.

'Fifty pound.'

What did he think I was, a moron? I'd paid nearly that much to get into the whole complex, and the scene outside the gate appeared to be nothing more than a field of piles of scrub and dust, so there was no way I was going to be screwed, not even if he *was* packing heat.

'Ten pound.'

'No, please, nothing to see, not allowed.'

'Nothing to see on top of ground, but much underground, yes? Statue?'

He smiled.

'Professor, yes, you know. But I must protect.'

My trusty akubra had weaved it's magic once again. Harrison Ford, many thanks, I take off my hat to you.

Clearly since the revolution theft of sites was a more public concern, and even more clearly, there was still stuff under the ground here in the Precinct of Aten. Eventually we agreed on thirty pound and he unlocked the gate, letting me through into what would have been a key part of my past.

The Precinct of Aten

Crystal was standing in the middle of nowhere, in the middle of nothing, in the middle of doing something that I had no idea about. And it was hot, damned hot! Scanning the surrounds, barely a trace remained of the past, just piles of sand covered in camel thorns.

Apparently at a previous date, the scant remains of Akhenaten's Karnak temple buildings to the Aten were discovered here. And when they were, of course the 'experts' had their say.

'It was here at Karnak that Amenhotep IV, after abandoning the traditional worship of Amun, taking up worship of Aten, and changing his name to Akhenaten, built a temple to the sun god out of standardized blocks called talatats. He also built an entire new city at Tel el Amarna. But, after his death, the Amun Priests of Thebes destroyed all signs of Akhenaten as well as any sun worship at Karnak and elsewhere.

Over sixteen thousand of the decorative talatats have been recovered from various locations at Karnak. About 27 x 27 x 54 cm, which corresponds to ½ x ½ x 1 ancient Egyptian cubits, they are being photographed by ARCE, so the scenes they depicted can be reconstructed.'

In principal it sounded great, but I was sure now, after my chats with Dwight and Randy, that ARCE was, and is, connected to the Illuminati. So, where are the talatats now, and what is the status of the reconstruction of the images? Maybe ACRE is, in some bizarre way, part of some secret lineage of the Amun Priests? Maybe the authorities just don't want us to know the truth about Akhenaten? It was just like the discovery of the Dead Sea Scrolls and their subsequent withholding from public scrutiny, until such time as the pressure became too much. But who knows what they have kept back, hidden from other independent non-Catholic, non-Judaic 'scholars'?

On another tack, maybe Amenhotep IV didn't abandon the Amun at all; maybe he *never* worshiped it, because maybe Amenhotep IV wasn't Akhenaten? One thing was certain; the Amun Priests probably had a major hand in the destruction of the temple and, compared to other temples, the Aten ones would have been easy to demolish as they were made of talatats, which, according to Egyptologists, were exclusively used during the reign of Akhenaten in the building of the Aten temples at Karnak and at Tel el Amarna further down the Nile.

As Crystal moved passed an area that could once perhaps have been a sacred lake, to a collection of granite fragments off to one side, I dutifully followed then stood beside her, closed my eyes, and called on Nemo to do his stuff. But it was proving difficult with nothing concrete to focus on, not even the granite fragments seemed to be helping. After a few minutes Crystal broke her silence.

'Anything?'

'Well, yes and no; I'm not really getting anything out here, but I had all sorts of things happen back inside.'

'You just need a little time to get over the shock and integrate the changes.'

And with that said, she turned and headed back towards the gate. I followed her like an ant after a strawberry-jam sandwich at a picnic.

'Changes? What changes?'

'Your whole body has been retuned?'

'What do you mean *retuned*?'

'To a higher frequency: the inner sanctum at the heart of the Temple of Amun is a molecular accelerator.'

I stopped dead in my tracks.

'What the ...'

I'd had a few jaw dropping moments in the last few days, and a few other experiences that left me breathless, but this one took the cake.

'...A molecular accelerator?'

'Yes, it was used by the Annunaki to rejuvenate their bodies.'

I rushed after her.

'Rejuvenate, you mean like, resurrection?

'Exactly.'

'How?'

'How is irrelevant. You would be better to ask why. '

'OK, why?'

'The energy on this planet vibrates at a much lower frequency than on the Annunaki's home world and, after a period of time, it compromises their cellular structure. So they need to spend time in the chamber to recharge on an atomic level.'

'Like a decompression chamber.'

'Exactly.'

'What does it to the cellular structure of human beings?'

She laughed.

'To most of them, very little, but to those with certain strands of DNA that have been laying dormant, it activates them and shifts the body, and then the consciousness, to a higher level in preparation for what is to come.'

We re-entered the main Amun complex and headed south of the temples towards the Sacred Lake.

'For what's to come? What do you mean, *"For what's to come"*? What *is* to come?'

'When the time is right, you will remember.'

Maybe it was the tone of her voice, but what ever it was, it sounded ominous.

Deep in thought, I shadowed Crystal as she walked beside the Sacred Lake; measuring about eighty metres long, forty metres wide and dating to the time of Thutmoses III, now it is filled with ground water whereas once it would probably have been connected to the Nile and supplied water for the priests' ablutions as well as for

270

other temple requirements.

As sacred lakes went it was huge, and I briefly wondered why it needed to be so large, but then everything was large in the 18th Dynasty. Actually, the lake could go back even earlier than that: who knows? It was lined with rough hewn stone and on its southern side had a stone tunnel through which apparently 'the domesticated geese of Amun were released into the lake from their yards further south'. Maybe the tunnel led somewhere else?

There were the ruins of some structure on the south side of the lake; perhaps they were connected to it? The structure was basically razed to the ground, perhaps obliterated by the tsunami: I wondered what might lay undiscovered beneath the surface.

Finally, in true 'modern' reconstruction and tourism, the seating for the temple's famous sound and light show was erected directly on top of the excavated remains of the housing for priests. Jesus!

Crystal strode on with a sense of purpose and I started thinking more about the inner sanctum and how a molecular accelerator might actually work. I figured it had to have something to do with the choice of granite for the chamber. Perhaps the silicon dioxide primarily worked much as it did in modern computers; storing data. If that were the case, then the stone would already have had to have been downloaded with the necessary data to reconfigure the DNA.

Christ, it sounded exactly like an episode of 'Star Trek – New Generation' I'd seen where they used the transporter to reconfigure someone who's DNA had been compromised by some microscopic entity.

And then there were the obelisks; did they provide the portals, the access points where information was downloaded, and, if so, from where?

Suddenly I had images of alien satellites in orbit around the planet, not just one or two, but a whole grid or network of them. Then I saw the first NASA space shuttle flying up into orbit to capture one and bring it back to earth. Shit, was the whole shuttle program a scam as well? By now nothing would surprise me. I wondered if I was going crazy, becoming a total conspiracy theorist, or if what Crystal had said was true, *'I just needed a little time to integrate the changes'*, and, *'When the time was right, I would remember'*. Was I starting to remember things already? I ran my hands over my arms and torso. No, I didn't feel any different.

Crystal walked onward, towards the northwest corner of the lake, passing an ascending tunnel that ran parallel to, and between, the sacred lake and the main temple, and towards the razed ruins of the Osireion Temple of Taharqa, penultimate pharaoh of the 25th Dynasty.

Tunnels led somewhere, and descending tunnels led underground. It just so happened this one led underground beside the Middle Kingdom Courtyard. My guess was it hit a T intersection and turned off to the sacred lake to the right, and who knows what beneath the old courtyard, perhaps the ruins of an even older temple dating back to the Old Kingdom, or beyond. The entrance was blocked in with a wire cage so I couldn't gain access, and it was too dark to see what lay at the lower end, but it tweaked more than just a passing interest in me. How strange it had not tweaked the interest of the Egyptologists; or was it firmly in the 'too hard' basket.

I followed along as it rose gently up towards the Osireion; about thirty metres long on each side, the structure looked more like the lower level of a mastaba-style tomb as it had no doors on any of its outer walls, and that seemed not consistent with the period. My notes also put the whole origin of the structure in question.

'Within the structure are additional support walls about 1.5 metres high containing a large number of reused stones from the Nubian period, of which several still retain the cartouche of Shabaka.'

The Shabaka stones clearly showed evidence of a later restoration, however, the real question was, just how far back did the structure go?

Circling anticlockwise around it so I could keep Crystal in sight, I noticed some blocks in the east wall were scored, while some were unfinished. That led me to believe an access ramp existed here that led to the terrace of the structure, and that made it start to look more and more like the structure that would have been at Deir el Bahri as part of the Middle Kingdom Temple of Montuhotep.

On the northern façade were several interesting scenes including the pharaoh, two falcons crossing their wings over his chest and under his three-row *user* necklace, purified by a double stream of the ankh and the *was* falling around him. To the left was another scene where the pharaoh, in a pleated loincloth with a triangular front panel, offered incense to Atum.

If I wanted to stay with Crystal, I wasn't going to be able to fully explore the Osireion, so I would have to rely on my notes.

'In the northwest corner of the monument is a staircase that descends along the inside northwest wall into the chambers below.'

I could just see over the ruins of the wall and into the staircase.

'On the wall next to the staircase are representations of androcephalic figures and mummified baboons, each of which correspond to a stair, climbing from north to south above a solar disk. Within the structure, in the northwest corner room, on its southern wall is a depiction of the pharaoh and, behind him, six baboons facing east. Called "the eastern souls who worship Ra when he rises", the Egyptians symbolically chose the baboon because it seems to greet the morning sun, and is said to give a howl at every hour and urinate twelve times during the day and twelve at night during the equinox.'

I don't know about the significance of the baboon pissing like a clockwork cuckoo, but what I did know was that the baboon was also a symbol for Thoth, and to me that smacked of a more distant connection to earlier dynasties. I wondered if the rising figures somehow bizarrely represented the ascent of Man, of Man's wisdom, or possibly even of Man's 'evolutionary' origins?

'On the north wall of the chamber is a scene depicting the solar barque proceeding from east to west, in the direction of the sun's daily path. The surface on which this bas-relief is sculpted has been flattened out, removing the base of a dozen columns of hieroglyphs from which the cartouches have been visibly removed or cut away.'

So, something existed on the stone beforehand; 'dozens of columns of hieroglyphs' and 'cartouches'. To me that meant an interference with history, and the finger pointed at the Amun Priests once again, but, in reality, it could have gone back way before even they stuck their noses in. If only the 'experts' could use modern forensic techniques to 'see' what lay beneath the barque relief, then we might get some real answers.

'To the southeast is another chamber containing descriptions of the sun-god's nightly journey through the netherworld and his rebirth each day as a scarab beetle.'

The scarab, Khebri, symbol of the Sun God, represented creation. Did that have any significance to the building?

'Further southeast is yet another chamber that leads to an inner chapel. Here, carved on the lintel to the doorway into the chapel, is a strange and extremely rare representation. On one side, a female figure draws a bow with her left arm pulled behind her back, while on the other side, a male figure, who holds a club in his left hand, is making the "great stride". In the centre is depicted a tree which juts up from a hemispheric mound drawn within a rectangle. Text here describes this as the shndt tree (spiny acacia of the chest). The name of Osiris is on the mound. A simulation on a Saite sarcophagus explains that "This is the mound that hides what it holds; this is the hill of Osiris".'

"This is the hill of Osiris" – That's the reason I was so interested, the location of the Osireion was right beside the inner sanctum, right beside the original primordial mound of the complex. That gave it geographical and historical importance. I was certain there were more answers below the surface, possibly even red and black granite walls, chambers, or structures. Now I really wanted to climb on top and check it out. It was only about six foot high so I climbed up on top for a better look.

The whole thing was covered in camel thorns. It was as if the Egyptologists had just turned a blind eye to it, as if it was unimportant. Hell, guys, 'This is the mound that hides what it holds; this is the hill of Osiris"! Surely that, the baboons indicating Thoth, its proximity to the inner sanctum and the Middle Kingdom courtyard, and the descending tunnel leading from it to who knows where were pretty good signs this place might just be important.

Well, that's what I would think; I certainly wouldn't let the Osireion become a plantation box for camel thorns. But that, I'm afraid, is exactly what it looked like had happened. I would have loved to stay and explore it further but two things made that rather difficult. The first was that Crystal was skating on, the second, one of the local self-appointed guardians was ushering me to get off. Guess why? Yep, 'It is not allowed'.

Were they afraid I was going to crush the camel thorns? Christ, as it stood, the Osireion was a platform of dirt with rock walls; I was hardly going to compromise its existence. In any case, I jumped down and followed Crystal as she walked to the western end of the lake towards a red granite plinth about six-feet high, three-foot square, with rounded corners. Atop it sat a worn figure of a scarab beetle, Khepri, the very deity I had just been contemplating.

It supposedly dated from the reign of Amenhotep III, and apparently was brought here from his west bank mortuary temple. I wasn't buying that for a minute: if it was that important it should have been here to begin with, and maybe it was.

I circled it slowly, examining the hieroglyphs and the four small rectangular holes half way up the front: it was like nothing I'd ever seen before. As I circled it, Crystal stood before it, and for the first time I saw her slightly perplexed and in deep thought.

'What do you think it's for?'

Crystal looked at me with a wry grin.

'According to the locals, if you circle it clockwise seven times you will find your true love.'

I suddenly felt foolish. I mean, I was already doing my second lap, but was I going in the right direction?

'I was thinking more of its original purpose.'

'I do not remember. All I can recall is that the scarab represents creation, or more specifically rebirth. That is why the ancient Egyptians used it to represent the sun being reborn every morning.'

I looked back at the camel-thorn ridden mastaba.

'Somehow, I think it's connected to the Osireion…'

Then an idea hit me like a lighting bolt from an obelisk.

'…This plinth used to be a part of the inner chamber; it's part of the molecular regeneration process. And the obelisks are part of it as well.'

Crystal intensified her focus on the scarab, then suddenly her whole body sort of jolted, as if she'd been hit by a short moderate electric shock. After a brief pause, she breathed in deeply, out, and relaxed, nodding her head in the process.

'Hmmm, yes, that feels correct; that is it.'

And then she was off.

'Where are you going?'

'Back to my hotel.'

'Aren't you staying to explore more?'

She paused and quickly looked around.

'No. Thanks to you, I have done everything I need to do here...'

I didn't know whether to cut my visit to Karnak short and invite myself to join her, or take potluck I would see her later. Thankfully Crystal made the decision for me.

'…You stay here and finish exploring. The others are gathering again at Bill's hotel around 5:00 pm, perhaps I will see you then.'

It was a bit of a long shot, but I took the opportunity to ask what her movements were in the long term.

'What are your plans beyond that?'

'As you are aware, Diane is holding another circle tonight.'

'And after that?'

She gave me the most sultry, steamy and wicked of looks.

'I would think bed.'

Was that an invitation? I was *so* tempted to invite myself to that as well, but again decided that discretion was the better form of valour.

'What about tomorrow?'

'I am travelling to Dendera and Abydos with Bill and Pernille.'

'Maybe I can tag along?'

'That would be up to Bill, it is his trip.'

'Then I'll ask him later on.'

'Enjoy the rest of your time here. Oh, and you might find the open-air museum worth a visit as well.'

If it was anything like her suggestion to visit the room beside the Akh-Menu, then it was probably going to open yet another can of worms.

'I might just do that.'

As she turned and made her exit, I followed her as far back as the Courtyard of Thutmoses I, between the Third and Fourth Pylons; this woman had the most hypnotic walk. Through her white muslin skirt the cheeks of her discernibly bare ass were gently giggling like a pair of ... well ... tight buns. For several seconds I wondered if she was wearing a G-string, or if she was going commando. Now *that* was hot! Oh to get my hands on those goddess globes; I would kneed them like two lumps of baker's dough. Things would get so hot it wouldn't just be the bread that was rising, that's for sure.

I needed cooling down in more ways than one, and fast, so once she had disappeared back into the temple and was out of sight, I finished not only my first bottle of water but made a considerable impression into the second. Then, refreshed and freed from any further visual distractions, I checked the time, 11: 20, gathered my faculties, and continued my exploration of Karnak.

Wandering around Karnak

The temples at Karnak are built along two axes: the original Middle Kingdom shrines, built on a mound in the centre of what is now called the Temple of Amun, run east-west, and pylons seven, eight, nine and ten run perpendicular on a north-south, or transverse, axis to the main temple. Then I remembered something unusual about Karnak and check my notes.

'The alignment of Karnak is such, that if it was built to align with the sun on the summer solstice, as would be expected, then Karnak, or rather the original parts of it, must have been built around 3,700 BC.'

Now, I know the Egyptologists have their dates all out of whack, but that really opened a can of worms. That was not only before the Middle Kingdom, it was six-hundred years *before* the 1st Dynasty. Or maybe it was even a complete precession of 25,920 years before that, around 29,620 BC, unless of course the poles shifted, and *that* was not so far fetched either. They may well have moved in 1,600 BC, and, if hey did, who knows how much they shifted, ten degrees, twenty? There was evidence everywhere that was at odds with the conventional history of Egypt. Either the Egyptologists were all mindless sheep, or someone was covering up and suppressing the truth, and my instincts told me it was a bit of both.

The transverse axis commenced with a badly ruined courtyard in front of what was the Seventh Pylon. On the east wall was a long inscription about Ramses II's son, Merneptah, and his battles with the Libyans, Etruscans and Achaeans, together with a relief showing Merneptah, smiting his enemies with a club before Amun. According to my notes:

> 'In this court once stood two temples, both demolished during the reign of Thutmoses III; one dated from the Middle Kingdom, the other built by Amenhotep I. The fine limestone blocks from these temples, decorated with reliefs, were built into the Third Pylon erected by Amenhotep III.'

Looking around the courtyard, I couldn't figure out where the two temples may have been. The Middle Kingdom temple, possibly dedicated to Montuhotep, could well have been made of alabaster and/or limestone, and been obliterated by the tsunami. The Amenhotep Temple may well have been reconstructed out of its remains and its destruction probably done by the Amun Priests. Amenhotep III then possibly resurrected the stones as the foundation for his pylon, sort of rebuilding the lineage, so to speak.

Anyway, all that was left now was an open courtyard.

> 'Now known as the Cachette Court, between 1902 and 1909, the French Egyptologist Georges Legrain (1865–1917) excavated the ground of the court before the seventh pylon and discovered a precious collection of 779 stone statues and stelae, along with over 17,000 bronzes, which now form a large portion of the Cairo Museum collections.'

I don't remember seeing any of them in Cairo, but then everything was so badly labelled, and I *was* in a bit of a daze. So what actually did Legrain find? Statues of who, made of what? And bronzes! That in itself had me wondering what the hell they were, and who made them? But, given the badly damaged Seventh Pylon beyond the courtyard was built by Thutmoses III, it would make sense that he and the Amun Priests disposed of all the previous references to Hatshepsut and Amenhotep I by just turning them into the ground like last season's husks.

As for the Seventh Pylon, the northern face celebrated the victories of Thutmoses III. In front of it were seven red granite statues of rulers of the Middle and New Kingdoms: in front of the eastern pylon, a figure of Osiris (with a later inscription by Ramses II) and a colossal statue of Thutmoses III, before the west tower, a colossal statue of Thutmoses III wearing the double crown, an Osirid statue of Thutmoses III, a seated figure of a pharaoh of the Middle Kingdom, a seated figure of Sobekhotep, and a fine statue of Amenhotep II.

None of them made any sense where they were, against the inner face of the pylon. And why put Middle Kingdom pharaohs alongside New Kingdom pharaohs? It was just a confusing hotch-potch. Normally, in most cases, the statues would be outside the pylon, on the southern face, to welcome visitors, but clearly the modern Egyptians had lined them up there for the aesthetic of the tourists; I hated that!

And what was Ramses II doing there anyway? Had he claimed one of Thutmoses III's Osirid statues as his own? I know he claimed almost everything, but even so, these statues were nowhere near where Ramses II would have had them placed. He would have had them set in a position of prominence, perhaps the opposite side of the courtyard leading into the temple proper, but definitely not where they'd been placed here.

Moving through the gateway into the next courtyard, the southern face of the Seventh Pylon also celebrated Thutmoses III's victories. In front of it, lay the lower parts of two colossal statues of Thutmoses III, and, in front of the more easterly of these figures, the lower part of a large obelisk erected by Thutmoses III.

Abutting the eastern wall of the court between the Seventh and Eighth Pylons was a small, badly ruined chapel dating from the reign of Thutmoses III. Further along, on the eastern wall were reliefs of Ramses II making offerings to the gods.

Moving on to the Eight Pylon, built by Hatshepsut, decorated, or rather 'claimed', by Thutmoses III, and later restored by Seti I, it became clear not many tourists visited this part of the complex, as it was in a poor state of repair and maintenance. However, there were still several scenes discernable on the façade of the pylon representing Hatshepsut with different deities, as well a religious scene featuring Thutmoses III.

'Hatshepsut's name was erased from the reliefs by Thutmoses III and Seti I restored the reliefs after their destruction by Amenhotep IV, in many cases inserting his own name in place of those of the earlier pharaohs.'

Well, I knew Amenhotep IV wasn't responsible for the damage, or was he? Akhenaten certainly wasn't, but maybe Amenhotep IV was? Maybe he was pissed off when Akhenaten arrived in Egypt and stole his thunder, relegating him to 'standby' pharaoh. Maybe when Akhenaten, and then Nefertiti, left Egypt, Amenhotep IV assumed the throne, changed his name to Smenkhkare, and sided with the Amun Priests; hell, he may even have been one.

But several other questions arose: 'Why did Seti I have to repair the pylon in the first place: an earthquake perhaps? Another tsunami? Or was it because the Amun Priests hacked the hell out of it?'

The eastern tower had reliefs of Seti I making offerings to various deities, and farther right, Thutmoses II, which would have originally been Hatshepsut, escorted into the temple by a lion-headed goddess followed by Hathor and priests bearing the sacred barque of Amun. Below that, Thutmoses I stood before the Theban divine triad.

On the west tower, Seti I, originally Hatshepsut, was being led into the temple by the falcon-headed god Montu, with priests bearing the sacred barque following. In addition, Thutmoses II, originally Hatshepsut, stood before Amun and Khonsu, behind him the lion-headed goddess and Thoth, who inscribes his name on a palm branch. Beneath that, in two rows, Ramses III stood before various gods.

Moving through the doorway, there were inscriptions on the doorjambs of the names of Thutmoses II, replacing the original Hatshepsut cartouches, and Thutmoses III. Against the right hand jamb was a badly-damaged red-granite stela recording Amenhotep II's campaigns in Asia. On the other side of the gateway, Ramses II was depicted in the presence of various gods. Hell, everyone was claiming a part of this pylon. The reliefs on the southern front of the pylon showed Amenhotep II seizing shackled enemies by the hair and smiting them with a club before Amun.

In front of the pylon were the partial remains of three seated colossi, similar to the Colossi of Memnon that sat outside the Temple of Amenhotep I on the west bank. Who they were, I wasn't completely sure, as they were pretty wrecked; apart from the most westerly one, Amenhotep I, which, even though it was made of limestone, was well preserved. I guessed the missing fourth colossi was also Amenhotep I as that would maintain the symmetrical approach employed by the Egyptians at most of the other temples.

I guessed the two other colossi, framing the gateway, were probably of Hatshepsut, after all this was her pylon, although from the waist up the body of each statue was missing. Of course, in keeping with the rest of the defacing, they may have been re-sculptured to represent Thutmoses II.

'The two central figures, lacking the upper part of the body, are of Thutmoses II (the more westerly of siliceous sandstone). According to an inscription on the back they were restored by Thutmoses III in the 42nd year of his reign.'

That was enough for me, 'restored' surely meant reformed from the image of Hatshepsut into that of Thutmoses II. It would be in keeping with the fact Hatshepsut built the pylon, was Amenhotep's daughter, and with who was responsible for the vandalism: the Amun Priests.

Moving on, the Ninth Pylon, built by Horemheb, was badly damaged. However, I found something interesting in my notes.

'A large number of bricks were found inside the 9th Pylon, being used as filling, that belonged to Akhenaten's Aten Temple.'

What better way to eliminate all traces of Akhenaten than to dismantle his temples and 'bury' the stones within the structure of another structure? But where are those stones now? Are they still in situ, or has ARCE got them hidden away somewhere?

Between the Ninth and Tenth Pylons was a square walled court. On the eastern wall were a number of reliefs of Horemheb, including him marshalling fettered prisoners from Punt and Syria, who were bearing costly gifts, before the divine Theban triad.

Further south were the remains of the Heb-Sed Shrine, the jubilee temple built by Amenhotep II and later decorated by Seti I. Originally it was positioned somewhere in front of the Eighth Pylon, but was probably removed, and rebuilt on a base topped by a cavetto cornice, during the reign of Horemheb, with extra decorations completed by Seti I, who used it as a barque shrine to Amun.

I walked up the ramp that led into the raised temple from the west, fronted by a portico of twelve square pillars decorated with reliefs. The first thing that caught my eye was the granite doorway, proof to me that this was part of a much older temple, even before the Amenhotep II temple that once stood either somewhere before the Eighth Pylon in the Cachette Courtyard.

The granite doorway led into a large five aisled hall, the ceiling of which was borne on twenty decorated square pillars crowned by cavetto cornices. A series of rooms led off in different directions; to the right, and south of the temple, a smaller pillared room contained the lower part of a colossal alabaster statue standing somewhat forlorn and abandoned among patches of overgrown camel thorn, yet another example of the lack of maintenance of the temples.

Given the temple was built by Amenhotep II, it might have meant the statue may well have been of him as well, and perhaps would explained why it was in such a dilapidated condition. However, as it was made of alabaster, to me it was even more proof that the statue belonged to the Middle Kingdom temple that existed *before* the Amenhotep II Temple, and the damage was more than likely as a result of the tsunami. So could it have been of Montuhotep?

The American Egyptologist Charles Van Siclen III had more recently reconstructed the temple, but it was still in pretty crap condition. Perhaps, because it received scant patronage from the tourists, it also received scant attention from the Egyptians in terms of maintenance and simple things like 'weeding'.

That said, the temple did have some finely carved reliefs on the walls and pillars, many depicting Amenhotep II before various gods. Mostly done in delicate low relief, with the occasional few in sunken relief, surprisingly, much of their original colour was well preserved. However a second glance at my notes confirmed Akhenaten was still getting the blame for everything.

'The images of the god Amun were destroyed during the reign of Akhenaten. They were later repaired by Seti I.'

I wondered if Akhenaten should go down as the first scapegoat in history? Ah, no, of course, that would be the snake in the garden of Eden.

On the eastern wall there was a large false door stele and, as I stood before it examining the detail, all of a sudden something got me thinking, 'Was it really a false door, or was it a real door, but a door into another world?' and 'Were these sorts of 'false doors' really portals into other worlds, or perhaps pathways into other dimensional levels of consciousness?' I guessed the only way to know was to go through one. Though I didn't feel any strong pull to know what lay behind this particular door, I thought maybe Nemo held the key and I made a point of putting him on notice that when the right door came along he was free to swim to the surface.

Leaving the temple in my wake, I reached the southern wall and the damaged Tenth Pylon, which served as the southern entrance to the precinct of Amun from the end of the 18th Dynasty.

'It was built by Horemheb using stones from a temple which Akhenaten had erected in Karnak in honour of his new god.'

Was it damaged because of the ravages of time and general wear and tear, or was it 'damaged' because the Akhenaten Project had removed all the talatats used to construct it?

A central granite doorway remained; a clear sign to me that this doorway was probably harvested from Akhenaten's Aten temple, which in turn may have used stone recovered from the jubilee temple of Amenhotep II, or more likely either the Middle Kingdom temple once behind the inner sanctum, or the one in the Cachette Courtyard.

As well as cartouches, the reliefs on the central granite doorway showed Horemheb making offerings to various gods and performing other rituals. It didn't mean Horemheb had excavated the granite, just that he had carved his name and deeds into it, just as he had into a stele, the remains of which sat in front of the pylon.

'The stele inside the 10th Pylon records a declaration by Horemheb designed to restore order in the land.'

Restore order? I may have been mistaken, but, Christ, he was possibly the one responsible for the chaos in the first place: assassinating his father-in-law, the spiritual and political ruler of the country; it was just like Ghandi. It seemed that was just like the Illuminati today, they want something to happen, so they create the problem first then magically have the solution. It was what they did with Pearl Harbor, the Gulf War, 9/11; Christ I must have been getting sun-stroke, I was sounding just like Randy. Time for a drink perhaps.

As I fished out a bottle I scanned the two limestone, yet headless, statues of Ramses II, that also sat in front of the north face of the pylon. The headless statues of Ramses II got me thinking about Jacques: I wondered how he was faring; I bet he was running around like a headless chicken without Pernille. I hoped she didn't change her mind and go back to him, she seemed so much happier with Bill. By now they were probably back at the Winter Palace quaffing pina coladas and planning the rest of their lives together: well, I hoped they were.

I downed the remainder of my second bottle of water in four or five healthy gulps. It was really hot out there in the middle part of the afternoon, more like a furnace. Everything was hot; the sun was hot, the air was hot, the ground was hot, the buildings were hot, I was hot, even the heat was hot. Thankfully my trusty akubra was doing the job keeping the sun from my tender complexion.

The gate in the Tenth Pylon was closed and locked, but through it I could see an avenue of sphinxes leading to the Mut temple complex. There was nothing in particular that drew me to explore it, other than the fact it was closed and off limits to visitors and the fact that in the space of a week or so I'd become a paranoid conspiracy theorist. Besides, it was highly unlikely I was ever going to pass this way again, I had plenty of time, and absolutely no one ever came out to this part of Karnak, so if I could find the guardian, then I was sure a little baksheesh would magically open the lock. And, sure enough, as if the rustle of notes or jangle of coins in my pocket had drawn him from his hiding place, the guardian mystically appeared.

'Closed.'

I shuffled the fingers on one hand; the universal opener for 'What if I cross your palms with silver?'

No language problems there: he looked around to make sure the coast was clear.

'Fifty pound.'

Now, I knew these guys took a bit of a risk letting people through the gates, but that was *in* to the complex, this was to exit, to let me through to outside to where everyone from the village had access. In fact there appeared to be considerable work going on unearthing and restoring the avenue of sphinxes. Eventually I negotiated him down to twenty pound to open the gate, then let me back *in* to the Amun Precinct half-an-hour later via the Khonsu Gate a hundred metres or so to the right. He agreed and, once again, I was off exploring.

Sitting to the east before the outer, or southern, face of the pylon was a plinth, on which stood, according to my notes, or rather would have stood, a massive colossus of Amenhotep III. Alas, only the feet remained.

'This mammoth statue, supposedly the largest royal statue ever erected in Egypt, was carved from a single block of red quartzite. A second plinth exists on the western side of the gate but archaeologists are uncertain whether a pair of colossal statues were ever erected here.'

Were they serious? Since when have the ancient Egyptians done things by halves? They are renowned for their preoccupation with structural symmetry; of course there would have been a second statue. Several questions arose. Firstly, 'Would it have been a second statue of Amenhotep III or a statue of Horemheb?'

My notes said the Egyptologists suggested the western colossus was of Horemheb. But that didn't ring true, because no other massive statues had ever been discovered of Horemheb, in fact I don't think many statues at all had been found of Horemheb. In addition, it was more likely Horemheb did not have access to the knowledge of how to make or transport such large works of art as he was of the Military and not an Amun Priest, and I don't think the Amun Priests were all that keen to help him. Finally, the statues guarding entrances seemed to always occur in pairs, and I think these two statues followed suit. I concluded they were appropriated from before the Eighth Pylon as there were only four colossi there, and there was room for six. It is highly likely that Amenhotep III added a colossus on each end of the pylon in deference to Hatshepsut.

The next question was, 'Where are they now?' My guess was, that unless the massive stones were carried away by subsequent tsunamis to the 1600 BC Thera tsunami, then the Amun Priests, in obliterating all references and connections to the Amenhotep/Akhenaten lineage, smashed them down and simply buried them where they lay.

That meant they were probably under the very avenue of sphinxes before me that had apparently been laid by Horemheb. It was like the Chicago gangsters burying the bodies of their victims in the concrete foundations of newly constructed buildings: in history, only the names change.

There was also the lower part of a huge Osirid statue beside the eastern colossus. Was it possibly of Horemheb, or was it more likely to have been of Ramses II, put there anywhere between thirteen to eighty years later? If it was, what happened to it? Or was it the partner to the Amenhotep III colossus on the opposite side? It seemed the later was the simple answer to that question.

The avenue of sphinxes extended from the Tenth Pylon to the Gate of Ptolemy II, which formed the entrance to the Temple of Mut complex. As I walked the route, I noticed the few sphinxes that were preserved enough to tell, had rams heads, and the cartouches of Horemheb on the base of most of them, and that of Pinedjem I on one.

Towards the end of the path were the ruins of two small temples, located to either side of the avenue of sphinxes. On the eastern side, the ruins of the Temple of Amun-kamutef, and to the west a barque shrine built by Thutmoses III and Hatshepsut, well, more likely built by Hatshepsut and claimed by Thutmoses III. I gave them a quick once over and, having decided there was nothing of great interest, headed for the Mut complex. A lot of restoration has been done here and many of the human-headed sphinxes, bearing the cartouche of Pinedjem I, were in good condition.

The Mut Temple Complex

Given its title, I was fairly confident Ptolemy II Philadelphus, and possibly Ptolemy III Euergetes I, probably built the entrance gate to the complex.

'During the Ptolemaic Period the precinct was given a new main entrance gateway and significant parts of the Mut Temple and the Temple of Khonsupakherod were rebuilt.'

On the eastern doorpost was the relief of a sistrum player, a harpist and a tambourine player standing before Mut on her throne. On the western doorpost was a scene of flowering papyrus emerging from water. But apart from that, there was little else to see, mainly because most of the gateway was missing. It was the same with the precinct of Mut itself: it looked like a bomb had gone off in a graveyard and levelled the place; only tombstones remained.

The enclosure measured about two-hundred-and-fifty by three-hundred-and-fifty metres, and according to my notes 'contained at least six sanctuaries'. I could only find four on my map and wondered if the 'six' included the Temple of Amun-kamutef outside the gate, and a small temple built by Nectanebo II outside of the eastern wall? But, clearly there were more.

'Ptolemies V and VII built a chapel, dedicated to both Mut/Sekhmet and only recently excavated, just inside the Taharqa gateway in the western wall.'

It didn't really matter, I didn't really have the time to thoroughly explore them all anyway, just do a walk through and see if anything jumped out and bit me on the ass.

According to my notes, there seemed some discrepancy as to who built the first temple here.

'Some experts believed the Temple of Mut was primarily built by Amenhotep III, but others propose that it went back to the reigns of Hatshepsut and Thutmoses III when the entire precinct probably consisted of just the Mut Temple and the sacred lake.'

It seemed the sort of thing that Hatshepsut would have built, and Thutmoses III usurped, but maybe its origins went even further back, maybe there was a Middle Kingdom connection as well.

One thing was certain though, having been consolidated in the middle of the 18th Dynasty, later rulers from the New Kingdom and into the Ptolemaic Period also added and enhanced the temple and the surrounding complex.

'By the Ptolemaic Period, it had grown to over twenty acres and included massive mud-brick walls surrounding three large temples, several smaller temples and chapels, and housing for priests and others.'

Time to check it all out.

Immediately ahead of me was a short avenue built by Taharqa in the 25th Dynasty that led to the actual entrance of the Temple of Mut. I decided to save the best until last and do a clockwise circuit of the complex; firstly taking in the Temple of Khonsupakherod, then circle the Sacred Lake to the Temple of Ramses III, and back to the Temple of Mut.

The Temple of Khonsupakherod

Heading left, located in the northeast corner of the complex stood the remains of the Temple of Khonsupakherod, Khonsu, the child of Amun and Mut, who was associated with the moon. There was some conjecture this temple was originally built by Amenhotep III, however, perhaps, like the Temple of Mut, it was also built by

Hatshepsut? It would make sense to build both temples at the same time: one to the mother, the other to the son. That made me think that they could also have been built when the original Amun Temple was built: but that would take a lot more investigation. Whenever it was built, it must have been important because it got the attention of Ramses II.

'It was renovated and expanded in the 19th Dynasty by Ramses II, who made the building a "temple of millions of years", adding a forecourt, a pylon, two colossal granite statues of himself, two colossal alabaster stelae proclaiming his achievements, and dedicating the temple to himself and Amun-Re.'

Nothing above a few feet tall seemed to have survived. Was it more evidence of tsunamis? I know some of the stones had been pillaged to build other structures in and around the complex over the three-and-a-half-thousand years or so, but there had to be another reason to account for the devastation I was witnessing before me.

On the way to the entrance, to the left, I passed the remnants of a headless, legless colossus lying lonely and helpless, like it had just stepped on a landmine.

Next was the remains of a large alabaster stela of Ramses II, Ramses II on which, according to my notes, 'his marriage to a Hittite princess is reported'.

Passing through what remained of the first pylon, I noticed a representation of the god Bes in the thickness of the doorjamb. The more I looked at this quirky little troll the more I was convinced the ancient Egyptians could not possibly have made him up, he had to be an actual being. The body morphology was very dwarf-like however the anatomy of the head was more ape-like. Was this creature a 'predecessor' of the human race? If so, the questions was, 'From whence did he come?'

That led me to consider the other gods: Osiris had green skin, Ptah's skin was blue, Hathor and Isis were mostly depicted with yellow skin, and then there was Anubis the jackal, Sobek the Crocodile, Hapi the hippopotamus, Horus the falcon-headed god, and of course Thoth, who was either depicted as a baboon or an ibis. I could accept that there was a certain amount of associating certain gods with certain human characteristics, and with the representation in certain animals, but only some of it, not all. There had to be some extra-terrestrial aspect to explain it better.

Inside the remains of the first court were numerous seated damaged statues of Sekhmet regularly spaced around the perimeter. I was a bit stunned actually: there were more statues in and around this complex than in any of the previous temples I had visited.

'Most Egyptologists believe that most if not all of these statues originally stood in the mortuary temple of Amenhotep III on the West Bank. They were probably brought to the Mut precinct during the 19th Dynasty when Mut and Sekhmet became more closely associated.'

Apparently, most of the statues of Sekhmet standing in the museums of the world were removed from this temple.

The first court appeared typically to have been colonnaded, and before each column stood a black granite statue of Sekhmet. There were even more Sekhmets in the second, smaller court, which had the bases of square-shaped pillars and also had numerous black granite statues of seated pharaohs. There were statues of Sekhmet everywhere, in varying states of repair, each one different in its own way, particularly in the variation of the headgear of the goddess from one statue to another.

Some, like the statue in the Temple of Ptah, had the solar disk atop their head. Others were seated on a low cuboid throne and had a more archaic facial and general appearance. The third group had a round cake-tin made up of uraeus cobras side by side around it.

'They embody the triple aspects the goddess could take:
Mut – Sekhmet – Eye of Re.'

The more I focused on Sekhmet, the more I was convinced there was a lot more to who she was, or even *what* she was. Then I realized that ever since I had 'seen' her in the Temple of Ptah, the spectres of the Amun Priests had been gone from Karnak. Well, maybe not gone, but they had left me alone. Was that because of her? Oh, I wished Crystal was here, she would know. I made a point to quiz her on it later. And what about all those black granite statues!

In amongst them were several seated statues of pharaohs: but statues of whom? Ramses II perhaps? No, far too small for him. Amenhotep III? Possibly. Thutmoses III? Maybe. But that means they would have been usurped from Hatshepsut, and that wasn't clearly visible. They had to be earlier, but how earlier? And all that granite, and yet the temples were made of sandstone? Something didn't add up, perhaps the answers were somewhere else in the complex.

In the far right corner of the courtyard were the ruins of a small chapel supposedly built by the 30th Dynasty pharaoh, Nectanebo I, and dedicated to Nitocris, God's wife of Amun. I wasn't completely sure but I think Crystal listed Nitocris as one of her past lives in Egypt. Nectanebo I had built a number of chapels throughout Upper Egypt, most memorably the one at Philae, and it appears he had a part in the restoration or enlargement here of the Temple of Khonsupakherod.

The second pylon seemed to have been constructed, in part, from the feet, torsos and heads of colossal statues.

'The stone was harvested from colossi that once stood in
the court of Ramses III's temple which was apparently no longer
in use.'

Nearby was the discarded cadaver: a headless, half buried colossus similar to the one laying on the ground that first greeted me.

Ok, who would have 'rebuilt' the temple at some time after Ramses III and been irreverent enough to carve up and dismember his statues to do the extensions? Simple: the Amun Priests of the 21st Dynasty. And of the 21st Dynasty Amun Priest pharaohs, Pinedjem I seemed to be the culprit, as his name was scrawled over several sphinxes and elsewhere around the site.

Ahead, I was drawn to yet another Osirian colossus, this one attached to a stela and leaning against the remains of a wall. Examining it, I discovered the edge carried the titles of Ramses II and that the vertical inscription that descended beneath the two crossed arms of the pharaoh had been overwritten.

'The origin cartouche belonged to Djehutymes /
Menkheperure, (Thutmoses IV) but had been overwritten by that
of Ramses II, superimposed in the reverse direction. The

inscription goes on to read, "King of Upper and Lower Egypt, master of the Two Lands, usermaatre Setepenre, Son of Ra". A second inscription reads, "Neter-nefer, master of the Two Lands, Menkheperre, Son of Ra, of his breast, Thutmoses IV, endowed with eternal life".'

It seemed Ramses II had claimed this statue as his own, and he in turn was about to have his ownership 'cut short' by Pinedjem I when something prevented it from suffering the same fate as those of his son, Ramses III.

Had I read anything about the *real* politics of ancient Egypt before? No, the Archaeologists were too busy with their heads in the sand, and the Egyptologist were too busy going with the flow. There was lots of guess work about who built what and when, but without understanding the politics and incorporating that into the actual physical evidence, then the picture that emerged of ancient Egypt was a very romanticized one. That may have been great for the throngs of snap-happy tourists who didn't see anything beyond the surface, but the reality was it was all a load of bullshit; the real history was proving to be far more interesting, and far far more controversial.

Moving on, through the remnants of the Hypostyle hall, littered with the scattered bases of its fluted columns, it reminded me of some of the ruins on the west bank and of those at El Kab. I was now so convinced of the Thera tsunami theory that I was doing exactly what the Egyptologists were doing, treating it as fact. The difference was, everywhere I looked, I saw more and more evidence supporting it.

All I wanted now was for some curious and interested geologist to dig a few twenty-to-thirty-metre deep holes in a few key locations up and down the Nile to examine the layers of soil and sand to see if there was any evidence of seashells, or Mediterranean marine life.

Amongst the 'rubble', I firstly discovered the remains of an alabaster stela, whose arch portrayed the figures of the Theban triad Amun, Mut and Khonsu, then an alabaster block of four baboons in worship before the rising sun.

That got me thinking Middle Kingdom again, not just the fact they were made of alabaster, but especially the presence of the baboons.

Heading on into the inner sanctum, it was very easy to make out the three inner chambers. On the walls, or on stones on the ground, were a few colourful painted reliefs, mainly of groups of gods, a rather rare effigy of Anubis, one of Mut in her form of vulture, and birth scenes of the pharaoh and Khonsu.

On the northern wall was the bottom half of an unusual scene depicting a circumcision ceremony. Flicking through my notes I found a quote from Herodotus around 400 BC.

"The ancient Egyptians have adopted circumcision in their search for cleanliness, and appear to think more highly of a perfect physical purity than any other adornment."

It was an interesting quote for two reasons: firstly, was circumcision merely done for an extreme of cleanliness, or was it to signify a rite of passage, or possibly even a sign of the lineage to the gods, to the *sang réal*, a practice reserved strictly for royalty. If the later was the case, then it had implication as to why the Jews still practiced circumcision, because they believed they were the chosen race. And that went back to Moses/Joseph and his upbringing in Egypt with the royal family.

Secondly, from whom did the ancient Egyptians adopt the practice of circumcision? Was it from the eastern invaders, the Hykos, of the 15th and 16th Dynasties? If the ancient Egyptians practiced circumcision as a matter of course *prior* to the Hyksos invasion, they would hardly take the trouble to represent it in a relief. However, if it was some new ritualistic practice introduced by the priests of the east then it would make perfect sense to represent it on the wall of the inner sanctum. Putting two and two together, it totally supported a Middle Kingdom connection to the location. Time to head around the lake to the Temple of Ramses III.

I was parched, and the proximity of the lake spurred me into cracking the seal on my final bottle of water. I wasn't concerned I would collapse of dehydration, but, still, I took a few measured mouthfuls just to ensure I wouldn't have to buy another bottle at cut-throat prices back at the shops near the visitors' centre.

The Sacred Lake, or to give the lake its proper name, Isheru, which is a term used to describe sacred lakes specific to precincts of goddesses who can be leonine in form, such as Sekhmet, surrounded the Temple of Mut on three sides. It was pretty clear from its kidney or horseshoe shape that the lake was not a naturally occurring body of water, rather it was constructed specifically the way it is, and where it is, wrapped around the Mut temple. The water looked pretty rancid; horrid and grungy, but, at one time it would have been fresh as there were apparently once fish in the lake. That meant it was probably fed by either an underground spring or an underground connection to the Nile.

On the other side of the lake, to the west, were the remains of the Temple of Ramses III. Almost gone, like the Temple of Khonsupakherod, it would also once have been outside the current precinct's walls.

'The temple has the same plan as the Ramses III's temple in the Amun precinct.'

I wasn't interested before, and, given the state of the ruins here, I hadn't changed my view. So, quickly moving through the ruins from the back and out through the entrance, I paid scant acknowledgement to the two headless colossi of the pharaoh with his queen standing in front of the entrance, which had probably been decapitated to provide stone for the Temple of Khonsupakherod, and set my sights on the main focus of the complex.

The Temple of Mut

Mut, the consort of Amun-Re, and mother of Khonsu, like many other goddesses, had both a human and a feline form. In her human guise, she was a protective mother. But, as the lioness-headed Sekhmet, she was a fierce defender of Egypt who could turn against humankind if angered. And it was here, in the Temple of Mut, she was most revered.

'The temple dates back to a possible Middle Kingdom foundation, however a more imposing structure was built by Hatshepsut in the 18th Dynasty.'

I wondered what evidence existed of the Middle Kingdom temple for the experts to make such a statement. But, what ever it was, it confirmed that something had happened to the 'old' temple that necessitated Hatshepsut to instigate a rebuilding process.

'Amenhotep III rebuilt the temple of Mut in sandstone, furnishing it with hundreds of statues of the goddess Mut in her leonine shape of Sekhmet (it is thought 720 or 730, one for every day of the year, morning and evening).'

There was of course another possibility; that the hundreds of black granite statues already existed on or around the Mut site, and had been there since the Middle Kingdom, and that Amenhotep simply removed several to his temple on the west bank.

That made more sense to me; that Amenhotep would acquire several statues to bring Sekhmet's special protection to his own temple. As for Amenhotep III's need to rebuild the temple, it may have been necessary due to the overzealous efforts of Thutmoses III and his Amun Priests.

'Later, Ramses II restored the building.'

'Remodelled it' and claimed it to satisfy his massive ego, more like it. Right, I'd had enough 'history'; it was time to see the temple for myself.

Facing north towards the Temple of Amun, the first pylon of the Mut temple, like the second pylon of the Amun complex, was preceded by a Kiosk of Taharqa. In the foundations of the two long-columned porticoes that remained were blocks containing reliefs and inscriptions that dated from the 18th through 20th Dynasties. Clearly they had most likely been harvested from the Ramses III temple.

The temple's first pylon was more like a wall that surrounded the temple and appeared to have been constructed primarily of mud-brick, replacing what would have been the earlier northern precinct wall. The gateway itself was constructed of stone and contained several texts as well as another relief of Bes

'In the remains of the entrance pylon, which was built by Seti II, there is a relief of the dwarf-god Bes and Ptolemaic texts of a Hymn to Mut.'

So, the pylon was built in the 19th Dynasty but had been repaired, with extra text added, by the Ptolemaic pharaohs, possibly Ptolemy II.

It was followed by a wide courtyard with the bases of two rows of four columns running down the centre, forming what would have been a covered walkway. The periphery of the external wall of the courtyard was again lined with numerous statues of Sekhmet that had been dedicated, or rather 'claimed', by various individuals, including Ramses II, Pinedjem, but most bearing the name of Amenhotep III.

'Each revealed a different inscription, such as, "Sekhmet, beloved of Ptah", "Sekhmet, mistress of the western desert", "Sekhmet in the house of Bastet", "Sekhmet the great" and "Sekhmet, beloved of Sobek".'

Like the first pylon, the second was also initially built of mud-brick, possibly part of an earlier precinct or temple wall, lined on the southern side by stone blocks.

'It was probably Ramses II who added a stone facing to the south side of the temples' mud brick second pylon.'

Of course he did, he wanted his temples, and his name, to live on forever. And blow me down he'd been pretty successful so far. I was guessing what remained of the further alterations and stonework probably occurred as part of the Ptolemaic restorations.

Exploring the ruins of the second, inner courtyard, I discovered even more Sekhmet statues, these situated before what would have been a colonnade of Hathor-headed columns. There were a few reliefs on the walls and, according to my notes, they were courtesy of ....you guessed it, Ramses II.

'Ramses II added new inscriptions and reliefs to the walls of the second court.'

Beyond the second court were the remains of a small hypostyle court, flanked by two chapels, which led to the inner sanctuary, in turn surrounded by a number of smaller chambers. Looking back towards the entrance, I could make out the floor plan, but there was little left of any statues, altars, niches or wall decorations.

A tiny elongated room, entered from before the lake, was tacked on to the rear of the main temple. It appeared to have been subdivided into three sections and my notes referred to it as an "Addorsed Temple", whatever that was.

I tried to work it out, but its badly ruined condition precluded me from discerning any specific detailed knowledge of its original form, decoration, or even its function. All that I could discern was that its addition must have had something to do with a more recent discovery at the site.

Apparently Archaeologists had found a 'porch of drunkenness', associated with Hatshepsut and erected at the height of her reign. The 'porch' was supposedly erected for one of ancient Egypt's most raucous rituals: the 'Festival of Drunkenness'.

'The festival was held during the first month of the year, just after the first flooding of the Nile. It re-enacted the myth in which the bloodthirsty Sekhmet nearly destroyed all humans, but the sun god Re tricked her into drinking mass quantities of ochre-coloured beer, thinking it was blood. Once Sekhmet passed out, she was transformed into a kinder, gentler goddess named Hathor, and humanity was saved.'

I was really taking a shine to Hatshepsut, not only was she a confident dildo-toting fully self-empowered women, but she was also a proponent of free-love and self-expression. I wondered if this small room was Hatshepsut's aforementioned 'porch', or perhaps the porch was another area I'd just spotted off to the east that was adorned with more statues of Sekhmet. If it was, then perhaps the Addorsed Temple was the bar, or where they stored the beer?

'The discoveries at the Temple of Mut parallel other historical references to drunken rituals during Egypt's Ptolemaic-Roman period. Some of the inscriptions uncovered here also link the festival with "travelling through the marshes", an ancient Egyptian euphemism for having sex. The sexual connection is further reinforced by graffiti depicting men and women in various sexual positions.'

I couldn't find *any* reliefs, let alone any pornographic graffiti; they had probably been removed by various 'expeditions' in the past.

'During the "Festival of Drunkenness" people come together in a community to drink huge quantities of beer made from fermented barley bread. They get absolutely knee-walkingly drunk, indulge in gratuitous sex, pass out, then wake up the next morning with the sound of music blaring and their friends praying that everything will turn out all right. Herodotus reported in 440 B.C. that such festivals drew as many as 700,000 people.'

Now that was a concept I could really handle: instead of all these tree-hugging, feather-waving, New-Age, Om-chanting gurus praying to Christ Consciousness or some disconnected higher-power extra-terrestrial 'angels' to come and save the planet and humanity, lets just all get pie-eyed pissed and fuck the brains out of each other in a senseless million-strong orgy of hedonistic self-expression. It was ancient Egypt's version of the Roman orgy, the hippie movement's 'love in', and a modern frat and sorority party of sex drugs and rock 'n' roll all rolled into one.

I started thinking that if Diane was Hatshepsut, then what else went on in her Goddess Circles? That was enough to get my imagination more than fired up, and me eager to move on and reconnect with them all.

I was nearly out of the complex when my eye spotted a curious but familiar shape sticking up out of the ground. I don't know how I hadn't seen it before, but now it drew me to it like a magnet. Like a leprous zombie, the half-buried faceless statue of a pharaoh was emerging from the ground. Made of timeworn red granite, I'd seen this type of statue before, positioned off to the side at Esna, having been dug up from beneath the level of the temple. I'd also seen this type and condition of stone before, in the columns and blocks randomly positioned in the surrounding grounds at both Philae and Esna.

Extending half way up the back of the statue was a narrow seat-back, telling me that beneath the ground the rest of the figure was seated: this was a throne very similar to the one used in reliefs and representations of Isis. There were the remains of some hieroglyphs on the seat back but they were too damaged to distinguish or determine anything of any note.

This was a major clue, in more ways than one; this statue was clearly much older than the alabaster stela or the baboons, or the colossi of Ramses II or anything else here. This went back far further than the Middle Kingdom. I was now betting these statues belonged to the Old Kingdom or even earlier. And if that were true, then it cast a completely different shadow over the history of not only the Temple of Mut, but also the whole Karnak site.

Leaving the Mut Precinct, I headed westwards down another short avenue of sphinxes to where it intersected with the main avenue that ran three kilometres all the way from the Luxor temple to Karnak. Or did it run the other direction, from Karnak to Luxor?

There are some Egyptologists who would suggest it may have been Tutankhamun who initiated this avenue, that the sphinxes had rams heads added to the bodies and a statuette of Tutankhamun placed between the paws. I briefly examined a few sphinxes but couldn't see that being the case. Maybe I had more information in my files.

'The latest research shows that the original heads of the crio-sphinxes had been human, with remains having been identified as portraying Akhenaten and Nefertiti, shown in equal size, making them unique, and that the sphinxes may have been transported from the Temple of Aten to the east of Karnak, since a possible processional way has been found there.'

Now, that I would have liked to see. Turning north and back towards the Amun Precinct, I couldn't help but think there was so much here at Karnak yet to be uncovered, not just physically, but more importantly, historically.

The road was lined with statues of seated rams larger than the crio-sphinxes of the other avenues and each bearing the cartouche of Pinedjem I on its plinth. That didn't mean the ram on top belonged to Pinedjem I.

'The rams are known to be the work of Amenhotep III, perhaps being brought from the Mut Precinct where other similar ram statues have been found.'

Just before I reached the gate I noticed a large curved excavation behind the western line of rams. It was an ancient embankment for the Nile, even more evidence of a much higher water level in the past, and that Karnak once sat on the banks of the Nile. If that was the case, then it was also strong evidence and reason to believe that almost every other temple would have been built on the banks of the Nile as well.

That was totally supported by what I had seen on the west bank, and a great explanation for the level of the devastation caused by a tsunami, or series of tsunamis, that swept up the Nile around 1600 BC.

Thankfully the guardian was true to his word and waiting for me at the Khonsu gate to let me back into the main Amun Precinct. I must have been totally in another world because I tipped him another twenty pound just for doing what we had already agreed to, and for what I had already paid him. From that moment I think I became his best friend forever and he wanted to marry me off to his youngest daughter, who, if she took after her father, probably looked like a hawk-nosed anorexic camel with rancid breath and rotted teeth: though I had to admit I would have been loved and respected by him and his wife, which is more than I could say about my relationship with my previous in-laws.

I started thinking if perhaps they were descended from Amun Priests, as they'd stabbed me in the back more times than Julius Caesar got knifed on the steps of the Senate. If there was blood spilled during the divorce, I had to admit most of it was mine and it dripped from their hands and their daughters'.

But now that seemed another lifetime ago and as I walked through the Khonsu gate, the Gate of Euergetes (Ptolemy III), I noted it looked very similar in structure to the Gate of Ptolemy on Philae. But that's where the similarity ended, as the decorations and detail on the interior of the gate here were stunning.

However, although they were initially very impressive, to be honest, unless the gateway was made of either alabaster, or red or black granite, I hardly gave it more than a cursory glance.

I did however take note of the extraordinary height of the doorway; that it would be totally in keeping with the passage necessary for a being who was perhaps fourteen to sixteen feet tall.

Leaving the gate behind me, I stood before the Temple of Khonsu, with the smaller Temple of Opet to its left, and my newly acquired father-in-law to my right. I decided to check out the larger Temple of Khonsu first and he willingly led the way.

The Temple of Khonsu

Supposedly built by Ramses III, the Temple of Khonsu looked almost complete and in pretty good condition. The reality was, that although Ramses III made claim to the construction of the temple, he merely began it.

'Only the seven small chapels surrounding the four-columned hall behind the sanctuary of the Hall of the Barque were completed during the reign of Ramses III and bear his cartouches. Even by the end of the reign of Ramses IV only the inner parts of the shrine were completed. Hence the temple continued to be renewed, using stones from other temples, well up to and including the Roman era.'

Despite all that, according to the 'experts', it was a perfect example of a New Kingdom temple, and that meant, given it was also on a north-south axis, I wasn't expecting to find anything of interest.

Fronting the temple, flanked on both sides by the remnants of a row of sphinxes, were the bases of a colonnade. According to their dedications, it, and the pylon that followed, were constructed, by the High-Priests Herihor and Pinedjem I, early pharaohs of the 21st Dynasty.

The pylon, built in the now usual paired-structure joined by a central gateway, was over thirty-metres wide, around twenty-metres high, and about seven-metres deep; tiny compared to Edfu.

'The reliefs covering the two wings of the pylon represent scenes of worship by Pinedjem, with the divine wife of Amun, Maatkare, Pinedjem's daughter, represented alone on the east wing and Maatkare and Henuttawy, Pinedjem's wife, worshiping Hathor on the west wing.'

Parts of the cornices around the doorway also bore the cartouches of one of the Ptolemies.

Heading through the pylon, the peristyle court that followed was bordered by a portico of twenty-eight identical columns, four pairs of two on each side, and two groups of six at the far end set upon a slightly elevated platform.

'Towards the rear of the peristyle court are columns that are presumed to have been taken from the great funerary temple of Amenhotep III on the west bank by Herihor some time after the reign of Ramses XI as the complete royal titulary of Herihor is all over the shafts of the columns.'

That was interesting: Ramses XI was the last pharaoh of the 20th Dynasty and Herihor the first of the 21st-Dynasty Amun Priests.

It confirmed my thoughts about the 21st-Dynasty Amun Priests not only claiming everything from the military dynasties that preceded them, but also their willingness to destroy the memory of the Amenhotep lineage, even after two-hundred-and-forty-odd years, which is interesting in itself considering that the High-Priests were commissioned with protecting the funerary monuments on the West Bank at ancient Thebes. Yeah, right, them, and the tombs in the Valley of the Kings.

At the rear of the peristyle court was a doorway, dedicated to Ptolemy IV Philopator, that opened onto a small hypostyle hall with eight columns; four similar columns in the middle about seven metres high, and two monostyle columns just under six metres to either side.

'All of the texts on the architraves of both the large and small columns are those of Menmaatre Setepenamun, Ramses XI, who is said to have built this hall.'

Though it had architraves and cornices similar to those in the great Hypostyle Hall in the Temple of Amun, the hall here was nowhere near as the impressive as that of Ramses II.

Just inside the doorway and to the left I discovered another statue similar to the one in the small chamber to the south of the Akh-Menu. I thought perhaps this one would reveal more of its secrets, but alas it was impossible to make out what it could have been: it looked more like an abstract from a modern 20th Century sculptor. I looked for an signs of reptilian vestiges, but to no avail. It was a mystery; that was for sure. What I could guess at was it was made of a sort of orangey-brown alabaster. The more I looked at it, the more I was convinced this belonged to a time way before Ramses III, more than likely to at least the Middle Kingdom, but possibly even earlier.

My thoughts were supported by the statue in the next gap between the columns; an extremely worn legless, but seated figure carved from red granite. Neither of the two statues belonged were they had been placed, or even in the temple.

Someone had even stuck a small baboon statue of Djehuty, Thoth, unceremoniously between two of the eastern columns. I was going to just walk straight passed it, until I saw the sun's rays illuminating the head and realized it was made of red granite.

It didn't belong here either, that was for sure. So where did it come from? Clearly it had been pilfered from another, earlier temple, but which one? The logical response was an older temple, perhaps the Temple of Opet right next door, but the truth was it could have been nicked from anywhere. It was getting hard to believe not only anything that I read about ancient Egypt, but anything that I saw as well.

That made me contemplate how mindlessly we accept the bullshit that is fed to us through the media; the papers, the television stations. Most of us let a handful of people, editors and producers, decide what is news for us, and what do we get - murders, riots, crashes, war, disease; death and destruction at every turn. All of it selected to keep us believing the world is a dangerous place to live in and that we can't trust anyone. I was with Randy on that one, there *was* a conspiracy, a conspiracy to keep the masses like mushrooms – in the dark and fed with tons of bullshit.

The guardian led me from the Hypostyle Hall into a column-less chamber known as the Hall of the Barque. The upper blocks and walls of the room were inscribed in numerous deeply-carved reliefs of Ramses IV; making offerings to Amun, Mut and Khonsu, being nurtured by Isis, purified by Thoth and Horus, and blessed by Mut. Some of the reliefs had been carved over older ones, either over Ramses IV's immediate predecessor, Ramses III, or more likely over the pharaoh from whose temple he 'appropriated' the stones.

In the centre of the room were the remains of a sanctuary made of sandstone, though there was a square vertical of red granite that could have been part of an original sanctuary either on this site, or relocated here from an older temple, possibly the Temple of Opet next door. In either case, clearly the priests hadn't passed-on the significance of the red granite to Ramses III.

To each side of the room was a small chapel, the eastern one with a staircase situated in the southeast corner. A relief of an upside-down chariot above the top of the stairs showed the extent to which stone from earlier buildings had been used in completing the temple. Although the stairs were gated and locked my faithful father-in-law to be graciously unlocked it and ushered me to the roof.

'Here, atop the temple, in a sun chapel, the "hour priests" would have recorded the movements of the sun, to ensure that the temple rituals were performed at the exact hour.'

That the temple rituals were performed at the exact hour was debatable, but the roof did provide an excellent panorama of the surrounding area of Karnak. Row after row of blocks, temple and statue fragments, stretched out across the precinct. I imagined three ten-thousand-piece jigsaw puzzles all mixed up together, and no box lids to tell you what the images were. I guess the Egyptologists had some idea, based on other temple sites in Egypt, but one thing was sure, progress in reconstruction was slower than a sleepy snail on Valium.

Returning to the ground level, the sanctuary of the barque led in turn through a doorway, constructed, or perhaps claimed, during the Ptolemaic period, to a pronaos, or inner sanctuary. The inner sanctuary contained four polygonal columns equally spaced around the centre of the room, each with a cylindrical bottom and slightly fluted at the top.

Between the posterior pair stood an altar. My first impressions were that it was vastly inferior to those I had seen elsewhere in the other temples, so I examined it closely, mainly to see if was made of red granite. It wasn't. I wasn't sure what it *was* made of, probably some type of red sandstone: again, where was Bill when you needed him?

The room also provided access to seven small chapels: two to each side and three chambers to the north, all built and decorated by Ramses III and bearing his cartouche. The rooms were currently being restored, however, as there was no one there, and, with my new faithful best-friend-forever beside me, locked doors were no obstacle.

Each room was dedicated to a separate deity; the south-eastern room dedicated to Ptah, Amun to the northwest, the central one for Khonsu, and the one in the northeast corner with a representation of Osiris, lying dead on a bier, Isis and Nephthys mourning on either side. While some rooms were faded and in fair condition, in many places the original colour was still present and in excellent condition. The reliefs were almost as good as the best I'd seen in the Valley of the Kings.

So, the question was, how was it that these reliefs survived relatively unscathed, while all the others here at Karnak copped a shellacking? The first possibility was that the tsunamis and flooding were *pre* Ramses III. That would explain all the 18th Dynasty damage, but not the later damage that occurred to the 26th to 30th Dynasties that needed to be repaired by the Ptolemaic pharaohs. So I quickly dismissed that option; time wasn't the issue.

It had to be the location of the temple itself, south of the main temple. If the main temple and outer wall acted somewhat as a storm wall, a sea-break, deflecting and diluting the effect of a tsunami, then it could possibly explain why this temple was not only relatively intact, but also why the interior wall decorations escaped any massive damage.

That meant the damage to the surrounding area could have occurred anytime between the completion of the temple by Ramses III's immediate successors, and its restoration by the Ptolemaic rulers eight-hundred years later. But it seemed to be pointing to a time after the visits by Herodotus around 400 BC and the arrival of Alexander the Great in 332 BC.

That just threw another curly spanner into the works. What the hell *was* the true history of Ancient Egypt? Would anyone ever really find out the truth? And, if they did, would they share it with the rest of the world if it were in conflict with what the mainstream population and religious fanatics believed, or were willing and ready to believe? I doubted it; I doubted it severely.

In one of the eastern rooms, the guardian showed me where work was being done to restore reliefs that existed on the wall *below* the floor level. That meant one of two things, either the floor had been added as an after-thought, or, there was an existing structure underneath. In the shadows of the room, I couldn't make out which was more likely, but it certainly added to my list of unanswered questions.

One final relief caught my attention, it was one of Sekhmet being offered an anointing oil or liquid of some description, and, in the other hand, something that looked like white powder on a spoon. Was this an offering of mono-atomic gold? Or was this even Sekhmet? The figure not only had very masculine looking legs and chest, but a rather obvious erect penis. Did this mean Sekhmet had a masculine counterpart, or was this a representation of something else all together? Was this a representation of a connection between fertility and mono-atomic gold?

I was tempted to spend a few minutes trying to put the pieces together, but I didn't want my new father-in-law to start thinking his son-in-law-to-be was some sort of weirdo, perving at an androgynous looking lion god/goddess with an erect penis, so I nodded my appreciation and we exited the inner sanctum area and made our way back out of the temple.

'Good, yes?'

'Yes, very good.'

I took out some water to top the tank and offered some to the guardian, who politely declined. However, he was rather keen to get some additional baksheesh for the guided tour. Quenching my thirst, I looked back at the Khonsu temple and decided to push my luck, pointing left of the temple to the ruins of another building I presumed to be the Temple of Opet.

'It is open, I can see?'

I gathered Pop wasn't so eager to let me in there, as a concerned look came over his face. He looked around, perhaps part of the performance, then held up a hand.

'Please, to wait.'

I nodded and watched as he headed off towards the western wall.

The Temple of Opet

'The hippopotamus goddess, Opet, also known as Apet, Ipet or Ipy, was venerated as a helper of women in childbirth. Her rather odd little temple was primarily built during the Ptolemaic Period by Ptolemy VIII Euergetes II.'

At first I wondered if Opet was also connected to Hapi, the hippopotamus god, as well. It made sense; perhaps Opet was simply the feminine aspect of Hapi? Then I thought, 'was the temple *really* built by Ptolemy VIII, or like many other temples in ancient Egypt, was it *re*built by him?'

If Ptolemy VII built the Temple of Opet, then he picked a dam stupid location for it, right beside and at right angles to the Temple of Khonsu, with its backdoor almost abutting the first pylon of the Khonsu temple. No, he must have re-built it.

So that means there was some original temple here, that was ruined by some event, and the tsunami fitted the bill there, then the Temple of Khonsu was built sometime between the Thera eruption at the end of the 17th Dynasty and the Ptolemaic period. After that, Ptolemy VIII came along and rebuilt the original Opet temple. Which meant he rebuilt what would have been the original temple on its original axis, which just happened to be the same as that of the Temple of Amun, the Temple of Ptah, the Osireion of Taharqa, even the Temple of Khonsupakherod. All the others were on the north-south axis. Wait a minute; there had to be some reason for that.

Almost everyone knew the ancient Egyptians were preoccupied with the stars and planetary alignments. The old temples all seemed to be aligned slightly off east-west. Was that because of an alignment with the rising and setting of the sun, or with some other celestial object, like Sirius, as some researchers would suggest?

I would have to take into account the precession of the planet earth around its 25,920-year cycle to trace back which temple aligned with which object at what time in the past, but I was guessing with an astronomical computer program it could easily be done. That reminded me about the alignment of Karnak: going way back before even the 1st Dynasty. Something wasn't adding up, or rather, lining up.

Why were the other temples on the north-south access? Sure, at Karnak they may have run out of room in front of the complex because of the river Nile, but maybe there was another reason. A north-south axis would mean the sun filled the temple with light from the east or west for most of the day, which might account for the 'windows' in the ceiling of the Hypostyle hall. But then maybe the windows were just functional in terms of air conditioning?

Maybe once the military rulers took over at the end of the 18th Dynasty with Horemheb, the Amun Priests withheld their astronomical knowledge and the significance of aligning the temple with the rising of certain stars? Hence the new north-south axis of pylons seven to ten, which interestingly also moved the earlier temples before the seventh pylon, that may well have run parallel on the east-west axis with the Temple of Amun, to positions between the Ninth and Tenth Pylons and on a north-south axis.

Any minor variations, those by a few degrees or so, could easily be accounted for by 'precession', thousands of years would simply translate as slight diversions from the axis of the previous temples. I wondered if this concept could be used to accurately date each and every temple in Egypt? Surely one of the experts has done that, right? Maybe not. I was no expert, but surely it was worth a try to see if it correlated.

But what about the major variations, how could you account for them: was there a bigger explanation right under my nose? At then it hit me: the pole-shift. If what Pieter was saying was true, then the crust of the earth would shift and rotate like a ball and socket joint anything from one to a hundred-and-eighty degrees in either direction.

If Africa was the oldest, thickest and most stable landmass, then it would basically act as the pivot point. Hell, it meant that if the crust rotated ninety degrees then temples that were once aligned north-south would now appear east-west, and vica-versa. If the pole-shift was one-hundred-and-eighty degrees, then the temples would have once been west-east, not east-west. Hell, the 'experts' may be lining up the temples with completely the wrong part of the sky.

I took a second look at the Opet temple, it may have been small but it must have been important because it was aligned east-west and had its own entrance gate in the perimeter wall, from which Pop was returning.

'Yes, we go, but must be careful.'

He led me initially passed the Opet temple to the western gate, all the time scouting the horizon like an Indian scout.

'Gate of Nectanebo, Dynasty Thirty.'

And what a gate it was, over six metres high at its outer frame with a passage about twice that in length, on which were numerous scenes depicting the 30th Dynasty pharaoh, Nectanebo I, making offerings of wine to the gods.

From the entrance he led me to the remains of a kiosk, a pylon, then two courtyards, the first of which had a second ruined kiosk. Next was the main body of the Opet temple that, unlike the sections before it, appeared completely intact and built atop a raised platform.

'The main temple building has several crypts hidden within its walls as well as larger ones built beneath ground level which served as a "tomb" for Amun-Osiris, a birth chamber, and as repositories for the equipment used in the Festival of the Resurrection of the god.'

Crypts that 'served as a tomb for Amun-Osiris' and 'The equipment used in the Festival of the Resurrection of the god'? That certainly got my attention; not only could there be a physical remnant of one of the gods who created the human race, but also part of the equipment the gods used to regenerate their bodies.

Perhaps the answers were buried under the temple, much as they had been with the Essenes and the Temple of Solomon in Jerusalem? It wasn't going to be that easy to dig them up however, as access to the main temple via its raised doorway was out of the question, partly because the staircase that would have led up to it was missing, but mainly because the entrance was locked with a barred gate.

To the side was a smaller gate and I was pretty sure Pops had a key, but I decided to leave the best until last, and skirted around the north wall.

The exterior of the building seemed adorned with reliefs primarily involving the Roman emperor, Augustus, who, having disposed of Julius Caesar and then been indirectly responsible for the death of Cleopatra and Marc Anthony, not only seized rule of Egypt, but obviously this temple. Why *this* temple, why not the others?

On the east end of the wall, introduced by Augustus, wearing a blue helmet on top and the crown of the North on the bottom, was a list of the provinces, or nomes, of Upper Egypt and Lower Egypt carved on the two tiers. On the lower register, Hapi, the symbol of the basin on his head, and a kneeling female figure, both bore the emblems of Lower Egypt, or the "flooded land". The upper tier proved far more interesting.

'Each nome is preceded by its particular god, the first being Ptah, symbolizing the first nome of Upper Egypt, "the White Wall", where the triad of Ptah-Sekhmet-Nefertum and the great deified sage, Imhotep, son of Ptah, were worshipped. The second nome, preceded by Horus, symbolized Letopolis, where the nape of Osiris's neck is preserved. While the scapula became symbolic of the second nome, the right leg, was symbolic of the third nome where Hathor was the principal goddess. A part of the dismembered body of Osiris was worshiped in each nome.'

Was this a burying place of one of the dismembered parts of Osiris? If so, what part, and what nome was Karnak? Perhaps the answer awaited inside and underground in one of the crypts?

I headed down a narrow alleyway, that separated the east façade of the Opet temple from the northeast corner of the first pylon of the Khonsu temple, and found an entrance in the back of the Opet temple. Low down, on either side of the doorway, were more reliefs of Augustus, wearing the red crown on the right and the white crown on the left, presenting an offering platter filled with vases and vegetables to Osiris. Behind him on both sides, Hapi wore on his head the symbolic flowers of reeds on the south and papyrus on the north. And there, above the doorway, was the winged-disk of Nibiru.

The door provided access directly into a small room with a niche in the rear wall. There were reliefs of Thoth in his baboon form and I wondered if the statue of Djehuty in the Khonsu temple next door would sit quite comfortably here. Or did the priests sit here? Maybe there was a secret sliding door, now sealed with concrete, that once allowed access to the main temple beyond the walls? Perhaps the answers were within the Temple of Opet itself?

Pop led me back around to the small gate, had a final scan of the land, then unlocked the gate and hastened for me to enter. I realized why he was edgy as there was considerable scaffolding and restoration work going on inside. The universities pay big bucks to get a concession to excavate and restore a site, so I don't think they'd be too impressed by plebeian 'novices' such as me wandering around their turf in the off-season. Actually I'm sure they were aware it happened, but couldn't really do anything about it. So, as long as nothing was disturbed, I guess they were OK with the guardians making some extra baksheesh on the side.

Straight away I felt I was on to something, as the first thing I noticed when I got inside was a strange right-angled groove, about an inch or so wide, cut into the floor. At each intersection were squares about two to three inches with a similar arch tracing around from one corner to another. My first guess was that something sat on top of the floor and rotated and moved through the grooves, but then I though it also could have been part of some secret floor trap that opened up to allow access to the lower crypts.

In and around the ladders, dust-sheets and scaffolding, I could see the Offering Hall had two elegant columns splitting centre, each having four faces of Hathor carved above composite capitals decorated with eight palm leaves and sixteen buds. On the cornice of the doorway leading into the sanctuaries was the cartouche of Ptolemy VIII. More importantly, a worn red-granite step divided the Offering Hall from the inner sanctuaries; the minute I saw it I knew I was on to something.

Within, to the left, was a side sanctuary, known as the "dwelling of User-menu". On the wall just to the left of the doorway were the cartouches of Ptolemy VIII Euergetes II and Cleopatra III, as well as a depiction of Isis wearing the vulture crown with two horns flanking a sun disk. Above the entrance, as it was with the other two inner sanctums, was the usual winged-disk and cornice of uraeus serpents.

Within the chamber, reliefs covered all the walls. Of special note was the north wall, with the resurrection of Osiris depicted upon it. Stretched out on a lion-shaped bed, he was in the process of waking up, bending his right arm and lifting his left foot. Hovering over Osiris is a bird vulture with the bearded head of Amun; the ka, essence of life, or sublime soul of Osiris.

At the back of the temple was the inner sanctum, or 'dwelling of the Golden One', containing a well-shaft currently covered with a heavy wooden grill. At the back of the room was a niche; I wondered if it aligned with the one I had seen in the outside room at the rear of the temple? I looked around to see if there were any hints of secret doors or staircases, but the light was not so good and I didn't have the time to see if Nemo could ferret any out.

On the walls were depictions of Opet.

'To the north, the pharaoh, wearing the red crown, stands before Opet on a pedestal of Ma'at. On the south wall, the pharaoh, wearing the white crown, offers the clepsydra to a head of Hathor supported by a small column on a cubic pedestal.'

Generally, the decorations, though blackened by the soot of ancient torches, were quite well preserved. But something in my notes grabbed my attention.

'The examination of their partitions with the aid of an ultra-violet light has revealed the existence of figures and texts that are totally invisible to the naked eye.'

That usually meant older hieroglyphs, perhaps relating to what lay in the crypts beneath the floor, where I presumed the well was heading. And that's where I wanted to head, underground to the crypts.

'Crypts?'

'Yes, yes.'

Fortunately Pops was eager to keep me moving as well and gestured for me to follow. I was right behind him as we headed to the next sanctuary, another small one to the right called "the high seat of the linked souls", in which "crypts had been worked into the north and south walls". That was great, but I wanted to get down and underneath. I pointed to the floor.

'Crypt, under temple.'

'Yes, yes, come.'

First he led me down a short narrow corridor to a room to the right showing me a section of floor that had been exposed. There were at least three layers of stone that had been either removed or broken through, revealing a rather large whole in the floor. Yes, there *were* crypts, underneath the temple. Who knows, perhaps there was a tomb containing the partial remains of Osiris.

Pops must have seen the excitement on my face and urged me to follow him to another location, where he pulled away a few boards covering an even larger whole in the floor. I say larger, but still not wide enough for my large western frame to squeeze through. I wondered if they sent down children, or trained monkeys, to check things out and do the dirty work?

Beside the hole were numerous statue fragments, mostly made of black granite. Clearly they had been rescued from the bowels of the temple. This was exciting, but I instantly wondered who was doing the excavation, and if they would ever reveal the truth to the rest of the world. I was here; I wanted to see it for myself.

'How to get down, to crypt?'

Pops nodded and took me into yet another short and narrow corridor. Here a complete rectangular section of floor was missing. My heart raced as I stepped forward, the depths revealing an old wooden staircase that descended into the void.

'I go down?'

His face suddenly turned to one of concerned consternation and fear as he pulled up his hand with two fingers poised to strike at me.

'No, no! Cobra.'

'I be careful, I will be OK.'

He stepped closer, an almost hypnotic glare in his eyes.

'No, no; COBRA.'

He reiterated the striking again towards my face, intent on making his message clear. Now I don't know if he had ever even been below, or if the Egyptologists had just told him there were cobras down there just to keep everyone away, but in the end I had to respect his position and, as much as I regretted it, as he covered the opening up, I resigned myself to moving on from the crypts of Opet.

However, now I knew there *were* chambers below, that there *were* crypts, and answers to be found; answers that were more than likely being suppressed or held back. Was part of Osiris there? Or rather was it once there, as no doubt it would have been removed by now? Why should the ancient Egyptians lie? And, if it was interred there, was it human, or something different altogether?

I followed Pops as we exited the corridor and headed back to the small gate. I knew he'd be hungry for more baksheesh, and this time I was not only ready, but willing. I gave him a fifty, then expecting the mandatory pitiful request for more, happily gave him another fifty. That brought a massive grin to his face and plaudits of gratification. Hell, it was probably the most money he'd seen in months, and probably the best value I'd had on the trip so far, excluding the felucca trip that is.

And that was it; that was the last of the temples. I checked the time, 3:21, stowed the iphone safely back in my pocket, and followed Pops as he led me behind the Opet Temple towards the Temple of Ramses III.

Sipping away at the last of my water, I spotted a modern brick storeroom off to the left that was bizarrely built adjoining the Khonsu temple. I shook my head, what a ridiculous place to erect a modern building. I wandered over to take a greasy eyeball in through the window.

OK, here they were; row after row, rack after rack, thousands and thousands of what I presumed were the missing talatats from the Aten Precinct. I guess it was here that ARCE were stabilizing each block, and photographing it before they reconstructed them somewhere. There didn't seem much happening inside, so I don't think the experts were in any sort of hurry. And why should they be when they get a nice little stipend from their respective universities to continue the work, so why do it fast and put yourself out of a job.

It reminded me of two things; a couple of local-council road-workers leaning on shovels contemplating what to have for lunch, and, the final scene in the first Indiana Jones movie, when the Ark of the Covenant is stored away in a giant warehouse never to be seen again. Apart from that, it was also a great way for the academics to withhold any controversial information: it happened with the Dead Sea Scrolls and it just may be happening again.

My curiosity satisfied, Pops led me back through the Khonsu temple and out through a narrow side door in the eastern wall of the Hypostyle Hall. He gave me a huge hug, then a blessing, and we bid each other farewell. It seemed I had escaped being made son-in-law. Hell, with what I'd just paid him he could probably go out and buy a half-dozen son-in-laws from the local village.

Making my way back along the outer wall of the courtyard, between the Tenth to Seventh Pylons, all that remained was for me to make my way back to the exit and then to the Nubian Hotel to rendezvous with Dwight; I wondered what he might have discovered.

It ain't over 'til it's over

I headed east and north of the Khonsu Temple snaking my way through row after row of 'block fields' that contained dozens upon dozens of Middle Kingdom temple stones 'stored' on plinths. I'd bet a king's ransom most of them belonged to what used to be the original Temple of Opet.

The whole area along and outside the transverse axis, from before the Seventh Pylon to the Tenth Pylon, was a gold mine, as the blocks were no doubt all awaiting identification, classification and restoration.

One particular piece drew my attention. It was an extremely worn statue made of black granite. It was so worn that I could barely make out any features. It was either a man seated on the ground with his arms around his knees, or it could possibly even have been a statue of Djehuty, or Thoth, in his baboon form.

The stone was so old it was almost crumbling, and that to me meant way before the Middle Kingdom, which I now associated more with the use of alabaster. Examining the facial features more closely reminded me of Roddy McDowell in '*The Planet of the Apes*', there was an apelike aspect to the appearance. But the piece was so worn I guess you could read almost anything into it. That wasn't the only problem.

The problem was, the blocks were either under the auspices of ARCE, the American Research Centre in Egypt, or under the Akhenaten Temple Project, begun by the University Museum of Pennsylvania and carried on jointly by the Egyptian Department of Antiquities and the Smithsonian Institution in Washington, D.C., both organizations I now believed were heavily influenced by The Illuminati.

Passing the outer west wall of the Cachette Court I briefly noted the inscription of Ramses II's peace treaty with the Hittites, before heading on passed the exterior southern wall of the Hypostyle Hall and the carved reliefs celebrating the military exploits of Seti I and Ramses II in Syria and Palestine, including Ramses II's famous battle of Kadesh.

Further along the wall, on the south face of the main temple, was another famous scene, but I needed my iphone to properly identify it.

'On the south face of the main temple's side wall, Sheshonq I, of biblical fame (Shishak, from 1 Kings 14: 25-26, the Egyptian pharaoh who conquered Jerusalem and plundered the Temple of Solomon), is depicted smiting his captive enemies in an important triumphal scene commemorating his victories against Israel and Judah. In another relief, Sheshonq offers a khepesh-sword to Amun, who stands before several rows of name-rings that represent a total of 165 captured cities.'

Beside that, was the famous 'Bubastite Portal', a monumental gate erected and dedicated by Sheshonq I, and my way back into the main temple. Reading on, I thought it was quite ironic that Sheshonq's gateway adjoined Ramses III's smaller Karnak temple.

'Sheshonq's ancestors were defeated by Rameses III six generations earlier, but, when Sheshonq assumed the crown, he became the founder of the 22nd Dynasty, taking power away from the Theban High Priests.'

The military usurped the crown from the *sang réal*, the priests usurped the crown from the military, and the foreigners usurped the crown from the priests. I guess what goes around comes around, or is that, 'what you sow you reap'?

I was totally in exit mode until I hit the massive alabaster block back in the first courtyard; something about it was different. It wasn't so much glowing, as brighter. It was hard to describe, but if it was a picture, it was like someone had photo-shopped it and increased the brightness and contrast. I paused and was going to put my hands on it again when suddenly I remembered what Crystal had said before she left, '*You might find the open-air museum worth a visit as well.*'

Maybe it was just a reflex, but it triggered me to look north, over in the direction of the museum, situated behind the triple-shrine Temple of Seti II, in far north-west corner of Karnak. Just like the alabaster altar, the doorway through the northern wall was alive with light. It was as if it were calling me, illuminating the path. I wasn't completely convinced I wasn't just seeing things, so I checked my notes.

'The open-air museum contains a number of small monuments that have been reconstructed from dismantled blocks found within the temple's walls and pylons where they were once used as filling. These include the limestone barque chapel of the Middle Kingdom ruler, Senwosret I, the New Kingdom shrines of Amenhotep I and II, and the "Chapelle Rouge" of Hatshepsut.'

It seemed there *was* something left for me to discover.

A room with a view

It cost me an extra twenty-five pound to enter, and at first I wondered if it was worth it as there were several broken and battered unidentified red-granite statues propped up to form the beginning of a sort of avenue of honour. To either side were shrines, comprising mostly concrete with a few blocks of alabaster here and there. It was hardly the sort of impact I was expecting, though I had to admit the use of alabaster blocks, and the scarcity of them, rekindled my perspective that the use of alabaster belonged to the Middle Kingdom or earlier.

The avenue itself was merely a succession of blocks and fragments stuck up on concrete blocks, with four black-granite Sekhmet statues, probably 'borrowed' from the Temple of Mut, set at the end as if standing guard. I presumed they'd been relocated from the Temple of Mut so as to create a little more variety of what to see, and some sense of 'life', in the museum. I had to laugh though, the Egyptologists had five square plates set up and only four of the spaces occupied, a trio taking prominence. Couldn't they just have grabbed another one?

For some reason I thought of giving them each names, and suddenly all sorts of famous threesomes filled my head: The Three Musketeers, Huey Dewey and Louie, The Bee Gees, The Three Stooges, the three witches of Macbeth, The Rhinemaidens, Ping, Pang and Pong, The Three Little Pigs, The Goodies, The Scarecrow, the Cowardly Lion and the Tin Man. In the end I let it go. It certainly wasn't Kansas, it was more like a ghost town, but I set off anyway on the yellow-brick-road as it wound its way around Munchkinland.

Across from the three ladies were more rows of blocks; various blocks from a number of periods. Further along was something quite simply stunning, a magnificent building in red and black; Haptshepsut's 'Red Chapel'.

'Haptshepsut's "Chapelle Rouge" is built of red quartzite, with doors and lintels of black diorite. But, as natural red quartzite varies in colour, the chapel was painted red to appear uniform.'

The overall effect was stunning. Quartzite, and diorite, I wasn't too sure about them, but if quartzite was anything like quartz, then the building would have been one huge resonance chamber. I'd have to run that one passed Bill.

'Originally a barque shrine, building probably started around four years before Hathsepsut's death, and may originally have been situated between her two obelisks by the 4th and 5th pylons. At the time of her death it was unfinished and Thutmoses III never completed it.'

A barque shrine? That didn't gel with me. Neither did it being situated between the two obelisks by the Fourth and Fifth Pylons. I think it was originally where the Middle Kingdom courtyard now was, as that would have placed it in the centre of Hatshepsut's four obelisks and right on top of the primordial mound.

And as to it being a barque shrine, that may be true later on, but I feel it originally had some other function, a function that related to it being a resonance chamber with four 'aerials' placed around it to receive, channel or transit energy.

I don't feel it was a case of Thutmoses III not completing it either, more likely that the Amun Priests actually had the chambers dismantled and the distinctive stones used to build the foundations of, and hidden within, the pylons. I did a lap of the Chapel, examining the reliefs. On the south side, carved into the black diorite, were rows of females making offerings.

'At the base of the shrine, around the outer walls is a frieze, once filled with gold paint, of Sepat deities, or nomes, carrying forward offerings to the gods. '

I could only begin to imagine how magnificent it must have looked. And gold too, did that have some part to play? It was a super-conductor after all.

On the northern side was an exquisite relief of a celebration. Dancers and acrobats were performing to a band comprising harpists and sistra being rattled, while food was being carried forward.

The entrance had been extensively 'reconstructed', meaning they had stuck what blocks they could find in a doorway of grey concrete. Having said that, it wasn't too bad a job and gave a good indication of the overall look of the doorway and the temple.

Inside were two chambers, each containing a low rectangular slab of stone in the centre of the room. In the first of these, a rounded sort of basin took pride of place in the centre of the floor. Did it belong there? It certainly didn't look like it.

'The basin in the first chamber functioned as a foundation for the bark.'

Bullshit! In every other temple the 'foundations' for the barque were in fact altars about three feet high. Suddenly this squat little hand-basin about eight inches high fulfils the same function? I don't think so. Do these 'experts' think we are idiots? Try this explanation guys, – 'The small basin WAS A BASIN, and it was used to wash one's hands, or possibly feet, *before* one entered the chambers'. Yes it may have been in the first chamber, *if* the chamber was a preparatory chamber for the second chamber, but guys, please, a foot bath is a foot bath.

The rectangular slab of stone in the next chamber probably did support a statue, but hardly in the centre of the room, and it looked ridiculous placed where it was. Hey guys, why not stick a statue on it? I mean you do have a few hundred Sekhmet ones lying around just up the road at the Mut Precinct, grab one of them and stick it on.

The 'temple' was apparently dedicated to Amun, and inside Hatshepsut is depicted making offerings and performing rituals to him. Other scenes include djed pillars, *was*-sceptres and ankhs, processions for Opet, the barque of Amun carried on the backs of priests, Thoth pouring purifying water over the pharaoh, Seshat recording events, and Hatshepsut conducting the barque of Amun across the river to the West Bank.

Even though there was quite a bit of concrete holding the actual blocks in place, the chamber still had amazing energy. I sat down on the empty plinth in the centre of the second chamber, closed my eyes and called on Nemo. For several minutes he swam back and forth without much success, it was almost as if he was confused, unable to connect. Perhaps it was the concrete, or maybe the chapel needed the four obelisks positioned at each corner to fire it up completely? I wasn't going to hang around flogging a dead horse, and moved on.

On the opposite side of the path a square clearing had been created, with an array of bits and pieces discovered elsewhere on the complex. To the left were a number of red granite blocks erected to look like columns. That doesn't mean that's what they actually were; they could have been parts of a doorjamb, or even been horizontal lintels or roof supports. The only thing that *was* definite about them was they were very very worn, much like those at El Kab, and lacked any obvious hieroglyphs or reliefs. To my thinking, that made them old, really old, way before the need for any 'human' graffiti or egotistical claiming by pretenders to the *sang réal*.

303

Beside it stood the reconstructed wall of Amenhotep IV; the one that supposedly once stood before, or in the vicinity of, the Third Pylon. On it was the typical scenario of the pharaoh grabbing a bunch of captured foe by the hair and, one would presume, preparing to cave their skulls in. I examined it closely. The head was missing but the rest of the body form seemed inconsistent with the statues of Akhenaten. Nor did I believe Akhenaten was into smiting people just because they came from a different part of town. And if Akhenaten went to all the trouble of building an entire temple just up the road, apparently out of talatats, then why build a wall here out of larger stones? No, this wall told me volumes; this wall *did* belong to Amenhotep IV, but *not* to Akhenaten.

To the right of the wall were a few more Sekhmet statues and a rather unusual piece of alabaster. It didn't look like part of a statue but was possibly part of a shrine. I was convince this belonged to the Middle Kingdom, possibly earlier, but I couldn't find any cartouches to seal the deal. But the more I looked at the hieroglyphs the more they looked of a much older style.

The next thing that stood out was a beautiful white barque chapel from the Middle Kingdom, belonging to Senwroset I, fourth pharaoh of the 12th Dynasty. Set on a squared base about a metre high and six metres on each side, a small gently sloping split staircase and 'wheelchair' ramp, similar in design to the ramps at Hatshepsut's temple, led up to the chapel, that had the typical curved cornice of New Kingdom temples as well as detailed reliefs on each of its sixteen squared columns. The entrance was roped off so I couldn't get close enough to tell if it was limestone or alabaster, but, what ever it was, it was stunning. In the centre was an altar, but again I was too far away to make out any details. Maybe it didn't even belong there?

I speculated on the chapel's use, as the positioning of the columns inside meant there wasn't even enough room to swing a temple kitten. Perhaps it was a place to go and meditate, or daydream? Maybe Nemo could find out?

No one was around so I jumped the rope and scampered up the ramp. I didn't get very far, just close enough to confirm the shrine was probably made of alabaster, snap a photo of the altar, and see it was made of red granite.

'No, please, not permitted.'

Where did he come from? He must have materialized out of thin air, or from under a rock. I flashed the now mandatory baksheesh gesture and the guard looked around. Things were looking good, that is until, wouldn't you know it, just at that moment a group of bloody snap-happy Japanese tourists flooded down the path. The guardian shook his head; I think he was definitely more disappointed than me.

'Come later, yes?'

I wish I could have, but my detour into the museum was now putting me under pressure to meet my deadline with Dwight. I shrugged and moved on, leaving the chapel to the incessant clicking of Nikons and Canons. Even with today's technologies, each of the Japanese tourists seemed to have the latest whiz-bang high-tech camera, with multi-whatsis lenses. I just had my trusty iphone, and I carried it on to my next surprise.

Further along the path was a barque shrine made of alabaster that apparently belonged to Amenhotep II, Thutmoses IV and Ramses II, as all their cartouches appeared somewhere on it. It would have been easy to assume, as the Egyptologists had done, that it was originally Amenhotep II's, then claimed by Thutmoses IV and later by Ramses II. That it was claimed by Thutmoses IV, and later Ramses II, is without doubt, but could we really be so sure it was originally Amenhotep II's? What if he appropriated it from someone earlier, someone in the Middle Kingdom? It was possible.

It seemed to be mostly constructed from new concrete with a few random chunks of relief cemented onto the walls. I wondered what the point was when there were so few original blocks remaining. But I suppose it did give some idea of what the original monument would have looked like.

To the untrained eye it could have looked just like a community shelter or toilet block, but suddenly I was struck by its dimensions. As I investigated the interior, my guesstimate was, that like the other 'barque shrines' and inner sanctums, it was 1.6 times higher than it was wider, and 1.6 times as long as it was high: just like the inner sanctum of Amun, this building was designed around the ratio of phi and the fibonacci spiral, only this chamber was in alabaster rather than red granite.

The real question was, 'What purpose did the chapel have?' And if I heard another frigging 'expert' say it was yet another barque shrine, I was going to stick the ceremonial barque right up their ceremonial nether regions. I took a moment to try and tune in with Nemo, tried to hum, but there was nothing doing, maybe all the concrete had scared him off.

Then, as I exited, I saw it, right alongside, shining bright like the alabaster block in the first courtyard; the chapel of Amenhotep I. Oh, wow! This must have been where the missing alabaster blocks from the Third Pylon finished up. As I circled it, the first question I had was, 'Did Amenhotep I build the chapel, or did he put his reliefs on a pre-existing Middle Kingdom building that had no decorations?' There wasn't really any way of knowing for sure. Being there were again no ropes or barriers preventing entry, I presumed we were permitted access to the chapel and strolled right in.

Unlike the previous chapel, which had a large percentage of concrete, suddenly I found myself almost fully surrounded by alabaster. On the inner walls, just as on the outer walls, were numerous reliefs of Amenhotep I before various gods. What made them particularly interesting were the striations of the alabaster. But, there was something else. I hummed a few different notes until one started to resonate in the space. Yep, this was a resonance chamber all right. The question was, 'For what?'

What was it Bill said about alabaster? Something about 'double refraction and the crystal splitting a ray of light into distinct beams'. Crystal then implied it was some sort of massive prism of diffraction that splits beams of energy up into it's visible components creating some sort of complex and expansive dimensional Doppler effect.' Well, sound was energy too, and I knew the Doppler effect from the difference between the sound of a police siren coming towards you, as opposed to the sound of it moving away. But how did that apply to the chamber? There was one way to find out for sure, call on Nemo.

At first I hesitated, I mean I didn't want another heavyweight title defence against the Amun spectres from the Hypostyle Hall. But then, again, I'd survived them once, and since my re-acquaintance with Sekhmet in the Temple of Ptah, the Amun Priests had left me well and truly alone.

Lying down in the centre of the chapel, I closed my eyes, and started to sing 'Ah'. Within a few breaths Nemo was leading me into the flow of energy within the stone. Suddenly, although my eyes were closed, I saw the chapel above me, then it became, at first translucent, and then totally transparent. A myriad of intensely coloured scenes then projected before me, some of my past, some of other lives, other planets. It was like a hundred TV monitors all playing at once, and not just visions, but sounds, smells and 'awarenesses'. I could actually feel what ever was happening on each screen. It was like a do-it-yourself 3D, or rather 4D, scratch-and-smell movie screen.

I don't know how long I lay there, it was at least ten minutes but it could have been half-an-hour, maybe even longer. Tens, maybe hundreds, of thousands of images, lives, events, were flashing before me, imprinting on my consciousness. I didn't have to remember them, I *was* remembering them, all of them, including scenes from the 'future'. But the one thing that stuck in my mind most was the sound of Japanese voices jolting me back into the alabaster chapel. The snap back reminded me of what other people described when they were astral travelling and suddenly called back into their bodies. Was that what I was just doing, astral travelling?

I think the Japanese thought I was just taking a nap in the shade out of the hot sun, but even then, had no consideration for that. They swarmed into the tiny space stepping beside, and even over me to bag a few happy-snaps. That was enough for me; I was outta there. Shit, 4:21, where did the time go? I had one last corner of the museum to explore, then I was on my way.

At the back of the museum was a huge twin portico and wall. This must have been the one that supposedly belonged to either Thutmoses IV or Amenhotep IV and apparently once stood before the Third Pylon. Something about all of that didn't sound right?

The Third Pylon would have been the original façade of the temple at the time of Amenhotep III, so any portico built in front of it would post-date it, and, to me, that ruled out Thutmoses IV as the owner. So it must have belonged to Amenhotep IV. But, the wall was made of sandstone blocks, not talatats, and as far as I was concerned that was more evidence that Amenhotep IV and Akhenaten were different beings. In any case it looked very impressive, with colourful reliefs of the pharaoh before various gods on the squared pillars.

Then, as I was leaving I spotted a perfect example of modern Egyptology; a section of red granite wall or door jam had been erected alongside a part of an alabaster wall, as if they belonged together. What was it with these guys, were they blind, stupid, or both? Pissed off, I hustled out of the museum, back through the courtyard and out through the First Pylon faster than a ferret up a trouser leg.

When I hit the visitors' centre I was briefly stopped for what I presumed was a random backpack check. I couldn't think why they would do it; unlike the tombs on the West Bank there were no areas off limits to photography, they didn't even ask to see my iphone. Maybe they were just checking that I hadn't stuffed a colossus of Ramses II away to sell on the black market?

Apart from that brief delay, I managed to avoid the hawkers circling like sharks outside the visitors' centre and flopped into a waiting taxi before he even had the chance to corner me.

'Nubian Hotel, ten pound.'

I couldn't believe it, he didn't even haggle! We were off and racing. Well, that was Karnak, it had taken me nearly eight hours to explore its secrets; but it would take me a lot longer to fully digest them, *and* what had transpired.

CHAPTER 20 – YOU TAKE THE HIGH ROAD

Arriving back at the Nubian Oasis I headed straight upstairs to the roof to meet up with Dwight. Eight hours of trekking around the fry-pan that was Karnak had taken its toll, and the four stories of stairs that led to the roof left me puffing and panting. I paused at the top of the stairs half expecting to see Randy lazing in a hammock surrounded by empty beer bottles and Dwight with his head still in Kareem's wad of documents. Instead, the roof was empty.

I stood there for a minute, then checked the time, 4:50 pm; damn, it looks like I'd missed them. No worries, I could always catch up with Dwight once I got to Cairo and, although the contemplation of a cool shower and cold beer was irresistible, the thought of a scantily-dressed Crystal awaiting at the Winter Palace was overwhelming. I decided the shower and beer could wait until after I'd joined the others at the Winter Palace.

Heading back down the stairs to my room, I wondered what happened to the documents? As far as I could figure at the time, there were three options; Dwight had taken them with him to Cairo to translate, he'd slipped them under my door before leaving, or he'd left them at reception. The moment I opened the door to my room I realized Dwight hadn't slipped the papers under the door, which meant he must definitely have taken them with him or left them downstairs at the reception desk.

Despite the late hour, the room still hadn't been made up. Though I didn't have many belongings, somehow I'd managed to leave them somewhat strewn across the bench and bed; I didn't really think about it at the time, I just figured I must have been in a rush getting out in the morning. I dropped off my backpack, stowed my laptop back underneath the mattress, and headed down to the lobby.

Seleh wasn't at reception but one of the other guys was; it seemed Seleh had breaks after all.

'Mister Dwight and Mister Randy, they have gone, yes?'

'Yes, yes, Seleh he take them to airport.'

OK, so Seleh didn't have breaks; he moonlighted as a shuttle driver for the tourists.

'Mister Dwight, did he leave a bag of papers here?'

'Paper? Yes.'

The 'concierge' leaned under the counter and emerged with a single sheet of A4 in his hand: it seemed we had a communication problem.

'No. Mister Dwight, he leave many paper in bag for me?'

He looked somewhat bewildered.

'No, Mister Dwight he go to airport.'

We weren't really getting anywhere, but, unless he left the bag of documents with Seleh, it was pretty clear Dwight hadn't left anything behind, which meant he must have decided to take them with him after-all, and, given the contentious nature of the contents, that was definitely a weight off my mind. At least *I* didn't have them, and for now that meant I could focus my attention one-hundred-percent on Crystal.

I hadn't really noticed him when I entered the hotel, but as I exited to walk the ten minutes or so to the Winter Palace, I caught a glimpse of a guy leaning against the wall of the mosque on the opposite side of the street about fifty feet away. Clean-cut well-dressed, shirt and trousers, about twenty-five to thirty, there was something out-of-the-ordinary about him, he was alone, and about what he was doing – nothing. This guy looked about as inconspicuous as the testicles on a prize-winning bull elephant.

I pretended not to be looking at him directly, but in his general direction and back down the street as if to look for a taxi, though it probably looked more like I was searching for some imaginary object suddenly floating off down the alleyway. As I did, he stood away from the wall and stepped towards me.

'Mister, please, I want talk to you about paper.'

At first my heart thumped, he was Egyptian Secret Police all right, no doubt about it. In a millisecond I ran through the scenario: I didn't have the papers, Dwight had them, and he was safely on a plane to Cairo, or at least I hoped he was. He must have been, because if they had intercepted him then why would they be here lingering outside my hotel. But what if Dwight had pointed the finger at me? No, if he'd done that then they would have just arrested me straight away. Dwight must have escaped undetected with the evidence and the Secret Police still been under the apprehension that I had them. Shit!

No, wait a minute, I was in the clear, they couldn't pin anything on me without the files, could they? Even if they arrested me, they had nothing without the evidence, unless somehow they did have the files. I thought it better to shake the tail rather than be stung by it and ran off down the street.

'Wait, I need talk to you about it paper.'

As soon as I hit the intersection I hailed down a passing taxi and dived in the back.

'Go, go!'

He took off: just in time to leave my pursuer pulling up at the corner scratching his head.

'Where to Cowboy?'

I looked back: the cop was hailing down a taxi as well. I could just hear him saying 'Follow that cab', well, the Arabic equivalent of it. Shit, I was about to be in one of those mad car-chase scenes from the movies, only I was the hunted. I couldn't head straight for the Winter Palace, I had to lose my unwanted attendant.

'The bazaar, as fast as possible.'

'Fifty pound.'

I didn't have time to haggle him down; it was only ten bucks anyway.

'Yes, yes, just go.'

He hit the accelerator almost as hard and as much as he hit the horn; talk about drawing attention to us. Well, actually that wasn't the case, as every cabbie honks their horn almost as much as they haggle over the price or pick their nose; an all to frequent habit I observed amongst the taxi drivers. It certainly made you think twice about shaking anyone's hand.

It was less than a five-minute drive through the streets but, through the rear window, I observed the smarmy gumshoe following us in his commandeered taxi and trailing us to the bazaar. Damn, there was no doubt now; they were definitely on to me.

Arriving at the Luxor Bazaar, I gave the cabby fifty pounds and told him to drive away, then come back in fifteen minutes and wait for me at the far end of the main street, and I would give him another fifty. He may have looked at me strangely, but naturally he agreed and I hustled in through the crowd, looking back to check if my shadow was following. In the distance I saw him jump from the cab and forge his way through the crowd; at best I had about a fifty-metre head start on him.

Dodging and weaving up side streets then back to the main drag I tried to shake my tail, but to no avail. Finally I backtracked and headed to the store where Saeed had purchased the original bag. Shit, I suddenly remembered I'd given it to Diane; for a moment I wondered if maybe she'd been caught up in all this mess as well.

The shop owner was delighted to see me and started showing me yet another of the horrendously tacky tourist carry-alls he had flogged to Saeed. I shrugged him off, grabbing a typically black and drab woman's dress and headdress, hijab or burqa, I didn't know the difference, and started putting them on. He was totally caught off guard.

'No, no, please, these they are for the lady.'

As he attempted to thrust more traditional men's attire in my direction, galebeya's and shirts, I tried to explain my situation.

'My friend, Saeed, yes? He buy bag, yes.'

'Yes, yes.'

'Secret Police, they follow me.'

'You no like bag?'

He had naturally, but erroneously, assumed I was upset with the bag so much that I'd called the Secret Police and that they were right behind me, ready to scold his unscrupulous butt. Suddenly he was offering me gaudy earrings and silken scarves as if I was one of those weirdo foreigners who cross-dressed.

'No, no, Secret Police after ME! I need to hide.'

Well, it was like I'd said I was carrying the plague; he couldn't get me dressed and out of there any faster than if he'd fired me out of a canon. He wanted to help me out, but I'm sure his real motivation was more that he didn't want to be *caught* in the act of helping me out. I tried to give him a hundred pound to ease the stress and cover the cost of the outfit, but he waved it off, so I pulled the headdress over and into place, and leered out through the letterbox-slot towards the door and into the street. I couldn't be sure, but I thought I saw my nemesis pass the shop; this was my best chance.

'Waiting please, Mister, your hat.'

In my rush, I'd left it on the counter and he went to hand it to me. There was no way I could carry it and remain unnoticed, but I daren't surrender it so easily.

'Bring it to Hotel Nubian Oasis tomorrow morning 8:00 am and I will give you one-hundred-fifty pounds. Yes?'

'Yes.'

'But first, you wait five minutes, then put on the hat and walk back to end of bazaar.'

I pointed in the direction where we had first entered. He seemed to comprehend my plan, and was momentarily hesitant, but upping the ante to two hundred quickly brought him on board. That done, I stepped out into the street.

I'd seen in a documentary on great white sharks where the seals actually followed directly behind the shark as it swam, as it's the least visible and safest position. It was a strategy I doubted that my adversary would be aware of, let alone consider, so I cowered in a hunched position as if I were a doddering but rather 'large' elderly local old lady, which fortunately was not that uncommon, exited the store, and fell into his wake.

I watched from my vantage point as he scanned each shop and side alley, occasionally asking a trader or local if they had seen a tall westerner with a cowboy hat. Fortunately they hadn't; my disguise was working, and I was getting closer to my destination.

His frustration growing, the cop made his way to the end of the market and made a scan of the passing street, before turning and looking back down the barrel of the bazaar. For a split second I thought he looked straight at me and that I'd been spotted. I almost had a heart attack as he rushed towards me, then almost knocked me to the ground as he pushed passed and set off after the millinery decoy; thankfully I realized he'd caught sight of my trusty akubra bobbing up and down above the crowd way back down the street. Escape plan right on schedule.

I spotted my taxi driver vigilantly standing beside his cab and climbed into the back seat. He fired off some sort of comment to me in Arabic, probably telling me that he was busy, but I opened the letter-box slightly and set him straight.

'No, it's me, Australian Cowboy, take me to the Winter Palace.'

I stayed in my disguise just in case, continually checking through the back window to see if we were being followed. We weren't, but just to be sure I got the driver to take a few detours. Even so, it only took five minutes or so to get to the Winter Palace. Once sure I was in the clear, I disrobed and alighted from the cab, handing over the promised fifty pounds.

'Wait, you leave clothes in back.'

'Keep them; a gift to your wife.'

He smiled and gave me his card.

'Anytime, you need tax, you call, Ahmed, I come. Yes?'

'Yes, thanks.'

I stuffed the card in my pocket and quickly headed inside, where again I was greeted almost as soon as I set foot in the foyer, though this time I was escorted out into the back garden where the others all sat leisurely by the pool. Shit, this place was an oasis like no other, luscious green lawns, palms, fountains, and a massive swimming pool.

Instantly I noticed Crystal, sitting at a table by the poolside bar with the others, her hair back in a ponytail and wearing a tight-fitting sleeveless purple top that nestled those breasts I had admired, adored and lusted after when she went swimming in the river; was I ever going to have the pleasure of seeing them again, let alone caress them?

'Alex! Nearly didn't recognize you without your akubra.'

Bill was genuinely pleased to see me and instantly flagged the waiter for a cold beer.

'Sorry I'm late, long story.'

'No dramas. How was your day?

'Exhausting, but amazing; I wouldn't know where to start.'

'I know what you mean. You'd better sit down, lad, and get a bit of the nectar of the gods into you.'

Naturally I sat down in the vacant seat next to Crystal.

'What about you guys, what did you get up to after you left Karnak?'

Pieter kicked things off.

'Yuko and I went to the Luxor Museum.'

'How was it?'

'OK; nothing particularly remarkable, but still worth seeing.'

Yuko followed on.

'After that we went back to the hotel to rest.'

'Did you see Dwight and Randy?'

'Yes, they were on the roof; Randy was asleep in a hammock while Dwight was still engrossed in the papers you left him.'

'What time was that?'

'About 3:00, maybe 3:15, I think.'

Bill chipped in.

'Are these the papers you were telling me about, the ones from Saeed's uncle?'

'Yep.'

I thanked the waiter for the beer he deposited before me and instantly savoured a deep first quenching mouthful. Meanwhile Bill continued.

'These papers must be pretty interesting if Dwight had his nose buried in them most of the day.'

'I think you're right, Bill, so much so I think he smuggled them with him to Cairo to translate.'

'Sounds like a wise move. Even so, I can't wait to hear what's in them.'

'Me neither.

'Maybe it explains Diane's little run-in with the local constabulary as well.'

'What do you mean?'

Bill sat back as Pernille took the lead, but he still threw in the occasional aside.

'We were just about to leave the visitors' centre at Karnak, when they stopped Diane and asked to look in her bag. At first we all thought it was just another ridiculous random check to see that she hadn't stolen something,...'

'... like a temple cat...'

'... but then we realized they were serious.'

'Diane calmly let them go through it though; she didn't have a clue what it was all about.'

'But they seemed mighty interested in that bag you gave her.'

'Shit, that's because it was the bag I had Kareem's papers in. What happened?'

'They started asking her specifically about the bag you gave her, where she got it, who you were and how she knew you.'

'Damn it, they must have followed me to Karnak. What did she say?'

'What could she say: she told them the truth; that it was a gift from you, and that she only met you a few days ago.'

'Then they asked the rest of us how we knew you and where we were staying.'

'What did you tell them?'

'How we met you for the first time on the felucca and that everyone was staying at the Nefertiti except Bill and Pernille, who were here at the Winter Garden, and Pieter and Yuko, who were at the Nubian Oasis.'

With a sense of trepidation I turned to Pieter and Yuko.

'Did you tell them where I was staying?'

'No, we didn't want to get involved.'

'Good thinking!'

Chew on this

Just then, the waiter arrived with a plethora of platters of tapas and scattered them across the table. I was famished but still able to focus on the events of the day.

'What happened next?'

It was Pernille who answered.

'That's when Crystal arrived. She spoke to the officer in charge and, within minutes, two of the police set off back inside the complex, and the officer let us all go.'

I turned to Crystal, who had been quietly sitting and sipping her juice.

'What did you tell him?'

She calmly took a sip of her drink and matter-of-factly related the details.

'Just that no one here knew anything about any special bag or any papers, that maybe you had them with you in your backpack, and, that as far as I knew, you were still inside the temple as the last time I saw you was near the Hypostyle Hall about ten minutes earlier.'

'So that's why they searched my bag on the way out; they couldn't find me inside because I'd headed off to the temples of Khonsu and Opet. But they must have waited in the visitors' centre for me to leave; they just didn't know I was going to be another couple of hours. Then, when I hadn't showed up after an hour or so, they probably gave up and just left it for the local guards to check out any tall Aussies wearing an akubra and a backpack.

They must have put a tail on Pieter and Yuko and followed them to the Luxor Museum, on to the Nubian Oasis, then checked the photocopies of the passports at reception. By the time I got back to the hotel, they had someone waiting for me outside.'

'Are you sure it was the police?'

'Yep, he even asked me about the papers. Who else could it have been?'

'Saeed's nephew.'

'What?'

'I overheard you telling Bill about the papers this morning, so once we'd left Karnak I called Saeed to warn him that the police were looking for the documents. He told me that he and his uncle had been arrested this morning by the Secret Police, who were trying to recover the files. Although Saeed had been released, they were still holding his uncle in custody. Saeed thought about coming to see you himself, but he was concerned they may follow him to your hotel. So he was going to arrange for his nephew to wait for you at your hotel and warn you to hide them.'

'Why didn't he wait in the lobby?'

'I don't know, maybe he went to, but the police turned up.'

'Well, whoever it was, I led them a merry dance through the bazaar before I lost them. Anyway, I don't have the papers any more, Dwight took them with him to

Cairo, and, to be honest, I'm glad they're off my hands. Once Dwight has translated them he can write a PhD or something and become and next Dan Brown or Julian Assange.'

I accepted Bill's offer to join the others and 'tuck in' to the tapas, then took a few deep swigs of my beer.

'And what about you, Bill, how are you feeling after your little "episode" in the Temple of Ptah? Do you remember it, or anything about it?'

'Well, at the time it was all a bit of a blur, like a strange dream you sort of remember bits and pieces of, but it doesn't make any sense. Then I finished up having a bit of a de-brief session with Diane, Crystal and Pernille this afternoon, and now it *all* makes sense.'

'Care to share?'

'Sure, so long as you won't get freaked out or think I've lost my marbles.'

'Bill, after everything I've seen, heard and been through on this trip so far, unless you're about to tell me you're the long lost love child of Kerry Packer and Ita Buttrose, then I think I can handle it.'

He gave a hearty chuckle.

'Well, actually ... no, that's even too freaky for me to contemplate. I guess it all started when I put my hands on the big block of alabaster in the first courtyard; I started feeling weird and my eyes sort of disconnected, like I was daydreaming.'

'Did you see any shadowy figures lurking behind the columns?'

'No, the opposite really; everything seemed to be brighter, shimmering.'

'I had a bit of that myself later on. Anything else?'

'After that, every time I touched a granite statue or piece of granite, the effect seemed to get bigger and I felt more disjointed. By the time we got to the Temple of Ptah I felt more like a mindless zombie than an intrepid explorer.

I was still here, but I wasn't, if you know what I mean, but that all changed as soon as we went into the inner chamber and stood before the statue of Ptah. I know the statue didn't have a head, but I remember seeing Ptah standing there, not seated, before us. Not the statue, but Ptah himself, all twelve or more feet of him.

After that, things got pretty blurry; it was like if my body was a car and I was the driver, then I suddenly jumped in the back seat and let somebody else do the driving. I had images in my mind of American Indians, tee pees, great meetings of chiefs and the ground being abused and raped by the white man. I felt like "the driver" was apologizing to Ptah for having not protected the land, and for not living up to his role as guardian of the earth and the ancient truths.

And that was about it; after that I literally passed out in the back seat like a drunken teenager at the end of a night out on the town.'

'That's pretty wicked. How do you feel now?'

'Oh, much better, Diane suggested I have a session with her to try and bring it all into the light, and that's what we did.'

'This afternoon?'

'Yep. Crystal and Pernille were there to help as well, and, with their guidance, I remembered that my purpose here is as a guardian of the earth, that I'd spent many lives both honouring and protecting it, as well as abusing it. It explained my whole life, well at least both my passion for geology and my involvement in the gold-mining industry; I was trying to walk the tightrope with one foot in each camp...'

He broke into a chuckle.

'... No wonder my balls were being busted all the time.'

'Do you know which Indian Chief you were; Geronimo, Sitting Bull, Pocahontas?'

'No, Pernille was Pocahontas.'

I turned to Crystal, who had a wry grin on her face; was she serious or not? 'And I guess Bill was John Smith?'

Once again Bill took Pernille's hand.

'It's not the only time she's saved my life.'

'Or Bill, mine.'

Discovering their past lives together had clearly brought them to a greater understanding of more recent events, and their attraction to each other.

'So which chief were you?'

'I don't know, we didn't figure out that, but we did get that I was a chief of the Hopi Indians.'

At that point, Yuko got to her feet, quickly followed by Pieter.

'Well, if you'll excuse us, we're going to get a bite to eat before the circle.'

I checked my iphone; 6:15, time was flying. Rather than run off, Bill had another option.

'There's plenty here, why not stay and order something off the menu?'

'No thanks; we're on a bit of a budget.'

'Please, my shout.'

'That's very kind of you, Bill, but we've been trying to do the trip as simply and true to the local people as possible.'

'I understand, no worries.'

'We'll see you at the circle though.'

'Yep.'

They disappeared into the luscious greenery of the gardens, and I for one, wasn't all that upset, as it left plenty of food for the rest of us, namely me!

'What about you, Alex, dinner?'

'I'm not proud. Thanks.'

I returned my focus to the tapas as Bill hailed the waiter. Within seconds I was licking my fingers and wading through the menu. Actually, the prices were pretty reasonable, especially when you considered this was the top place in town.

'Hell of a couple of days, hey Alex.'

'You can say that again.'

Bill smiled as he took Pernille by the hand.

'It's certainly turned my world around.'

Cheekily, Pernille withdrew it.

'For the better I hope.'

'Oh, without a doubt.'

She returned her hand to unite with his, leaning in to give him a kiss; they were the embodiment of bliss. I stole a glance at Crystal who had a smug sort of contented look on her face; I think she took a little pride in perhaps having been part of bringing them together.

Dinner was soon ordered and I took the opportunity to turn my thoughts to my prime concern.

'What about you, Crystal, has the trip changed your world?'

'That's an interesting question…'

I felt another eye-opening conversation about to happen.

'…It's one of the dichotomies of the universe.'

'How-so?'

'Change implies a state existing in the past, and that state ceasing to exist and modifying into a different state, and yet there is no past, no future, there is only this moment, there is only *ever* this moment.'

Pernille was quickly drawn in to the discussion.

'So how can things change and yet always be the same?'

'Things *appear* to change because your perception shifts.'

'I'm sorry, I don't understand.'

'There is no need to apologize for the perception you have, nor that you are not yet able to yet see the perception you desire.'

'So how do I gain the new perception?'

As Crystal looked at me, I realised I should have seen it coming, but I was caught as unprepared as a nervous teen on his first heavy date.

'Well, Alex, do you have any thoughts?'

She'd thrown down the gauntlet and, though somewhat caught on the hop, I readily picked it up.

'First you must let go of the perception you have.'

'And how do I do that?'

I fumbled with the napkin, contemplating whether to let Nemo loose and go into the whole Nile river thing, but somehow the setting was wrong. I needed something present and tangible. Then I had an idea.

'Bill, do you have a pen I may borrow?'

'Most certainly.'

As he took the requested article from his shirt pocket and handed it to me, I spread out one of the white cloth serviettes that had come with the tapas, then made a mark on it with the pen.

'If I put a tiny black dot on this cloth, has it changed?'

'No, not really.'

I picked it up and held it at arms length way back behind my head.

'And if I held it way back here, you probably wouldn't even notice the black dot.'

Pernille leaned forward and squinted.

'You're right; I can't even see it, so I would assume the cloth hadn't changed.'

I laid it out on the table before her, and closed my hands in around the dot.

'But if I got a magnifying glass, or microscope, and zoomed right in on the dot, so that's all you could see…'

'…Then the whole thing would look black.'

'The complete opposite of what you first perceived it to be.'

Suddenly I had images of fractals, zooming out, thinking the pattern was changing, when in fact it was just repeating over and over and we were observing a different part of it. I was drifting out, but it seemed Pernille was tuning in.

'I get it…'

She picked up her glass.

'If I drink this glass of champagne, the champagne may appear to be gone and the glass appear to be empty, but if I shift my point of perception to the moon, then the earth hasn't changed.'

Taking her glass and refilling it, Bill had some thoughts of his own.

'At the sub-atomic level, things are changing all the time, millions of electrons are circling all over the place in the atomic structure of this glass, but the glass still looks and acts like a glass...'

As Bill handed the filled glass to her, he inadvertently knocked his own from the table and it broke on the tiled floor.

'...Oops, unless of course you cause a cosmic catastrophe.'

'Alex?'

Crystal pulled me back from my fractal adventure.

'Hmm?'

'How would you explain the broken glass?'

I looked at the shattered pieces on the ground.

'A tragic loss of a cold beer.'

The tragedy was quickly wiped away as the waiters swooped in to collect the broken glass and replace it with another glass of golden nectar. My fate was not so easily avoided.

'So, Alex, what's the significance of the broken glass?'

I mulled it over, searching for an answer.

'Well, the glass is still there, it's just *diversified* its existence.'

By the look on her face I could tell Crystal was not yet convinced; I needed to raise the stakes.

'If there's only Oneness, then it doesn't matter how the drops of water in the river or ocean arrange themselves, the river is still the river and the ocean is still the ocean, and so it is for everything in the universe, including consciousness.

Things don't really *change* they just rearrange and assume a different possibility, and thus create new possibilities. It all depends on your frame of reference and the perspective you choose to see things from. You see, creation can't happen without the *de*-struction of what already exists; creation is merely the *altering* of universal structures into other possibilities, into different points of perception.'

Crystal smiled.

'Very profound.'

'In this way, instead of trying to change the world, trying to force your views on others through your actions, your words, your intentions or prayers, and mostly failing, when *you* change, the universe changes by default. But it *is* still the universe, not changed, just different; its awareness has shifted. It hasn't *changed* so much as it has reconfigured *because* of its shift in perception and broadened awareness.'

'Phew, that's quite a lot to digest, Alex.'

I took a deep swig; he was right, it was. Yes, I'd said it, but the truth be told, I had no idea where it came from. Thankfully, the meals arrived, as I wanted some control over my mouth, if I couldn't control what was coming out of it, at least I could control what was going in. But, from the look on Crystal's face, she knew a lot more than she was giving away so, after we had all sufficiently chowed-down to arrest the pangs of hunger, I redirected the bullet she had so eloquently and efficiently dodged ten or so minutes earlier.

'So, Crystal, things have clearly *reconfigured* for Bill and Pernille, and I don't think I will *ever* look at the world the same way again, but what about you, how has the trip changed *your* world?'

She paused and took a deep breath; I wasn't sure if she appreciated the fact I had just cornered her or not.

'How has the trip changed my world? It hasn't. The *world* has modified my trip, exactly as it is meant to be.'

'Can you explain that?'

'Of course I can.'

We all held our breath waiting for the explanation until she looked at each of us quizzically.

'Oh, you *want* me to explain.'

'Please.'

Was it possible this paragon of German temperament and sensibility had more than just a dry-wry sense of humour?

'Each of you has followed the guidance of your Higher Selves to be in Egypt at this time of my confronting my fears and reawakening to my Higher Self. Each of you has fulfilled you intention to be aboard the White Rose and embrace the challenges *your* Higher Selves has set for each of you, and to fulfil the agreements entered into by our collective Higher Selves for awakening and re-membering.

And, as our time together in Egypt draws to a conclusion, we shall each reflect on the influence the others have had on our thinking, our feelings and our lives.'

I was really just thinking out load, but I think it came out somewhat confrontational and condescending.

'How can our time draw to a close if there's only the moment?'

'Time is just as big an illusion as space, possibly bigger.'

That said, Crystal returned to her meal. Her words, like my dinner, were substantial, meaty, somewhat satisfying, if at time bland, but I'd started something and now I wanted dessert.

'So, is that it?'

She looked up.

'Perhaps, perhaps not; perhaps the greatest *changes* are yet to come.'

I think somewhere in that warped German mind she actually enjoyed her ironic reference.

'So where to from here?'

'Diane's circle.'

'I meant, after that.'

'As you know, tomorrow we are all going to visit Dendera and Abydos.'

I turned to Bill.

'Yeah, I was wondering if you minded if I tag along?'

'Wouldn't have it any other way.'

'Cool.'

Time was fast racing passed and before I knew it 7:00 had come and gone.

'I hate to eat and run, but I really should have a shower and clean up a little before the circle.'

'You can have a shower here if you want.'

'Thanks, Bill, but I need a change of clothes as well. How much do I owe you?'

'My shout, mate.'
'Then here's fifty towards the tip.'
'Much appreciated.'
'I'll see you all soon.'

Doing the rounds

Leaving the hotel, I couldn't help but wonder if maybe I'd pushed the envelope with Crystal a bit too far and pissed her off for all time. I laughed it off. 'Well, if I had, then that was just an illusion as well'. And if I hadn't, then I had the rest of tonight and at least another day to see where I stood with this astonishing woman.

Stepping out the front door, I had a look around to see if there were any dodgy characters lurking in the shadows; thankfully there weren't. I guess they'd realized I didn't have Kareem's documents and had left me to my own devices.

Naturally Ahmed was still hovering around the Winter Palace and spotted me the minute I set foot in the street. My discarded disguise was still sitting in the front passenger's seat as I climbed aboard and he took me briskly to the Nubian Oasis. He tried it on for another fifty for the trip, but this time I was no fool and told him a tenner was more than sufficient for the 3 or 4 minute ride, but if he waited ten minutes he could take me to the Nefertiti for another tenner.

'Oh no, much further, twenty pounds.'

"Much further" was about another minute, so we settled on fifteen and I headed inside.

No one was at reception as I raced up the stairs, surged into my room, and ignoring the unkempt status of the room and not even bothering to take off my clothes, just my shoes, I emptied my pockets and walked straight in under the shower. It was like standing under a magical waterfall, the cold water soaking me to the skin. The advantage was, as the cold water cascaded over my head and face, my saturated clothes clung to me like a reverse wetsuit; it was divine. My skin gasped at the welcome hydration as my body cooled down and revived. I wanted to stand there for eternity, but the thought of Crystal in a white muslin dress, which I assumed she would once again wear to the circle, quickly gave me an increasing reason to hustle on.

I took my shirt off and washed the powdery Karnak dust out of it, quickly followed by my trousers, socks and Calvins. A final rinse of the hair and within minutes I was revitalized, recharged, and dressing. Then it hit me. Shit, my room was a mess. Now maybe I was running a deep thread of paranoia, but as I scanned the room I concluded it was a mess that was not of my making, and that meant it had to be a thief or, yes, of course, the Secret Police. And if it was them, what happened to Dwight, and what happened to the papers?

If Dwight was still looking through them when the police arrived, he would have shit himself. He probably stuffed them in the back of his pants and high-tailed it out of the hotel as fast as his scrawny little legs would carry him. Seleh probably warned him and got Randy and him out of the place while the fuzz were busy turning over my room. Hell, these papers must be dynamite; thank God *I* didn't have them, and thank God I'd taken my laptop with me; if they'd read my notes I'd be stuffed; I'd be hung, drawn and quartered. The good news was that for now it meant I was in the clear and could head to the Nefertiti and focus my attention one-hundred-percent on

Crystal.

I grabbed my iphone, 7:23, plenty of time. I retrieved my laptop from under the bed and headed down to the lobby.

'Is Seleh back yet?'

'He will be back around 8:00 pm?'

'Egyptian time or Western time?'

The poor fellow looked totally bewildered so I quickly set him at ease.

'Don't worry, can you put this somewhere safe?'

I gave him the laptop and he nodded.

'Yes, yes, of course.'

'Oh, and please, my room, can you make it up?'

'Yes, of course. When is it you will be come back?'

'Not before 10:30 I wouldn't think.'

Normally I wouldn't have bothered, but I was being extremely optimistic and didn't want the room looking like a tornado had hit should I strike it lucky and convince Crystal to spend the night with me. Optimistic? Hell, who was I kidding, after my performance over dinner I had no chance. But, hope springs eternal, and within seconds I was out the door and into the back of Ahmed's taxi. It was the first time I'd had the chance to relax all day, and yet, as I sank back into the seat, I was as excited as a Nubian slave being invited to his first Temple orgy.

Arriving at the Nefertiti I paid off Ahmed and entered the hotel, quickly finding my way to the 'circle room' where I was greeted by Diane.

'Alex, I'm glad you could come. I wasn't sure you'd make it, I wasn't sure *I* would make it, what with the police having all that interest in that bag you gave me. They asked an awful lot of questions; are you trafficking drugs or something?'

'No, no. I'm sorry, it was all a misunderstanding.'

'Good, then let's get started.'

As before, cushions were arranged in a circle, ambient music was playing, and the air bathed in fragrances. Everyone was there, much as there had been in the previous circles, and surprisingly enough everyone seemed to sit in exactly the same positions, with Crystal and me directly opposite Diane, Bill and Pernille to one side, Pieter and Yuko to the other.

The circle opened the same as before, with Diane hold out a large clear-quartz crystal in both hands and declaring it a circle of love and awakening.

'Divine Aset, Highest Goddess, we gather here in your name that we may fully re-member our Highest Self and our true purpose here on this planet at this time. We meet in the eternity of this moment to fully embrace and embody the creative Goddess Source that is at the heart of each and every one of us....'

This time I actually listen to what she said; "fully re-member our Higher Self and our true purpose on this planet". That's exactly what Crystal had been talking about at dinner. I wasn't in Egypt for a holiday, my Higher self had brought me to the Nile to re-member, to connect to who I really was, or rather really *am*. And, if that was the case, then everything that had happened, that was happening, that was going to happen, and everyone I'd met, or was going to meet, was in some way a part of that awakening.

OK, so I had remembered I was an alien: Akhenaten, Amenhotep, Imhotep, a whole lineage of Annunaki-related beings, that was pretty obvious to me now. But what was my purpose? *That* was still unclear. Perhaps the circle had some answers for me.

Following her introductory prayer, Diane instigated a discussion about Karnak, with each person taking their turn relating their experience. Of course, everyone was interested in Bill's experience and he retold it as succinctly as he could. Firstly he told them about his reaction at the alabaster altar, then about his experience with Ptah. Many of the women related totally to his visions of American Indians and to the need to save and protect the land, waters and animals. It led to a brief discussion on Spirit Guides and animal totems; eagles, wolves, deer, bison, owls, bob-cats, cougars, my God, if my ex-wife could see me now, she'd be having kittens.

Several of the women, including Crystal, spoke passionately about their connection and experience with Sekhmet in the adjacent chamber. I contributed how I'd seen her face and eyes come to life and how moved I'd been by her warmth and strength, though I refrained from revealing that I'd scratched her on the chin. Somehow the thought of scratching the whiskers of a granite statue was just a little *too* 'out there' to admit to. Then it was Crystal's turn to speak.

'The most powerful moment for me was in the inner sanctum of Amun. Thanks to everyone's toning I have been able to activate certain dormant strands of my DNA and shift the vibrational frequency of my consciousness to a higher level.'

Several of the women were curious as to how it happened; Crystal's response was matter-of-fact.

'Thanks to Alex, I remembered that the granite chambers and sarcophagi are rejuvenation chambers. When the sympathetic harmonic of the granite is triggered, by an act such as toning, the subsequent vibrations accelerate the atoms and molecules of everything within them.'

They all looked at me as if I were some mighty guru and started firing questions left right and centre. I simply told them what I'd realized about the golden mean dimensions of the chambers, the silicon component in granite, and how I believed the plinth of Khepri was not just a symbol of rebirth, but some sort of control panel connected to the inner chamber; that the symbol of Khepri was more appropriately viewed in respect of recycling rather than simply rebirth, as it reflected the cyclic nature of the universe and that all creation is the recycling of matter rather than a rebirth of the same matter.

There was a brief moment as they all paused to absorb the concepts, then one of the younger women spoke up.

'Does that mean the rest of us have been recycled and shifted as well?'

It was a good question and everyone looked at me, hanging on the answer. I didn't have a clue, but thankfully Crystal saved my butt.

'No, only those of you who have the dormant strands of DNA, and of those, only those of you who are not running blocking patterns that short-circuit the acceleration.'

'Do you know which of us have the dormant strands?'

Before Crystal could respond, Diane stepped in.

'It is not for Crystal to tell you, but for each of you to discover your own path. What if she were to say you don't have the DNA? You may then choose to feel inferior, which is not the case; you are simply different. What if she said you *had* the DNA? Then your ego may kick in and you may feel superior, which you are not. What if she said you were, but you weren't, or, that you weren't, when in fact you were? It is not wise to listen to the words of others above your own inner, or Higher, voice.

The awakened path is to first and foremost ask of oneself, then take responsibility for not only the answers you receive, but for the actions you take. You are all *what* you are and *where* you are at this moment, it's as simple as that. What path you take from here is your choice. If you desire to be something other than what you are now, then you must set your intent and set off on your journey. You, and only you, can do that.'

As Crystal passed the baton to me, I felt a lot more comfortable sharing my experiences and thoughts. Starting with how the Amun Priests had tried to prevent me from entering the complex, and my experience at the alabaster altar, I moved on to relating my experiences of the inner sanctum and particularly inside the barque shrines of Amenhotep I and Hatshepsut in the open museum.

The conversation quickly led to how I remembered all this, how I had been here before, and if I remembered who I was. I was cornered and confronted with 'publicly owning' that I had been Akhenaten in a previous incarnation. Though I didn't go as far as to reveal my thoughts on Amenhotep and Akhenaten being Annunaki aliens.

'Akhenaten, I thought so…'

I expected challenges and sceptical doubt but, to, the contrary, received nothing but confirmation, and it started with the eldest of the group, the woman in her late sixties, whom I'd previously tagged as the spiritual matriarch of the group.

'…I knew it the first time I saw you.'

One of the younger women was not so ready to accept it.

'How can you be so sure?'

'Because I was Queen Tiye.'

Another of the women chipped in.

'Akhenaten's mother?'

'No, Tiye was the mother of Amenhotep IV.'

'But weren't Amenhotep IV and Akhenaten the same person?'

The elder woman was quick to answer.

'No. Amenhotep IV was the son of Amenhotep III and Queen Tiye. Akhenaten was somebody else altogether.'

I knew it! And she knew it too, I could tell by the look on her face. The younger women wanted more convincing.

'But how do you know?'

'Because I was there, I saw him, I knew him.'

Within seconds they were all suddenly declaring their identities.

'I was Akhenaten's daughter, Meritaten.'

'Me too, I was Anhkesenamun.'

'The wife of Tutankhamun?'

'Yes'

'I think I was a daughter as well, Neferneferuaten.'

'I was Khiya, Akhenaten's sister-in-law and one of Amenhotep IV's wives.'

By now Pernille had remembered she was Queen Ashotep, wife and sister of Seqenenre Tao, great grandmother of Hatshepsut and probably the last keeper of the sacred knowledge, while Diane of course acknowledged she had been Hatshepsut; granddaughter of Amenhotep I and great great great grand-matriarch of the 18th

321

Dynasty.

By the looks on their faces, Bill and Pieter obviously felt a bit left out; but not for long.

'Don't fret, guys, you belong here too. At the last circle I looked around the room and realized it was a big family reunion from the 18th Dynasty; Bill, you were Ahmose, son of Ashotep and Seqenenre, and first pharaoh of the 18th Dynasty, and later Senenmut, consort of Hatshepsut. Pieter, you were Amenemhat, son of Thutmoses III and half-brother of Amenhotep II. In your lives as Senenmut and Amenemhat you were both High Priests of the Tat Brotherhood, entrusted with the protection of the sacred knowledge of the skies and land.'

One of the younger women had a sudden light-bulb moment.

'And what about you Crystal, you were Nefertiti, weren't you?'

'Yes, but she was previously known as Iset, a misinterpretation of Aset, or who the Romans called Isis.'

'The goddess Isis?'

'Yes, but in that incarnation Aset was a half-breed, a hybrid you might say; part human, part Annunaki.'

'You mean aliens?'

Suddenly the cat was out of the bag. I decided to try and at least keep it on a leash.

'Yes, aliens...'

I looked around the circle.

'...To some degree, we were all aliens, *are* all aliens. And for some reason, all of us here chose to incarnate at that time in history.'

Diane knew why.

'That's because it was a key time in the re-establishment of Goddess energy.'

I scratched my chin.

'I think there may be more to it than that. I think it was about consciousness as well. Contrary to what the experts in the book may say, I believe Akhenaten didn't worship the sun as an object, he honoured that all earth-born consciousness on this planet, and in fact consciousness in the solar system, originated from the sun. He was aware of the corruption of the Amun Priests and tried to set the human race back on the correct path. Isn't that why you are all here, what you have all strived for you whole lives?'

The words had flown out of my mouth without me even thinking, but suddenly I saw how what I had said related to my entire life. Looking around I realized it was having the exact same effect on everyone else as well.

'We're all here not just to remember who we are, but remember our purpose, to bring the higher path of consciousness to the human race. Each of us might have a different way, a different path, but the message is the same.'

'Alex, are you saying we are all aliens?

'I, er, well,…. Yes, I suppose I am.'

Now that hit me like a run-away Mack truck fully laden with neutron stars. Could it be, that while my body may have appeared to be human, some part, or *all* of my soul was from somewhere way out in space. If that were the case, then what the hell was I doing here on Earth?

'What an interesting concept, especially as tomorrow we head to Dendera and the Temple of Hathor.'

Whatever it was, Diane saw it as an apt time to move on. She changed the music on her ipod and invited everyone to close their eyes and make themselves comfortable. I laid back on the floor and took a few deep breaths; hell, I was exhausted.

'Hathor was not one god; she was one of a group of inter-dimensional, intergalactic beings, the Hathors, who originally came from another universe and another dimension via Sirius, which acts as a portal between Universes. From Sirius they made their way to our solar system, inhabiting the etheric realms of Venus. As well as interacting with several other pre-history cultures, they connected to ancient Egypt through the temples of the Goddess Hathor. As we are visiting the temple tomorrow, let us take this opportunity to open our hearts to them…'

My mind was suddenly filled with the image of the cow-eared woman with the Asiatic eyes, who looked down from atop the capitals of the columns in so many of the temples.

'…Picture your heart opening like a blossoming flower; each petal unfolding to both offer its sweet fragrances, pollen and nectar, and in grateful reception of sunlight and the caressing breezes that bring the many birds and insects that will spread your seeds of truth and wisdom around the globe.

In the centre of your heart, the centre of your flower, visualize the eternal flame of creation that burns within you, from which you have emerged. See its flickering flame rise from the deepest red, through orange, yellow, green, blue and to the highest violet light of knowingness. See it extend out through your feet and out through the top of your head, infinitely reaching into, and connecting you completely with, the Source of All That Is.'

The face started to become real; it was as if *it* were speaking the words, not Diane.

'It is time for Goddess energy, the pure creative energy of Love, to reclaim the planet. This it must do through the feminine, through the women, who must first fully awaken and embrace their *own* Goddess energy, before men can see it in themselves, remember not to fear it, before awakening it fully within *them*selves.

Totally relax, for Goddess awakening does not require you to acquire anything, nor to *learn* anything, for the answers are not external. Nor are they internal, for there are no answers to seek, only truths to become aware of. Your responsibility is to *be*, nothing more, nothing less, nothing else.'

And then Diane's voice started to drift completely into the background and I totally tuned out, or should I say, tuned in to the smiling face before me.

'Welcome.'

'Who are you?'

'I am Hesat, emissary of the Hathor mission to this planet.'

'Where are you from?'

'I am one of a group of beings existing at a specific vibratory field far beyond that of human perception.'

'A higher consciousness?'

'You could see it that way. In terms of the vastness of the universe, we are a little higher on the spiral of awareness and consciousness than human consciousness; we are like elder brothers and sisters. We have grown, as humans are now growing, ascending to the awareness of One Source, though we are all part of the spectrum of love that binds the universe together as One.'

'Are you here to save mankind?'

'No, we are not saviours, nor are we the messiahs many religions speak of.

That humans hold the belief some ascended master or advanced alien intelligence is going to save the human race, that humans will not have to make any changes in their thoughts and actions, that they will not have to be responsible, is unrealistic and just a projection of the need of human consciousness to rely on others to bring in their ascension without any work on their part. The belief humans can continue running patterns of lethargy and unawareness, then take something or have something given to them that will transform them, without any effort on their part, is sheer absurdity. It just won't happen, and there are many who are going to be very disappointed.'

'Then why *are* you here?'

'We come in love, heralding the possibility of a new age for the earth. We simply offer our understanding and what we have learned as friends, mentors and fellow travellers on the path of ascension that leads back to remembrance of All That Is.

In offering our assistance, we do not wish to interfere in any way with any other spiritual helpers or cosmic advisors, nor with any earth-bound religious beliefs, affiliations or organizations of help. We simply offer the choice of our perspectives. If human consciousness is ready to build the new world, then there is a great deal we would like to share. In the end, the human race is free to take it or leave it, but we offer it freely.'

'How do you present these choices?'

'Through the vibratory nature of the cosmos, we aim to encourage spiritual ascension in two main ways. We use sound, supersonic and subsonic, as well as audible, to stimulate and activate psycho-spiritual experiences, and visually through the use of sacred geometry as a means to excite and arouse brain performance through the stimulation of retinal receptors that will trigger activation of sub-atomic neural pathways.'

'Sacred Geometry? So, are the Hathors responsible for Crop Circles?'

'Some, but not all; we are not the only race contributing to the assistance of the rise of human consciousness.'

'So why aren't we getting the message?'

'You are no more human than the driver of a car is the car itself. You may have incarnated into a human form, but who you *are* is not what you *appear to be*.'

'Am I a Hathor?'

Hesat smiled.

'No, you have different origins, though a similar mission.'

I reflected on my incarnation as Akhenaten.

'Am I Annunaki?'

'Are you the car you first drove as a youth, the car you drove at twenty-five, or the car you now drive?'

'I'm none of them, but I was the driver of them all.'

'Exactly; the actor wears many many costumes in his career, but it does not mean he is the character who wears them.'

'I get it. So why am I here then, what is my purpose? What role do I play this time?'

'The same as ours; to assist humans in raising their vibrational existence.'

'So that they follow the enlightened pathway and ascend to the Higher realms?'

'Ascension is not a pathway, it is a process of self-awareness and mastery on, and of, all levels, all of which occur in the same moment of the Oneness that is the universe and in the localized perception that is space/time.'

'And how do I do that?'

'That is for you to remember.'

'Is it through truth?'

'It is not for us to say; it is your script and sometimes the script must be left to unfold of its own course. And with that I shall leave you.'

'Will I see you again?'

'Of course: in the pattern of every flower, in the ripples on the water, in the singing of the birds. We wish you well on your journey, my brother.'

The face and voice faded into the distance as I became aware of Diane and then Crystal's voice.

'Alex?'

'It's alright Diane, I'll look after him; you go to bed.'

'OK, I'll see you tomorrow. Goodnight.'

'Goodnight.'

My mind started trying to make sense of why Diane was going to bed in the middle of the circle. Unable to come to a resolution, I slowly opened my eyes and quickly became aware that I'd done it again, drifted off to Neverland.

'I did it again, didn't I?'

'Yes. Are you OK?'

'Yeah, I'm fine.'

Slowly sitting up, I scanned the room and realized that the circle had not only ended, but that everyone except Crystal had gone.

'What time is it?'

'Just after midnight.'

'Midnight?'

'Yes, you've been out for about three hours.'

'No way!'

'The others were worried and wanted to bring you back, but I convinced them you were in no danger and that I would look after you.'

'You won't believe this but I just had the most amazing conversation with an emissary from the Hathors.'

'Why would I choose not to believe you, are you lying?'

'No, but … I'd better get going.'

I tried to stand, but clearly I was still not fully *compos mentis*.

'I don't think so. You'd better stay here tonight.'

I was wasted; totally spent, so didn't have the energy to argue the point. It wasn't that I'd actually slept, I'd just been 'out of it' for three hours, and that seemed more exhausting than the eight hours I'd spent trekking around Karnak. Besides, wasn't this what I wanted, a night alone with Crystal? Hell, yeah!

She guided me down the corridor and to her room, which was thankfully on the same floor as the room in which we'd had the circle. Heading inside I vaguely remembered her room was much nicer than mine, before I collapsed on the bed.

'Let me get you something to drink, then you can tell me all about it.'

Before she could return, I fell into a deep sleep.

Also in this series

RED GRANITE
The Grains of Truth Beneath the Sands of Egypt
I
Abu Simbel - Wadi Hillal

RED GRANITE
The Grains of Truth Beneath the Sands of Egypt
III
Dendera - Dahshur

RED GRANITE
The Grains of Truth Beneath the Sands of Egypt
IV
Saqqara - Abusir

RED GRANITE
The Grains of Truth Beneath the Sands of Egypt
V
Giza - Alexandria

Other books by this authior

PIAHNA'S GIFT

12 FOOT FENCES

www.ingramcontent.com/pod-product-compliance
Lightning Source LLC
Chambersburg PA
CBHW071531260626
47170CB00002B/586